The Rabbi's Knight

The Rabbi's Knight

Michael J. Cooper

FIVE STAR
A part of Gale, Cengage Learning

Farmington Hills, Mich • San Francisco • New York • Waterville, Maine
Meriden, Conn • Mason, Ohio • Chicago

Copyright © 2015 by Michael J. Cooper
Bible Scriptures are taken from The King James Bible.
Other quotes are from the works of Yehudah Halevey and Rumi
Map Design by Ricardo Passalacqua
Five Star™ Publishing, a part of Cengage Learning, Inc.

ALL RIGHTS RESERVED.

This novel is a work of fiction. Names, characters, places, and incidents are either the product of the author's imagination, or, if real, used fictitiously.

No part of this work covered by the copyright herein may be reproduced, transmitted, stored, or used in any form or by any means graphic, electronic, or mechanical, including but not limited to photocopying, recording, scanning, digitizing, taping, Web distribution, information networks, or information storage and retrieval systems, except as permitted under Section 107 or 108 of the 1976 United States Copyright Act, without the prior written permission of the publisher.

The publisher bears no responsibility for the quality of information provided through author or third-party Web sites and does not have any control over, nor assume any responsibility for, information contained in these sites. Providing these sites should not be construed as an endorsement or approval by the publisher of these organizations or of the positions they may take on various issues.

LIBRARY OF CONGRESS CATALOGING-IN-PUBLICATION DATA

Cooper, Michael J., 1948–
The rabbi's knight / by Michael J. Cooper. — First edition.
pages cm
ISBN 978-1-4328-3100-4 (hardcover) — ISBN 1-4328-3100-3 (hardcover) — ISBN 978-1-4328-3094-6 (ebook) — ISBN 1-4328-3094-5 (ebook)
1. Knights Templar (Masonic order)—Fiction. [1. Knights and knighthood—Fiction. 2. Palestine—History—13th century—Fiction.] I. Title.
PS3603.O582725R336 2015
813'.6—dc23 2015009923

First Edition. First Printing: August 2015
Find us on Facebook– https://www.facebook.com/FiveStarCengage
Visit our website– http://www.gale.cengage.com/fivestar/
Contact Five Star™ Publishing at FiveStar@cengage.com

Printed in the United States of America
1 2 3 4 5 6 7 19 18 17 16 15

For my parents, Emanuel and Buni Cooper,
who set me on the road to Jerusalem.
And for Teri, Matthew, Elana, and Daniel,
with me on the journey.

ACKNOWLEDGMENTS

I want to offer my profound gratitude to all those who read the manuscript in its various forms and offered their comments and encouragement. Most notably I wish to thank my mentor, Penny Warner; my former agent, Laurie McLean; my friend Herma Lichtenstein; my big sister Adrienne Cooper; and my wife, Teri.

Special thanks are due to the long-suffering members of my critique group, Critical Mass: Margaret Dumas, Janet Finsilver, Claire Johnson, Rena Leith, Ann Parker, Carole Price, and Gordon Yano. Without their relentless attention to detail this book could not have been written.

I'm also indebted to Deni Dietz of Five Star for bringing *The Rabbi's Knight* in from the cold, and to Diane Piron-Gelman of Word Nerd, Inc. for cleaning him up.

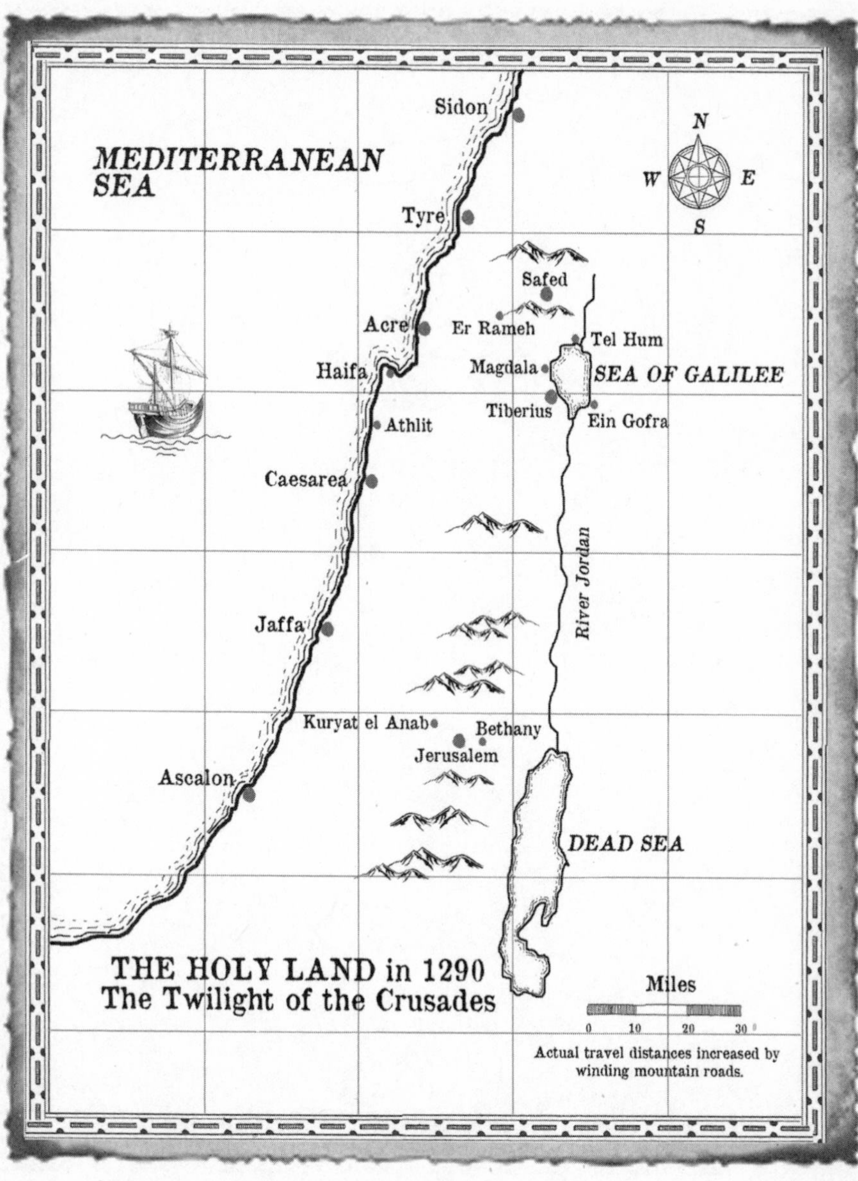

MEDITERRANEAN SEA
N
W
E
S
Sidon
Tyre
Safed
Er Rameh
Acre
Tel Hum
Magdala
SEA OF GALILEE
Haifa
Tiberius
Ein Gofra
Athlit
Caesarea
River Jordan
Jaffa
Kuryat el Anab
Bethany
Jerusalem
Ascalon
DEAD SEA
THE HOLY LAND in 1290
The Twilight of the Crusades
Miles
0 10 20 30
Actual travel distances increased by winding mountain roads.

CAST OF CHARACTERS

(Historical figures in CAPS)

Abdullah ibn Sayid ibn Elias—Emir of Safed by order of the Mamluk SULTAN BAYBARS after the defeat of the Templars at the citadel in 1266

Abu-het, Karim—Viceroy to the emir of Jerusalem

ABULAFIYA, ABRAHAM BEN SAMUEL (1240–1291?)—Founder of the school of Prophetic Kabbalah. In 1260 journeyed to Acre in search of the legendary Sambatyon River and the lost Ten Tribes. After a lifetime of study, writing, controversy, and wandering, fled to the island of Comino and, after completing his last book, *Words of Beauty,* disappeared from history.

Abu-Rahman—Master silversmith in Jerusalem

Ad-Din, Ayoub—Emir of Jerusalem

Al-Hasani (Abu Muhammad ibn Hasan)—Seventy-year-old mathematician, cartographer, and physician who fled Baghdad after the Mongol conquest and settled in Jerusalem. This character is based on historical pioneers of optics, mathematics, physics, and medicine such as IBN QURRA, Al KHWARIZMI, AL KINDI, and ALHAZEN.

Al-Hasani, Sha'ima—Sixty-five-year-old wife of al-Hasani

Al-Hasani, Tarek—Nineteen-year-old son of al-Hasani

Buscarel—Merchant of Genoa

Cosimo—Merchant of Pisa

DE BEAUJEU, WILLIAM—Twenty-first Grand Master of the Knights Templar, from 1273 until his death during the siege of Acre in 1291

De Rogé, William—Master of the Templar citadel at Safed; mentor of Jonathan St. Clair

Elijah ben Azariah—English merchant and synagogue *gabai;* one of the thousands of English Jews exiled by order of KING EDWARD I in 1290

ISAAC BEN SAMUEL of ACRE—Nineteen-year-old student at the yeshivah of SOLOMON PETIT. Left Acre when it fell to the Mamluks in 1291, and went on to gain fame as "Isaac of Acre," a prominent Kabbalist in Spain beginning in 1305.

MAIMONIDES, MOSES (1135–1204)—Preeminent rabbi, physician, and philosopher in Spain, Morocco, and Egypt. Wrote religious, philosophic, scientific, and medical texts in Hebrew and Arabic. Beginning during the final years of his life, a sometimes-violent controversy developed around a number of disputed cultural, religious, social, and philosophic elements of Maimonides' writings. This became known as the Maimonidean Controversy, and it went on for centuries.

MAIMUNI, DAVID BEN ABRAHAM (1233–1301)—Grandson of MOSES MAIMONIDES, he followed in the footsteps of his grandfather as Nagid or "Prince" over the Jewish congregations in Egypt

Nehemiah ben Azariah—Young Jew exiled from Jerusalem to the leper colony of Tel Hum

PETIT, RABBI SOLOMON—Sixty-eight-year-old French rabbi who emigrated to Acre in 1288 where he founded an academy. His hatred of MAIMONIDES led to burning his writings and desecrating his tomb in Tiberius. These actions led the Baghdad Gaon, RABBI SAMUEL, to excommunicate PETIT.

RUMI (JELALUDDIN BALKHI, 1207–1273)—Born on the eastern shores of the Persian Empire, Rumi was one of the world's most revered mystical poets. Although a Sufi scholar of the Koran, his appeal reached across religious divisions, and at his funeral, many Jews and Christians were in attendance.

SAMUEL BEN DANIEL HAKOHEN, GAON of BAGHDAD—Seventy-year-old rabbi, the last of the heads of the Baghdad Academy with authority over all cultural, legal, intellectual, and political aspects of Jewish life in the Levant. After writing a letter around 1290 to RABBI DAVID MAIMUNI regarding the excommunication of SOLOMON PETIT, he disappeared from history.

St. Clair, Jonathan—Forty-eight year-old Knight Templar

SULTAN AL-ASHRAF KHALIL (1262–1293)—Mamluk sultan who succeeded his father, QA'LA'UN, in 1290, and led Mamluk forces against Acre in 1291

SULTAN AL-MANSUR QA'LA'UN (1220–1290)—Mamluk sultan who succeeded BAYBARS. He drove the Crusaders out of much of Palestine and was preparing the campaign against Acre when he died in 1290.

SULTAN AL-ZAHIR BAYBARS (1223–1277)—First of the Mamluk sultans, a Kipchak Turk, captured as a child by the Mongols and sold as a slave in Damascus, converted to Islam and trained as a soldier. Rising rapidly in the ranks because of his valor and ambition, he became commander of the Mamluks. After assassinating the Ayyubid Sultan Qutuz in 1260, BAYBARS became Sultan and began a lifelong struggle against the Crusader kingdoms.

Tewfiq Ayoub, Viceroy—Master of shields and cupbearer to the emir of Safed

WALLACE, WILLIAM (1272?–1305)—Eighteen-year-old Scot who went on to lead the resistance as Guardian of

Scotland against KING EDWARD I during the Wars of Scottish Independence

YEHIEL BEN JOSEPH of PARIS—Arrived in Acre with his son and 300 pupils from Paris in 1260 and opened the academy, MIDRASH HA'GADOL

Yosef ben Asher, Rabbi—Spiritual leader of the Sephardic Jews of York; one of the thousands of English Jews exiled by order of KING EDWARD I in 1290

Zahirah—Thirty-four year-old woman of Safed, encountered by Jonathan St. Clair and RABBI SAMUEL in the leper colony of Tel Hum

The place that Solomon made to worship in,
called the Far Mosque,
is not built of earth and water and stone,
but of intention and wisdom
and mystical conversation and compassionate action

—*Jelaluddin Balkhi, "Rumi"*
1207–1273

. . . for night shines as the day and darkness is as light.

—*Psalm 139*

PREFACE

The Rabbi's Knight is set at the twilight of the Crusades in the year 1290. At this point in history, the once proud "Latin Kingdom of Jerusalem" no longer included Jerusalem. At its height in the mid-12th century, the Kingdom encompassed what is now Israel, Jordan, Lebanon, Syria, and the Sinai. By the year 1290 it was reduced to a few fortress cities clinging to the Mediterranean coast—and their days were numbered.

The world of Islam was also in transition. The powerful Ayyubid dynasty, founded by the great Saladin, was riven by civil war and the invasion of the Mongols from the East. The Ayyubids lost power to their former slave-soldiers, the Mamluks, and it was the Mamluk sultans who would vanquish the Crusaders as the 13th century drew to a close.

Throughout the years of the Crusades, Jews in the Holy Land led a tenuous existence—caught between the great armies of Moslems, Mongols, and the Cross. In Europe, Jews were occasionally attacked by knights of the Crusade on their way to fight in the Holy Land. A notable exception was the French abbot, Bernard of Clairvaux, who came to the aid of Rhineland Jews in 1140. His protection of Jews became a central code of conduct for the Knights Templar. The "Rule of Bernard" allowed the Jews of Acre to flourish with great academies of learning and renowned scholars before it all came to an end with the final destruction of the Latin Kingdom of Jerusalem.

Chapter One

Safed, Palestine
4 May, 1290
Dawn

Cloaked in a hooded robe, the rider stared into the gorge through trailing fingers of mist, watching for any movement on hills that rose and fell beneath the dawn sky. Turning, he urged the mare up the slope between boulders and scrub brush, toward the mountain village. The mare's hooves thudded into the muddy earth. He crested the hill and dismounted. With a final glance into the gorge, he led the mare into a maze of deserted cobblestone lanes. The dull clatter of her hooves echoed in the silence.

The rider stopped at a shuttered building of limestone blocks. He pushed back the hood of his robe to reveal close-cropped black hair, salted with gray and parted by a scar along his left temple that ran down his cheek and was lost to sight in his beard. He reached behind his head, feeling for the hilt of his broadsword, making sure it was hidden by the robe. He stepped to a door of weathered planks and knocked.

No sound came from behind the door.

He pushed against it and it opened, rasping over a stone floor.

Peering into a darkened room, he saw a low table with a few scrolls and two candles that guttered at the wind's touch. At the edge of the wavering light stood two bearded men in striped robes. One of them bowed.

"Noble sir," the man said in accented Arabic, his voice quavering. "We travel under the protection of the Sultan Qa'la'un—"

"As well you should in these dangerous times." The rider stepped forward.

"What do you seek here, sir?" The man straightened his turban and took a step back.

"I discern by your speech that you come from Baghdad," the rider said.

"You are perceptive. We are indeed from Baghdad."

"That is well, for I seek the Gaon of Baghdad—Rabbi Samuel ben Daniel ha-Kohen. Are you his servants?"

"His disciples, sir. But our rabbi is not here—"

"Then I shall await his return." The rider bent and picked a scroll off the table.

"If you will but tell us your name, noble Arab, we'll inform the rabbi . . ."

The rider parted the scroll and peered at the Hebrew script, recognizing passages from the book of Isaiah. "Tell him that Abd al-Qadir al-Jilani desires an audience."

A side door creaked open and light filled the room. A figure stood silhouetted in the doorway. "You are Abd al-Qadir?"

"I am." The rider stepped forward, squinting against the light.

"Then I would speak with you. I am Rabbi Samuel. Please, come into the study."

Bowing his head to duck beneath the low lintel, the rider entered a study warmed by a fire that burned in the hearth. He saw that the rabbi's dark turban matched a long robe of black satin, and a tasseled cord circled his ample body.

"Rabbi," the rider began, "Thank you for—"

"Don't speak." The rabbi pushed the door closed and turned. "First, I must know who you really are. Why do you call yourself by the name of Abd al-Qadir, who has been dead for two hundred years? Why do you use the name of a mystic blessed with extraordinary wisdom?"

"Because I aspire to obtain wisdom," the stranger said and fixed his eyes on the rabbi. "It is for that reason I come to you."

"You come to *me*?" Rabbi Samuel raised his hands, palms up. "To a Jew? Why do you not seek out one of your own teachers?"

"Only you can teach me what I need to know."

"What do I know of the Koran?"

"I do not speak of the Koran. I want you to teach me the inmost secrets of Kabbalah—"

The rabbi shook his head as he turned and, limping slightly, walked toward the hearth. "Come and sit with me."

The rider saw an overstuffed chair and footstool by the hearth. "Please, have a seat," the rabbi said as he settled into the chair and pointed at the footstool. "How can I accept you as a pupil? You haven't even told me your true name!"

The rider remained standing. "Then you shall know me, Rabbi, and you shall know my purpose." Standing before the rabbi, the rider reached beneath his robe.

The rabbi sat forward in his chair. "What have you there beneath your habit?"

The stranger looked down and saw the edge of his chain-mail shirt, glinting in the firelight. He drew a deep breath and let the robe fall open to reveal a coat of shining mail.

"What? That's a soldier's hauberk! What is your purpose, sir? To mock me and then kill me?" The rabbi jabbed his finger at the stranger. "Know that I travel under the protection of the Sultan! No Mamluk may harm me."

"I am not a Mamluk." The stranger pulled off his robe.

Beneath the mail shirt was a tunic of white silk, a splayed red cross emblazoned over the chest.

"A Knight Templar?" The rabbi fell back in the chair, staring up at the Crusader. "I am mocked and twice deceived—and now I die."

The stranger reached over his shoulder and grasped the hilt of his broadsword. The blade slid from its leather scabbard with a smooth whisper.

"Your sword is not sufficiently covered with Jewish blood?"

Towering over the old man, the knight grasped the shining blade and rotated the sword, extending the hilt toward him. "Take the sword, Rabbi."

"No. I won't give you the amusement of participating in my own death." The rabbi closed his eyes and began to chant in a quiet voice, "Hear, O Israel, the Lord is our God, the Lord is One . . ."

The knight recognized the *Shema,* a Jewish prayer recited upon waking and upon going to sleep, and also a prayer traditionally spoken when death appears imminent. "Rabbi Samuel," he said sharply, switching from Arabic to Hebrew, "You haven't given me the opportunity to explain myself. Take the sword and I will."

The rabbi opened his eyes. "You speak Hebrew."

"Yes. And Aramaic also." The knight extended the sword hilt further, holding the rabbi's gaze.

The old man hesitated, then grasped the sword. Apparently finding it heavy, he rested it across his knees.

The knight lifted a leather pouch that hung from a lanyard about his neck. "Allow me to show you why I have come." He carefully drew forth a roll of yellowed parchment and handed it to the rabbi.

The rabbi spread the scroll open upon the flat of the broadsword and stared at the script in silence. When he finally spoke, his voice was a whisper. "Where did you get this?"

"Two hundred years ago, my grandfather's grandfather was among Knights of the Crusade who took Jerusalem—"

"This is from *Jerusalem*?"

"No. It's from the ruined city of Petra beyond the Valley of Moses."

The rabbi looked down, studying the scroll. Only when an ember snapped in the hearth did he look up. "What do you understand of this?"

The knight raised his shoulders. "Only that it bears a few passages in an ancient Hebrew script—of no special significance according to most of the scholars who have seen it. But many years ago I met a man who thought otherwise. He was sure that, hidden within the inscription, was a meaning of great importance. Though he himself couldn't understand it, he knew of one who could. You."

The rabbi again lowered his eyes to the scroll.

The knight stood, waiting, looking down at the rabbi as the fire burned low in the hearth. His heart pounded in his chest as he watched the rabbi nod and mutter, in silent conversation with himself as he studied the scroll. Seeing that the rabbi wished to keep his own counsel, the knight quietly lifted his gray robe from the floor and put it on over his hauberk. Stepping to a window, he pushed open the casement and looked out at an overgrown garden partially enclosed by a broken fence. The leaden sky brightened to silver-gray where the cloud-hidden morning sun stood over the eastern hills. The cool air heralded a wet spring.

A small white cat crossed the yard and jumped up on the windowsill, purring loudly. The knight took the cat in his arms and stroked its head.

Minutes passed.

"Very interesting . . ." the rabbi murmured.

With the cat still in his arms, the knight turned back to the rabbi. "Do you understand its meaning?" he asked quietly.

"In part, yes."

"Will you tell me?"

"Only when I know more about you." The rabbi looked up and saw the cat in the knight's arms. "I see you've met my little *shoonrah.*" He smiled as he fixed his eyes on the knight. "Why don't you tell me your *real* name?"

"Jonathan St. Clair."

"Tell me, Jonathan St. Clair—how did you know to find me here on my way to Acre? My academy was in Baghdad. This place," he encompassed the building with a sweep of his hand, "which was once the Academy of Rabbi Jacob, has been deserted for years. How did you know to come here?"

"You have in Acre friends who know of your coming and follow your progress. Among your friends is Rabbi David ben Abraham Maimuni. He sent me."

"Why?"

"That we might help each other—in return for teaching me, I provide you safe passage to Acre."

"Does Maimuni believe I am in need of protection? I carry a letter of safe conduct from the Sultan—"

"That letter will avail you nothing." St. Clair stepped away from the window, still stroking the cat's head. "For just as you have friends in Acre, so too do you have enemies. One of them has contracted with the emir of Safed to kill you. If you remain here, your life is forfeit—"

"And we sit here talking?" The rabbi sat forward. "The palace of the emir is less than a league from here! If what you say is true, we should get away now!" He struggled to rise from the chair, but couldn't with the heavy broadsword still across his lap.

"We have time, Rabbi," St. Clair said. "The missive to the

emir mandating your death comes hither with a certain merchant of Genoa who travels slowly with the caravan for Damascus. We'll leave tonight under cover of darkness. By the time the letter arrives, we'll be well away."

"I'll instruct my disciples to immediately make ready for our departure." The rabbi again tried to rise, then looked up at the knight and tapped the heavy broadsword. "Please, Jonathan, let's make a trade. You take the sword, and I'll take my cat."

St. Clair gently handed the cat to the rabbi, then easily lifted the sword and slid it into the leather scabbard behind his back. "Maimuni said you would know the one in Acre who seeks your death. Do you?"

Rabbi Samuel nodded. He stroked the cat with his free hand as he gave the scroll back to St. Clair.

Chapter Two

ב

Latin Stronghold of Acre
Northern Coast of Palestine
4 May, 1290

With morning prayers drawing to a close, Isaac ben Samuel sat at the end of a worn wooden bench next to the synagogue's whitewashed wall, wrapped in his prayer shawl and phylacteries. As other worshipers raised their voices in a responsive chant, Isaac silently indulged his interest in searching liturgy for hidden connections between one sacred concept and another. He scanned his handwritten copy of the *Shema,* a central prayer declaring love and faith in God, counting the number of words.

Exactly two hundred and forty-eight . . .

He turned the number over in his mind, recalling a passage in Talmud stating that the human body contained exactly two hundred and forty-eight bones. *So, the number of our bones is identical to the number of words in the Shema. Thus, the Shema reflects the wholeness of our physical body . . .*

Isaac was a slight young man with piercing black eyes, a sparse beard, and a matchless memory. Despite his age of only nineteen years, he had already gained a measure of fame; scholars in faraway Provençe and Spain already knew of him as Isaac of Acre.

Resting his eyes on the word *Shema,* Isaac calculated in a glance the sum of the numerical value of each letter utilizing gematria, a system to interpret hidden meanings of liturgy.

Four hundred and ten is the gematria of the word Shema. *Interesting—it's identical to that of the word* mishkan, *the holy sanctuary.* Isaac knew it wasn't a coincidence when different words had the same gematria. With Torah, there was no coincidence. An identical gematria denoted a connection—one only had to find it.

With pounding heart, he glanced at the prayer's opening lines: *And you shall love the Lord your God, with all your heart and with all your soul and with all your being.* He smiled as he brought all aspects of the revelation together in his mind. *When we give ourselves completely to the love and service of God, we become His sanctuary. Thus—*

"Isaac."

Startled, he looked up.

Rabbi Solomon Petit, his mentor, was standing over him. All the other worshipers had finished prayer and departed. He and Rabbi Petit were alone.

"Do you plan to finish morning prayers anytime this morning?"

Rabbi Solomon Petit was a grizzled septuagenarian with a scraggly white beard and old skin. Even after ten years in the Holy Land, he still affected the striped robe and fur hat worn by Jews in his native France.

"I'm sorry, Rabbi, but I just realized some wonderful connections in reference to the *Shema*! May I share them with you?"

"Later." Petit sat on the bench across from Isaac. "For now, I have a certain matter to discuss with you." He leaned forward; looking at Isaac from beneath heavy, gray eyebrows. "You are a gifted student, Isaac, but one thing concerns me." Petit raised a gnarled finger. "You consort with the uncircumcised."

Isaac blanched. "I assume, Rabbi, that you refer to the Knight Templar known as Jonathan St. Clair."

"Indeed."

Isaac shrugged. "Rabbi Jacob of Safed, may his memory be blessed, vouched for his character. I merely assumed the knight's instruction after Rabbi Jacob died."

"Jacob was a fool!" Petit snapped. "Equipping our enemies with knowledge of Torah is dangerous folly."

Isaac's heart thudded in his chest, stung by the rebuke. He raised his shoulders. "I'm not sure I understand your meaning, Rabbi."

"Don't you know our faith is under attack throughout Europe? In Paris and Aragon, these assaults often take the form of disputations."

"But isn't a disputation merely a harmless debate?"

"It's not harmless and it's not a debate! It pits a rabbi against a Christian cleric or some apostate Jew—a contest we can never win." Petit sat back and crossed his arms. "This St. Clair is a Knight of Christ. His only allegiance is to his order and to his god. What's to keep him from turning on us at the first opportunity?"

"I'm sorry, Rabbi."

Petit's voice softened and he patted Isaac gently on the knee. "You are young, Isaac. Though you are rich in knowledge, you lack understanding. As it is written, 'Wisdom is before him that has understanding.' Learn from me, Isaac. I give you the wisdom that comes from understanding."

"Yes, Rabbi. I will give the knight no more instruction."

"No." Petit shook his head. "For now, I want you to continue."

"But . . . but, Rabbi," Isaac stammered, confused by the contradictory directives. "I thought . . . you said—"

"For the present, this knight and his comrades may be of some use to us."

"Use, Rabbi?"

"Yes." Petit nodded and leaned forward. "Are the Templars aware of all who enter the city?"

"Yes, Rabbi—especially since the fall of Tripoli. No one enters but through the land gate and it's guarded night and day."

"What of deliveries, letters?"

"All are closely watched . . ."

"Good. Now, listen well, Isaac. There is one coming hither from the east, from the maw of the great abyss. This man comes in the guise of a rabbi, but he is manifestly a demon son of Ashmedai!" Petit turned his head and spat three times. "This *sitra ahrah* is our sworn enemy, Isaac, determined to destroy our way of life. As he draws near, the stench of his apostasy grows stronger. He must be stopped!" He jabbed a gnarled finger at Isaac. "Toward this end, I require your assistance."

"Of course, Rabbi." Isaac had no idea of whom the rabbi spoke, but he was afraid to ask.

"I have made certain *arrangements* to stop this snake before he can spread his venom here. However, there's a small chance he may elude the fate I've planned for him." Petit leaned further forward. "We can't afford to take any chances! Your Templar friends must watch for him, Isaac—this one called Rabbi Samuel of Baghdad. Indeed, they must be alerted to watch for any missive from his hand. This is what I require of you; I want you to bring me guards who speak good French and may help us in our purpose. Tell them there will be gold in it for them, Isaac. Bring them to me with dispatch. Today."

"I will, Rabbi."

"I know you will." Petit flashed a yellow smile within his beard as he reached out and patted Isaac's knee. "I know you will."

Chapter Three

ג

Safed
4 May, 1290
Morning

"Will you be ready to leave by nightfall?" St. Clair asked as Rabbi Samuel entered the study followed by the white cat and one of his students carrying a wooden chest.

"Well before nightfall." The rabbi pointed toward a shelf crowded with scrolls. "Put the chest over there, Yitzhak."

Once done, the student turned to leave. "Will you require anything else, Rabbi?"

"Only that you and Ya'akov finish packing and prepare some repast that we may eat before we depart. And bring a bowl of *lebiniyah* for Master Shoonrah." The rabbi knelt on the floor by the chest and began removing scrolls from the shelf.

"Can I help with that?" asked St. Clair.

"No. Ya'akov will bring the *lebiniyah* for Master Shoonrah."

"I mean, with the scrolls.

"No, thank you, Jonathan. These are correspondence and official documents. I need to arrange them myself, and besides, you're not here to be my personal secretary." He glanced up at St. Clair and smiled. "You're here to protect me."

"Indeed I am, Rabbi."

"A single knight?"

"A company would attract attention."

"And in exchange for this *protection,* I'm obliged to teach you?"

St. Clair nodded as he leaned on the wall by the window.

"When?" Rabbi Samuel asked as he continued to place scrolls in the chest. "Now?"

"At any opportunity you deem appropriate, Rabbi. Clearly, once in Acre, we'll have more time."

"To teach you—toward what end?"

"To understand *this.*" St. Clair patted the pouch tethered around his neck.

The rabbi glanced up and shook his head. "I could try to explain that inscription to you right now, but without an understanding of Kabbalah, it will hold no meaning for you."

"That's precisely the reason I've sought you out. I want to study Kabbalah."

"A study of Kabbalah is not Kabbalah," the rabbi said without looking up as he continued to arrange scrolls in the chest.

"I don't understand."

"Of course you don't. How could you possibly understand?" The rabbi got to his feet and limped over to the hearth. "To what may the thing be likened?" He took a blackened iron rod from its place against the hearthstones and stirred the glowing coals. "Look at this fire, Jonathan. I did not grow the tree that burns here. I did not cut it down. I didn't even strike the flint to light the spark. I tend the fire, nothing more. So it is with this." Rabbi Samuel leaned the rod against the hearth. "I can only tend a fire that burns in you. Do you have a soul that burns with the light of the divine emanation? Do you have the spark, the fuel, and the fire within you? You ask that I teach you, but this isn't about teaching. This is about you."

The rabbi settled into his armchair opposite the hearth and pointed to the padded footstool. "Please, Jonathan, sit down."

St. Clair shifted his leather scabbard to the side and sat. "Look what God hath wrought, Rabbi. He has made your enemy to sit upon your footstool."

The rabbi laughed and smoothed his beard. "I can see that you wish—"

Three taps came at the door. "Rabbi Samuel?"

"What is it?"

"I have the *lebiniyah* for the cat."

"Thank you, Ya'akov," the rabbi called, and turned to St. Clair. "Could you get it for me?"

As St. Clair unlatched the door, the cat brushed back and forth against his legs, purring loudly. "I'll take it," he said and held out his hand.

As Ya'akov passed the bowl to St. Clair, he looked past him at the rabbi. "We're nearly finished packing, Rabbi. Would you like some tea? We have a fresh pot."

"No, thank you, Ya'akov."

"Rabbi Samuel," the disciple persisted. "Is there *anything* at all that you require?"

"Only that you finish packing."

St. Clair pushed the door closed and set the latch. He knelt, scratched the cat on the head, and set the bowl on the floor. As he settled back on the footstool, the rabbi shrugged. "My disciples—they worry about me."

"That is as it should be—but where are your other disciples?"

"These two are all I have left." The rabbi frowned. "With Mongols in the East and wars of the Cross in the West, the region is too unstable, which is why I closed my academy and sent my pupils to study in Provençe and Spain—" The rabbi left off speaking as the cat began to growl and hiss. St. Clair turned and saw the cat edging away from the door, crouching low with flattened ears, baring its teeth.

"What in the name of heaven—" the rabbi began.

St. Clair jumped to his feet as the door shook with frantic pounding. "Rabbi Samuel! Guards of the *halka* are at the door. They demand to see you."

In a flash of white fur, the cat leapt out the window.

"Ask how many!" St. Clair instructed as the rabbi limped to the closed door.

"How many are there?" Rabbi Samuel asked through the door.

"I'm not sure—perhaps four. What should I do?"

"Tell him not to open to them!" St. Clair whispered, and vaulted out the window. He reached over his shoulder, drew his sword, and rounded the edge of the building.

The rabbi's disciple had underestimated the number of guards. There were six.

All wore the yellow robes, shining breastplates, and pointed helmets of the emir's personal escort. As St. Clair watched, they began to hack through the door with their scimitars, cutting away the splintered wood and pushing through the gap.

St. Clair darted forward and drove the point of his sword deep into the side of the trailing guard, between the leaves of brass armor. As the man fell, St. Clair leapt over him, slashing down at the next yellow robe. He felt flesh and bone give beneath his blade. From his right burst an ululating war cry, and he ducked as a curved blade hissed over his head. He swung his sword and the guard's cry strangled into silence. Another guard charged from the shadows, swinging his scimitar. St. Clair twisted his body away. The blade glanced off the shoulder of his mail shirt.

He fell backwards, crashing onto a wooden table. It splintered beneath his weight. He lifted his sword in time to deflect the slicing arc of another stroke. Again and again, the weapons clashed in a shower of sparks. He struggled to his feet and shunted off a thrust. In one fluid motion he rotated his sword and brought the blade down, splitting the guard's shining helmet and cleaving the skull.

As the guard's body dropped to the floor, St. Clair saw light filling the room. The rabbi's study stood open, the doorframe shattered.

"Rabbi!" He rushed forward, nearly tripping over a guard who lay facedown just past the door. At the far end of the study, St. Clair saw another guard advancing toward the rabbi with drawn scimitar. The rabbi stood with his back to the hearth, gripping the black iron poker in his hands.

As the guard raised his scimitar, St. Clair lurched forward, fearing he was already too late. In the next instant, the iron rod whirled in the rabbi's hands like a stave, striking the guard in the abdomen, then snapping against the yellow plumed helmet.

The guard collapsed at the rabbi's feet.

St. Clair stared down at the guard, then quickly surveyed the room before lowering his sword. "I didn't realize jousting was part of rabbinic training."

"I was one of five brothers," the rabbi said and leaned the rod against the hearth. "When we weren't studying Torah, we were hitting each other with sticks. I used to be pretty good at it."

"You still are," St. Clair said and nodded down at the guard.

"He's only stunned." The rabbi knelt and pulled off the tasseled cord girding the guard's yellow robe. "I'll bind his hands. What about the one by the door?"

St. Clair went over to him, knelt, and felt the guard's neck for a pulse. "This one won't need binding." He wiped his sword clean on the dead man's robe.

"Oh, my God! What of my disciples?" The rabbi rushed past St. Clair and out the door.

Following him out of the study, St. Clair crossed to the front doorway where a dead guard lay across the threshold. Grabbing hold of the bloodied robe, he pulled the body into the room. What remained of the door hung by a single hinge, and he pushed it closed as best he could. Turning, he saw the rabbi kneeling by one of his disciples. "Dead?"

Rabbi Samuel nodded.

"And the other?"

"Also."

"I'm sorry." St. Clair checked the bodies of the other guards.

"You said the emir wouldn't come for several days," the rabbi said as he climbed to his feet.

"They must have sent the letter with a rider ahead of the caravan."

The rabbi looked down at the bodies of his disciples. "We must bury them."

"There's no time, Rabbi. We must away, and quickly."

"I won't leave them like this."

"More guards will come."

"There's a shovel in the yard outside the study, and the earth is soft. It won't take long. I'll prepare their bodies for burial. You prepare the earth to receive them."

"You don't understand—"

"No, Jonathan, *you* don't understand. I *will* see these beloved boys properly buried."

"But, Rabbi—"

"Do as I say, Jonathan. If you truly wish to be my pupil, you must learn to do as I say."

Chapter Four

ד

La Rochelle
French Atlantic Coast
4 May, 1290

With dawn a faint blush along the eastern edge of the cobalt sky, Rabbi Yosef ben Asher looked toward the only world he had ever known—England—wreathed in darkness, somewhere beyond the Bay of Biscay. Banished by order of King Edward along with all the Jews of England, Reb Yosef sat astride a low stone wall, high on the cliff face beneath the walled city, looking over the water with no idea of where to go next.

In the pale half-light he saw someone approaching, mounting the steep flight of steps that intersected the terraced lanes of rough cobblestone that ran back and forth across the cliff face beneath La Rochelle. He looked closer and recognized the fashionably short cut of the black robe, the wide-brimmed black hat, and the trimmed black beard of Elijah ben Azariah. The rabbi stood up and waved.

Elijah, a successful merchant, had also served the rabbi as synagogue warden in York. For years Reb Yosef had relied on Elijah to manage day-to-day synagogue affairs, just as he depended on him when it came to dealing with gentiles. Now, with their world shattered and their future uncertain, Reb Yosef depended on Elijah all the more—for his own family and for the extended family of his congregation, more than a hundred souls.

"It's all arranged, Reb Yosef," Elijah called out as he paused on the steps to catch his breath. "We leave tomorrow for the overland trip to the Templar port of Collioure."

"Collioure?" Reb Yosef asked anxiously. "Where might that be?"

"On the Mediterranean coast of France . . ." Breathing heavily, Elijah finished the climb. "From Collioure we'll have passage on a Templar vessel . . . bound for the Land of Israel . . . and with fair winds . . . we should be there . . . well before Rosh Hashanah . . ."

Reb Yosef felt a rush of joy. *Could this be possible?* It seemed too good to be true. *There must be a catch* . . . "What will this cost us?"

"One talent of silver for each man, woman, and child."

"That's not cheap."

"We're paying for more than transportation, Rabbi," Elijah said as he removed his hat and wiped perspiration from his forehead. "The Templars guarantee our lodging, our victuals, and our safety."

"Excellent! But how did you manage to arrange all this? You don't speak the Franks' language."

"I had help—from a young Scotsman, a gentile."

"Really?" The rabbi made no attempt to conceal his skepticism. "And what does the young gentile ask in return?"

"Only that we pay his way. He wants to come with us."

"What does a Scotsman want in the Land of Israel?"

"He yearns to see Jerusalem, Rabbi. He's been in France for a year, studying for the priesthood." Elijah drew a deep breath. "I'll warrant there's no guile in him, Rabbi. He has such a fondness for the Psalms of David, he carries a copy in his pocket. I'll warrant he's a good lad . . ."

"Lad, you say? How old is he?"

"Just eighteen, but a head taller and stronger than most men."

"And this *boy* negotiated with the knights for our passage to the Land of Israel?"

"He did indeed, Rabbi. He's quick and seems to speak excellent French."

Reb Yosef frowned. "These Templars concern me, Elijah. I've heard they're just as eager to kill Jews as Moslems."

"I voiced the same concern, Rabbi. But the lad claims the Templars are different from common knights. He says they follow the example of Bernard, a priest who protected Jews from the excesses of the early Crusades." Elijah raised his shoulders. "But if you feel the risk is too great, we could stay here in France. Many of our brethren from York have so chosen—"

"No, we cannot stay in France." Reb Yosef sat back on the low wall bordering the stone steps. For a few moments he stared out over the bay as the sun rose and lamplighters extinguished the lights along the pier. He shook his head. "I don't trust the French. It hasn't been that long since the Disputation of Paris when they burned the Talmud. Mark my words, Elijah—next time it will be us they burn!" The rabbi looked down at the orange badge stitched to his black coat, stone tablets of the law in saffron taffeta. "I don't want to go anywhere where we'll have to wear a mark like this."

"I already cut off my badge, Rabbi. Why don't you do the same?" Elijah drew a knife from his belt and handed it to Reb Yosef.

"I've worn this blasted *tabula* for almost twenty years . . ." the rabbi murmured as he cut the stitches away and threw the bright orange badge to the ground. He handed the knife back to Elijah. "You've done well in securing our passage. Better we should go to the Land of Israel than anywhere else. But tell me more of this young Scotsman. Of what region is he?"

"Of Elderslie, Rabbi—sent to church school to become a priest, first to Dundee, then to France. He's been a year at a scriptorium, but the lad's not cut out for the priesthood—a cheerful giant of a boy, nine quarters large he is, no less, and strong—you should see him."

"Indeed! When do I meet him?"

"Any minute now. I sent him to get his hair shorn yesterday," Elijah said with a smile. "I told him that with long hair and a full beard, he could be mistaken for one of us. But with a shorn head he'll fit in nicely as a Templar."

Reb Yosef squinted down the terraced mountainside. "Is that him?"

"Indeed. Even at this distance, I'm certain." Elijah stood up, waving his hand. "Up here, lad!"

Taking the stone steps three at a time, a broad-shouldered youth moved quickly toward them. Drawing near, he pushed back the hood of his habit. "Master Elijah." He rubbed his head and laughed. "You didn't tell me my head would feel so cold!"

"Come, lad. I want you to meet our rabbi, Yosef ben Asher—another refugee from England and cruel King Edward."

"I'm honored to make your acquaintance, Rabbi!" With an easy smile, the boy extended a large hand.

Reb Yosef was surprised at the gentle strength in his grasp. "Tell me, son, do you plan to keep on growing?"

"I think I'm near done, sir."

"By what name are you called?"

"Here in France the monks call me Willelmus Wallensis."

"Good Lord, boy! What's that in plain English?"

"My name is William Wallace."

Chapter Five

ה

Safed
4 May, 1290
Late morning

As St. Clair finished digging the first grave, Rabbi Samuel appeared in the window overlooking the garden. "Jonathan, help me bring them out."

The bodies of the two disciples, shrouded in their striped and fringed prayer shawls, lay side by side in the study. St. Clair saw that the surviving guard was still unconscious, lying where he had fallen by the hearth. Wrenching the splintered study door off its hinges, St. Clair used it as a bier, and soon had both bodies in the garden.

He straightaway began digging the second grave. Again and again, the spade bit into earth and a second mound rose next to the deepening hole. Between each shovel stroke, he listened for footsteps. He was anxious to finish—to leave Safed.

The rabbi stood silently over the bodies of his disciples.

The sun had risen and the morning was warm. As St. Clair paused to strip off his hauberk, tunic, and lambskin undershirt, he looked up at the rabbi. "You see now that Maimuni did well in sending me to protect you. It is as he said—someone has persuaded the emir to take your life—"

"Solomon Petit."

"I've heard of him." St. Clair grunted as the grave grew deeper. "Something about a disagreement over Maimonides—"

"It's far more than a disagreement, Jonathan. Those who oppose Maimonides cannot be reasoned with, and Petit is one of their most violent leaders. He has exhorted his followers to erase all memory of Maimonides—to burn his manuscripts and to destroy his tomb in Tiberius. It was because of this that Maimonides' grandson, Rabbi David Maimuni, sought my assistance."

"Assistance?" St. Clair asked as he wiped the sweat from his forehead, his body flecked and smeared with dirt. "What assistance?"

"To stop Petit's rampage by issuing a ban against him, and if necessary, to excommunicate him. I've already completed a first draft of the writ of excommunication. Petit knows this. That's why he doesn't want me to reach Acre alive."

"Are there others who join you in this action?" St. Clair asked as he continued digging.

"Yes. A total of twelve rabbis."

"Does Petit mean to have you *all* killed?"

"I believe he has reserved this honor only for me. As the Gaon of Baghdad, I am the final word on Jewish law in the Orient. The others are under my authority. Petit's thinking is logical; kill the shepherd and the sheep scatter." The rabbi leaned over and looked into the grave. "That's deep enough."

Using ropes, they lowered each body down, and each time St. Clair heard the rabbi intone a benediction. "May he take his place in peace in the world to come."

St. Clair quickly covered the bodies with earth and packed the soil down.

This done, the rabbi threw a handful of grass and dirt in the direction of the graves with a final benediction. "Remember, O

Lord, that we are dust." Then, turning to St. Clair, he shook his head. "You're a mess, Jonathan. Draw water from the cistern and wash off. I'll bring you a cloth."

The gourd came up full of clear water. After taking a drink, St. Clair poured the rest over his head, feeling the cool water coursing down his chest and back. As he waited for the rabbi to return with a towel, he saw the small white cat in the yard, preening himself in the sun.

"Here you are, Jonathan," the rabbi said and handed him a white cloth.

St. Clair nodded toward the cat. "Did you bring Master Shoonrah with you from Baghdad?"

"Heavens, no. He's from here—a neighborhood cat and an excellent mouser." The rabbi lifted the cat in his arms and scratched him gently on the chin. "He did well before we came, and he'll do well after we leave. Though I will miss him very, very much." He placed the cat on the ground and looked at St. Clair. "Get your clothing and let's go inside."

St. Clair gathered his lambskin undershirt, tunic, hauberk, scabbard, and sword. Rounding the building toward the front entrance, he made certain the lane was deserted before beckoning the rabbi to follow.

Once back inside, the rabbi pointed to the clothing in St. Clair's arms. "I hope you're not thinking of wearing those things."

"You think it preferable I go about half naked?"

"Not at all," the rabbi said and handed him a striped robe. "Put this on."

"No."

"If you aspire to be my disciple, Jonathan, you must dress the part."

"Very well, but I'll wear my own clothing beneath."

"If you insist, but not the sword."

"I keep my sword," said St. Clair.

"No, Jonathan. You must travel with me as a disciple, not as an armed Templar. And we will be better served by our wits than by your sword. Give it to me."

St. Clair shook his head.

"Jonathan, as my disciple, you must trust me and do as I say—"

"As your *disciple*?" St. Clair asked with a smile.

"Yes—as my disciple."

"Very well, Rabbi. I will do as you say." He handed Rabbi Samuel the sword in its leather scabbard. Over his own clothing, he donned the striped robe and put the turban on his head. "How do I look?"

"It shouldn't cover your eyes. Wear it higher on your head. Like this." The rabbi reached up and made the adjustment.

"It's too big for me."

"Your hair is shorn. The turban will fit better once your hair grows out."

A low groan came from the study.

"The guard must be waking up," said St. Clair. "We should be off—"

"No. I want you to question him. We should know the emir's mind—"

"But Rabbi," St. Clair began.

"Disciple! Please question the guard." The rabbi pointed toward the study.

St. Clair stared at him and drew an impatient breath, then stepped swiftly through the doorway into the study where he found the guard struggling to free his hands.

St. Clair grabbed the guard's arm and turned him onto his back. "On whose authority did you come here?"

"Curse you for an infidel dog!" the guard shouted defiantly, his eyes blazing as he struggled to rise. "Coward! Untie me and fight me like a man!"

St. Clair placed his boot on the guard's shoulder, pinning him to the floor. "I ask you again, on whose authority?"

"Damnable Jew! May Allah rain curses as scorpions upon you!"

With his boot still on the guard's shoulder, St. Clair took the iron poker from its place by the hearth and placed the tip among the glowing coals. "On whose authority?"

The guard's eyes fixed on the rod in the hearth. "Who else's?" he spat. "The emir's!"

"Why? What does the emir want with the rabbi?"

"A letter came from Acre," the guard muttered.

"Who dispatched the letter?"

"One who wants the old man dead and offers a rich bounty. One of his own—a Jew."

St. Clair felt the rabbi's hand on his shoulder. "A word with you, Jonathan."

St. Clair looked down at the guard as he turned to leave. "Don't go anywhere."

Once outside the study doorway, St. Clair asked, "Should we gag him or kill him?"

"Neither. We should make an arrangement with him."

"An arrangement?" St. Clair asked, his voice rising in disbelief.

"Yes. We'll bribe him and have him take us to the emir at the palace."

St. Clair's jaw dropped. "What in the name of heaven are you talking about?"

"Making sure we get out of Safed alive."

"But I told you, Rabbi." St. Clair slapped his chest, his face reddening. "That's *my* part!"

"Don't be foolish, Jonathan. There are legions of Saracen troops between here and the coast."

"But ensuring your safe passage to Acre is *my* end of the bargain. And why would you ever trust our fate to the emir?"

"Because he answers to the Sultan and I carry the Sultan's promise of protection. Furthermore, the Sultan Qa'la'un is known to be a devout Moslem, and Moslems look upon Maimonides as one of their own—they call him Abu Amran and hold him in the highest reverence." The rabbi put his hands on St. Clair's shoulders. "Hear me, Jonathan! I'm sure that once the emir hears we are defending the legacy of Maimonides against Petit, he will side with us."

"But you heard the guard. What of the rich bounty the emir stands to receive from Petit?"

"I've considered that as well. Petit is not a wealthy man, and whatever gold he has promised the emir, I'll be able to match. With that, and the matter of Abu Amran, I'm certain we'll put ourselves in the emir's good graces."

St. Clair sighed and shook his head. "Well, just in case you're wrong, we may have another way out." He leaned close to the rabbi and said in a low voice, "The emir's palace used to be the citadel where I was posted when I first came to the Holy Land. We had a hidden passage from the main hall down to the valley at the base of Mount Safed. That passage is very likely still there . . ."

"Good. In the unlikely chance I'm wrong, I hope you're right about that passage."

"I hope so, too," said St. Clair and led the way back into the rabbi's study.

Chapter Six

ו

Safed
4 May, 1290
Midday

"Remember, you receive the other half of the gold once we're safely away from Safed," Rabbi Samuel whispered to the guard as they drew abreast of two courtiers lounging on a bench in the palace gardens.

"Hold your tongue or you'll get us all killed," the guard hissed as he prodded the rabbi and St. Clair forward, adding loudly, "Go along you two, keep moving!"

They quickened their pace along the broad path of crushed limestone that meandered through the gardens.

"And bear this in mind, my friend," Rabbi Samuel added, "once the emir hears you spared our lives out of reverence for Abu Amran, even greater will be your reward."

The guard grunted in reply.

St. Clair adjusted the turban on his head as he surveyed the hedgerows, green lawns, spreading pines, and tall cedars of the palace gardens. In the twenty years since the defeat of the Templars by the Mamluks, little had changed in the lower city, but the area on the summit of Mount Safed surrounding the citadel was unrecognizable. Of the order's stables, church, and dormitories, there remained only chunks of masonry scattered among the flowerbeds and lawns. The citadel came into view and St. Clair whispered to the rabbi, "There it is. But so changed—I hardly recognize it . . ."

As they passed through the arched doorway, St. Clair stared up at slabs of polished marble and multicolored mosaics. In the main hall, tall columns of veined gray marble held up a vaulted ceiling. In his day, this had been the Templars' dining hall, infested with black rats that ran along the dusty ceiling beams. Now rich tapestries hung from the rats' former domain.

As they advanced through the pillared hall, St. Clair searched with his eyes for the doorway to the passage that led down to the base of the mountain. Among the rugs and tapestries adorning the walls, he saw one that raised his hopes—a large woven rug bordered with elegant flourishes of the Koran.

The guard led them between two rows of Kurdish lancers with surcoats of yellow silk, gleaming breastplates, and helmets tufted with yellow plumes. Each held a long lance tipped with a double-edged steel blade. From the far end of the hall, a wiry Saracen in the splendid robes of a prince approached. Behind him were three men in white turbans, white robes sashed in red silk, and boots of red leather.

The guard stepped forward. "My Lord Viceroy, I bring to audience with the emir, Rabbi Samuel, Gaon of Baghdad, and his disciple."

St. Clair saw a trace of confusion flit across the viceroy's face.

"You are most welcome in our court, Rabbi. I am Viceroy Tewfiq Ayoub, master of shields and cupbearer to the emir."

The rabbi made a little bow with his head. "We are honored, my Lord Viceroy. May Allah preserve you and your master."

"And you also, Rabbi." murmured the viceroy. "You have some business with his Excellency?"

"Most assuredly, my lord." The rabbi held up a scroll. "This is an *irade* of safe passage from the Sultan Qa'la'un. We would be honored to receive a similar writ from the emir's own hand."

"I will make inquiry for you, Rabbi," the viceroy said and took the scroll. "In the meantime, these servants will attend you."

The rabbi bowed. "The emir is generous."

The viceroy turned and strode down a hallway that St. Clair remembered as the Templars' ambulatory, leading from the chancel to the cloister. Once he was gone, the guard leaned forward and whispered, "When do I get the rest of my gold?"

"I told you," Rabbi Samuel replied, "once we're away from Safed."

After a minute, the viceroy reappeared with a flourish of silk. "Fortune favors you, Rabbi. The emir will see you and your disciple." The viceroy glanced at the guard. "You will come also."

Passing through tall doors of beaten copper, they entered a sun-washed room with a cream-colored carpet. It bore little resemblance to the Templar chancel where St. Clair recalled gathering with his comrades in late afternoon for Vespers Mass on a rough stone floor. A cubical altar had stood in the center of the room, with four horns around the open Bible within a triangle of three candles. In its place now was a large table with inlaid wood polished to a golden glow. At the room's far end, the emir lounged on a high dais. Wearing a white turban and a flowing robe of white silk, he was flanked by a dozen advisors. As St. Clair drew near, he saw how the emir fingered his thin beard, gazing at them with one dark eye and one eye that was blind and white.

Viceroy Ayoub proclaimed with a low bow, "May Allah preserve the most excellent Emir Abdullah ibn Sayid ibn Elias, beloved of Allah, Master of Realms and Dominions! Begging your indulgence, Great One, I present to your eminence the Gaon of Baghdad, the most reverend Rabbi Samuel, and his disciple."

Rabbi Samuel made a token inclination of his head. "I bow before the magnificence of the Emir Abdullah."

Watching how the rabbi bowed, St. Clair did the same.

"And may Allah smile upon you, Rabbi. Your writ of passage is quite in order." The emir lifted the *irade* in a limp hand and regarded them with half-closed eyes. "My viceroy tells me you would speak with me."

"Yes, beneficent one. I am bound for Acre on a matter of great importance. Since I pass through your dominions, it is imperative that you know the nature and gravity of my mission."

"Please, continue."

"O Emir, there is one whose memory is sacred to your lordship and to his eminence, the Sultan Qa'la'un, may his days increase. I speak of one known to you as Abu Amran, the one we Jews call Maimonides."

One of the emir's courtiers leaned toward him, whispering in his ear. The emir waved him away. "I am well aware of Abu Amran, Rabbi. I have studied the *Guide for the Perplexed* in the exquisite Arabic in which it was written. And my physicians are schooled in Abu Amran's writings concerning every aspect of the body's health and disease. His memory is, indeed, as precious as carbuncles to the children of Islam."

"It delights my ears to hear this, great one. Verily, Abu Amran's legacy is one of many treasures that our people share. It is to protect this precious legacy that we are bound for Acre."

"His legacy requires your protection?"

"It does, great one. There is one in Acre of my faith, a renegade Jew, who seeks to erase the memory of Abu Amran. This same man has burned his writings and sent his spawn to destroy Abu Amran's tomb in Tiberius, which I believe is within your domain—"

"These foul acts are indeed repugnant in my eyes. If it were possible, I would reach out my hand and crush this faithless villain! But alas, I cannot, since Acre remains in the grip of the accursed barbarian crusaders. But tell me, Rabbi, who is this villain?"

"A Jew who brings his heresy from the land of the infidel Franks—my brother in the faith and my enemy—Rabbi Solomon Petit. It is against this man that I, as Gaon of Baghdad, will issue a ban. It is my hope that the threat of excommunication will force him to end his rampage against the legacy of Abu Amran."

"It is well that you have told me this, Rabbi, and I will offer you every assistance in the fulfillment of your mission."

"Thank you, great one, for we indeed require your help."

"Speak your need, Rabbi, and it is done."

"It is clear that our journey will become more treacherous as we approach the coastal frontier. An *irade* from your hand together with that of the Sultan might assure our safety."

"You will have it. Scribe, make ready your quill for a letter of safe passage for the worthy rabbi and his disciple. Furthermore, we will provide you with fresh horses, victuals, and an escort. Your mission demands no less."

The rabbi bowed. "O Emir, you are the very picture of beneficence and honor. Only let us repay your lordship's generosity. As our father Abraham once said, *I will not take a thread nor a shoe-lachet nor aught that is thine . . .*"

The emir sat forward and fixed the rabbi with his good eye. "What do you have to offer?"

The rabbi held up a leather pouch. "Gold dinars, great one. We pray you, accept this from our hand."

"That is well," said the emir. He motioned to a courtier who stepped forward, took the pouch, and brought it to the emir. St. Clair felt troubled as he watched the emir weigh the gold in his hands, a strange smile on his lips.

Rabbi Samuel spoke again. "We need only return to our academy to retrieve more gold, great one."

The emir nodded his assent. "When you return, the letter and all else will be ready for your departure. May peace be upon you."

The rabbi bowed. "And upon you, peace."

They left the throne room preceded by three courtiers, and passed amid the thick marble pillars of the main hall. The rabbi whispered to St. Clair in Aramaic, "Quickly, where's the hidden passage?"

"Why?"

"It's manifestly clear to me that I was wrong. The emir will, indeed, destroy us. Quickly! Where is it?"

St. Clair's eyes fixed on the decorative rug that hung on the wall to his left. "Follow me."

The emir tapped the armrest of his chair with long bejeweled fingers.

"My quill and ink are ready, Great One," announced his scribe.

"Leave me," said the emir.

"But Sire, the letter of safe conduct—"

"There will be no letter!" He waved away the scribe and courtiers. "Leave me. All of you. Except you two." He pointed to the guard and the viceroy, then curled his index finger at the guard. "Come here." The emir fixed the guard with his good eye. "How is it that this rabbi lives?"

"Sire, they . . . they . . . were armed . . ." the guard stammered, beads of sweat forming on his brow.

"Armed? This old Jew and his disciple? Do not try my

patience! Where's the rest of your company? Did they bribe all of you?"

"No, your eminence. All the others perished. I alone survived and prevailed against them."

"Silence, cur!" The emir sat back in his chair and pulled at his beard as he stared malevolently at the guard. "How much did they give you?"

"A . . . a few coins. . . ."

"Give them to me."

The guard lifted a pouch from beneath his armor. The viceroy snatched it away and gave it to the emir. The emir opened the pouch, scattered the coins on a satin cushion, and shook his head in disgust. "And for *this,* son of dogs, you brought them to the palace?"

"There was the matter of Abu Amran, Sire. I thought this was of importance—"

"You *thought*? It is not your purpose to think! But the old man does remain in our grasp, and in recognition of your long service to our person, Sergeant, we forgive you."

The guard fell to his knees. "Thank you, your eminence—"

"On one condition." The emir raised a slender finger. "You will accompany them to that hovel they call an academy with my lancers, and, once they have given us more gold, you will dispatch the old man and his disciple. Do you understand?"

"Yes, Sire. Thank you, Sire." The guard climbed to his feet and backed away, bowing. On reaching the doorway, he turned and disappeared into the main hall.

"Now, good viceroy, inform the lancers to kill the three of them once we have the gold."

"To hear is to obey." The viceroy strode to the doorway and stopped.

The three courtiers who had left with the rabbi and St. Clair were back. Breathing heavily as they approached the dais, they looked anxiously about the throne room. "Oh Emir, may you live forever," said one, bowing low. "The rabbi and his disciple did not follow us out of the palace. Did they perchance return here?"

The emir was quickly on his feet. "What are you talking about?"

"They were just behind us, Sire. But as we passed through the Hall of Pillars, they were gone, as if by some evil magic."

"Nonsense! They must be somewhere within the palace or on the grounds." He turned sharply. "Viceroy, alert the guards. It should be quick work to find them."

"And when they are found, Great One, shall they be brought back to the palace?"

"Only their heads, viceroy. Just bring me their heads."

Chapter Seven

ז

Safed
4 May, 1290
Early afternoon

St. Clair led the rabbi through the colonnade toward the tapestry as doubts stabbed through his mind; *is the passageway still there*? Lifting the edge of the pungent, goat-hair fabric, he reached out and felt the textured grain of a wooden door. He gave it a little push and sighed with relief as the door opened beneath his hand. "Quickly," he whispered as he slipped under the rug and through the door. In the weak light he could see the first steps of a stairwell descending into blackness.

The rabbi called to him softly. "Jonathan?"

"Rest your hand on my shoulder and step carefully, Rabbi. The stairs spiral to the left."

St. Clair blindly led the way, his right hand tracing the damp stone of the stairwell. After a minute, he asked, "What made you believe the emir wasn't going to help us?"

"He would have refused to take our gold, or at least made a good show of it."

"That's all?"

"Trust me, Jonathan. When you have lived long in the Orient, you learn to listen to the silence between words, to understand intention from the unspoken."

Descending slowly in the darkness, St. Clair listened for any sound of pursuit. He heard nothing but the drawing of their breathing and the rasping footfall of their boots on the rough stone steps. The dark smell of lichens hung in the air.

After a time, the rabbi spoke. "Jonathan—what was the name of that man who sent you to me?"

"Rabbi David Maimuni—"

"No, the one from long before, the one who saw the scroll when you first came to the Holy Land."

"Oh, him—Abraham Abulafiya. He had come from Saragossa on a quest to find the legendary River Sambatyon—"

"Shhh!" The rabbi's hand tightened on St. Clair's shoulder. "Do you hear that?"

St. Clair held his breath and listened. The silence was as perfect as the darkness. "I hear nothing, Rabbi. Perhaps it was just the echo of our own footsteps."

Continuing slowly down the stairwell, the rabbi asked, "Where did Abulafiya think to look for the legendary River Sambatyon?"

"Among the mountains of the Lebanon. But with Sultan Baybars on a rampage along the frontier, none could leave Acre. After a few weeks, Abulafiya gave up and sailed for Greece. I never saw him again."

"And it was during that time you showed him the scroll . . ."

"Yes, Rabbi. Do you know him?"

"Only by his reputation and his writings. And I know that he's now in hiding on the island of Comino—accused of claiming to be the Messiah. His opponents have issued a ban against him."

"Is that akin to excommunication?"

"A ban is the *threat* of excommunication. But tell me, Jonathan, are you not concerned about *your* excommunication?"

"For what offense?"

"I should think that your order would not look with favor upon your consorting with Jews . . ."

"I've been guilty of that offense since I first came to the Holy Land . . ." St. Clair laughed softly as he continued moving down the dark stairwell, the gentle pressure of the rabbi's hand on his shoulder. "Beginning with Abulafiya, I sought out any who might help me comprehend the meaning of my scroll. When I was dispatched to the garrison in Safed I learned the rudiments of Hebrew and Aramaic from Jewish shopkeepers. I then began coming to the academy of Rabbi Jacob. It became my habit almost every day to listen outside the window in the study that looks out to the garden. From there, I could hear the lesson well enough and eventually, I learned to follow the discussions."

"Were you ever discovered?"

"Yes, I was. Actually, it was my own doing. One day Rabbi Jacob posed a question that none of his pupils could answer. I couldn't restrain myself, and from my place of concealment in the garden, I answered the question. That was the first time I spoke, and once Rabbi Jacob and his pupils overcame their fear of me, I regularly joined in the lessons, leaning in at the window." St. Clair drew a deep breath. "But all that ended when the Mamluks conquered Safed. Our entire garrison was put to the sword."

"How did you survive?"

"I was struck on the head by a lance and covered with blood. They thought me dead and placed me among the corpses." Tracing the stairwell wall with his right hand, St. Clair stared into the darkness as images of that day flooded his mind. "From where I lay, I watched as they butchered my brothers—the beheadings. My commander, William de Rogé, who was my teacher and my friend, was flayed and burned." St. Clair drew a deep breath as he continued to descend, step-by-step in the darkness. He seldom thought of that day. Whenever he did, a sense of guilt stung his mind like nettles—*I watched and did nothing.* He shook the thought away. "Afterwards, the Mamluks forced the Jews of Safed to bury the dead. A pupil of Rabbi Jacob saw that I lived and brought me to the academy. They hid me and tended my wounds until I was well enough to travel. Then Rabbi Jacob closed the academy in Safed, leaving it with a caretaker. He moved all his pupils and their families to Acre where he joined the great academy—Midrash Hagadol."

"Don't tell me you became a student there—"

"Not officially. But I no longer needed to eavesdrop. Rabbi Jacob spoke no French, and wished to converse with his brethren at the academy on worldly matters. So we struck a bargain. I taught him French, and he continued to guide me in studying the Hebrew Bible . . ."

"Any instruction in matters of Kabbalah?"

"Not really, but after Rabbi Jacob died, I continued my studies with a young scholar named Isaac. He had a growing interest in Kabbalah and gave me a book to read—the Book of Brightness, called the *Bahir.* At first, I thought it was a book like other books—that I might read and understand—a book that would instruct me. Indeed, the *Bahir* seemed to speak of ordinary things, but when I tried to comprehend the text, all meaning slipped from my grasp. I understood nothing."

"The text is enigmatic on purpose—to tease the reader—to invite you to understand and then to defy understanding. Do you believe the Torah is any less mysterious than the *Bahir*?"

"I'm familiar with Torah, Rabbi. Even before my studies in Safed and Acre, I studied the Five Books of Moses as a Cistercian monk."

"So the meaning of the Torah is clear to you?"

"Yes. The Torah speaks of the history and laws of the Jews.

It's quite straightforward."

"Is it?" Rabbi Samuel asked with a soft laugh. "Is that what you think Torah is, Jonathan—ordinary language about ordinary things? If you believe Torah is merely a collection of laws and nice stories, you have understood nothing."

"I'll grant there's a greater witness, Rabbi. Indeed, as Christians, we discern foreshadowing of Jesus Christ in the text—in such types and symbols as the Pascal Lamb, the brazen serpent, the Tabernacle, Isaiah's suffering servant, Ruth's kinsman redeemer, and Daniel's fourth man in the furnace—but apart from such as these, the Torah appears quite unambiguous—"

"Not so, Jonathan. I tell you that in *every* word, indeed, in every *letter,* Torah conveys sublime secrets of God's inner being."

St. Clair smiled to himself as he continued to descend slowly, feeling for each step, groping forward. "Given my level of understanding, Rabbi, it seems total darkness is an appropriate setting for this discussion."

"An apt metaphor, Jonathan. And just as you are compelled to move through this darkness toward light, I would suggest that the light, itself, compels you."

"The light compels me? What's your meaning, Rabbi?"

"Let me illustrate with a parable from your own world—the parable of the knight and the hidden maiden . . ."

The rabbi paused and St. Clair waited for him to continue, listening to the echo of their footsteps, feeling the constant and gentle weight of the rabbi's hand on his shoulder. Finally the rabbi began to speak.

"There is a knight who travels through a strange land and chances upon a remote castle in a hidden valley. There is a beautiful maiden in the castle's high tower with one small window looking out to the world. On this particular day she opens the casements and shows her face for an instant, then retreats back into the tower. The only one who sees her face is the knight who happened to pass by the castle and look up at that particular moment. He believes it was out of love that the maiden chose to reveal herself to him. And in his heart, he becomes her lover. He sets up camp near the castle and every day passes by the tower. He spends hours looking up at the window, and every so often, he catches a glimpse of her, and with every glimpse, he is drawn to her all the more. Day after day he returns in hope of seeing her, despite the barriers—a deep moat, high walls, guards. He perseveres. He cannot do otherwise, and over many years, the maiden slowly reveals more and more of herself to him—every glimpse carrying a message of love. And the barriers fall away." Rabbi Samuel fell silent.

"The knight showed great love," St. Clair whispered.

"Even so the maiden, Jonathan, though her love is not apparent to the outside world. She does not reveal herself to everyone. She shows her secret love only to him."

St. Clair felt the rabbi stop, his hand gripping his shoulder, his voice close to St. Clair's ear.

"Very few Jews are aware of the love with which the Torah calls to those of her choosing, Jonathan. How is it that *you* have heard this calling? How is it that you have seen the maiden's face?"

St. Clair felt the rabbi's hand relax, followed by two gentle pats on his shoulder. As he continued down the spiral steps, his heart pounded with a strange and familiar joy. Rounding a turn, he cleared his throat. "I think I finally see some light."

"You speak metaphorically?"

"No. I really see light below. We're almost there."

"Good."

They descended the final rough-hewn steps, dropping steeply toward a bright patch of light. As they stood in the mouth of a crevasse, surrounded by limestone boulders, blinking in the sunlight, the rabbi turned to St. Clair.

"We should continue on our way with all haste, Jonathan. They'll be looking for us."

St. Clair frowned. "And we won't be able to retrieve anything from the academy. We have no mount, no money, and no food. It will be difficult to reach Acre."

"We're not going to Acre. We're going to Jerusalem."

"We *are*?" St. Clair couldn't hide his surprise. "But I had planned to be back in Acre within a fortnight. And what of your ban against Petit? You told me you had already written a draft of the writ—"

"I did. It's back at the academy with everything else, but no matter. I'll write another and find a way to have it delivered to the rabbinic court in Acre."

"But I thought this matter of Maimonides was of great importance—"

"It is, but it's more important for us to go to Jerusalem!"

"When did *that* become important?"

"When I saw your scroll, Jonathan. That's when."

St. Clair's shock gave way to curiosity. "You've told me nothing of the inscription, Rabbi. Please tell me now."

"No." The rabbi shook his head. "Only when I myself understand more of it, and only when you are able to comprehend."

"But you must tell me why it leads us to Jerusalem. You must at least tell me *that.*"

Rabbi Samuel fixed his gaze on St. Clair. "The inscription leads us to Jerusalem to find a certain gateway—a gateway to the Upper Jerusalem."

St. Clair shrugged. "There are any number of gateways to the upper city . . ."

"No, Jonathan. I speak of another place altogether. *Yerushalayim shel ma'la*—the Upper Jerusalem—a place not of this world."

"I don't understand . . ."

"You don't now, but you will."

Chapter Eight

Acre
4 May, 1290
Late afternoon

Rabbi Solomon Petit was hungry. Sitting at the table in his study, he drew an impatient breath and contemplated his hands. The fingernails, ridged and yellowed with age, needed trimming. The skin, tethered over heavy blue veins, had acquired the dry aspect of the scrolls he had studied since youth. He had washed his hands and recited the requisite blessing, fully expecting that his dinner was ready. But there was no dinner on the table, only the ponderous copper candleholder with twelve thick candles. And his hands.

Heavy footfalls sounded from the hall and the door scraped open. Petit's steward, Menahem Mendel, filled the doorway. "Your dinner, Rabbi," Menahem intoned. He shuffled forward and carefully placed the tray on the table. Petit snatched up the bread roll, mumbled the appropriate blessing, tore off an olive-sized piece, and stuffed it into his mouth. The steward retreated toward the door.

"Will you require anything else, Rabbi?"

Petit surveyed the tray. "No. You may go."

"Yes, Rabbi. Thank you, Rabbi," the steward mumbled and

backed out the door.

Petit tore off another piece of bread and began to spoon the lentil soup into his mouth. The soup was tepid and lacked salt, the bread stale and flavorless. *How I miss the bread of France.* Though ten years had passed since he left Paris, there were still a great many things he missed about France—bread was one of them.

Yet he was glad to have left. Glancing at the burning candles, he remembered how the flames had devoured thousands of holy texts after the Disputation of Paris. He could still recall the acrid smoke, the black cloud shrouding the sky. He sighed and lifted the bowl to his lips, finishing the soup in a noisy swallow. He was cleaning the bowl with the last of the bread when there was a knock at the door.

"Who is it?" he called.

"Isaac," came the reply.

"Come." Petit stuffed the last morsel of bread into his mouth as Isaac pushed the door open. "Sit with me," Petit said with his mouth full and nodded at the chair to his right. He wiped his mouth with the back of his hand, then lifted a small brass bell from the tray and shook it. The sharp, joyless ring was swallowed in the shadows that hovered at the edges of the candlelight. "Will you join me in some bitters?"

"I would be honored, Rabbi." Isaac sat down and folded his hands on his lap. "Do you wish to speak with me in reference to our discussion in synagogue this morning?"

"Indeed, I do," Petit said as he brushed breadcrumbs and stray bits of lentil from his beard. Sitting back, he stared at Isaac, relishing this particular opportunity to challenge and test his pupil. "Answer a question for me, Isaac; which is greater, the wisdom of God or the wisdom of man?"

Isaac drew a deep breath and replied, "The wisdom of God is greater than that of man, Rabbi Petit. Indeed, the wisdom of

God is beyond all human comprehension. Though the Greeks claim otherwise, it is self-evident to anyone of discernment that the Torah of Israel is far above the wisdom of man, far above the foolishness of the Greeks."

"You answer well, Isaac." Petit smiled through the thicket of his beard. "But, as you know, we contend with certain heretics in a bitter struggle over the very soul of our faith. They believe that man, a vessel of clay, can fathom the wisdom of God. Polluted by their study of mathematics and philosophy, these heretics insist that man is able to comprehend the mysteries of nature. Their secular studies only *diminish* their love of Torah and their devotion to God. Truly, this is arrogance of the worst sort. And this arrogance leads to heresy."

Isaac nodded his assent. "It is as you say, Rabbi."

"Other facets of the controversy are more troubling . . ." Petit began when the door scraped open.

"You rang, Rabbi?" Menahem Mendel asked as he shuffled into the study.

"I rang long ago. Bring a bottle of bitters and two cups."

"Yes, Rabbi." The steward bowed and backed out the door.

Petit spoke again to Isaac. "Greek foolishness is only one of the many facets of our controversy with the apostate, Maimonides, and his spawn. For example, do you believe it is proper for the community to support scholars who study Torah?"

"Of course, Rabbi," Isaac answered.

"Well, according to the heretics who follow Maimonides, financial support for those of us who devote our lives to Torah is somehow *wrong.* They would have us working as porters or tailors, studying Torah in our spare time." Petit rolled his eyes. "Like common laborers, Isaac. Can you believe such insanity?"

"No, Rabbi."

"But that's not the worst of it. In their arrogance, the followers of Maimonides brazenly promote his writings over those of the Talmud—placing Greek philosophy over the Talmud! Is this not apostasy of the highest order?"

Isaac nodded and mouthed one of Petit's favorite slogans. "It is written that the wisdom of the Greeks bears flowers with no fruit."

"Exactly! The followers of Maimonides would have us polluting our minds with Greek foolishness—substituting this heresy for our faith in the one true God of Israel!" Petit leaned forward, his face flushed, perspiration beading on his forehead and along his nose. "In France, we issued a ban against this sower of discord. Now we must extend the *herem* to the Holy Land. We are the last hope of the true faith!" Petit shook his finger at Isaac. "We *must* prevail in this struggle. That is why I need your help."

"Of course, Rabbi."

"Then hear me well, Isaac." Petit lifted the skullcap off his head, fringed by gray stubble, and wiped away the perspiration. "The demon grandson of Maimonides is recently come to Acre. A cast-off of his own community, he has brought his grandfather's poisonous heresy here."

"Do you speak of David Maimuni, Rabbi, the Nagid of Egypt?"

"He is the Nagid of nothing!" Petit snapped and patted the skullcap back on his head. "Even the Jews of Egypt reject him."

The door rasped open and Menahem sidled in, carrying a wooden tray with a bottle and two cups. The candle flames wavered, casting a shifting lacework of shadows over the table as the steward set the tray down. "Your bitters, Rabbi."

"Menahem, see to it that we are not disturbed."

"Yes, Rabbi," the steward said heavily and pulled the door closed as he left again.

The cork squeaked as Petit twisted it out of the bottle. "By himself Maimuni is nothing." Petit measured the amber liquid into each of the cups. "However, he has enlisted the help of other apostate Jews of the Orient to force their heresies upon us." Petit took his cup, threw his head back, and drank. "That is why I asked you to send your Templar friends to speak with me."

"Yes, Rabbi. I have conveyed your request to the knights."

"So where are they?" Petit banged his cup down on the table. "Where are they? The heretic from Baghdad who comes to Maimuni's aid might soon be at the gate! Where are the knights?" He poured himself another cup, tilted back his head, and emptied the cup. Then, reaching into a pocket of his coat, he produced a leather purse full of coins, which he slammed down on the table in front of Isaac. "Here! *This* is a language the knights understand. I want a dozen of them here before nightfall. I want them to begin watching this very night—for that snake from Baghdad, or for any communication from his hand!" Petit leaned close. "Do you understand me?"

"Yes, Rabbi," Isaac replied, his voice barely above a whisper.

"Good, good." He patted Isaac on the arm. Then, leaning back, he poured himself another cup of bitters, gulped down the liquor, and turned his face to Isaac. "There is a second thing I require of you," he said and handed Isaac a folded piece of parchment.

Isaac unfolded the stiff, light brown parchment, turning it over in his hands. "It's blank, Rabbi."

Petit leaned forward, his face glistening with perspiration. "See that it's filled."

"Filled, Rabbi?"

Petit pointed a crooked finger at the parchment. "I want a careful accounting of the strength of Acre's knights."

"I . . . I'm not sure I understand . . ." Isaac stammered.

"These knights protect us, Isaac. Our lives are in their hands. In view of this, we can perhaps advise them how best to defend

Acre against the Mamluks. In order to insure their strength, we must know their weaknesses. I wish to know how many knights are billeted here, how many heavy horse, weaponry, siege engines, and the like. I want to know how and where they guard the city wall. Show me all this in writing—with maps and tables." Petit poured himself another glass of bitters and winked at Isaac over the glass. "You fill the parchment with an accounting of *that*."

Once back in his room, Isaac sat on the edge of his bed and breathed a deep sigh. He hated himself for pretending to agree with Petit.

Looking down at the evenly stitched seam along his sleeve, he frowned as he recalled how Petit had derided those who worked for a living and studied Torah in their spare time. *Common laborers, he called them. My father is a tailor, and this frock coat I wear is his work.* He ran a finger along the seam. *There is nothing common about my father. He's a good Jew and a good tailor, and I'm proud of him . . .*

Isaac looked at the whitewashed walls of his room, at his writing table, and out the window at a tall palm tree standing against the blue sky. *Soon I'll be free of Rabbi Petit, his anger, and his foul breath. But for now, he is my teacher. And I have a job to do.*

He stood up and felt for the parchment and sack of coins in his coat pocket. *I'll start with the Templar guards at the land gate.*

Chapter Nine

ט

Safed
4 May, 1290
Late afternoon

Viceroy Tewfiq Ayoub glided swiftly forward, his robe of white silk billowing behind as he made for the throne-room door. Even though he knew his master, the emir, was at supper, he never brooked delay in bringing him news—good or bad.

Without hesitating, he pushed on the beaten-copper door and it swung open. He stepped forward and bowed flawlessly. "O Emir, I beg your forgiveness—"

"Have they been found?" the emir asked as he lounged on velvet cushions by a shiny platter, deftly molding shredded lamb and semolina into a neat ball with his long fingers.

"There is no trace of them, my lord," the viceroy replied, "not in the palace and not in the garden, not at their academy nor along the road to Acre—"

"Bah!" The emir threw the morsel down. "Food holds no savor for me with the old man out of my grasp!" He climbed to his feet and paced along the dais.

The viceroy watched the emir pace, knowing that in this manner he kept his own counsel, and at such times, one did not speak. He felt proud that he knew the emir's mind. *But, know-*

ing his mind as I do, how I loathe him . . .

For years, Ayoub had chafed beneath the emir's arrogant whims. A false demeanor of obsequious deference had served him well, and he had risen swiftly. Starting as table-setter, he had ascended to slipper holder, then lord of the chair, and finally to his present duties as cupbearer, master of shields, and viceroy. The years of flattery had gained him much, including a measure of the emir's trust—but only a measure. Ayoub knew the emir didn't trust him completely. Indeed, he didn't trust anyone. But Ayoub also knew he had done nothing to betray the emir's trust. *Not yet . . .*

"How could they have escaped the palace?" the emir muttered as he stopped pacing and fixed Ayoub with his good eye. "I am deeply vexed, good Viceroy—do you know why?"

"Great One, I believe the source of your vexation is not the loss of gold."

"You are correct, my most sapient viceroy—it isn't about the gold. In exchange for the life of the old man, Rabbi Petit of Acre has offered me something far more precious than gold . . ." He descended the steps leading down from the dais. "Can you imagine what he offered me?"

"Diamonds, my lord? Precious stones?"

"A far greater jewel," the emir whispered and draped a long arm across Ayoub's shoulders. "Listen well, good viceroy, for what I now impart to you must be held in the strictest confidence. If you were ever to repeat this to anyone, your life would be short and your death would be slow."

"Great One, my discretion and my life are yours."

"Your sentiments are correct and elevated." The emir drew closer, breathing his lamb-scented breath in the viceroy's face. "Know this—for the life of Rabbi Samuel, Petit has promised me Acre."

"Acre, Sire?"

"Yes." A smile spread over the emir's face. "The secrets of Acre's defenses."

"Ah!" The viceroy nodded. "Now I understand."

"Then you also understand that the man who conquers Acre might command loyalty in many quarters . . ."

"Indeed, Sire, and your eminence is already held in the highest esteem by the Sultan Qa'la'un, may he live forever—"

The emir's face darkened. "May he most certainly *not* live forever!"

"My . . . my lord?" stammered the viceroy.

"Qa'la'un is old and weak." The emir sneered. "He has squandered our natural advantages and made treaties with the infidels instead of crushing them. The victor of Acre would stand above this dotard like the great Salah ad-Din over a donkey."

Ayoub could scarcely believe his ears. *To speak thus of the sultan is the very height of treason.* His heart pounded and his mind raced with the implications of the emir's words. Betraying none of his excitement, he bowed his head. "I believe I follow my lord's meaning . . ."

"And?" The emir gripped the viceroy's shoulders.

"And I stand at your side, my lord, now and always."

"That is well." Giving the viceroy's shoulders a final squeeze, the emir stepped away. "And for your loyalty and service, you and your family will prosper . . ."

The beaten-copper doors creaked open and a herald announced, "The captain of the guard, your Lordship!"

Doffing his yellow-plumed helmet, the guard bowed. "Your Excellency! We have found no sign of the rabbi or his disciple at the academy of Rabbi Jacob."

"What *did* you find?"

"Five dead guards of the halka, Sire, and *this.*" The guard held up St. Clair's sword in its leather scabbard. "I'll warrant it belonged to a Templar—there's a device upon the hilt."

"Give it me!" Taking the scabbard, the emir grasped the hilt and unsheathed the sword. He frowned as he studied the blade. "Now, what would Jews be doing with a weapon of the infidels?"

"In all likelihood, my lord," the viceroy offered, "this sword was hidden years ago, during the time of the Templars in Safed. The Jews apparently came upon it, and seeing it might have some value, they kept it."

The emir slowly shook his head. "No, Viceroy. The infidels have been gone for some twenty-five years, yet see how the blade shines . . ."

The captain cleared his throat. "Begging your royal pardon, Sire, but there's something else . . ." He pointed at the sword. "I'll warrant several of my dead comrades were dispatched by this very weapon—one man's helmet and skull were cleaved through. Only a heavy broadsword in strong hands could have struck such a blow."

"But who?" the viceroy asked. "Certainly not the old man . . ."

"What of his disciple?" asked the emir. "A rather large fellow." He slowly rotated the blade, looking at his reflection in the shining metal. "I wonder . . ."

Along the road from Safed to the Galilee
4 May, 1290
Afternoon into evening

"Please, knight," the rabbi pleaded. "My old body can't maintain this pace."

"We'll rest in yonder grove, Rabbi. The trees will give us ample cover, and we'll be able to see if any follow us."

St. Clair paced swiftly down the muddy track between clumps of scrub brush, beneath an overcast sky. Beside the path coursed a thin rivulet of water. He entered a stand of cypress, then turned and eyed the valley and hills to the northwest.

"Do you see anyone?" asked the rabbi.

"No. But we have far to go. It's thirty leagues to Jerusalem—"

"But only three to the encampment I told you of on the shore of the Galilee. We should be there before nightfall, and there we'll find friendly hosts and warm lodgings for the night . . ."

"I hope so," St. Clair said as he studied the lowering sky. "We're in for foul weather." Turning, he saw that the rabbi had taken off his turban and was fanning himself as he leaned against a tree. "Are you ready to go on?"

"I'll need a few minutes for afternoon prayer." Rabbi Samuel replaced his turban and pointed to the south. "Jerusalem is that way?"

St. Clair nodded and watched as the rabbi clasped his hands behind his back and began murmuring—the words coming quickly as he began to sway, bending at the waist.

St. Clair realized it was time for Vespers. Kneeling on one knee, he closed his eyes, crossed himself, and bowed his head. When he finished, he opened his eyes and saw the rabbi step backward and bow as if leaving the court of an unseen king. St. Clair genuflected and rose to his feet.

Rabbi Samuel chuckled and shook his head. "Forgive me, Jonathan. It's just that, dressed as you are, as a pious Jew of the East—to see you kneel and cross yourself like that . . ." The rabbi shook with laughter.

St. Clair looked down at his robe. "I'll be careful about that. Since I'm dressed as a Jew, I should appear to pray like one."

"At least outwardly. How you actually speak to God is your own business."

They left the grove and plunged through long grasses waving beneath a cold wind that bent the trees and keened through bare branches. The sky glowed as the setting sun hovered on the horizon beneath the heavy clouds, setting them afire.

Cresting a hill, they stopped short. The smooth mirror of the Galilee stretched to the horizon, shining scarlet beneath the sky.

"There she is," the rabbi whispered.

For a few moments, St. Clair could not speak. When he found his voice, he whispered, "The beauty of heaven is, indeed, reflected on earth." He looked at Rabbi Samuel and added, "As it is written—as above, so below."

"Very apt, Jonathan." The rabbi patted St. Clair on the back and nodded toward the lake. "To what may the thing be likened?"

"You speak of the lake, Rabbi?"

"Yes. But night comes quickly. Let's talk of this as we continue on our way."

St. Clair started down the hill through the tall grass. Rabbi Samuel, following in his wake, began to speak.

"From here we see only the surface of the lake, Jonathan. So it is with Kabbalah. Why is it you wish to immerse yourself in the deepest water? Would it not suffice to observe its beauty from afar?"

"Would that suffice, Rabbi?" St. Clair asked as he pushed forward. "You've told me each letter of Torah conveys hints of God's hidden mysteries. Is it not vital that I go deeper?"

"Perhaps, but what you ask is daunting, Jonathan, and I must warn you—for those who are untested, these hidden matters can create much confusion . . ."

"I thought Kabbalah was a way to clear away the confusion."

"For some it's a way to *catalogue* the confusion, to guide one in navigating the mysteries. But for the uninvited, for those without the proper abilities, Kabbalah may confound and mislead into madness, even unto death. Those who suggest that Kabbalah is for everyone create a snare for the unprepared."

St. Clair stopped walking and turned to face the rabbi. "How is one deemed able to receive this knowledge?"

"That's up to the teacher."

"What does the teacher look for?"

"First and foremost, a certain level of life experience, maturity. In the *Gemara* it states that one should be at life's halfway stage before any other considerations."

"What other considerations? Such as being Jewish?"

"That's perhaps assumed. It's not mentioned specifically."

"So what *is* to be considered?"

Rabbi Samuel placed his hand alongside St. Clair's face. *"Hakarat panim*—the initiate's bearing, his expression, his eyes. Also, the lines on the palm—*sidrei sirtutin* . . ."

"I thought palm reading was the domain of Arabs and Greeks, not of Jews."

"On the contrary, Jonathan. It's long been a Jewish tradition. Is it not written in the book of Job: *He seals up the hand of every man, that all men may know His work* . . ."

St. Clair extended his hand. "Read my palm, Rabbi."

The rabbi peered closely at St. Clair's hand, then looked away. "There's not enough light. Come. We're almost there. The village of Tel Hum is at the bottom of this hill . . ."

St. Clair stood, watching how the rabbi limped as he moved through the tall grass down the hill. Suddenly, it came to him. "Wait!"

The rabbi turned. "Yes?"

"Is Tel Hum not the site of Kfar Nahum—that which the Vulgate calls Capernaum?"

"It is."

"Is it possible?" St. Clair murmured as he looked over the grassy hill that sloped down to the Galilee. "Rabbi, if the site of Capernaum is at the bottom of this hill, then *this* must be the Mount of the Beatitudes! The multitude would have been right here, listening, when the words of Jesus' blessings were first spoken . . ."

"How many blessings did he speak here?" Rabbi Samuel asked as he took a few steps up the hill toward St. Clair.

"Eight—the same number of points on the splayed Templar cross."

"Could you recite them for me?"

"Certainly." Switching from Arabic to Aramaic, St. Clair began; "*Too-vey-hon le-mis-kney va-roah*—Blessed are the poor in spirit, for theirs is the kingdom of Heaven. Blessed are they that mourn, for they shall be comforted. Blessed are the meek, for they shall inherit the earth. Blessed are those who hunger and thirst after righteousness, for they shall be filled. Blessed are the merciful, for they shall obtain mercy. Blessed are the pure in heart, for they shall see God. Blessed are the peacemakers, for they shall be called the sons of God. Blessed are they who are persecuted for righteousness' sake . . ." St. Clair bowed his head. "For theirs is the kingdom of Heaven."

The rabbi slowly exhaled. "Wasn't this also the place where Jesus chose his disciples?"

"It was."

Rabbi Samuel placed a hand on St. Clair's shoulder and whispered, "Here also will I choose my disciple."

Chapter Ten

י

Approaching Bordeaux
Southern France
4 May, 1290
Evening

Eleven hours out of La Rochelle, the road began to climb through Gascony toward the Pyrenees. William Wallace, tired of sitting in the wagon with his Jewish patrons, rode one of the Templars' extra horses. He glanced into the deep gorge where the Garonne ran, turbid and green-yellow, toward the sea. Behind him, the wagons rattled and lurched along the rutted road, skirting the edge, at times by no more than a hand's breadth.

The sun had nearly set when a city wall came into view, high on a steep hill, shining in the scarlet evening through the dust. Tattered gray clouds edged in crimson unfurled like banners above the battlements.

"Bordeaux!" came the hoarse voice of Imbert Blake. Wallace watched as the Templar wheeled his horse about, his face and beard covered with a fine dusting from the road. "We'll quarter there for the night."

Wallace urged his horse forward. "How far to Collioure and the great sea?"

"At least three days, but our voyage over sea will wait upon the west wind, William. On its wings, with God's grace, we'll be carried to the Holy Land. Now get back and keep the wagons moving."

After a year in the cold scriptorium, Wallace thrilled at the freedom of the journey, and the certainty that he would soon see Jerusalem. The words of a psalm rose in his mind: *Let us go to the house of Adonai. Our feet will stand in your gates, O Jerusalem!* As he rode through the dusty heat, his imagination was filled with vague notions of the Holy Temple, the Sepulcher, a perfect City of God.

Once past the ramparts of Bordeaux, onlookers crowded the streets; cheering the Templars and gawking at the Jews with their dark robes, black hats, and side locks. William Wallace rode next to the wagon with Rabbi Yosef ben Asher and Elijah ben Azariah.

"Dieu vous bénissent, chevalier!" a shrill voice sounded from the crowd and a corpulent gentleman bustled forward. Mistaking Wallace for a Templar, he began walking alongside his horse. "Assistant Constable Guillaume at your service, *chevalier.*" He saluted smartly. "Another group of pilgrims for the Holy Land?"

"Yes, good constable," Wallace replied, though the man's Norman French dialect wasn't easy to understand.

The man squinted into the wagon. "And what manner of people are these?"

"Sons and daughters of Abraham."

"Jews, then." He nodded. "I thought as much. We don't have many Jews around here anymore." He smiled brightly and waved to them.

"These Jews are from York, good constable," Wallace added.

"We bid you welcome, Jews," the constable called.

"Not so fast, my dear constable." A Dominican friar, apparently coming from supper, wiped greasy hands on his cowled brown robe as he strode forward. Raising a pudgy hand, he called out, “Halt!”

The wagon driver, looking from the friar to Wallace in confusion, pulled back on the reins, and with his free hand set the lever, locking the wheels.

The friar bowed. “We bid you and your company welcome, *chevalier.*”

“You are gracious, Father.” Wallace didn’t attempt to correct the misconception that he was a Templar. He rather enjoyed it.

“Will you be staying long?”

“I believe . . .” Wallace began and left off speaking when Imbert Blake rode up.

“What’s this about, then?” the knight asked sharply in English.

Wallace nodded at the friar. “The good Father was asking how long we’ll be staying in Bordeaux.”

Blake reined his horse around and looked down at the fat priest. “Only for the night, good friar,” he said in French. “We depart on the morrow for Collioure.”

“In that case, sir, I wish to address your Jews in the brief time given to us.”

Blake drew a deep breath and rolled his eyes. “Get on with it, then.”

Stepping around to the side of the wagon, the friar looked up, shading his eyes against the setting sun. “Who is your leader, Jews? Is there a rabbi among you?”

Reb Yosef made no response.

“I charge you, sirs, I . . .”

“Excuse me, Father,” Wallace said and moved his horse forward. “These people are newly come from England and have no knowledge of the French language.”

“Then you shall translate, *chevalier.* Please inquire if there is a rabbi among them.”

After William repeated the question in English, Reb Yosef rose to his feet.

"Greetings, Rabbi. We are empowered by the Holy Father to present you with the word of God."

Wallace glanced at Blake and muttered in English. "Can he force them?"

Imbert nodded wearily. "And the sooner he begins, the sooner he'll be done." He wheeled his horse about. "I'll see to our lodgings."

The friar wiped beads of perspiration from his clean-shaven face. "Tell the rabbi that we will speak to the lot of them. For they are compelled to gather at our call. Have them follow me to yonder church." He pointed a sausage-like finger. "There we'll present them with the word of God."

Wallace translated the friar's words.

When he finished, Rabbi Yosef frowned. "Must we endure this, William?"

"According to the Templar, Imbert Blake, you must, Rabbi. But let me see what I can do . . ." Wallace dismounted and approached the friar, forming what he hoped was a believable excuse. "The rabbi is most anxious to hear the learned friar, but bids you consider that they have been traveling all day. The rabbi is certain that their comprehension of your sacred doctrines will be much improved after they have rested. He therefore requests that they be allowed to hear you after *nones* tomorrow." By that hour in the midafternoon, Wallace was sure they would be far from Bordeaux.

"Quite out of the question." The friar's chins shook. "We have an edict, sir. If the Jews will not come of their own will, our officials," he nodded at the constable, "will compel them to attend our discourse, putting aside all excuses . . ."

"Very well." The rabbi shrugged when Wallace finished translating, "Let's get this over with."

Satisfied, the friar turned, and, with a wave of his hand, grandly led the way toward an imposing cathedral.

The rabbi placed a hand on Wallace's shoulder and nodded toward the cathedral. "I fear what may befall us here, William."

"Be assured, Rabbi, you travel under the protection of the Knights Templar."

"Come along, then," said the constable. "Mustn't keep the good friar waiting."

The cathedral with its attached cloister loomed gray against the sky, its stone façade decorated by rose windows. Wallace and Rabbi Yosef mounted the steps, followed by the rest of the flock. Passing the main portal, Wallace saw that the buttresses flanking the door were carved with the contorted figures of saints, and along the length of the tympanum there was a representation of the Last Supper.

Within the cathedral, tall pillars extended into darkness, and lofty windows of colored glass, weakly lit by twilight, glowed with the images of patriarchs and apostles. One narrow window displayed a fully armored knight with sword and shield; another showed a strange-looking man holding a poorly proportioned child. The air was heavy with the pungent memory of incense.

The friar led the way into a nave lit by a dozen candles. The Jews were instructed to sit in the wooden pews facing the choir. They separated into two groups on their own; men and boys taking seats in front, women and girls behind, just as they were used to sitting in synagogue.

The friar mounted an elevated platform in the choir. The candles wavered as the church doors closed. He gripped the sides of the lectern and began to speak. "Jews, your fathers have inherited falsehood and have followed foolishness." He paused, waiting for Wallace to translate.

The words, as Wallace spoke them in English, left a terrible taste in his mouth.

"We will show you, beyond any doubt, that in Jesus there is a fulfillment of all Scripture; the Crucifixion is the center of faith, the death of Jesus is the death of sin, and the Resurrection is the heart of redemption . . ."

The instruction, cajoling, and haranguing went on for better than an hour, with the friar regularly pausing for Wallace to translate. Finally, the end was in sight.

"In conclusion, Jews, we bid you, as Zechariah the Prophet has written, to look upon Him whom you have pierced. Look upon Him and mourn for Him, as one mourns for an only son. Look at the prints of the nails in His hands." He held up both hands, his shrill voice rising. "Ask Him, Jews—what are these wounds in your hands? And He will answer you, saying; with these I was wounded in the house of my friends—wounded in the house of my friends . . ." He dropped his arms and heaved a large sigh. "Jews, do you not see? You can yet be friends of Christ if you will but accept His finished work. There need be no disagreement between us. You are not pagans. We are all sons of Abraham. You must simply understand that the Church has replaced you as the chosen people of God, just as the New Covenant has replaced the Old Covenant. The new supersedes the old. The Torah did its work—with types and shadows foretelling His coming. But now it's done. Now it's time to let the Torah go . . ."

As Wallace translated, Reb Yosef stood up.

"Yes, Rabbi?" asked the friar.

"Good friar, we are the people of this Torah. How can we let it go?"

Wallace translated and held his breath.

The friar smiled benevolently. "When you accept Christ, you *must* let the Torah go, Rabbi. To cling to this relic is an *affront* to Christ. It offends all Christians . . ."

His mind weary, Wallace mechanically continued to translate.

"Indeed," the friar continued, "your very existence as Jews is offensive. It is time for the Jew to disappear."

Wallace formed words that fell from his mouth like burnt ashes, floating irretrievably toward Reb Yosef and his congregation.

A short uneasy silence was followed by the rising voices of the Jews, standing and speaking at once.

"Silence!" The friar's face reddened as he shouted. "I compel you to listen. The edict will . . ."

A gust of wind swept through the cathedral. The candles guttered and a few went out. Imbert Blake with two other Templars strode into the nave.

"Are we finished here?" Blake asked.

"Chevalier!" the friar cried. "You tell them—the edict requires them to listen!"

"And they have, good friar. And now it's time for dinner, and then for rest."

"Most definitely! Hot food and warm lodging await all who would be baptized—"

"You would force them?"

"Of course! How can I allow them to remain in darkness?"

"You are aware, good friar, of the encyclical against forced baptism?"

"And are you aware, sir, that as a friar, I am an instrument of the papacy? Are you aware that I sit on the court of the Inquisition? Are you aware—"

"Come, William," Blake cut in. "Let us escort these good people out of here."

As the Jews began to file out, the friar moved as swiftly as he could from behind the lectern and confronted Blake next to the baptismal font in the vestibule. "I adjure you, *chevalier*! I must—"

"Good friar," Imbert said through clenched teeth, "I am a

simple monk and a Poor Knight of the Temple. I follow the rule of Bernard of Clairveaux, the peacemaker who rose from his sickbed and traveled to defend the Jews of the Rhineland. I do as Bernard taught. I adjure *you* to join me in this. Let us devote ourselves to offer prayers for the Jews' salvation. Does the Lord not teach us to render such love? Remember this in your orisons, good friar. Remember this and remember me!" Blake smiled and, with his hand on the hilt of his sword, he made a little bow. "I bid you good night, sir."

Chapter Eleven

Safed
4 May, 1290
Night

The viceroy smiled and bowed smoothly, hoping his true thoughts were well concealed. *Is the emir actually stupid enough to believe that a Knight of the Temple would fight on behalf of a rabbi? Yet he requires and expects my counsel*—"Your eminence, how can this be so?" he began, choosing his words carefully. "The Templars are the very bane of the Jews. Have we not heard that the road from Europe to Jerusalem is littered with Jewish corpses?"

"All you say may be true, my good viceroy, but look again." The emir slowly rotated the sword. "This is no antique. See how the blade shines, and though the hilt is worn, the leather is quite supple." The emir pointed the sword's tip at the viceroy. "There can be no question. This is manifestly the sword of an accursed Templar!"

"But, Great One, is it not more likely that this sword was merely used by the Jews to defend themselves?"

"And the helmet and skull of a royal guard cleaved through?" The emir slashed the air with the heavy sword. "That was not the lucky stroke of a novice, Viceroy. Though it defies all reason, there can be no other explanation; a Knight of the Temple defended Rabbi Samuel here in Safed. What's more, we've seen the man . . ."

"We . . . we have?" the viceroy stammered. "Where, Sire?"

"Right here." The emir pointed with the sword. "He brazenly stood before us—in the guise of the rabbi's disciple."

"But . . . but what manner of Christian knight masquerades as a Jew?"

"One who wishes to live." The emir leaned over the copper platter, reaching for a morsel of lamb. "Such a pity . . ." he murmured as he popped the lamb into his mouth, chewing as he spoke. "The sergeant I had executed might have told us something of this knight—"

A herald pushed open the high double door and announced, "As you commanded, O Emir, the captain of the halka has returned."

The emir waved him in. "Have they been found?"

"No, Great One!" The captain brushed past the herald and bowed. "But we've found a war horse stabled at the Jews' academy—fifteen hands and scarred by lances."

"And was there a device upon the saddle?"

"Yes, Sire, though it was concealed—the stamp of the Temple in Acre."

The emir fixed his good eye on the viceroy, a smile playing on his lips. "Thank you, captain. Have the beast brought to my royal stables."

"It is already done, Sire."

"Good. Leave us now."

As the throne-room doors closed, the emir threw back his head and laughed. "My one eye sees that which your two eyes cannot . . ."

Damn him! The viceroy's face grew red and he made a little bow. "I am honored to serve so wise a master." He drew a deep breath. "But where are they—the rabbi and the knight, Sire? We've searched every inch of Safed—"

"I think they are no longer in Safed," the emir said and picked another morsel from the copper platter. "You're ignoring the obvious, my good viceroy—the rabbi knew we would be looking for them to the west. So, they went east. And it is there we must seek them out. Dispatch the mounted guard."

"Certainly, my lord." The viceroy bowed and turned to leave. "You are wise to stretch out a wider net to catch these slippery fish."

"Now that you mention nets and fish, Viceroy, have the guard also search the shore of the Galilee. It's only natural for slippery fish to go to the sea."

Tel Hum
4 May, 1290
Night

Rabbi Samuel and St. Clair hurried forward in a driving rain. On both sides of the muddy track, black stones shone darkly as a splinter of lightning flashed along the heavy clouds. Thunder shook the air, and out on the water, whitecaps churned beneath the lowering sky.

"Welcome to Tel Hum, Jonathan!" Rabbi Samuel called over his shoulder. "The village is this way."

St. Clair followed the rabbi past a stand of cedar buffeted by the wind and rain into a field of bramble with scattered boulders—shining pale and white in the darkness. *That's odd,* St. Clair thought as he moved quickly through the field. *I've always heard that the stones of the upper Galilee are black . . .*

Once past the field and after stumbling through a grove of trees, St. Clair was relieved to see dozens of tents, lit at intervals by wavering lantern-lights.

"Wait here," the rabbi said and ducked into a nearby tent,

leaving St. Clair standing in the rain.

He stood, watching the sides of the tents billowing and snapping in the wind. He wondered who the villagers were. A ribbon of lightning lit the sky, and St. Clair saw that the tents were black. He caught hold of a loose tent flap and felt the texture against his cheek, inhaling its scent. *Goat hair—they must be Bedouin.*

After several minutes, the rabbi emerged, carrying a brazier with glowing red coals. He wasn't alone. Next to him walked a man who was a good deal taller than the rabbi. St. Clair squinted through the rain and saw that the stranger held a kettle in one hand, and in the other, a rattle, which he shook as he walked.

They soon came to a tent that stood apart from the others. The stranger laid the kettle on the wet ground, turned, and, without a word, left them. The rabbi entered the tent, but St. Clair remained standing outside, watching the man disappear into the darkness, listening to the receding sound of the rattle.

The rabbi's head poked out of the tent. "What are you waiting for, Jonathan? Come inside, and bring the kettle."

"You didn't tell me they were Bedouin," St. Clair muttered as he entered the tent and placed the kettle on the ground next to the brazier.

"They aren't Bedouin," Rabbi Samuel said as he took off his robe and hung it on a rope that was stretched along the side of the tent.

St. Clair took off his turban and shook the water from his hair. "Only Bedouin live in tents such as these."

"The Bedouin gave them the tents," the rabbi said and handed St. Clair a blanket. "Here. Get out of those wet clothes."

St. Clair pulled off his mail shirt and jerkin, hanging his sodden clothing on the rope next to those of the rabbi. Naked to the waist, he unfurled the blanket and wrapped it around his shoulders. "If they're not Bedouin, who are they?"

"They're our hosts," replied the rabbi. Wrapped in his blanket, he crouched on the ground next to the brazier. From a box next to the tent's central pole, he produced two earthenware cups.

"And why does our host shake a rattle?" St. Clair asked as he sat cross-legged next to the rabbi, warming his hands over the brazier.

"It's their custom, Jonathan." The rabbi tilted the kettle and carefully poured steaming broth into the cups. "Please, no more questions tonight. We've had a very long and difficult day. Let's enjoy a quiet drink and get some sleep."

St. Clair closed his eyes and sipped slowly, letting the warmth spread through him as he listened to the sound of the rain pelting the tent. He cradled the cup in his hands and drew a deep breath. "Just one more question, Rabbi; how are we going to repay our hosts for their kindness? You gave the emir all our gold."

The rabbi put down the cup and wiped his mouth. "I am confident we will find a way to compensate them." He stood up, took his turban from the rope where it hung, and wrung the water out of it. Placing it on his head, he turned to St. Clair. "It's time for me to pray—*Ma'ariv*—and you, knight?"

St. Clair put down his cup. "The prayer office at day's end—Compline."

Together they prayed, Rabbi Samuel standing and St. Clair kneeling. Then, wrapped in their blankets, they placed their pallets on either side of the brazier and slept.

Chapter Twelve

יב

Tel Hum
5 May, 1290
Morning

Turning on the edge of sleep, St. Clair reached out for the solid comfort of his sword. Not finding it, he awoke with a start, angry at the rabbi for forcing him to leave it behind.

He sat up and looked around. In the orange glow of the brazier he saw the rabbi's empty pallet, the woolen blanket folded in a neat square. "Rabbi?" he whispered. There was no answer. Indeed, there was no sound at all. The storm had passed.

The blanket slid from his shoulders as he climbed to his feet. He wondered how long he had slept as he groped along the sides of the tent for his clothing, gratified to find his cotton jerkin warm and dry. He slipped into his boots, chain-mail shirt, and the disciple's robe. With the slightly damp turban on his head, he pushed through the tent flap, sending drops of night rain into the cold morning air. Squinting in the light, the first thing he saw was the lake, a silver mirror less than a stone's throw away, and the rabbi in silhouette, standing in prayer at the water's edge. St. Clair walked forward, his boots crunching on the smooth pebbles along the shore.

The rabbi turned at his approach. "Good morning, Jonathan.

You slept well?"

"I'd sleep easier with a sword at my side."

"And I'd pray easier with my phylacteries. We'll both have to make do."

"Have you finished morning prayer?" St. Clair asked.

"Not yet. Please, join me."

St. Clair stood alongside the rabbi and smiled. "I'll be doing *lauds*—but standing instead of kneeling—your form, my substance."

"Good. And if you pray and dress as a Jew, you should also have a Jewish name—how does Yonatan ben Avraham sound?"

St. Clair nodded his assent and the two men stood together as the sun rose over the Galilee, bowing back and forth in cadence with their separate prayers.

After several minutes the rabbi finished and St. Clair saw him pace along the shore and stretch. Quickening his pace through the remainder of the prayer office, St. Clair soon joined the rabbi sitting on a smooth boulder, still cool in the warming sun. The morning was very quiet and the lake quite still, the water barely moving along the shore.

The rabbi was the first to speak. "I wanted to ask about something you told me yesterday—about the time you listened to the lessons of Rabbi Jacob from outside the window. You told me he posed a question that only you answered. What was that question, Jonathan?"

"He asked about a passage from the book of Malachi—about how God is a refiner and purifier of silver . . ."

"An excellent metaphor," the rabbi said as he bent and picked up a flat stone from the shore. He drew back his arm and threw the stone, which skipped over the smooth water, its path marked by a chain of ripples. "And you alone were able to answer?"

"I had an advantage," St. Clair replied. "At the garrison in Safed, there was a smith, Abu Hamid, from among the renowned silversmiths of Damascus. I had watched him practice his craft many times, and I had questioned him about the process. Thus, the *mashal* was clear to me, and I was able to advance the metaphor without difficulty."

"And your answer?"

"I began by explaining that the smith holds the silver in the middle of the fire, where the flames are hottest, so as to burn away the dross. He keeps his eyes on the silver while it is in the fire because it would be destroyed if left a moment too long. The smith knows when the silver is truly refined at the moment when he can see his image reflected in the silver. Thus it is with the silversmith, and thus it is with God who sits as the refiner and purifier of our souls." St. Clair moved his hand, thumb extended, in a circle, as he had learned to do when concluding a Talmudic argument. "When we feel the heat of God's fire, we know that our dross is burning away. We also know that He will not leave us too long in the fire, because He is watching—waiting to see His image in us."

"You answered well, Jonathan."

"Thank you, Rabbi. But, again, I had an advantage over other students. I had seen the process performed many times."

"Others may have seen, but not understood."

St. Clair stood up and stretched. He looked past the sunlit tent where they had slept. The tents of the encampment were shrouded in the shadows of willows and pine that grew along the shore. "We should thank our hosts and be on our way, Rabbi. The emir's guard might seek us here."

"The guard won't come here, Jonathan. No one comes here. No one dares."

"What?" St. Clair caught a glimpse of movement among the trees. His gray eyes narrowed. "Who are they?"

"Our hosts. Let's go meet them."

Striding away from the water, they approached the trees.

Suddenly, the sound of rattles filled the air. Then St. Clair saw them—beneath the hanging tendrils of a large willow. "Dear Jesus, I think I understand. The rattles warn the healthy of their approach . . ."

"That is so," said the rabbi.

A disconsolate group shuffled forward, clutching wooden rattles and cheerless rags.

"I remember such as these in Europe," St. Clair whispered. "Shut away in the *lazarettos*—thousands of them. When they ventured out, they wore bells to mark their approach. We called them Christ's poor . . ."

"Here we call them lepers," Rabbi Samuel stated quietly.

At a distance of about four cubits the lepers halted and the sound of rattles stopped. The ensuing silence was complete but for the sibilant murmur of a breeze through the sweeping branches of the willow.

A man wearing a tattered robe stepped forward. "Welcome, Rabbi," he whispered. "We are again honored to receive you among us."

That's the man from last night, St. Clair thought, now able to see a reddish discoloration bordered by a silvery scale along the left half of his face.

"Thank you, Nehemiah. Your kind hospitality is again most appreciated, especially considering the foul weather."

On either side of Nehemiah disfigured men and women nodded in agreement. A few used withered stubs of fingers to hold masks of brown bark over their faces. Most didn't bother. St. Clair's breathing quickened as he stared at them.

"We did not expect you to return so soon from Acre, Rabbi, and I remember two disciples," Nehemiah whispered and turned his brown eyes on St. Clair, "and this tall gentleman was not one of them, though you are most welcome here, sir."

St. Clair bowed at the waist. "I . . . I thank you," he stammered. "Those two went on, and . . . and I came from Acre to join Rabbi Samuel."

"This is Yonatan ben Avraham," the rabbi said and rested his hand on St. Clair's shoulder. "Yonatan, this is Nehemiah ben Azariah of Jerusalem."

"We are honored to have you as our guest, Yonatan."

St. Clair bowed. "The honor is mine."

"Honor, indeed! I would introduce you to the other living dead," Nehemiah whispered and gestured at those about him, "but names matter little here."

And the whispering—St. Clair recalled that lepers were forbidden to speak above a whisper in the presence of a healthy person. He hadn't seen a leper since leaving Scotland. He recalled seeing a few at a market in Edinburgh, wearing bells and strange gay masks mocking the horror of their disfigurement, which he may have glimpsed but couldn't remember. Now he forced himself to look—at ruined hands of dead clay, faces of uncooked meat, a cavity in place of a nose. He found himself staring at the remains of a face with one eye puckered closed, and the other opaque and blind. Then the eye blinked.

The sound of rattles began again and St. Clair was startled to see the rabbi moving toward Nehemiah.

"Forgive me, my son, but your face . . ." he murmured and stepped closer. The sharp sound of the rattles rose in the air.

The rabbi pointed toward the lake. "Please, Nehemiah, walk with us. I should like to speak with you apart from the others."

The rabbi and St. Clair moved toward the shore. Nehemiah followed, staying a good distance behind.

At the water's edge, the rabbi turned and beckoned to Nehemiah. "Come closer."

"You know that is not permitted, Rabbi. Why do you ask of me what I cannot?"

"The discoloration on your face is unchanged, Nehemiah.

There is no loss of hair, nor any whitening of the hair."

"Which means . . . what?" asked Nehemiah testily.

"My son, are you aware of the holy writings concerning leprosy?"

"I'm all too aware! These writings stripped me of my bride just after our marriage. These writings condemned me to the isolation of this living death—lest my pestilent breath pollute the salubrious air."

"My son," the rabbi said and took a step toward Nehemiah.

"Come no closer, Rabbi!" Nehemiah shook his rattle as he tried to back away, but found his path blocked by a fallen tree.

The rabbi continued moving forward, raising his hands, his eyes fixed on Nehemiah's face.

"No! You mustn't touch me!" Nehemiah shouted as he lurched to the side, tripped on a branch, and fell to the ground.

The rabbi knelt beside him. "Listen to me, my son. You know of the writings regarding Miriam, the sister of Moses . . ."

St. Clair hung back, listening and watching. Nehemiah struggled to rise, but the rabbi restrained him with a hand on his chest.

"You know that all that might be called leprosy is not true leprosy. You know there are other skin ailments that are distinct from it. Listen to me now! I believe you do not have leprosy."

"How can you be so sure? Perhaps my case is just less advanced—"

"No. I studied your face when I passed this way before. The Book of Leviticus is very specific regarding every aspect of the illness—the skin, the hair, the scalp . . ."

"But how many cases have you actually seen?" Nehemiah challenged. "I'm told that in Babylon leprosy is practically unheard of."

"That's true. But I know the descriptions in the Torah, and I know the other holy writings concerning leprosy. I bring you the gift of this knowledge, Nehemiah. Accept it!" the rabbi shouted, and stood up. "I do not believe you have leprosy!"

Nehemiah sat up and stared out over the water, saying nothing.

The rabbi put a hand on his shoulder. "My son," he began.

"I lost everything," Nehemiah cried, burying his face in the rabbi's black robe, "my home, my bride . . ." He pulled away and looked at the rabbi, his eyes filled with tears. "What must I do now?"

"You will separate yourself from the others." The rabbi pointed along the shore. "We'll have a tent pitched for you over there. You will remain under observation for some weeks, according to the Levitical precepts that govern the determination of the illness. It's all clearly prescribed by law. Do you understand?"

Nehemiah nodded. "But what of the others?"

"We'll examine them all." Rabbi Samuel patted Nehemiah on the back. "And you will assist us. In a few hours, I'll determine exactly what I'll require for this task." He turned to St. Clair. "Come, Yonatan."

As they walked along the shore toward the encampment, St. Clair asked, "Rabbi, did I hear you aright? Did you just tell Nehemiah that you will examine *all* the lepers?"

"That is my intention."

"Have you taken leave of your senses, Rabbi? Do you want to catch the disease?"

"I told you, Jonathan—the contagion of leprosy is actually quite low—it takes months, even years, of close contact."

"Even if that's so, it will take many days to examine these people, and during that time, aren't we likely to be discovered by the emir?"

"No, Jonathan. The Mamluks avoid this place as they would the plague. We're quite safe here. This will be our city of refuge."

"But what of Jerusalem?"

"Staying here for a time improves our chances of reaching Jerusalem. Indeed, if we stay here for some weeks, the emir's guard will likely give up searching for us altogether. It is well that we stay here. Besides, last night you asked what we might give our hosts to show our gratitude for their hospitality." The rabbi rested his hand on the knight's shoulder. "We can give them hope, Jonathan, and perhaps for some, release from this living death. And don't worry—when I perform the examinations, I'll cover my hands with cloth."

"But I can't believe you're not more concerned about catching the disease . . ."

"Don't worry, Jonathan. Leprosy is rarely seen among those from Babylon."

"And why is that?"

The rabbi smiled at St. Clair. "According to my brethren in the Land of Israel, we're protected because we bathe in the Euphrates, eat turnips, and drink beer."

Chapter Thirteen

יג

Templar Port City of Collioure
Mediterranean Coast
12 May, 1290
Morning

At first light, William Wallace stood on the quay beneath the tall gray walls of the Château Royal, looking out to sea. Still wrapped in the woolen blanket in which he had slept, he drew a deep breath, tasting the cool sea air as he watched the triple-banked galley, called the *Falcon,* roll in the swell. Beyond the harbor, he could see the sails of a few other Templar galleys moving like ghosts upon the mist.

And now the *Falcon*'s great square accaton billowed in the wind, snapping and straining along the yard, its splayed red cross lit by the rising sun. Wallace drew the blanket close about his shoulders and watched the *Falcon*'s prow swing to shore, driven by the dawn wind and three men to the oar.

Wallace turned at the sound of footsteps and saw Elijah in his short, black coat walking toward him. "A very good morning to you, sir," he called out.

"And to us all, William, if this be the happy day we sail for the Holy Land."

"Then set your face for sadness, Master Elijah."

"What's your meaning, William?"

"Look to the flags." Wallace pointed up at the streaming black and white Templar pinions along the battlements of the Château Royal. "The same east wind that blows those banners bars our path. It is only upon the breath of the west wind that we may sail to Acre."

"When might the wind turn, William?"

"Very soon, now. The Templar mariners tell me the time of the west wind is at hand."

Elijah motioned with his head toward a group of white-mantled knights, kneeling on the promontory at the end of the landing. "Are they praying for the wind to change?"

"Nay." Wallace laughed. "They perform the morning prayer office of *prime*."

"You Christians pray even more than we do."

"But you Jews seem to have special blessings for everything."

"That we do." Elijah smiled. "We have a special blessing for eating, drinking, washing the hands, putting on a new garment, for seeing a falling star or a rainbow or a beautiful woman. We even have a blessing for relieving ourselves. However, we don't have a blessing for being thrown out of our homeland. For that we have only curses for your good King Edward."

"He's not my king, Elijah. I'm a Scot."

"And you Scots have no king at all." Elijah shook his head. "And with the throne empty, who's in charge?"

"A gaggle of nobles who call themselves Guardians of the Peace or Protectors of the Realm, whichever title sounds grander." Wallace shrugged. "They'll rule Scotland till it's determined if the bloodline is stronger in John Balliol or Robert the Bruce."

"And as long as your countrymen fight among themselves, Edward has more time to plot and scheme his way to Scotland's throne. He's already seized Wales and the Isle of Man. Mark my words, William—Scotland will be next. Your nobles would do well to stand united . . ."

"William!" A white-robed knight beckoned from the promontory.

"Pray for the west wind, Elijah," Wallace said as he made his way toward the knight through a plume of sea spray. Out in the harbor, he noticed the galleys ranging themselves along the quay like horses at their pickets. As he drew closer, he saw that the knight calling him was Imbert Blake, his red hair sticking out from beneath the hood of his cowled robe.

"We need all able-bodied men from among the Jews. And you as well, William."

"Why, sir?"

"We sail today, lad, may God grant us His blessings."

"But, what of the wind, sir. I saw the flags just now . . ."

"Look again, William!" Blake pointed up at the black and white standards along the Château Royal, snapping in a strong west wind.

Safed
12 May, 1290
Midday

Tewfiq Ayoub lifted a parchment from the pile of documents on the polished table in the throne room. "The next missive is an urgent request . . ."

"My good Viceroy . . ." The emir yawned loudly and leaned back on a lavender mountain of satin cushions. "The royal harem requires my attention. I grow weary of these petitions, and I will not look upon another request for clemency . . ."

"This is not such a request, Great One. It comes from the sultan's eldest son, the Prince al-Ashraf Khalil."

"Really? What does he want?"

"To inform you that his father, the Sultan Qa'la'un, has

charged him to rebuild the great city of Tripoli, razed by the accursed infidels before their defeat. For this purpose he wishes to harvest trees in the northern reaches of your domain."

"To harvest trees," the emir repeated as he fingered his beard. "How many?"

The viceroy scanned down the scroll. "Ten thousand *dunam,* Sire . . ."

"Let me see that!" The emir extended a bejeweled hand and took the scroll, frowning as he read. "There's something going on here, and I think I know what it is." He looked at the viceroy and breathed out the words, "Siege engines."

"My lord?"

"With this lumber, Khalil intends to build towers and catapults. I'm certain of it. For he wishes to be the one to conquer Acre." The emir stood up, muttering. "And I'm determined that this will not come to pass. It is I who will drive the infidels from our shores. It is *my* name which is inscribed in the Book of Fate!" He turned back to the viceroy. "Any word from Rabbi Petit?"

"Only that he holds to our bargain, Sire, and demands proof of Rabbi Samuel's death."

With a curse, the emir threw down the parchment and began to pace. "Once Khalil has constructed sufficient siege engines to ensure victory, he'll make his move. He knows the prize of Acre will seal his ascension to the throne and bequeath him an honored place in history. I am determined that he shall have neither, and I shall have both!" He turned to Ayoub and slapped his chest. "It is I, the champion of Allah, who will finish the work of the magnificent Sultan Baybars. Did Baybars not bequeath me this province after I slaughtered the Templars on this very hill? I am his true heir, not the dotard Qa'la'un or his indolent son. I am Allah's chosen instrument. Khalil is as craven as his father and will only move against Acre when he has *double* the number of engines required for a siege. This will give us time." Ayoub placed his hand on the viceroy's shoulder. "So, we will graciously grant him leave to take all the lumber he desires."

"But Sire, won't we also require siege engines to snatch Acre from his grasp?"

"Must I remind you, my prudent advisor?" The emir drew Ayoub close and whispered in his ear, his words coming slowly. "We will let Khalil have his wood, because we have the keys to the gates of Acre, compliments of Rabbi Solomon Petit. Therefore, let us send a messenger by our swiftest horse to the western march. We will convey to Petit that, by my word, Rabbi Samuel is dead, and we demand our due—the secrets of Acre's defenses." The emir fixed Ayoub with his eyes, smiled, and stepped away.

"But he'll require proof, Sire."

"And we will give him proof, good viceroy. Do we not have the bloodied vestments of the rabbi's disciples? Was the academy of the Jews not filled with scrolls of the law and the rabbi's writings? Do we not have the sword of the Frankish knight who traveled from Acre to be the rabbi's defender? We will convey all these to Petit with that Genoese merchant who sojourns here. What was his name?"

"Buscarel."

"Yes. Buscarel will present these articles to Rabbi Petit as evidence that we have kept our part of the bargain. We will then insist that Petit keep his."

"But if he remains obstinate?"

"If he will not be induced to aid us by the death of his enemy, then we will promise him his own."

Chapter Fourteen

יד

Acre
27 May, 1290
Afternoon

Seeking relief from the heat of a sultry day, Isaac sat astride the crenellated battlements of the sea wall, the rough stone warm beneath his hands. Pushing his face into the cool breath of the wind, he could hear doves cooing from within the stonework of the wall, and in the distance, a sentry called and another answered, passing the word. Then the sentries began to shout, and others took up the call: "The fleet comes."

Isaac could see them—the gray sails of galleys clustered like gulls upon the azure water beneath a bright blue sky. The Templar fleet was flying to Acre on the wings of the west wind. The cheering grew louder and louder.

He recalled prior arrivals and knew that the tall Templar galleys would soon fill the outer harbor, joined by heavy-laden cargo ships of the Pisans, Venetians, and the Genoese. He knew pilgrims and cargo would fill the long boats and these would fill the inner harbor. The pilgrims would disembark, weeping and kissing the soil of the Holy Land. He knew the unloading of the ships would go on for many days—timber for siege engines, fine fabrics and sewing needles for his father, weapons and wondrous foods, bottles of wine and books. For, in this manner, nourishment flowed on the pulse of the wind, through the twisting channels of the sea like the dark blue veins that sustain a fetus. Thus, Mother Europe nourished her orphaned outpost clinging to the edge of the Orient.

As Rabbi Petit had instructed, Isaac had spent the past few weeks gathering details about Acre's defenses. He had easily gleaned information from knights he chanced to meet on his way about the city, pleased to offer reassurance. Indeed, anxious questions about the city's defenses were not uncommon, especially after the Mamluk conquest of Tripoli earlier in the year. Isaac gathered details from a hundred conversations; numbers of heavy horse, men, ordnance, and weaponry, the manner of the watch along the walls, and the manner of passing the land gate. The details, caught in the fine web of his memory, all recorded in the report he prepared for Rabbi Petit.

Isaac looked down at the inner harbor. Soon, he would go down to the quay and be among the throngs cheering the arrival of the long boats. And there he would catalogue the added men and weaponry for his report.

He turned his back to the sea and looked over the teeming lanes by the harbor. Since the fall of Tripoli, there had been a steady migration to the fringe of coastal land that remained under Christian control. Remnants of the crusaders and their allies filled the city and its suburbs. Here were gathered all the rich lords of Outremer who had left their hill castles—the Prince of Galilee and members of his household, the great families of the Ibelin and the Lusignans. And in Acre they would not be separated from their wealth. Palatial villas dotted the city like bright jewels, with ornamental windows of colored glass and gates of intricate iron grille.

Bells began to toll across the city.

Isaac turned and saw the tall galleys enter the outer harbor, splayed red crosses on their sails billowing in the wind, long oars flashing in the sun. *Time to go down to the quay and cheer the knights who came to reinforce the garrison, and to tabulate their numbers.*

Isaac picked his way down the steep mural steps built into the wall, to join the multitude surging toward the port. Between the crowding buildings, with tall walls of beige limestone shouldering high against the sky, the mob flowed toward the sea like a swift stream in a deep canyon, and the air rang with songs and prayers of thanksgiving in a dozen tongues.

Once on the quay, Isaac climbed upon a barrel to watch the long boats moving away from the galleys. A cool breeze ruffled his black frock coat, and crying gulls wheeled above the pier and the blue-green water. As the boats drew near, he saw that two were filled with people whose appearance was familiar to him; men with beards and side locks like his own, skull caps and wide-brimmed hats, women with shawls covering their heads.

"Blessed are those who come!" he called out in Hebrew, and waved as the boats passed out of his sight to dock at the far end of the quay.

Pushing through the crowd to the landing, Isaac saw the Jews stepping from the boats, assisted by Templar mariners. Many dropped to their knees, ignoring dried bits of fish entrails and swarming black flies as they bent and kissed the landing. An elderly Jew in a long black robe led the others in prayer. Isaac caught the final words: ". . . that you have granted us life and sustenance and permitted us to reach this season."

Amid shouts of *amen* and joyful weeping, the old man, apparently the group's rabbi, turned, his cheeks wet with tears above his white beard, his eyes shining.

Isaac pushed his way forward and welcomed him in Hebrew. "Blessed are you in your coming to our Holy Land! I am Isaac ben Samuel."

The rabbi spread his arms and hugged Isaac. "Words cannot express our joy at being among you, Isaac. I am Rabbi Yosef ben Asher and this is my *k'heela,* all of us exiled from England." He reached out to a robust man in a broad black hat standing nearby. "Elijah!" he called and drew the man near. "Isaac ben Samuel, this is our *gabai,* Elijah ben Azariah."

"Greetings to you, sir!" Isaac beamed. "Do any of your *k'heela* have family in Acre?"

"No."

"You do now!" Isaac said with a broad smile. "Once you have your belongings together, it will be my honor to bring you to the synagogue at the time of *mincha.* There you may refresh yourselves while we arrange for your dinner and lodging with host families. For just as Abraham made welcome the angels by the oaks of Mamre, even so we welcome you."

"And as the angels blessed Abraham and Sarah," said Elijah, grasping Isaac's hand, "so may you be blessed with fine children."

"I'm not yet prepared for that blessing, Master Elijah. I should first need a wife, I think."

"How old are you, my son?" the rabbi asked.

"Nineteen, sir."

"And not yet betrothed?" The rabbi glanced at Elijah. "We shall have to remedy that . . ."

Elijah nodded. "There are a few very marriageable young ladies in our *k'heela,* Isaac."

"You have outdone the angels at Mamre, *rabotai,*" said Isaac, laughing, "not only do you promise progeny, you bring the bride."

The rabbi waved toward a tall young knight and called to him in English, "William, come and meet a lad of your own years." As he approached, the rabbi asked Wallace, "Do you speak any Hebrew?"

"I learned to read a bit at the scriptorium, but I've never spoken the language." Wallace turned to Isaac. "Do you speak any English?"

Isaac raised his shoulders and shook his head.

"Français?"

"Oui!" Isaac smiled up at the young giant. *"Je m'appelle Isaac. Quel est votre nom?"*

"William Wallace." He extended his large hand in greeting. *"Enchanté!"*

"Bienvenue, William!"

Elijah cut in, speaking Hebrew to Isaac. "Young Wallace arranged our journey from France with the Templars. We wouldn't be here if it wasn't for him." He smiled at Wallace and repeated the testimonial in English.

Wallace bowed his head. "Master Elijah is too generous with his praise."

"Not at all." The rabbi patted Wallace on the shoulder. "You boys stay here and get to know one another. We'll see to the belongings."

The rabbi and Elijah moved down the quay toward a growing mountain of bags and luggage at the end of a chain of porters.

Isaac turned to Wallace. *"D'où venez-vous, William—la France?"*

"No. I was studying there for the priesthood. I'm actually from Scotland, a small country north of England. And it is from England that these Jews were expelled."

"Expelled?"

"Yes. All the Jews of England were expelled, thousands of them, by royal decree."

"For what offense?"

"For the offense of being Jews."

"How can this be?" The color drained from Isaac's face.

"Where do they go?"

"Wherever they can. Most are finding refuge in France, Flanders, and Germany. When I met the rabbi and Elijah in France, they didn't know which way to turn."

"And you helped them find passage to the Holy Land—a fine thing you did for them."

"It wasn't completely altruistic." Wallace shrugged. "I arranged the trip so that I, too, could come here." He fixed his eyes on Isaac. "I have it in my mind to see Jerusalem."

"Put such thoughts aside, William. Jerusalem has been outside the domain of the Latin Kingdom for a hundred years."

"Perhaps, but the Templars told me I might be able to get on with a merchant from Genoa or Venice. Such as these pass freely across the borders, no?"

"Yes, but the danger is great and the price is high. How is your purse?"

"What purse?" Wallace smiled and canted his head. "Tell me, Isaac—wouldn't *you* like to see Jerusalem?"

"More than I can say."

"And you know how to speak the dialect of the merchants?"

Isaac nodded warily.

"Well, there it is then!" Wallace patted Isaac on the shoulder. "We'll go together!"

Isaac pulled at his beard and smiled. "An interesting thought . . ."

"We're ready, lads," Elijah called as he came down the quay, carrying large bags.

Wallace leaned down and whispered, "It's more than just an interesting thought, Isaac. My heart is set on it. Let us speak further on this when we meet again."

"You're not coming with us?"

"No. I've accepted the generosity of the Templars to join them at their commandery."

"Good. I'll call on you there tomorrow."

Wallace said his goodbyes to the rabbi and Elijah, embracing them both. Then, with a nod at Isaac, he was gone.

"Rabotai," Isaac said with a gesture. "This way to the Jewish Quarter." As he led the new arrivals into the city, he glanced at the dock teeming with activity, and made a mental note to return that evening to amend his estimates of Crusader strength.

Chapter Fifteen

טו

Tel Hum
27 May, 1290
Late afternoon

Only three occupants of the colony remained to be examined. They had begun, three weeks before, with seventy-five.

St. Clair spread a new sheet of parchment over the table and secured the corners with four smooth stones he'd selected from the shore of the Galilee. He placed the clay inkwell by the edge of the parchment and began to sharpen his quill.

The storms of late spring had passed and the skies had cleared. With the tent sides raised, St. Clair could see down to the shore where two black cauldrons squatted over bright orange flames, boiling water for laundry. Sheets of white muslin billowed between trees like low clouds and the aroma of burning cedar scented the breeze off the lake.

The familiar footfall on the pebbles outside the tent door announced Nehemiah's approach. He pushed through the tent flaps, followed by a portly man with a sparse black beard and sharp eyes shaded by thick shaggy brows. Nehemiah pointed to a chair covered by a white cotton cloth. "Please, Ibrahim, sit here."

Rabbi Samuel stepped forward. "Welcome, friend. I am Rabbi

Samuel of Baghdad, and"—he motioned toward St. Clair—"this is my pupil, Yonatan, who will assist in your examination."

St. Clair removed the cap from the clay inkwell.

The man managed a smile and whispered, "I am Ibrahim ibn Elias."

"Ibrahim," said the rabbi, "would you care for a cup of mint tea?"

The man shook his head.

St. Clair dipped the quill into the ink and wrote the man's name on the parchment.

"Ibrahim," continued the rabbi, "please cease from whispering and speak in your normal voice."

"As you request, Rabbi," Ibrahim replied in a clear voice.

St. Clair made a note regarding the absence of hoarseness, which afflicted many with leprosy. The examination had begun.

Nehemiah stood close, watching and listening. Rabbi Samuel had insisted that he become familiar with the various manifestations of the disease since subsequent examinations would fall to him once the rabbi was gone. To do this, Nehemiah would require knowledge born of direct observation, as well as St. Clair's written record of initial findings.

"Tell me something of yourself, Ibrahim," the rabbi said gently, "your city of origin, your vocation, your family."

"I was sent hither about a year ago from Bet She'an when my affliction was discovered. I was thirty years old and a cobbler." Ibrahim paused and drew a deep breath. "I had a wife and two children."

St. Clair inscribed the information in an even script. The story was all too familiar. Torn from their families, lepers were cut off from all connection with their former lives. Many told of burial rituals as they were cast out of their villages.

"Ibrahim, I would ask that you step behind the partition, remove your clothing, and put this on." The rabbi held up a white cotton gown.

Once Ibrahim emerged from behind the partition, the rabbi wasted no time. Wearing white gloves and using pine twigs, he started with the scalp and moved down. In describing the various skin lesions, the rabbi departed from Arabic and used Biblical Hebrew terms. Since the nature and degree of penetration of the skin marked the degree of the disease's severity, special importance was attached to the subtleties of these lesions. St. Clair was by now familiar with the terms; a thickening within the skin was a *se'et,* a crusted skin lesion *sa'pahat,* a whitish spot *ba'heret.*

"Look here," the rabbi said to Nehemiah, "over the left aspect of the forehead there is an olive-sized, irregular *se'et* with no discoloration." He scratched the skin over the spot with a pine twig. "Does that feel the same as this?" he asked and did the same over unaffected skin.

"Yes."

"Sensation, normal," the rabbi murmured as he continued to study Ibrahim's skin. "And look here—another *se'et* at the nape of the neck, about half the size of the first."

St. Clair entered the finding.

"Note that apart from the normal thinning of Ibrahim's hair, there are no irregular patches of hair loss, and no discoloration. Eyes appear clear." He handed the man a small piece of pine bark. "Please, Ibrahim, cover your left eye with this." He pointed at St. Clair. "Tell us how many fingers Yonatan is holding up."

St. Clair held up two fingers.

"Two," said Ibrahim.

"Good. Now cover the other eye. What about now?"

"Four."

"Good. Tilt your head up, please." The rabbi peered into each nostril. "No lesions in the nose. Open your mouth, please. Good. No lesions there. Please lower the robe to your waist.

Look here, Nehemiah, over the front aspect of the right shoulder. This may be a *ba'heret,* about the width of a garbanzo bean. You'll need to recheck that."

St. Clair made the notations as Rabbi Samuel continued to carefully examine the man's body, cataloging every possible vestige of the disease. All the while he spoke gently to Ibrahim as he had to all the others, making every effort to maintain a sense of their dignity. For his part, St. Clair concentrated on recording the observations without looking up; he found the appearance of some of the afflicted an unsettling distraction.

At the conclusion of the examination, St. Clair set about preparing the scroll for the rabbi's signature.

As Ibrahim stood up, the rabbi said, "We would ask that you separate yourself from the main colony."

"Why? Is something wrong?"

"You have some sores that will require further inspection. To facilitate this, we require that you stay in one of the tents by the lake."

Always careful to avoid raising false hopes, the rabbi never stated that the skin lesions might prove not to be leprosy.

"Will you effect my healing through prayer, Rabbi?"

"That's your responsibility, Ibrahim. It is not in my ability to heal you, but to see that precepts of the Scriptures are appropriately applied."

"I understand. How long will I remain apart?"

"At least several weeks." The rabbi led the way to the tent door. "All you can do is follow our instructions and pray that you may live well or die well. Now go in peace."

After escorting the man out of the tent, Nehemiah turned to Rabbi Samuel. "Do you think he has true leprosy, Rabbi?"

"I doubt it, but, as with the others, it depends how the changes in the skin and hair look over time. If it's true leprosy, you'll know." The rabbi tossed the white gloves into the laundry basket.

"I'd feel better if you could stay and make these determinations yourself, Rabbi."

"That's impossible, Nehemiah. We've been here three weeks, and we have pressing business in Jerusalem. Let us proceed with the next subject."

Nehemiah left and the rabbi turned to St. Clair. "Have you finished?"

"Yes, Rabbi, the scroll is ready for your signature."

Sitting down, Rabbi Samuel read St. Clair's neat Arabic script aloud. "The bearer of this scroll, Ibrahim ibn Elias of Bet She'an, has been examined by myself, Rabbi Samuel ben Daniel ben Abi al-Rabia ha-Kohen, Gaon of Baghdad, on this day, 16 *Jumaada al-awal 689.* By my signature, I hereby propose that this man's skin condition may not be true leprosy. My pupil, Rabbi Nehemiah ben Azariah, will render a subsequent examination. His note and signature below will confirm my impression." He dipped the squib in the inkwell and signed the document with a flourish. After blowing softly over the parchment, he looked up. "Our time here is nearly done, Jonathan. How stands the count?"

"Of the seventy-three people examined, you determined twelve men and ten women to be questionable. All the rest have true leprosy." St. Clair leaned back in the chair and smiled. "We're almost finished. Only two left—"

"Begging your pardon, Rabbi," Nehemiah said as he pushed through the tent flaps.

"The next subject is here?"

"No, Rabbi." Nehemiah raised his shoulders. "It's an old woman who is pretty far gone. I wouldn't bother with her—"

"There will be no exceptions. Bring her in." Once Nehemiah was gone, the rabbi turned to St. Clair, who sat at his writing table. "I wish we had more to offer these people."

"Such as healing?"

"Yes, Jonathan. In your Scriptures, it's written that Jesus had the power to heal them. It's also recorded in the histories of Josephus. That was probably the reason the priests hated him—jealousy. The priests could do only as we do—separate the sick from the healthy. While this is a very important function, which limits the spread of the pestilence, I'm sure many of them found it frustrating. They could offer nothing more than isolation."

"Do you think Jesus taunted the priests?" St. Clair asked.

"What do you mean?"

"By Jesus telling the healed lepers to show themselves to the priests."

"No. He was just following the Law. It was the priest's job to examine any such person and perform ritual sacrifices before allowing them back into society. But I suppose some priests felt they were being taunted, which is why some refused to acknowledge the healings or declared them works of the devil."

"But wouldn't the priests consider that all healing comes from God?"

"Or one of his anointed surrogates," agreed the rabbi, "like Moses or Isaiah, but they didn't choose to put Jesus in that category."

"Actually, Rabbi, Jesus gave them two choices—to consider him a deluded heretic or God incarnate."

The rabbi rested his hand on St. Clair's shoulder. "I know what you believe, Jonathan—infinite God strikes a tent in human flesh and dwells among us, the willing servant who is pierced, the Pascal Lamb sacrificed—all the types and shadows of Scripture neatly fulfilled . . ."

"And what do you believe?"

"What do I believe?" Rabbi Samuel drew a deep breath, his hand still resting on St. Clair's shoulder. "I believe you and I share the same hope and the same love of the same God. I believe we serve the same God when we help the poor and raise up the afflicted. And I believe that, at the end of our days, when we search for our reflections in a glass darkly, we will see the same face."

Nehemiah poked his head through the tent flaps. "She's here," he announced. Then, standing aside, he gave wide berth to a bent and ragged figure, shuffling slowly forward. A thin stick swept back and forth, clutched by a nearly fingerless hand. Opaque eyes skittered sightlessly in sockets crowded by folds of pale flesh. Where a nose should have been there was an open cavity bounded by sores.

St. Clair winced and lowered his gaze to study the blank scroll spread out on the table.

The old woman hesitated just past the tent door, waving her stick back and forth.

"Please come forward, Mother," said the rabbi. She didn't respond and he repeated the request in a loud voice. The old woman moved forward. St. Clair knew her hearing was all but gone. As leprosy advanced, the senses were extinguished, one by one, as the disease eased its host toward the final oblivion.

"That will be fine. Stop there." The rabbi moved a cloth-covered chair behind her. "Here, Mother, you may sit now. What is your name?"

"Rachel Ezra." Her voice wheezed up like something squeezed out of her as she sat down.

St. Clair wrote the woman's name on the scroll. As with other advanced cases, he knew there would be no examination beyond the interview.

The rabbi sat down opposite the old woman. "When did you come here, Rachel?"

"Many years now, many years . . ." Her voice trailed off, like a dying wind through dry cornhusks.

St. Clair entered the sparse details of the old woman's life on the scroll—seven children, a widow from Tiberius, a midwife until her affliction.

"Rabbi!" She leaned forward suddenly. "Are you the one that is come to heal us?"

"Only God can heal you, Mother."

"I thought you might be the one," she murmured and settled back in the chair. "We wait for such a one as healed here long ago, in this place of leprous stones."

"I am not the one. I'm sorry."

"That's all right," she wheezed. "Soon I will be released from the bondage of this life. Perhaps in the world to come . . ." Her body shook with a fit of dry coughing.

"Tell me, Mother, how is it with you? Have you enough to eat?"

"There's a girl who cares for me now. Before she came I did the best I could."

"That is well. We will see to it that you continue to receive all the care you require from those who are able." The rabbi stood up. The interview was over. "Thank you for speaking with us, Rachel. May God be with you."

"And with you, Rabbi."

Shielding his hands with cloth, Nehemiah helped the woman out of the tent.

When she was gone, the rabbi turned toward St. Clair and sighed. "I'm reminded of how powerless the priests must have felt."

"Leprous stones . . ." St. Clair murmured. "What did she mean by that?"

"I'm not sure. Leprous refers to a whiteness, but the rock in this part of the Galilee is black—"

"Not all of it, Rabbi. On the night we came here, we passed a place with white stones."

"We did?"

"Yes. In that heavy rain just before we reached the colony." St. Clair tossed Rachel's scroll among those of the other incurables.

Nehemiah shuddered as he reentered the tent. "I told you she was far gone, Rabbi."

"So you did, Nehemiah. Please bring in the last subject."

"I can't, Rabbi."

"What do you mean, you can't?"

"It's the girl who cares for Rachel Ezra, Rabbi. She insists she must stay with the old woman and refuses to come."

"Arrange for someone else to assist Rachel Ezra, and have the young woman here by sundown. I'm determined to complete our task today."

Once Nehemiah was gone, the rabbi turned to St. Clair. "Show me this place of leprous stones, Jonathan."

Chapter Sixteen

טז

Tel Hum
27 May, 1290
Late afternoon

St. Clair led the way through a stand of ancient pine trees on a hill north of the colony. "The white stones the old woman spoke of are just beyond this hill, Rabbi. I'm certain of it."

Afternoon sunlight filtered through spreading branches inscribing shifting traceries of light on a ground cover of pine needles. A screech owl perched on a low branch regarded them with huge eyes and blinked once. Its head rotated smoothly as they passed.

St. Clair saw that the rabbi's breathing was labored as they moved uphill, his limp more noticeable. "We can rest awhile, if you like."

The rabbi leaned back against the thick trunk of a large tree, fanning himself with his turban.

St. Clair leaned against the rough bark next to him. "Aren't you afraid?"

"Afraid of what? That I'll die trying to keep up with you?"

"No, afraid of catching leprosy."

"I've told you, Jonathan, it's not so easily acquired, and we've taken appropriate precautions."

St. Clair looked up at the towering canopy, spreading above them like flying buttresses. "I feel so uneasy when I'm near them."

"That's understandable, but rest assured, I've known people who worked closely with lepers for years and never acquired the disease. Indeed, a baby born to a woman with leprosy will not be afflicted if there's no further contact with the mother after the birth. So don't trouble yourself, Jonathan. We've done all that's necessary to avoid contact."

"But the customs pertaining to lepers in Europe are so very different—"

"Many such customs have no basis in common sense. They're just driven by fear and superstition."

"Sometimes fear and superstition come in handy. The emir's halka hasn't dared search for us here—just as you predicted."

"You can always depend on fear and superstition, Jonathan." The rabbi smiled as he replaced his turban. "Come. I've recovered my breath. Lead on."

The ground rose and the trees thinned. Finally, cresting the hill, they looked down on a sloping field where chunks of white limestone were scattered among patches of thorn brush.

"Leprous stones . . ." the rabbi murmured as he wiped sweat from his forehead.

St. Clair started down the hill. As he pushed his way through tangled weeds, he startled a family of badgers that slid away like sleek brown arrows into the brush. Nearing the jagged white stones, which were partially concealed by bramble, he held back. "Is there any danger in touching leprous stones?"

"These aren't stones," the rabbi replied.

"What do you mean? Of course they're stones."

"Not exactly. Look at this." The rabbi crouched on his heels and pulled away dry weeds and thistles. "See? Decorative carvings—like a capital that once graced the top of a column." He stood up, brushing soil from his hands. "Do you know what place this is, Jonathan?"

St. Clair shielded his eyes with his hand, squinting against the setting sun. "A ruin?"

"Yes, but of what? Look at the sections of columns." The rabbi pointed. "One row here, another over there, and between them another. And in what direction are they aligned?"

"North-south," St. Clair replied and scratched his beard.

"South—toward . . ." prompted Rabbi Samuel.

"Toward Jerusalem." St. Clair looked over the field as realization dawned. He turned slowly about, looking at the broken columns, his heart pounding, his mind racing. "We're standing in the ruins of a synagogue—the synagogue of Capernaum. This is the colonnaded courtyard." He drew a deep breath. "Jesus came here with the sons of Zebedee, John and his brother James, with Simon called Peter, and his brother Andrew." He crouched down and began cleaning the casing of dirt from a column with his hands. "It's written that Jesus taught here, Rabbi. It was here he healed the sick. It was here he restored the daughter of Ya'ir to life. *'Talitha kumi'*—'Arise, little one,' and she was healed."

Rabbi Samuel knelt on the ground next to St. Clair. "That's what the old woman meant when she spoke of her hope of healing in this place. After all this time, Capernaum is still thought of as a place of miracles and healing."

"Look, Rabbi," St. Clair said as he peered at the decorative carving emerging beneath his hands. "This appears to be a triangle of some sort."

"There's more to it, Jonathan. It's a Star of David."

"So it is." St. Clair shook his head and stood up. "To think this place has been desolate for a thousand years . . ."

"Not that long. From Talmud we know this was the synagogue of a thriving fishing village. For centuries, Jews lived here side by side with Sectarians."

"Sectarians?"

"That's what Jewish Christians are called in the Talmud."

"Were they accepted as Jews?"

"No. Even though Sectarians considered themselves Jewish, they weren't regarded as such."

"Jews who weren't considered Jewish?" St. Clair asked in disbelief.

"It's the same today, Jonathan. There are sects that have arisen over the centuries that aren't considered to be really Jewish—Karaites, Samaritans, the Hadhrami, and others. I know of isolated communities high in the northern mountains of the Caucasus, others in the southern mountains of the Hindu Kush. All these sects—whether separated by high mountains, deserts, or their beliefs—they're all considered outside the mainstream. Only the Judaism of the Pharisees, Rabbinic Judaism, is considered *real* Judaism."

"And all *real* Jews follow these beliefs and practices?"

"To varying degrees, and with some differences. You see, Jonathan, Rabbinic Judaism teaches that the Torah revealed at Sinai reflects what God demands of us, and that God's will is reflected in a system of laws and practices we call *halakha,* and halakha differs in different communities."

"At what point do differences in halakha become too great to still be considered Jewish?"

"An excellent question." The rabbi raised his shoulders and walked toward the lake. "I have no answer."

"But is Rabbinic Judaism, itself, unified?"

"Not at all. Look at Petit and myself—we're both rooted in the rabbinic tradition. But here am I threatening to excommunicate him, and he's trying to have me killed!" The rabbi smiled. "So much for the unity of *real* Judaism."

"And if there is such dissension *within* Rabbinic Judaism," St.

Clair said, switching from Arabic into Hebrew, "*kal ve'homer*—how much more so, between divergent sects of Judaism." He emphasized the point with a twist of his hand, thumb extended.

"Jonathan!" the rabbi exclaimed, "you're sounding more Jewish by the day!"

"Just don't let the Master of the Temple hear of it."

They turned and walked slowly along the shore. Out on the lake, St. Clair saw a few of the colony's fishermen drawing their sails and bringing in the nets, while others waded to shore, wicker baskets balanced on their heads. A few women of the colony, in white robes, tended bright fires beneath a half-dozen black laundry cauldrons set along the water's edge. They reached the pine grove and St. Clair noticed a fine gray haze suspended in the green foliage of the trees as cooking fires flickered in the darkness of the main colony. He felt the rabbi's hand on his shoulder.

"It's beautiful, no? Life goes on in the shadow of death . . ."

St. Clair nodded and they continued walking, passing a thicket of oleander with white flowers shining like porcelain. With the sun a finger's breadth over the horizon, streaks of crimson reflected off the lake. The air was very still. A snow-white egret stepped carefully from a thicket of reeds.

Suddenly Nehemiah emerged from among the pine trees of the colony. The egret startled clumsily into flight, flapping its great wings.

"Rachel Ezra is near death, Rabbi," Nehemiah called out, "and the young woman still refuses to leave her side."

"This is unacceptable, Nehemiah. We must conduct her examination now."

"Why bother, Rabbi? You saw the state of the old woman. You can be sure the young woman who tends her is just as bad. That's the way it is here."

"Must I remind you that the presence and degree of the

disease can only be established through direct observation? Please, Nehemiah, bring her at once!"

"I'll try, Rabbi." Nehemiah turned and walked back toward the encampment among the trees.

The rabbi bent to pick a stone from the shore. "Let me show you something of different sects and religions, Jonathan, an idea central to Kabbalah." He drew back his arm and threw the stone in a high arc over the water. It broke the smooth surface with a splash. "See how the ripples spread in widening circles over the water? To what may the thing be likened? At the center of our yearning is a point so subtle that it is hidden from view, the depths of depths. But as one moves away from that point, things become more layered, more revealed . . ."

St. Clair watched the ripples spread toward shore, passing through a thicket of papyrus at the edge of the marsh, the slender stalks swaying in the current. Then the ripples faded into smooth water and the silence deepened. On a bluff overlooking the lake, a dark blue cormorant perched on a *dom* tree. As St. Clair watched, the great bird spread its wings and took flight, soaring over the water. Out of the silence, he heard the rabbi speaking.

"From that hidden, inmost point of God's being there is an emanation that goes forth, like these ripples—extension upon extension—each becoming a garment to the layer beneath it. This is the process within God's self-unfolding, Jonathan.

"God has layers and layers, and depths within depths. By moving back, through the levels of our own soul, we may hope to glimpse the structure of His inner world." The rabbi threw a second stone, and another circle of ripples spread over the water. "It is as the poet Yehudah Halevi has written, *when I went out to come to You, I found You coming to me*. This is the essence and journey of Kabbalah. There's an unbroken flow of holiness from the inmost essence of God's being to the outer reaches of his most remote emanations. It doesn't matter what you look at: this lake, your religion, a flower—they all reveal the same pattern. We don't lead separate lives—God, the soul of man, and each part of the created universe—whatever touches one part, ripples through the whole."

The rabbi turned and looked at St. Clair. "In this manner, what the human soul does affects the rest of creation, no matter where we find ourselves in the path of emanation, no matter at what distance from the source. There is a profound effect of human behavior on God's own realm."

"Some philosophers wouldn't agree with you, Rabbi. According to them, God is self-sufficient, unaffected by anything we do."

"What do *they* know? I contend that the relationship between God and man goes both ways. Thus, *our* conduct has a profound effect on God. What *we* do in this world is for the sake of God—*le'shem sha'mayim*—for the sake of heaven. Didn't Jesus teach that our relationship with God is determined by our relationship with each other?"

St. Clair nodded. "Perhaps this is what he meant when he said, *inasmuch as you have done it unto one of the least of my brethren, you have done it unto me.*"

"How could it be otherwise?" the rabbi asked. "God in His wisdom, or in His folly, made us partners in creation. What *we* do either sanctifies or desecrates His work. We have the freedom to do one or the other. He waits for us to choose."

"And the religions of men help us choose?"

"They do if they guide us to be good partners with God—to love God as we love one another. But more often than not, religions divide us. We Jews with all our different stripes and, for that matter, Christians, Moslems, all religions—we are all emanations from the same divine point. But, unfortunately, we tend to harp on our differences." The rabbi bent down, scooped up a handful of pebbles, and threw them into the water. The smooth surface broke into a dozen ripples, overlapping and colliding in turbulent waves. "Look at the mess we make of things."

A wind came up and whitecaps spread over the surface of the water.

"As below, so above," the rabbi sighed. "Let's go to the tent and get ready to examine the last leper."

With the sky darkening over the plain of Batiyeh, they followed the shoreline toward their tent at the edge of the colony.

Nehemiah, his white robes lifting in the wind, came toward them with a lantern in one hand. "The old woman is dead," he called over the wind. "The last leper will come soon."

Chapter Seventeen

יז

Tel Hum
27 May, 1290
Evening

Nehemiah lifted his lantern to light the way for Rabbi Samuel and St. Clair as they approached the tent. They pushed through the tent flaps, and Nehemiah set his lantern on the table.

"While we wait for the last subject, let's review some scrolls so you'll better know to complete the work we've begun." Rabbi Samuel gestured with his hand. "Please, Yonatan, bring us the scrolls of those who may not have true leprosy."

St. Clair placed a crate on the table.

"How many are there?" asked Nehemiah.

"Twenty-two," St. Clair replied as he spread out one of the scrolls under the lamplight. "Notice how I've arranged the information. Here in the first column, beneath the name, I list personal information—family, city of origin, date of arrival. The second column indicates the quality of the voice. The third notes involvement of the skin. The fourth, the hair. And the last column lists other findings: eyes, nose, mouth, and any deafness."

As St. Clair spoke, the rabbi lit a candle from Nehemiah's lamp. Bending over the table, he squinted at the scroll. "We need more light."

Nehemiah and St. Clair gathered candles from around the tent and brought them to the rabbi, who lit each one with his candle.

As he lit the last one, the rabbi smiled up at St. Clair. "Yonatan, you once asked me if God is not diminished by His emanations. To what may the thing be likened?" He raised the candle in his hand. "See how we have illuminated the whole tent from this single candle, and see how the candle burns as brightly as before? So it is with the divine emanation—like a candle that is not diminished even though it lights a thousand candles, even though it lights all the candles in the world. In this manner God ignites everything with His essence, without being in any way diminished. Indeed, His emanations magnify and glorify His power and His holiness."

The rabbi turned back to the parchment. "Look here, Nehemiah. You must compare each detail of our examination with your own. Only then will you be able to determine if any aspect of the disease has progressed, and thus, you will determine if the person has true leprosy."

"I will execute the task faithfully, Rabbi."

"And remember, those you determine to have true leprosy must go back to the colony. It may take some months to be certain, and you owe it to each of them to be certain; they either go back to the colony, or they go home. And, before any leave to rejoin their families, you must sign and date the confirmation of healing here, just beneath my signature."

"Do you believe this will be sufficient to insure their acceptance back in their villages?" asked Nehemiah.

"I shouldn't be surprised if some are rejected. Warn them of this. And, of course, tell them that they may be returned to Tel Hum if a future suspicion of leprosy arises." The rabbi raised his shoulders. "All we can do is provide them with a chance."

He drew three scrolls from within his robes and placed them on the table. "These are for you—to take with you when the time comes for you to leave the colony." He handed one of the scrolls to Nehemiah and smiled. "This one affirms that your skin condition is not leprosy. With this, you will return home to Jerusalem."

"Thank you, Rabbi."

"But before you return home, you must do something for me." The rabbi placed his hand over the two remaining scrolls. "I need you to first deliver these . . ."

St. Clair recognized the scrolls. One was his report to the Master of the Acre Temple regarding Mamluk siege preparations. The other was Rabbi Samuel's finished writ declaring a ban against Rabbi Petit.

The rabbi continued. "Listen well, Nehemiah. This is of the utmost importance. When you leave here you must bring these two scrolls to Acre."

"To . . . to Acre?" Nehemiah stammered. "But, Rabbi, when may I return home to Jerusalem?"

"After you deliver these scrolls to Acre. This one you will bring to the Templar commandery, and this one you will deliver to Rabbi David ben Abraham Maimuni at Midrash Hagadol. To him and no other. Only after completing this task may you make your way to Jerusalem." Rabbi Samuel patted Nehemiah on the shoulder. "And who knows? Perhaps we'll meet there. Now, go and see what's keeping our last subject."

Nehemiah turned to go, but no sooner had he pushed aside the tent flaps than he turned back to the rabbi. "She's here," he whispered. "Right outside."

"Excellent! Show her in."

St. Clair sat down and readied the quill. Glancing up as Nehemiah escorted the woman into the tent, he saw that she was covered with rags as was customary with advanced cases. With a heavy heart, he spread out the parchment.

"I hope you haven't been waiting long, my daughter," the rabbi said and gestured toward a chair draped with a white cloth. "Please sit down."

Moving like an old woman, she shuffled over to the chair.

After quickly introducing himself and St. Clair, the rabbi asked, "What is your name, my child?"

"Zahirah," she whispered.

"You don't have to whisper, Zahirah. Please speak in your normal voice."

"This is all the voice I have left," she whispered in reply.

St. Clair made note of the hoarseness.

"Where are you from, Zahirah?" asked the rabbi.

"Safed."

"How long have you been here?"

There was a pause before she answered. "About a year, I think."

"Were you ill for long before you were sent here?"

There was no immediate response.

The rabbi repeated the question loudly.

"Yes," she finally whispered. "My mother hid me for years before I was discovered and sent here."

St. Clair noted the approximate duration of the disease and the apparent loss of hearing.

"And since you arrived, I am told that you have devoted yourself to caring for Rachel Ezra."

"Yes."

"You were a blessing to her. God is pleased with such acts of loving-kindness."

The woman coughed. "God is not here, Rabbi."

"Do you feel so abandoned, my child?"

"Yes."

"I am sorry for that." The rabbi drew a deep breath. "How

old are you?"

"Four and thirty years," she whispered.

St. Clair noted the age.

"You were married?"

"No."

"What of your family?"

"My father died when I was a child. It was just me and my mother."

"Did your father die of leprosy, Zahirah?"

"No. He died a warrior's death at the citadel many years ago."

St. Clair's breath caught. *Could it be?* Though almost twenty-five years had passed since the fall of the Safed Citadel, St. Clair could vividly recall the full horror of the battle. His hand shook as he made the entry about the woman's father. *Was it my sword that dispatched her father?* The images rose in his mind and he shut his eyes. Again he could see the ballistas spewing iron darts, the trebuchets hurling boulders, and the Mamluk Sultan Baybars leading the charge through the breach. Again he heard the shouts of his comrades—*Deus lo volt! God wills it!* He heard himself, his own throat raw from shouting. In the fierce abandon and power of his youth, he saw himself, wielding his heavy claymore, cleaving a wide swath into the Mamluk cavalry like a reaper with a scythe, to the right and to the left, the screams of men and of horses, banners torn and fallen to the earth, soaked in blood. Again he felt the lancers pressing in, hemming him round, and he heard his own voice roaring in his ears—then the quiet as he lay among the dead, the heaviness of bodies pressing him down.

He couldn't move and could only watch as they taunted his mentor, the Master of the garrison, William de Rogé. He could only watch as they scraped away Rogé's skin with iron combs. There among the dead, not wanting to be discovered, he stayed silent. But now, in the quiet tent, he heard his own voice cry out.

"Yonatan!" The rabbi's voice startled him.

St. Clair looked up. The rabbi and Nehemiah were staring at him.

"Yonatan," the rabbi repeated gently, "may we proceed?"

"Certainly, Rabbi." St. Clair struggled to steady his voice and wiped the sweat from his forehead. He felt the woman's eyes on him from within her rags. *It may have been by my sword . . .* The thought echoed in his mind. He heard the rabbi speaking.

"Put aside your rags and show me your hands, Zahirah."

She didn't respond.

"Please," he repeated loudly. "Show me your hands."

St. Clair hated seeing the deformities of the severely afflicted, but this one was different. He was compelled to see. He looked up from the parchment, watching as the woman hesitated, then slowly raised her arms. He cringed in anticipation as Nehemiah slowly drew back the sleeves.

Her hands were . . . perfect.

He looked closer.

In the candlelight, her olive skin was smooth and even. There were no lesions. *Nothing.*

The rabbi was silent, staring at the woman's hands. Presently, he spoke. "Zahirah, show me your face."

Now, without hesitation, she pushed back the rags covering her head.

St. Clair gasped and dropped the quill as he stared at her.

The woman's full lips turned up slightly at the corners in a bemused and defiant smile. Her dark skin was smooth without blemish. With calm gray eyes, she regarded the rabbi and Nehemiah. Then she looked at St. Clair.

According to his vow of chastity, he averted his eyes, staring down at the scroll. His heart pounded and his throat felt tight.

He could scarcely breathe. He heard the rabbi speaking, as if from far away.

"Do you have *any* sores of leprosy, Zahirah?"

"None that I know of," she replied evenly with no trace of hoarseness.

"You weren't really sent here, were you?"

"No, Rabbi, I wasn't. I came here on my own volition."

"Why in the name of heaven would you do that?"

"To hide. I was sold to the emir." She spat the words out bitterly. "I determined that I would rather die than be a concubine in his harem."

The rabbi laughed. "You came here to hide from the emir."

"You find that amusing, Rabbi? I assure you, there was nothing amusing in the degradation fated for me as an object of the emir's lust." She stood up and added, "I thought I might be able to trust you . . ."

"Ah, but you can, Zahirah, because . . . I am also hiding from the emir."

"You are?" Her voice rose in disbelief. "For what possible offense?"

"That is not your concern, my child. But I will tell you this; it wasn't because I refused to join his harem."

St. Clair heard her laugh. He looked up and saw her smiling, her teeth white and even, her hair thick with a golden brown color, like a grain field in summer. She glanced his way and again he lowered his eyes.

"Tell me, Zahirah," said the rabbi. "You chose this place rather than accept a pampered life in the emir's harem? Were you betrothed to another?"

"No. But I'm *intended* for another."

"This was arranged by your mother?"

"No."

"Then who arranged the union?"

"No one."

The rabbi scratched his beard. "I don't understand. You said you are intended—"

"I know what I said," Zahirah answered sharply. "When I am betrothed, it will be *my* intention, it will be *my* choice."

Chapter Eighteen

Tel Hum
28 May, 1290
Before dawn

St. Clair lay upon his pallet as the dark hours passed. Sleep did not come. As he listened to the sound of the rabbi's even breathing, he yearned for the oblivion of dreamless sleep. Turning onto his back, he stared into the darkness, his mind racing with thoughts of the woman—the unblemished smoothness of her olive skin, the feral beauty of her eyes . . .

Enough! He sat up and crushed his hands against his closed eyes, his heart pounding in his chest. *I must not give rein to such thoughts!*

He lay back and drew a deep breath as he willed his thoughts away from her. *All our provisions are packed and we'll leave after dawn—finally to complete the journey to Jerusalem. I'll observe the Mamluk preparations along the way and make report to the Temple . . .*

But his mind's eye turned again to the woman—the surprising perfection of her, but more than that . . . *the fierce conviction of her mind with such speech as I have never heard from a woman . . .*

He recalled her words; *it will be* my *intention, it will be* my *choice.* In the darkness before dawn, he could hear her speaking in his mind.

He got up, shrugged into his robe, and pushed through the tent flaps, the night air cool on his skin. The Galilee was a dark glass beneath the fading canopy of night, silent but for the sound of water sliding over smooth stones. Standing by the lake, he closed his eyes and sought the shelter of the day's first prayer office. He began to feel better—more like himself. Once done with Lauds, he sat on a boulder waiting for dawn. High in the eastern sky, a leering crescent moon with upturned horns obliterated all but the brightest stars. The moonlight dimly lit the tents along the shore. In one of the tents was the woman.

I can't stop thinking about her.

The smiling moon seemed to mock his misery. As he stared at it, he remembered a phrase often spoken by his mentor, William de Rogé—*Je vais regarder al badra—I'm going out to look at the moon.* St. Clair, then a novice in Safed, had heard Rogé say it each evening upon leaving the Citadel after Vespers—always alone, and always the same words—*Je vais regarder al badra.*

It was not unusual to mix French with Arabic, but the word Rogé always used for moon was not the generic *al-qamar,* but the word that referred only to the full moon—*al badra.*

Why was that?

It wasn't as if Rogé didn't know the difference—he spoke Arabic like a Mamluk.

Why did he refer only to the full moon—al badra?

On most of those nights, the moon had not been full, but waxing, waning, or new, or not yet risen, or already set. Yet Rogé always said the same thing. St. Clair stared at the moon and whispered, "*Je vais regarder al badra . . .*"

Along the unbroken line of the horizon pre-dawn light shown like the gray-pink color inside a seashell, only more luminous.

At sunrise, we'll leave, and I'll never see the woman again.

From behind, he heard the rabbi's sandals clicking on the stones along the shore. "You're not praying this morning, Jonathan?"

"I did Lauds early." He felt the rabbi's hand on his shoulder.

"Did you sleep at all?"

"No."

"It's the woman, isn't it?"

"My vow forbids any commerce with women."

The rabbi sat on the boulder next to St. Clair. "This woman is dangerous."

"All women are dangerous," murmured St. Clair. "But this one stands between me and God." He looked out over the Galilee, brightening under a russet sky and the fading crescent moon.

"Is the lake not beautiful, Jonathan?"

"Yes, Rabbi, it is beautiful."

"Do you not love to bathe in it?—to feel the water on your body—"

"All right, Rabbi," St. Clair cut in, smiling. "I grasp your meaning . . ."

The rabbi put his arm around the knight's shoulders. "Jonathan, do you believe God is served when you deny the beauty of His creation?" Pulling St. Clair closer, he asked, "Do you truly believe that God wants you celibate?"

"What manner of question is *that*?" St Clair shrugged off the rabbi's arm, hopped down from the rock, and trudged down the shore to the edge of the marsh. Then, as quickly, he returned, planting himself in front of the rabbi. "How can you ask me such a thing? Am I not a knight of Christ? Celibacy is central to my calling."

"Why? Where is that written?"

"In the Rule of the Templars!" St. Clair barked and turned away. "Set down long ago at the Council of Troyes."

"And is there a scriptural basis for this celibacy?"

"Of course there is!" St. Clair paced angrily, his boots crunching on the pebbles along the shore. "In the Epistle to the Hebrews."

The rabbi stroked his beard. "I don't recall any directive in the Epistle to the Hebrews concerning celibacy, and I've studied it very carefully—"

"You have?" The knight stopped pacing and glared at the rabbi. "Why?"

"Because I'm a Hebrew. It was addressed to me, so I read it." Rabbi Samuel raised his shoulders. "Tell me, Jonathan, where do you believe the epistle speaks of celibacy?"

"In the verse . . ." St. Clair waved his hands in the air as he paced, *"Strive to bring peace to all, keep chaste, without which no one can see God . . ."*

"Keep *chaste*?" The rabbi shook his head. "No. The Aramaic word used in that phrase is *ka'deeshoo'tah* meaning sanctified, not chaste. That's the word I recall—"

"Who cares what you recall?" thundered St. Clair, startling a flock of mud hens that pattered away and labored into flight. "Come! We must leave this place." He turned and began walking back to the tent, shouting. "Come, Rabbi! Let us gather our things, bid Nehemiah farewell, and we'll be off."

Chapter Nineteen

יט

Acre
28 May, 1290
Morning

Isaac's hands trembled with excitement as he wound up his phylacteries and placed them in their velvet bag. Leaving the synagogue quickly, he went directly to see William Wallace at the Templar compound. Isaac found him at the pells in the practice yard, hacking at the wooden posts among a half-dozen knights. Wallace wasn't hard to spot, standing a full head taller than the others. The dusty air was filled with the thud of heavy swords. Other knights threw spears at hay-filled Mamluk effigies hanging on quintains. Isaac moved into the shade of a wall to watch.

"William!" called a knight with red hair who was working the pells next to Wallace. "Are you chopping vegetables or fighting?" The knight swung his sword full hard, burying it deep in the wooden post, then shook a mailed fist at Wallace. "You've got the strength, lad, use it!"

"Quickness is also a virtue," another knight chided, deftly raining short strokes on his post.

"You'd best have both," said another.

On the far side of the yard, Isaac recognized an old knight

sitting on a bench in the sun. Grizzled and lean, Claude d'Urbot wore a hooded mantle of white linen. His beard was mostly gray and his face deeply lined and darkened by decades under the desert sun. He was staring intently into the yard as he absently twirled the point of his sword in the dust. As Isaac approached, he glanced up, a flash of recognition and a smile in his eyes. "Isaac! Good to see you again."

"And you, *Chevalier.* May I share your bench awhile?"

"Aye, lad, rest yourself."

"Thank you, *Chevalier.*" Isaac sat on the bench at a respectful distance from the knight.

"We haven't seen much of you lately with St. Clair gone."

"Has there been any word from him?"

"Nothing yet, but he's only been gone for a month. I'm certain we'll hear from him when he has something to tell us." D'Urbot nodded toward Wallace. "Have you met this young giant from Scotland?"

"I have, indeed, sir—yesterday on the quay. I was hoping I might speak with him."

"Soon enough. The boy's nearly spent. But he has promise—with his height and strength, he may amount to something." A smile creased d'Urbot's face as he squinted out at the yard and shook his head. "I didn't know they grew them that big in Scotland." He turned to Isaac and his smile faded. "We'll need more swords like his when Qa'la'un decides to end the truce."

Isaac nodded. "We were all relieved at the arrival of the fleet, sir."

"As were we. *Merci soient à Dieu.*"

"My mother has been worried sick about the Mamluks," Isaac said casually, sensing an opportunity to troll for details of Acre's defenses. "I've tried to reassure her that the garrison is well fortified."

"That you can, Isaac, especially with the arrival of the fleet.

We've gained about fourscore fighting men, the same number of heavy horse, double the weaponry with lances, enough lumber for a dozen siege engines, and more than a hundred barrels of Greek fire." He lifted his sword and studied the blade, tracing its edge with his left hand. "Things may not be as bleak as they seem. There's talk of the Holy Father raising another Crusade, and some say King Henry may bring troops from Cyprus. I've even heard rumors about the Mongols opening an eastern front against the Mamluks." He smiled at Isaac. "Who knows? This time next year, we might be sitting together at a teahouse in Jerusalem."

"That is my greatest wish, sir," Isaac replied as he committed the information to memory—more details for his report to Rabbi Petit.

A bell sounded, and the steady pounding of the swords gradually ceased. Isaac watched as Wallace swung his sword with two hands and buried the blade deep in the post with a final blow. Then he turned and headed in Isaac's direction, breathing heavily, his shirt drenched in sweat. He stood before d'Urbot. "May I sit down, *Chevalier*?"

"You've more than earned your rest, lad. That was hard work you did at the pells."

"That it was, sir." Wallace sat down heavily between Isaac and d'Urbot and wiped perspiration from his face with his shirtsleeve.

"First time with a broadsword?"

"No. My father taught me a bit before he sent me off to become a priest."

D'Urbot smiled. "Do you think he'd approve of you becoming a warrior?"

"Aye, sir—for Scotland. When the time comes, he's expecting me to do my part."

"Yet he sent you to become a priest?"

"Priest or no, he thinks that once a Christian is smitten on both cheeks, it's time to fight."

"That's the spirit, William! And next time you're in the yard, ask for a claymore. With your height, you can handle the extra length." D'Urbot stood up and pointed toward a corner of the yard. "Go have yourselves a cool drink." Then, turning to Isaac, he added in a low voice, "If you hear anything of St. Clair, let me know."

"I will, sir."

Wallace made his way to a barrel where a clutch of knights stood drinking in the shade. Returning with two earthenware cups, he handed one to Isaac. "Lemon squash, not half bad." Tilting his head back, Wallace finished the drink in a gulp and wiped his mouth. "I heard Master d'Urbot ask you about someone named St. Clair. Is he a knight of Scotland?"

"Yes he is. Jonathan St. Clair. Do you know him?"

"No, but I know of his family. I believe his father was once ambassador to France. What manner of man is this Jonathan St. Clair?"

"A most unusual one. He came to the Holy Land about thirty years ago when he was our age. He was sent to the garrison in Safed, where he somehow found time to learn Hebrew and to study the Holy Scriptures with a rabbi. When Sultan Baybars laid waste to the garrison, St. Clair was the only survivor. He was brought to Acre to recover from his wounds, and he continued to study the Hebrew Scriptures. After the rabbi who taught him died about two years ago, I continued his instruction."

"Where is he now?"

"No one knows exactly—somewhere in the territory of the Mamluks."

"For what purpose?"

"That depends who you ask. To his brother knights, he is the perfect spy, passing among the Mamluks with full command of their language and customs, determining the timing and strategy of the coming siege." Isaac took another drink of the lemon squash. "But I know he has another purpose: to seek out and learn from a certain learned rabbi."

"But you said *you* were teaching him."

"I was, but he desired a knowledge beyond my own—hidden things in the realm of Kabbalah—secret knowledge of the Temple Mount in Jerusalem."

"But what of *our* plans about Jerusalem, Isaac? Have you thought of the matter?"

"I've thought of little else!" Isaac smiled broadly. "I could hardly sleep." He took a step closer to Wallace and continued in a low voice, "I've come up with a plan!"

Wallace nodded. "Go on."

"The first thing we must do is leave Acre without raising suspicion. You'll tell the knights you're going to seek the fallow deer in the fields near Haifa, and after the hunt, you wish to visit the stronghold of the Templars at Athlit, built upon the black rock at the sea's edge. It's natural that you would want to see it. For my part, I'll tell my parents and Rabbi Petit that I am compelled to join the small community of Elijah's followers for some weeks at the foot of Mount Carmel in the Cave of Elijah—"

"For some weeks in a cave? Why would they believe that?"

"Many believe that anyone suffering from a nervous disorder can be cured by staying at the Cave of Elijah. I'll tell them my mind is troubled and I cannot sleep or study. They'll likely encourage me to go. In this manner, no one will wonder about our whereabouts while we're in Jerusalem."

"But how long is the journey?"

"Only about four or five days, but dressed as we are, we'll never make it." Isaac paused, relishing the prospect of the adventure. "So we'll go disguised as Genoese merchants. My father has some long-unclaimed articles of clothing at his tailor shop. Once we're beyond the land gate, we'll put on merchants' clothes."

"But if we're questioned—?"

"I'll do the talking. I know the manner in which the Genoese speak Arabic."

Wallace nodded, a pensive look on his face. "Aren't we a bit young to be merchants?"

"We'll say we're apprentice merchants."

"Then shouldn't we have some . . ." Wallace paused, searching for the word, "merchandise?"

"This will require some doing." Isaac frowned as he twisted a side lock and tucked it back behind his ear. "We'll need the *appearance* of goods in some sort of a cart. And we'll need horses." He looked up at Wallace. "Do you think you might borrow a couple of horses from the Templars?"

Wallace shrugged. "They have some old war horses out to pasture. I might be able to borrow a couple of those, but they're pretty worn out."

"The more worn out the better. Chargers pulling a cart would attract attention—"

"Very good. I'll see to the horses and the cart, and I'll borrow water skins and field provisions from the Templar storehouses. You figure out what merchandise we put in the cart. Once we get everything together, we're on our way!"

Isaac finished the lemon squash, wiped his mouth, and winced. "Oh, I almost forgot. Before I can leave, I must finish a report for my rabbi."

"A report?"

"About Acre's defenses. My rabbi wants to make sure we're adequately protected from the Mamluks. I'll finish that by tomorrow." Isaac drew a deep breath, his face shining, "William, in less than a week we could be in Jerusalem!"

"Om'dote ha'yoo rag'lay'noo be'sha'arayich, yerusalayim," Wallace whispered in Hebrew heavily accented by a Scottish brogue. "Did I say that properly?"

"You said it fine. Do you know what it means?"

"Oh, yes! We shall stand in thy gates, O Jerusalem!"

Chapter Twenty

כ

Leaving Tel Hum
28 May, 1290
Morning

Following a narrow path along the shore, St. Clair and Rabbi Samuel left Tel Hum wearing the cowled gray robes of wandering Moslem scholars. The air rang with the song of blackbirds hidden in the marsh grasses. At a rock bluff that left no room along the shore, the path led away from the lake, winding upward between thistles and boulders of black basalt.

St. Clair turned, waiting for Rabbi Samuel to labor up the low hill. As he drew near, St. Clair could hear the rabbi speaking.

"The Aramaic is quite unambiguous. Perhaps it's a question of translation—sanctity or chastity." The rabbi shook his head. "Strange to think how lives can turn by the translation of a single word—"

"It's not the single word, Rabbi," St. Clair snapped. "It's the *discipline*! Our life in the order is bound by *discipline*."

"Discipline?" The rabbi raised his shoulders. "And do all knights follow this discipline?"

St. Clair kicked at a stone.

"Since you took your vows, have you always observed this discipline?"

"Is this to be a proper confessional?" St. Clair asked as he moved along the road, the rabbi following close behind.

"This is not about confessing, Jonathan. This is about rectification—"

"Rectification? What are you talking about?"

"In your study of the canon, I assume that you read 'The Song of Songs'?"

"Of course." St. Clair replied, relieved to discuss something other than celibacy.

"And what is your opinion of this erotic love poem?"

"It's neither erotic nor a love poem, Rabbi. It's a *mashal,* an allegory for the love that God holds for Israel, that Christ holds for His Church . . ."

"Do you think God would divorce allegory from the thing itself?"

"I've studied 'The Song of Songs' with my order and with Rabbi Jacob of Safed. It has *nothing* to do with erotic love."

"Really? What about the passage—*your breasts are like two fauns that feed among the lilies*?"

"Rabbi Jacob taught that this is a reference to Jewish history. The two breasts represent Aaron and Moses who provide Israel with nourishment—"

"Please!" Rabbi Samuel exclaimed. "Do you actually *believe* that?"

St. Clair stopped and turned. "Are you saying this interpretation is untrue?"

"True, untrue, it doesn't really matter. In the best traditions of *midrash,* there is no attempt to decide which interpretation is true and which is untrue. What matters is the process of interpreting the Bible in order to extract relevance. What matters is *relevance.*"

"So what's your interpretation, Rabbi? What do *you* say the breasts represent?"

"In my learned opinion, Jonathan," the rabbi replied as he frowned and stroked his beard, "the breasts represent breasts."

St. Clair turned away, barely suppressing laughter as he continued along the road, walking slowly since he could see the rabbi was tired. The ground to the left of the path sloped down sharply into marshland with the blue water of the Galilee stretching to the horizon. Without turning, he asked, "Is there no relevance to other interpretations?"

"All interpretations have value. But in the context of this beautiful love poem, I believe that it's irrelevant and even silly to suggest that the breasts of a beloved woman represent Moses and Aaron, no matter how one embellishes that suggestion. On the other hand, it is appropriate for *midrash* to dissolve the literal text into different contexts. But for myself, this process should be a way to be *relevant* to the real world, to *sanctify* the real world, to enhance our awareness of the divine presence in *this* world. This is what I call *relevant* mysticism."

"As opposed to . . . ?"

"*Self-indulgent* mysticism—created for the sake of itself rather than for the sake of heaven—*le'shem sha'mayim.* I believe self-indulgent mysticism is invented by men with too much time on their hands, men who sit and read all day, men who have never bathed in the Euphrates or the Galilee, men who never really loved a woman—"

St. Clair came to a stop, raised a finger to his lips, and pointed. "Look," he whispered. Perched on a scraggly myrtle a stone's throw away was a bright blue kingfisher.

The rabbi stifled a cough, and the bird startled from its perch and glided down toward the lake. St. Clair watched the kingfisher until it disappeared into the marsh. The only other movement was out on the lake where a northern wind etched whitecaps on the water.

St. Clair turned to the rabbi and saw that he was flushed, breathing heavily, his forehead covered with perspiration. "Are you very tired, Rabbi?" he asked.

"I was very tired an hour ago. Let's rest awhile over there." He pointed toward a large boulder next to the myrtle. As the rabbi sat down, he pushed back the hood of his robe and wiped his brow. "For the sake of Jerusalem, I will not rest, but for my sake, I must." He unstoppered the water skin and took a long drink. Then, with a deep sigh, he handed the skin to St. Clair and asked, "What do you know of gematria?"

"Rabbi Jacob used it on occasion. He taught that Kabbalists use gematria to extract meaning from text by assigning a number value to every letter of the alphabet." St. Clair shrugged and sat next to the rabbi on the boulder. "I always thought it a tortured path to understanding."

"True, but what matters is the *relevance* of the discussion to the real world. The idea at the heart of gematria is that each word, indeed, each letter, *matters.* In short, *words count.* Gematria is a way to link text to a divine dimension in our world. Let me explain with another passage in 'The Song of Songs'—one that speaks of the woman going to meet her lover in the garden—*el ginat egoz yaraditi.* With gematria, the letters of the passage add up to five hundred and one. We can link this passage with one in the book of Ezekiel, which also equals the same number—*this is the depth of the merkavah*—the exalted chariot of God. Thus, the going down of lovers to the garden is likened to the ecstatic descent to the most intimate heart of the divine realm. In this way relevant mysticism celebrates the divine in everyday life. And by this, it suffuses the loving relationship between a man and a woman with a divine dimension—"

"Rabbi," St. Clair cut in, "are you deliberately bringing the discussion back to the loving relationship between a man and a woman just to torment me?"

"Perhaps . . . well, yes." The rabbi smiled and rested his hand on St. Clair's shoulder. "Don't be cross with me, but I want you to comprehend the idea of rectification. Remember, Jonathan, as above, so below. All things in the world point to God. Within the depths of all things is a reflection of the divine, just as the lake reflects the sky. Thus, men and women mirror male and female aspects of God, and when they join in a loving and sacred union, we glimpse the majesty and holiness of God becoming one. We witness the reflection of a unity we wish to see throughout creation. Thus, the coming together of the lover and the beloved reflects God made one in a perfectly restored world. As it is written, *in that day God will be one and His name will be one.*"

St. Clair looked out over the lake. He took off his turban and ran his fingers through his hair. His hair felt thick, and he knew it was much longer than the order allowed. He closed his eyes and felt the richness of it. When he spoke, his voice was a whisper. "I understand your meaning, Rabbi, and it shakes me to the core. You suggest that my celibacy separates me from the world of the chariot, the *merkavah.* You suggest that it is not the woman, but my denial of her, that stands between me and God . . ."

The rabbi nodded as he climbed stiffly to his feet. "Yes, Jonathan. But you're now free from the temptation of that particular woman." He turned and began walking down the shore. "Come. We must hasten to cross over. The far shore of the Galilee is outside the emir's domain. We'll be safer there."

"Why didn't we cross at Tel Hum?"

"The water is wide there and the winds are changeable. Besides, the fishermen of the colony are not permitted beyond . . ."

"Wait!" St. Clair pointed. "Look there!"

"What . . . ?" the rabbi asked, searching.

"There's someone in that thicket off the path. Wait here." Gripping his wooden staff, St. Clair rushed toward a tall stand of oleander. After threading his way between walls of green leaves and red flowers, he emerged and walked slowly up the hill, stopping several times to glance back. "I could have sworn I saw a flash of white—like . . ."

"An egret?"

St. Clair starred at the thicket. "Perhaps it was an egret."

They continued down the bluff and came upon a ruined house in the shade of a fig tree, growing wild among the tumbled limestone blocks. The morning was well on and warm, and the air sweet with the perfume of rotting fruit. Heavy black flies buzzed in the silence.

St. Clair picked a fig off a low branch, split the rubbery outer husk, and smiled. "These are perfect." He stuffed the sweet, red center into his mouth.

The rabbi looked up into the dusty green canopy as he unshouldered his leather pack. "It's a shame to let this fruit go to waste. We should stock up for the trip."

They stood together picking figs, eating some and putting others into their packs.

"What place is this?" St. Clair asked.

The rabbi had just eaten a fig and answered with his mouth full. "Since we've come about a league from Tel Hum, this might have been Tabgha."

"How far must we go to find a boat for passage across the lake?"

Wiping his mouth, the rabbi stepped from the shade and looked down the coast, squinting against the bright glare off the water. "I'm sure we'll find a vessel in Tiberius, but that's six leagues from here. There are smaller villages closer at hand—Gennesar, Migdal Zobaiya . . ."

"Let's be off then, Rabbi. We have all the fruit we can carry, and I'm not keen on meeting the emir's halka without my sword."

"They've probably given up looking by now," the rabbi replied and followed St. Clair down the path. "Besides, can you imagine a better place to die?"

"If it's all the same to you, Rabbi, I'm not keen on dying today—I should like to complete our journey to Jerusalem."

"I would agree. But it's not in our control—there's a time to be born, a time to die, and a place for each. Tell me, Jonathan, what death would you like?"

St. Clair stopped and turned. "A soldier's death—with my sword in my fist—a death swallowed up in victory. I don't want to take years to die in little bits. And you?"

"Well," the rabbi raised his heavy eyebrows and smiled, "since I've been relegated to dying, as you say, in little bits, my hope is that, at my final dissolution, I may be granted a more intimate knowledge than I have yet known. As Saul of Tarsus wrote, *For now we see in a glass darkly, but then, face to face.*"

St. Clair smiled as he turned, then froze, looking down the shore, shading his eyes. "What's this?" he muttered, squinting into the glare.

The rabbi was at his side. "What are those flashes of light?"

"The emir's halka!"

"What should we do?"

"Hide. Now!"

Chapter Twenty-One

Acre
28 May, 1290
Early afternoon

Seeking refuge from the heat of a spring day that felt like summer, Isaac mounted the rough mural steps of the sea wall to the high battlements. Shining fronds of bending date palms and flat green leaves of tall poplars rustled in a cool breeze off the water, while Acre baked in the heat between her walls where no wind stirred.

Isaac reclined on a cushion of camel thorn netting that covered a mangonel and looked down at the Templar galleys and the Italian trading ships listing lazily in the outer harbor. Grotesque dragonheads with huge eyes and impassive women with bare breasts peered from the lofty prows over sparkling blue water.

Isaac closed his eyes. He listened to the wind in the netting and considered how to organize his report for Rabbi Petit.

Since visiting Wallace at the Templar commandery that morning, Isaac had spent several hours at the docks. The port master had personally shown him hemp sacks full of ordnance, stacks of timber for siege engines, and barrels of Greek fire ranged along the quay. He seemed as anxious to reassure himself as he was to reassure Isaac about the strength of the garrison.

Isaac drew a deep breath and opened his eyes. From where he sat, he could see most of Acre and the harbor. Built upon a promontory, the fortress city stuck out from the coast like a clenched fist. Its outer land wall was studded by square towers and crowned by a circlet of crenellated battlements, and beyond the outer wall was a ditch so wide and so deep as to confound any scaling ladder or tunnel. And if this perimeter were not defense enough, Acre's inner wall, contiguous with the sea wall, was wide enough for two carts to pass abreast along its summit. Thus, it was believed no siege engine could breach the city walls, and with its superior navy guarding the sea-lanes, Acre was considered impregnable. These facts would also find a place in the report to Rabbi Petit.

Isaac drew a folded piece of parchment from his trouser pocket. Sitting forward, he smoothed the parchment open upon a flat limestone ledge. Using a fine piece of charcoal, he added numbers to his previous totals, so that his report would reflect yesterday's arrivals. Upon completing his calculations, he refolded the parchment and tucked it away. He felt proud to be involved in the defense of his city and wondered how much time Acre had before the Saracens attacked.

Despite the ocean breeze, perspiration beaded along his forehead, and beneath his black frock coat, his white shirt was wet and clung to his body. He stood up, took off his coat, and placed it in a slot along the seaward battlements. Glancing along the wall's summit in both directions, he made certain he was alone. Then he faced into the wind and lifted his shirt. Wreathed in the cooling pleasure of the wind on his body, he drew a slow breath and gazed through half-closed eyes over the outer harbor, watching the high masts and slanting yards of the galleys tipping drowsily from side to side under the pulse of the swell. Leaning against the sea wall, he closed his eyes.

"You there on the wall! Jew!"

Isaac froze, then slowly lowered his shirt and turned. On the lane below he recognized the beefy Templar with the blond beard and bald pate, whom the other knights called Tiny.

"Isaac, isn't it? You're just the one I was seeking. Come down." Tiny waved a thick hand. Like many common knights, he spoke a strange mixture of French and Latin, with odd bits of Arabic thrown in. The splayed red cross adorning his jerkin was barely visible through layers of dust. "You're to come with me. There's a delivery at the land gate."

Isaac breathed a sigh of relief and called down, *"Merci, chevalier!"* He picked up his coat and carefully began to descend the steep flight of mural steps.

Rabbi Petit, concerned about apostates as well as Saracen spies, had instructed Isaac to convey all correspondence addressed to any of Acre's Jews to him for review. To this end, he provided Isaac with silver and gold to compensate the guards. Apparently, the rabbi had yet to detect any suspicious communication. Following the rabbi's review, all correspondence was duly delivered to the designated recipient. Isaac had been to the gate more than a dozen times over the past week.

While Petit's rivals bitterly resented his meddling, especially angered by his breaking of seals, they were ill at ease around the knights, and had not yet mustered the courage to approach them about stopping the practice. They had, however, no hesitation in complaining to Isaac, and this they did regularly. While Isaac attempted to defend Petit, he also harbored deep misgivings about the arrangement.

"A Genoese merchant with a crate," Tiny explained as Isaac alighted from the last step.

"Who's it for?" Isaac asked as he shrugged into his coat.

"Petit himself. The merchant says it's paid for, and he's already given me something for my trouble." Tiny smiled and patted the purse hanging from his leather belt. "Come, young master." He led Isaac through the city square toward the land gate.

As they passed a brothel, two prostitutes called out to Tiny by name from a balcony. He glanced at Isaac. "That's just my nickname, mind you, not a description." He guffawed and clapped Isaac on the back. "Haven't seen you about much since St. Clair left."

"Ah, St. Clair." Isaac nodded. "Do you have any idea why he left?"

Tiny smiled mysteriously. "Do you?"

"No," Isaac lied. "One day I called for him and he was gone."

Tiny leaned his head close to Isaac and said in a low voice. "Truth is, St. Clair's our eyes and ears out there. You've no doubt heard us tease him about going native. All in good fun, of course, but fact is, the man speaks Arabic like one of them. He's out there now, blending in, spying out the land."

They left the square and passed *Khan el-Faranj,* the caravanserai of the Franks.

"Have you heard anything from him?" Isaac asked.

"Nothing yet, but that's small wonder. Our pigeon post was finished when the Mamluks trained their falcons to kill our birds. We'll have to wait till he gets back to hear what he knows."

Entering a narrow lane, they passed the tower of the Venetian Quarter.

"Mark my words, Isaac, the signed truce we have with the Saracens isn't worth the parchment it's written on. They'll probably attack in the next spring. It's St. Clair's job to ferret out the details." They ducked beneath a low-vaulted passage and found themselves jostled by a dusty entourage of animals entering the city.

"Venetian caravan!" Tiny shouted to Isaac over the din. "Just arrived from Damascus."

They flattened themselves against a stone wall to avoid being trampled by swaying camels with tinkling bells, bleating herds of pungent sheep, skittering brown goats, and patient donkeys with straddling baskets bulging with fruits and vegetables. Amid the shouts and curses of the drivers, the beasts claimed right of way as the caravan flowed toward the warehouses and comforts of *Khan el-Faranj*.

Edging along the wall, Tiny disappeared into a recessed doorway, his large hand beckoning Isaac to follow. Standing with Tiny in the shadowed alcove, Isaac watched the caravan pass by, relieved to be sheltered from the noise, the dust, and the smell. "How do you know that there aren't Mamluk warriors stealing in among the drivers and porters?" Isaac asked, only half in jest.

"Unarmed?"

"They could conceal their weapons."

"We check them at the gate." Tiny wiped the sweat from his bald head. "Besides, Mamluk warriors are too proud to go skulking about disguised as camel drivers."

"The Sultan Baybars used to delight in such disguises."

"The way I heard it," Tiny cleared his throat and spit into the dust, "he only did that for sport."

Once the caravan finally passed, they threaded their way among a human throng that replaced the animals in the narrow lane: peddlers with trays of cakes and nuts, porters carrying tubs of olives and pickled vegetables, and butchers bending beneath great slabs of meat. The crowd thinned as they passed beside the long wall surrounding the arsenal house and approached the land gate, which was guarded by a mixed contingent of Knights Hospitallers and Templars.

"Where's the box for the rabbi?" Tiny asked.

One of the guards motioned with his thumb.

Isaac saw a wooden crate resting on a cart in the shade of a porter's alcove where a heavyset, bearded man lounged, cracking and eating sunflower seeds. The striped robe and black velvet cap marked him as a Genoese merchant. Seeing Isaac, the merchant got to his feet.

"Are you Rabbi Petit?" he asked in Italian-flavored Arabic.

"I am his pupil and authorized to accept anything you might have for him."

"I'm sorry, young master, but I'm charged to deliver this only to Rabbi Petit." The merchant frowned and rested a thick hand on the crate.

"Then I shall take you to him."

"Very good! Let's be off, then." The merchant tipped his cap. "I am Buscarel of Genoa." He bent at the knees, gripped the cart's handles, and grunted as he lifted. The wagon settled back on its two large wooden wheels. The merchant pulled and the wagon creaked forward.

"Not so fast, Master Buscarel." Tiny raised his hand. "You may bring that into the city only *after* I have a look at your wares. Can't be too careful, you know." He smiled teasingly at Isaac. "You might have a division of the Sultan's guard hiding in there. Open the crate."

Buscarel stopped. "Sorry, sir, but I was instructed to deliver this to Rabbi Petit unopened."

Tiny planted himself in front of Buscarel, his hand resting on his sword hilt. "And I am instructing you to open the crate now."

The merchant smiled. "I will comply with my new instructions." Buscarel lowered the cart, took a wooden mallet, and with a few well-placed taps, loosened the crate's cover.

Isaac stepped around Tiny's considerable frame as the merchant lifted the lid. He saw that the crate was filled with frayed scrolls and bits of parchment. Inhaling the sweet effluence of an old library, Isaac surveyed the jumble of miscellaneous fragments. He reached out his hand, then paused and looked up at Tiny. "May I?" he asked.

The knight nodded.

Isaac picked out a scrap of parchment and saw that it was crowded with Hebrew script. Looking closely, he recognized a passage from the book of Leviticus. He returned the scrap and dug deeper into the crate, emerging with the worn black strap of old phylacteries winding like a thin snake among scraps of parchment, and entangled with a frayed prayer shawl.

"What do you make of this junk?" Tiny muttered.

"It's *holy* junk, Knight," Isaac said and flashed a smile. "Clearly, the contents of a *genizah*—a burial chamber for sacred texts and articles that are damaged and can no longer be used." He looked at Buscarel, noticing that the merchant's face glistened with perspiration. "Where is this from?" he asked.

"Safed, I think."

Isaac smoothed his thin beard, nodding as he picked through the upper layers of the crate. "There was an academy there, long abandoned. This must have come from there."

"That's the place, exactly." Buscarel smiled and took hold of the crate's cover. "May we proceed to the rabbi now?"

"Only after I make certain you don't have a Mamluk spy in there." With that, Tiny drew his sword. He thrust it into the crate three times.

Isaac saw Buscarel cringe with each thrust.

Chapter Twenty-Two

Western Shore of Galilee near Magdala
28 May, 1290
Evening

Between the lake and a stand of pine trees, Rabbi Samuel sat by a bright campfire warming his hands. The sun had set and the sky was ribboned with crimson clouds.

St. Clair dropped an armful of pine branches by the fire. He crouched on his heels next to the rabbi and began breaking the rough branches in his hands, carefully feeding the flames beneath an iron pot. "This will bring our tea to a boil."

"Your resourcefulness impresses me, Jonathan."

"In thirty years of soldiering one learns to live with simple pleasures." St. Clair pushed back the hood of his robe and ran a hand through his hair.

"Aren't you worried about someone seeing our fire?" asked the rabbi.

"No. The cove shelters us from Magdala. This fire can only be seen from the other side of the lake."

"With any luck that's where we'll be tomorrow," the rabbi said. "On that further shore, safely beyond the grasp of the emir."

"But how are we going to secure passage? We gave the emir

all our gold."

"Not all." The rabbi smiled. "I kept a little. It should be sufficient to persuade a fisherman to take us."

St. Clair peered into the pot, then moved it off the fire. "The tea is ready." He filled an earthenware cup and handed it to the rabbi.

Taking the cup, the rabbi inhaled deeply. "Ah, plenty of mint."

"It alleviates foul breath," St. Clair said as he ladled a cup for himself.

"And beneficial for passing water." The rabbi took a drink. "You know, between this tea and your command of Arabic, I'd say you've adapted to the region rather nicely."

"I had a good teacher," St. Clair said as he sat cross-legged on the ground next to the rabbi. "My commander at the Safed garrison, William de Rogé, encouraged me to learn Arabic and to respect that which was noble in the Saracens." Staring into the fire, he took a sip of tea. "And when he learned of my visits to the academy of Rabbi Jacob, he arranged my watch so I could continue." He paused, a smile playing on his lips. "He was my mentor and my friend." St. Clair drained his cup. "And he died with the others."

A wind moved through the pine trees and St. Clair turned his head. Holding his breath, he stared into the darkness, listening. The fire's light played on the spreading branches above them.

St. Clair turned back to the fire. "After the Mamluks took the citadel, Baybars promised clemency to all Templars who laid down their arms. Once they surrendered, he had them pile our dead along the tower keep. With my head wound," St. Clair ran a finger along the scar on the side of his head, "I was cast in among the dead. When I awoke, I found myself beneath the bodies of my comrades. I couldn't move, but from where I lay, I saw everything. I saw Baybars line up the prisoners. I couldn't move so I prayed. And as I watched and prayed, each of my brothers was put to the sword. They saved the worst for Rogé. While I watched and while I prayed, they flayed him and then they burned him, but with wet branches so he would not die quickly." St. Clair drew a deep breath. "My prayers meant nothing. God wasn't listening." He snapped a twig and fed the fire. "That was the last time I tried to speak to God in prayer."

The pine trees whispered and creaked in the night wind. St. Clair turned to look into the darkness. He felt the rabbi's hand on his shoulder.

"And yet, you continue to perform one prayer office after another. Why?"

"Discipline, Rabbi—like my celibacy—just discipline."

"Prayer has no other meaning for you?"

St. Clair paused before he answered. "Prayer is my way of saluting God. He is my king. I am his soldier. When I pass him, I salute. But we don't speak. Not since that day."

"Did God say no to your prayer, Jonathan? Was it His will that your friends die? These are good questions." The rabbi climbed to his feet and ladled himself another cup of tea. "More for you?" he asked.

St. Clair shook his head.

"I've seen the innocent die, Jonathan—earthquakes, floods, disease. I lost my wife and a child to a pestilence. I've questioned God's justice. I've questioned His goodness. I've even questioned His existence." The rabbi eased himself down to a sitting position next to St. Clair. "These questions raise a dust of doubt, and these doubts cast long shadows over our lives. It wasn't easy for me to dispel the dust. It wasn't easy to come out from the shadows."

"How did you do it?"

"Let me answer with a *midrash.* Seeing you bring sticks for the fire just now reminded me of one." The rabbi took a sip of tea before he began to speak. "There was once a very poor man. Weak with hunger, he went to gather wood for a fire. After hours of searching, he had just managed to fill his old sack with sticks of wood when the sack tore open. All the wood fell out. In anguish, he prayed to God, 'Lord, I am wretched and full of sadness. Send the Angel of Death, I beg you. Take me from my miserable life.' No sooner had he uttered these words than the Death Angel appeared. 'You called for me?' he asked the man. 'Ah, well . . . yes,' the poor man stammered, looking for a way out of his predicament. Then he pointed to the wood on the ground. 'I need some help gathering up these sticks.' "

St. Clair smiled. "An amusing story, Rabbi, but what's the relevance."

"The notion of God granting our wishes, however noble and altruistic, like some *jinn* that leaps from a magic lamp, is ridiculous."

"How can you say such a thing?" St. Clair challenged him. "Is it ridiculous to pray for those who are innocent and good? Is it ridiculous to pray for those you love?"

"Let me tell you another story, Jonathan. When I was a boy in Baghdad, there was a magician who performed in the great *suk.* He would use special incantations to make coins or doves appear or disappear. He was amazing! One time he made a donkey disappear! His magic tricks seemed to defy nature." The rabbi scratched his beard and then smoothed it with his hand. "Many people treat prayer like magic tricks. It's an easy mistake to make, especially when one is young. One uses prayer like one who rubs a lamp and expects God to pop out and do your bidding. But, magical thinking invites false hope." The rabbi paused and leaned toward St. Clair. "To pray means to ask intelligently, to *respect* the world God has created. Prayer cannot be wishing for results. When we ask God to alter events that have occurred or are already in motion, we are making a vain petition."

"Really, Rabbi!" St. Clair snorted. "I've studied your liturgy.

You Jews flatter God like any Christian. You beg for healing, for wisdom, progeny, wealth—"

"I don't deny that," the rabbi cut in. "You're right. Even when we speak of ourselves as *servants* of God, we set up the problem of pleading for a result, and this lowers us." The rabbi paused and took another sip of tea. "God didn't intend for that. We are, after all, created in His image. And *this* is key. If God created us in His image, then the divine image is implanted in us. Therefore, prayer becomes a way of discovering God's image within us, and what we must do to know His will. Prayer becomes far more than a petition. In true prayer, God is both the one to whom we pray and the one who prays through us. It becomes a two-way relationship, a covenant. We are not passive supplicants begging a master for something. We are active partners with the divine. This is what I tell my students when they petition or praise God—occasionally put your own name into the prayer in God's place."

St. Clair turned sharply. "What blasphemy is this?"

"Wait and listen. It is not that we, God forbid, claim to be God. It is, as I told you of Kabbalah—as above, so below—from an activity below, there is a corresponding activity on high. Without the impulse below, there is no stirring above. You say correctly that much of prayer is flattery, petitioning God with words of praise and adoration. You are correct. But this is not idle flattery if, in praising God, we aspire to emulate His attributes."

"I'm familiar with that concept, Rabbi. We call it *imitatio dei*—in ascribing compassion and mercy to God, we define our own moral imperatives."

"That's it *exactly.* When we pray and we walk after His attributes, we become good partners with God. In this way, prayer becomes a two-way bridge on which we meet the divine that is reflected within us. And on that bridge we don't just salute, we *embrace* God. We embrace the notion that we are created in His image, with the freedom and the responsibility to inquire, to think, to love, to work, and to create as if we're doing God's part in this world . . ."

"Shh!" St. Clair looked into the darkness among the pine trees. "Did you hear that?"

"No."

After listening intently for a minute, St. Clair let out his breath. "I'll be glad to put more distance between us and the emir. I have an uneasy feeling."

"Is that why you put on your mail hauberk this morning?"

"I thought you were sleeping."

"I was, but the racket you made putting it on woke me. Why—"

"Shh! There it is again." St. Clair stood up, staring into the darkness among the trees, beyond the circle of firelight.

He bent down and grabbed his stave from where it lay by the fire.

"The emir's halka?" the rabbi asked in a soft whisper.

St. Clair put a finger to his lips as he stared into the shadows, his eyes gradually accommodating to the darkness. Then he slowly pointed with his stave. "There."

A hooded figure stood motionless between two oleander bushes on the path to the shore.

St. Clair gripped the stave and rose to his full height. "What do you want of us, sir?"

There was no response.

He took a step forward. "I charge you. Show yourself and tell us what you want here."

Firelight flickered on the cowled robe, the face in shadow. Then a whisper. "I'm hungry."

"Then come and eat! Only tell us who you are."

"I cannot." The figure turned away and took a few steps

toward the shore.

"Wait! Tell us who you are."

There was no response.

"You try my patience, sir! I charge you to show yourself!" St. Clair ran forward, reached out with his hand, and roughly turned the stranger about. Then he staggered back as if burned by fire.

Gazing at him serenely with her calm gray eyes was Zahirah.

St. Clair's throat suddenly felt thick. He looked away and swallowed hard. "You . . . I . . . I don't understand," he stammered. "You must return to Tel Hum!"

"No." Her voice was clear and resonant, like the gently plucked string of a lute.

St. Clair stalked back to the rabbi. "She must go back!" he said with a sudden ferocity, trying to mask his joy at seeing her again.

Chapter Twenty-Three

כג

Acre
29 May, 1290
Before dawn

By the light of a single candle, Isaac sat writing at his desk. He had worked for hours and yearned to sleep. Leaning back, he yawned and rubbed his eyes. Along the city wall, he could hear the guards calling the final watch of the night. He had yet to complete the second draft of his report for Rabbi Petit.

In rejecting Isaac's first draft, Petit had flown into a rage—waving the parchment in Isaac's face, shouting, *Where are the details? Where are the diagrams?* He had never seen the rabbi so unsettled. Petit had crumpled the parchment into a ball and flung it into the wastebin by his desk. Then he grabbed Isaac's lapels, shrieking invective punctuated with malodorous spittle. *I charge you to do it properly. And I must have the report before daybreak. Do you hear me? Before daybreak!*

Isaac sat forward in his chair and continued writing, but after a few minutes, he began to doze off. Shaking himself awake, he forced himself to concentrate, but a heavy lassitude settled over his mind, and his thoughts began to drift. He wondered about the contents of the crate the merchant had brought to Petit. He sat without moving, his mind lingering on the edge of sleep, or perhaps he *was* asleep. He wasn't sure. When the quill fell from his fingers, he started awake and opened his eyes wide. The length of candle looked the same as before. *If I slept, it wasn't for long.*

He pushed away from the writing table and stood up. Leaning over the basin next to his bed, he dipped his hands into the cold water, splashing his face again and again. He dried his eyes with the fabric of his white cotton robe, then pushed open the window casements and leaned out. The cool air on his face helped clear his head.

The only sound was the distant roar of the sea pounding the breakwater at the edge of the outer harbor. A gust of wind slid off the dark waters of the Mediterranean with a dry rustle of palm fronds. Isaac looked up at the curved trunk of the palm in silhouette against the sky, the sharp edges of the fronds waving like curved scimitars. The stars were beginning to fade. The inquisitive *bulbul* that lived among the fronds high up in the palm tree had not yet begun its morning song.

As he stood at the window, misgivings about Rabbi Petit's behavior rose in his mind, confusion at having to complete the report so quickly. Then, rebuking himself, he shook away the doubts. *The rabbi must have received knowledge of an impending attack by the Mamluks from the merchant, Buscarel. And now, privy to this terrible knowledge, he requires the complete report with dispatch so as to warn the Christian knights and offer counsel.*

It made sense, but he couldn't rid himself of the feeling that something wasn't right.

Leaving his doubts unresolved and the window open, Isaac returned to the writing table and put the finishing touches on a map that showed the precise locations of the Templar armory and watch stations along the wall. He then completed the report with a discussion of what he felt was a lack of security when it came to caravans. He concluded with recommendations as to how surveillance might be improved.

And now it was done.

And none too soon. Through the open window came the fluty staccato of the bulbul, welcoming the dawn. Isaac put down the quill. The gregarious bird with its dark head and long tail was perched on the windowsill. "Good morning, little friend. I thank you for your song."

The sky had turned a dark blue and was streaked with wisps of dull rose-colored clouds. Isaac stood up and the bulbul flew off.

He threw on his clothes—black trousers, white shirt, and his black frock coat. He pinched off the candle flame, then held the parchment carefully in his hands as he blew the ink dry and headed for the door. Down the dark hallway, he came to the rabbi's study. He balanced the parchment on the flat of one hand and knocked on the door.

"Come." The rabbi's voice bit through the silence of the sleeping academy.

Isaac pushed the door open with his shoulders. He was surprised to see the rabbi fully dressed in his favorite striped robe, sitting at his writing table.

"The report is now as I requested?" Petit asked warily.

"Yes, Rabbi." Isaac carefully placed the parchment on the writing table in front of Petit. "The ink is just drying."

The rabbi scanned the parchment, nodding. "Good. The map and tables add a nice touch." He took a blotter and carefully dried the ink.

"I added some recommendations about caravans at the end," Isaac offered.

"You have done well, Isaac. You have insured our safety, and we are all in your debt." Petit put down the blotter and rang for his manservant.

Isaac watched, confused, as Petit began to roll the parchment into a tight scroll. "Are you not going to read it in detail, Rabbi?"

"I know your capabilities when you're properly motivated, Isaac. I'm sure the report is flawless." Petit fastened the scroll with a bit of twine, then began to melt sealing wax over the lighted taper on his desk. "Go and wash up, my son. We'll go to synagogue together."

Isaac didn't move, watching in disbelief as the rabbi sealed the scroll with the wax. His mind was foggy. He tried to comprehend why the rabbi wasn't reading the report.

Menahem Mendel was at the door. "You rang for me, Rabbi?" he asked thickly.

"Summon Buscarel."

"Certainly, Rabbi. Good morning, Rabbi."

"Buscarel?" Isaac's confusion mounted. "The merchant is still here?"

"He's to convey this directly to the Templar commandery," Petit said as he finished sealing the binding. "Don't trouble yourself with further questions, Isaac. Go wash up."

Isaac turned toward the door, his head spinning with confusion and fatigue. Had the merchant spent the night at the yeshiva? Given the availability of comfortable appointments at the Genoese caravansary and Petit's disdain for gentiles, it made no sense.

Isaac pulled the door closed and turned down the darkened hallway toward his room. Then, hearing footsteps, he stopped and turned.

Buscarel bustled down the other end of the corridor toward the rabbi's study. There, he stopped and knocked. The door opened and he went in.

Isaac stepped back toward the study, listening to their voices through the doorway. He heard the merchant's greeting in his Italian-flavored French. "A glorious morning to you, Rabbi."

"And a very good morning to you, Buscarel. I trust you're

well rested."

"Yes, and anxious to resume my travels. Is it not written in the proverbs that in all labor there is profit, but in talk there is only poverty?"

"And far from poverty, good merchant—here's for your pains."

There was a sound Isaac recognized as a bag of coins striking a wooden surface. He stepped closer to the door.

"It's all here?"

"As we agreed. Do you wish to count it?"

"I think not, Rabbi. You know better than to trifle with my trust."

"Then, my good man, take your wages and the scroll, and Godspeed to you."

Isaac stepped back into the shadows as the door creaked opened. Buscarel emerged and turned down the hall as the study door closed.

Isaac followed. Watching from the front door, he saw Buscarel in the dim, pre-dawn light step through the yeshiva gate just as a black-robed Knight Hospitaller passed by in the lane.

"A good morning to you, sir," the merchant called out cheerily and doffed his cap. "I bid you farewell."

"What's this, Buscarel? With the west wind bringing you opportunity for profit here in Acre, you're *leaving*?"

"Yes, *Chevalier,*" Buscarel replied. "Profit calls to me more loudly from Safed!"

Safed? Isaac's confusion mounted as he watched Buscarel disappear down the lane. *Where's he going? That's not the way to the commandery.* His skills of logical deduction, honed by the rigors of Talmudic reasoning, reeled in the face of the contradictions and his lack of sleep. He shook his head, trying to clear his thoughts. It didn't help.

"This makes no sense," he whispered to no one as he leaned

against the opened door. Then the merchant's parting word to the knight tugged hard on the loosening threads of contradiction, unraveling the garment of lies. *Safed.*

His eyes shot open as the full horror of what he had done struck him like a stone.

Chapter Twenty-Four

כד

Western shore of Galilee
29 May, 1290
Before dawn

In the fading darkness before dawn, St. Clair stepped back and bowed as one who departs from the presence of an unseen king. Crossing himself discreetly, he looked out over the lake. A light gray haze hovered over the water, and wisps of rose-colored clouds hung in the pale eastern sky.

"Good morning, Jonathan," Rabbi Samuel said, stepping to the shoreline, smooth stones clicking beneath his sandals.

St. Clair didn't turn. "This is wrong, Rabbi. The woman is unclean."

"We don't know that for certain."

"That's exactly the point. We *don't* know for certain."

"The situation does raise certain challenges." The rabbi cinched a woolen blanket around his shoulders. "But I think we can overcome them easily enough. We have, after all, established that she has no blemish, and it is well known that one with no physical trace of the disease cannot infect others. And in the time it takes to reach Jerusalem, we'll continue to watch for any blemishes."

Over the lake, the sky brightened, and the clouds glowed.

St. Clair closed his eyes and drew a deep breath. The dawn wind slid toward them, bringing smells of the desert and of fish. "This isn't right," he muttered and stalked away shaking his head. "This isn't right." He stopped, turned, and jabbed his finger at the rabbi. "She *must* go back to Tel Hum. If Nehemiah finds her clean, she can return to her home in Safed."

"No, I can't." The woman had quietly joined them at the water's edge. "I'm a fugitive from the emir, just as you are. When I'm declared clean in Tel Hum, where am I to go?"

St. Clair turned and looked at her. The hood of her robe was down, resting on her shoulders. Her head was shorn, according to the rabbi's injunction in Tel Hum for those awaiting determination of their sickness or health. When she caught his eye, he turned away.

The rabbi raised his shoulders. "She could come with us . . ."

"What are you saying?" St. Clair glared at the rabbi. "You yourself determined the manner of purification. How can you—"

"You saw me, Rabbi," Zahirah cut in. "You know I am clean. Even though I cared for the old woman, I was ever careful to shield my hands with cloth. You know I am free of the disease. You just said I cannot infect anyone. Please, let me travel with you—"

"No." St. Clair crossed his arms. "It's out of the question." His vow hung upon his heart like ill-fitting armor on a hot day.

"Please," she pleaded. "I have nowhere else to go."

"I feel like the father of two squabbling children," Rabbi Samuel murmured as he limped past St. Clair. "Come, Yonatan. A word with you in private."

A dozen paces down the shore, the rabbi stopped and looked up at St. Clair. "Her reasoning is sound, Jonathan."

"But, Rabbi . . ."

"And there's this. The emir seeks two men, correct? If we travel with the woman, we're two men and a woman. This affords us more protection. So, it's my decision that she comes along." Without waiting for a reply, the rabbi limped back toward Zahirah. "Come, my child. The fishermen of Magdala sail with the dawn. We must hurry if we are to secure passage."

"Thank you, Rabbi," she whispered and turned toward the campsite.

St. Clair stalked to his pallet, where he made a great show of snatching his blanket off the ground and shaking off the soil and pine needles. He stuffed the blanket into his pack and cinched it closed, his jaw muscles bunching as he clenched his teeth. Straightening up, he secured the pack on his shoulders. With his eyes resting on Zahirah, he whispered, "But she must remain apart from us."

The sun rose over the eastern mountains and the woman's skin glowed in the soft light. Her eyes, like brushed gold, challenged him.

He did not look away.

Acre
29 May, 1290
Dawn

Isaac skidded to a halt by a Templar sitting in the shade at the land gate. "The merchant, Buscarel," he panted. "Has he been here?"

"Been here and gone," the knight drawled. "Rode off in his cart not fifteen minutes ago." The knight squinted up at Isaac and scratched his beard. "Unfinished business?"

"Yes, sir." Isaac sighed. "Unfinished business."

The knight nodded toward the gate. "Go ahead. You might yet catch him. Only don't go past the frontier."

Isaac pelted out the gate, holding his skullcap in place with one hand, his black coat spreading out behind him like a cape. Once beyond the outer city wall, he followed the well-traveled caravan road to the east. Skirting a herd of dusty goats, he was soon past the few houses and villas that stood outside the city walls. At the edge of the frontier, marked in fading French and Arabic on a wooden sign, he stopped, exhausted. Gasping for air, he stared down the dull brown ribbon of road, past long rows of palm trees where farmers plodded through a blue mist drifting over morning fields. There was no sign of the merchant.

What have I done? Panic clutched at his heart. *What have I done?*

In a daze, he returned to Acre and passed back through the city gate.

"Catch up with him, did you?" asked the guard.

"I fear not, sir."

Isaac wanted to tell the knight to organize a squad and pursue Buscarel, to retrieve the scroll. But he said nothing. He knew they would never pursue Buscarel into Saracen territory. Such an incursion would violate the terms of the truce.

And I can't catch up with Buscarel on foot, and not dressed as I am . . .

He wandered into a broad marketplace, one end open to the sky, the other covered by a domed roof sprouting dry grass. The suk was lined with arcades covered by awnings, their bright colors muted by years of dirt. *How could I have been such a fool?* He passed a table piled high with sheep heads at the entrance to a meat shop festooned with dangling carcasses and swarming with black flies.

Leaning against the splintered wood of a shuttered stall, he struggled to think clearly through a fog of anxious fatigue. In a stall across the way an aged cobbler tapped nails into a black boot, the sound echoing in the silence. Isaac drew a deep breath and closed his eyes. *All that time, I thought I was helping to save Acre; Petit tricked me into bringing its destruction!* The bitter irony burned in his chest. *He used me!* Seething with rage, Isaac lurched forward. *He lied to me!*

Dodging past porters, he broke into a run, and was soon sprinting through the yeshiva gate. He careened down the darkened hallway and, without knocking, burst into the rabbi's study.

The room was empty.

Of course—morning prayer at the synagogue. He'll be gone for another hour or two.

Isaac staggered to the rabbi's writing table, and with a snarl of rage, brought the flat of his hand down with a bang on the wooden surface. "How could you *use* me so?" Crushing his eyes shut, he bowed his head and leaned forward, both hands on the desk, his mind seething with angry thoughts. *I know. I'll confront him at the synagogue. I'll expose him there.* Turning, he half-sat on the writing table and shook his head. *For what purpose? The report is written in my own hand. I'll only implicate myself and accomplish nothing . . .*

He rubbed his hands over his face and forced himself to think. *I must repair what I have done. But how?*

He began to pace. *Wallace and I are ready to leave for Jerusalem. Instead, we can try to retrieve the document from Buscarel.* He paced faster. *It's more than ten leagues to Safed and much of it mountainous. And he'll be stopping somewhere for the night. I'm certain we can overtake him!*

As he turned to leave the study, Isaac glimpsed the crate Buscarel had brought from Safed on the floor behind the writing table. Since its arrival, Petit had seemed unsettled and anxious.

Why? The crate contains only torn prayer shawls, worn-out scrolls, and scraps of parchment fit for burial in a genizah.

He hesitated at the door. *No. There must be something else.*

With the rabbi at synagogue, this was his chance to find out.

He dropped to his knees and lifted off the crate's cover, letting it clatter onto the clay-tiled floor. He pawed through scrolls and fragments of parchment, evoking the pungent memory of an ancient library. He lifted out a prayer shawl, followed by a long tangle of phylacteries. Digging deeper, he discovered a cloth garment, the fabric stiff and stained a red-brown color. He shook it open, scattering scraps of parchment onto the floor like dry leaves. It was a striped robe, like those worn by Jews of the east. He looked closer. The robe was covered with dried blood.

This has no place in a genizah.

He laid the robe gently on the floor.

He turned back to the crate, sifting his hand back and forth through deeper layers. His hand hit something hard, covered in what felt like leather. Trying to lift it from the crate, he found it too heavy. He reached in with his other hand and, straining, lifted it up, out from beneath layers of parchment.

A broadsword!

It was tall as a man and sheathed in a leather scabbard. The pommel of the hilt was embossed with a design. Isaac looked closer.

"Oh, my God!" He dropped the sword and fell backwards as if he had been struck. "I know that device. This is the sword of Jonathan St. Clair!"

He looked from the sword to the bloodied robe. The message seemed clear.

Jonathan St. Clair was dead.

As he climbed to his feet, he glimpsed a crumpled ball of parchment in the wastebin by the writing table. Recognizing it as the rejected first draft of his report, he picked it up and saw there was also a scroll in the bin. He took them both.

He smoothed out the crumpled parchment and saw that the draft included most of the information of the final report. *This might help turn a curse to blessing,* he thought. *Many of the knights are known to me. I can convey this to such as these. Then, knowing what the Mamluks know, the Templars will be ready.* He folded the parchment and tucked it into the pocket of his jacket.

Next, he took the scroll. It was unsealed. As he spread it open, his eyes locked on the Hebrew word emblazoned across the top.

Herem.

"My God," he whispered. "This is a writ of excommunication."

And on the first line was the subject of the action.

Rabbi Solomon Petit.

With pounding heart, he scanned through the Hebrew script smudged with corrections and crowded with addenda along the margins. It was clearly a working draft. Bits of text leapt from the parchment . . . *violence against the followers of Maimonides . . . burning of manuscripts . . . destruction of libraries . . . desecration of Maimonides' tomb.* Isaac could scarcely catch his breath. And at the bottom of the page was the name of the author.

Rabbi Samuel ben Daniel ha-Kohen, the Gaon of Baghdad.

As the fog of early morning vanished beneath a rising sun, so the haze of Isaac's perplexity began to lift. A picture was emerging—undeniable, yet incomprehensible.

It was widely known that Rabbi Samuel had disbanded his academy in Baghdad, and was coming to Acre to lend his support to the pro-Maimonides faction in the city. But Isaac hadn't realized it had come to this—a decree of excommunication. And while he knew of Petit's antipathy toward Maimonides and his adherents, he never imagined the old man capable of such acts as mentioned in the writ. But all that paled in comparison with the fate Petit had arranged for Acre.

Isaac rolled up the writ and placed it in a deep pocket on the inside of his jacket, his mind racing. *So, it was Rabbi Samuel St. Clair went to meet in the land of the Mamluks—in Safed. And the sword and the bloodied robe point to only one conclusion—they're both dead, undoubtedly by order of a local emir to whom Petit promised the secrets of Acre's defenses . . .* His heart clenched with sadness as he looked down at St. Clair's sword and the rabbi's bloody robe. *It's too late to save them, but it isn't too late to save Acre—but I must make haste.*

Isaac quickly returned the sword, robe, and most of the fragments of parchment to the crate and replaced the cover. He left the room and headed for the Templar commandery, going by way of Midrash Hagadol, the home of Petit's adversaries. He stopped at the iron gate and pulled the chain, sounding the bell.

Within seconds, the chief rabbi's steward bustled out of the academy's doorway, fumbling with a heavy ring of keys. "Isaac," he exclaimed. "How good to see you. You must come in."

"Another time," he said and passed the draft ordaining Petit's excommunication through the bars of the gate. "Please convey this with dispatch to your rabbi."

"Certainly, Isaac," the steward fussed. "But wouldn't you like to give it to him yourself?"

"I haven't the time."

Without another word, Isaac turned and hurried away.

Chapter Twenty-Five

כה

Magdala
29 May, 1290
Dawn

Zahirah followed the rabbi and his disciple out from among the trees toward the harbor of Magdala. She saw that the rabbi was limping forward as quickly as he could, leaning on his disciple's arm.

"Hurry!" he shouted. "The fishermen are about to put in."

Though the air was cool upon her face, she felt warm in her hooded robe. Glancing across the lake, she saw a low bank of clouds along the eastern edge of the sky hiding the morning sun. Near the water she could make out a group of men moving within the morning mist.

The rabbi quickened his pace. But it appeared they were too late.

A half-dozen boats had already pulled away from shore, their oars flashing in the weak dawn light. Zahirah saw only a single boat at the water's edge, its hull resting among reeds, water lapping the bow.

"Now what?" asked the rabbi's disciple, frowning as he looked over the water. "How are we to get across?"

The rabbi nodded at the empty boat. "This one would suit

us well enough."

"With no crew, Rabbi? No rigging?"

Zahirah turned toward the village, staring into the mist. "Do you hear that?" she asked, pointing along the path to Magdala. "Someone's coming this way."

Emerging from the mist, two fishermen moved slowly forward beneath the weight of lines, nets, and sails. As they drew nearer, Zahirah saw that their dark hair and beards were long, their robes simple, and shawls covered their heads against the morning chill.

The rabbi raised his arm in greeting and called out in Arabic, "Good morning, gentlemen."

"And to you, sir," one of them replied with a quick bow. "What do three Mamluk scholars seek this fine morning?"

"If it's fish you like," interjected the other as he tossed nets and lines into the boat, "we'll be returning by midday with as fine a catch as any in Galilee."

"No. It's not fish we want," said the rabbi.

"What is it, then, venerable father?"

"We require passage to Ein Gofra on the eastern shore of the lake."

The men exchanged glances. Then one spoke.

"Begging your pardon, sir—we are but simple fishermen, and it is only by honest commerce that we fill our bellies and care for our families. As you can see, the sun is well up, and we need make haste to put in and be about our work."

"I well understand, and we'll gladly pay a fair wage for your troubles."

"A fair wage?" the man said as he stepped the mast. "What's it worth to you, then?"

"Ten silver *dirhams* now, and ten more upon arrival. A month's catch of St. Peter's fish would not fetch you such a price . . ."

As the men rigged the sail, they spoke to one another in a language the woman recognized but did not comprehend. The rabbi, on the other hand, immediately began speaking to the men in the same tongue. Zahirah stood by the boat, listening and watching. The rabbi appeared to introduce himself, and with that, the men immediately stopped what they were doing. In what appeared to be an attitude of stunned reverence, they came near the old man, bowing and giving homage as to a sultan. The rabbi received them and, first gesturing toward his disciple, he then pointed at Zahirah and switched his speech back to Arabic.

"This young lady, on the other hand, is indeed Saracen. Destitute, she is, having recently lost her family."

One of the men stepped forward. "I am Shmuel, and this is my brother, Yosef. It will be a rare honor to assist you, Rabbi Samuel, but we will not accept anything in return."

"Ah, but you will," the rabbi argued. "We will not permit you to forego your wages on our account. Our offer stands firm."

"But, Rabbi—"

"No, Shmuel." The rabbi gave him a friendly pat on the shoulder. "I'll hear none of it. We'll pay you for your pains."

The men soon had the boat in the water. Zahirah, the rabbi, and his disciple sat with their belongings among the coiled lines and nets. The boat was well balanced, though it rode low in the water. Zahirah settled herself against the rounded planks of the bow away from the men.

Since there was not yet wind, they left the sail furled about the mast and fitted the oars onto the pins. As the sun lifted its countenance above the clouds, the fishermen plied the oars for Ein Gofra on the far shore. After an hour of rowing, a west wind began to blow and the fishermen rejoiced, speaking excitedly in what Zahirah now recognized as Aramaic. They shipped the oars and unfurled the sail.

The boat moved swiftly upon the lake, and Zahirah leaned over the bow, watching the bright fish move beneath the surface, the clear water parting smoothly at the prow. She smiled into the cool wind. But after a space of half an hour, the wind stopped, the sail went slack, and the boat listed in the water.

"We had hoped for increase of the wind, my masters, but it was a dying breath." Shmuel sighed as he looked out over the flat surface of the lake. "The Greeks call this *ghalini,* for a calmness." He shook his head. "We'll wait a bit before we set the oars—perhaps the wind will blow again."

As the skiff drifted lazily in the quiet water, Zahirah saw that they were very, very far from shore—the larger houses of Magdala barely discernible over the smooth water of the lake to the west. Feeling warm beneath the hood of her robe, which concealed her shaved head, she reached down and cupped cool water from the lake in her hand. She splashed her face with the water again and again. With a sigh, she settled back in the boat and her heart swelled with joy.

The rabbi leaned toward her and pointed over the lake. "Does it not seem that the water is a sheet of molten silver, my daughter? Is it not as we are wandering between two skies?"

"Yes, Rabbi." She smiled. "It is written in the Koran that such water is a palace made smooth with glass."

"Let's set the oars, Yosef," Shmuel said, his voice as flat as the water. "We have far to go to Ein Gofra."

As the men leaned to the oars, the sun rose higher and the day grew hot. In the clear sky above, a single tern circled, gray-white with a black head. *Kaa-uh, kaa-uh,* it cried. Again and again it dove down with backswept wings into the water. To the east, Zahirah saw clouds rising like mountains, and the shore they sought came in sight—a long green line with a veil of gray-green hills behind.

The rabbi pointed toward the clouds. "Perhaps the day will

cool and there will come a wind."

"I don't much like the look of those clouds, Rabbi." Shmuel frowned as he rowed. "The first sign of foul weather."

The disciple rose from his place and said to the fishermen, "Let me lend a hand with the rowing that you two might rest." Taking the place of both brothers, he leaned to the oars and the boat gained speed. He rowed for an hour without pause or respite. Though his face ran with sweat, he did not remove his robe. Zahirah saw that he had great strength, and she was much amazed.

Past midday, the sky clouded over, and she felt a wind. The disciple shipped the oars as the wind rose aft of the boat.

"Finally!" Yosef exclaimed as he began to unfurl the sail.

"Have a care, brother. The wind rises," Shmuel said, his brow creased with worry. "We should square-rig the sail after the manner of the Rum—that which they call *musallabah.*"

"Ay," Yosef replied. "This wind will move us to that further shore soon enough. It's a good wind."

"A bit too good for my taste . . ." Shmuel muttered, his eyes on the sky.

Acre
29 May, 1290
Early morning

At the portals of the Templar commandery, Isaac clenched his fist and knocked on the thick-grained oak door.

A panel slid open. "What do you want?" asked the guard.

"I must speak with William Wallace," Isaac replied.

"He's in the yard," the guard said and the gate swung open.

Isaac saw Wallace among a group of novices and beckoned to him. Seeing Isaac, Wallace smiled and waved.

Isaac waved again, pointing to where he stood. As Wallace approached, Isaac stepped forward and whispered, "We must leave

Acre with all haste!"

"So we spoke, Isaac." Wallace clapped his friend on the shoulder. "Our fervor for Jerusalem draws us—"

"You don't understand, William—we must leave now!"

"What are you saying?"

"Walk with me apace, and I'll explain." Isaac led Wallace to a secluded corner of the yard. "We must leave Acre now, but not for Jerusalem."

"Why? What changed?"

"Time and circumstance conspire against us," Isaac replied quickly. "A certain merchant came hither yesterday with a crate from Safed for my rabbi. At first glance, it seemed to contain only worn-out texts, but this morning, I found therein bloody vestments and the great sword of the knight, Jonathan St. Clair, my sometime student and my friend."

Wallace's face darkened. "What means this?"

"I fear St. Clair is dead," Isaac replied grimly and drew a deep breath. "But there's more, William. It seems my rabbi has conveyed, by this same merchant, a missive to the Mamluks in Safed. And this is the very heart of the matter, for this letter contains such detail that will lay Acre's defenses bare before her enemies." Isaac stepped closer to Wallace, his voice edged with tension. "It is not an hour since the merchant left Acre through the land gate. We must overtake him, William. We must wrest this letter from his grasp."

Wallace clenched his fists. "Even so, but are we already not too late?"

"I think not, for the merchant is fat and travels slowly. But we must leave soon. I have set aside our disguises. Did you arrange for the horses and cart?"

"Aye. All that and supplies for the journey."

"Good. Now only one thing remains. I must quickly speak with that same knight with whom I sat when you were at the pells yesterday."

"That was Claude d'Urbot. He's here with the novices. Come."

Hurrying forward with Wallace at his side, Isaac saw that d'Urbot had gathered the novices about him and was beginning instruction.

Clearing his throat, Wallace stepped forward and bowed. "Sir Knight, I'm sorry to interrupt, but Isaac and I must speak with you on a matter of grave urgency."

"Certainly." D'Urbot came toward them, as he addressed the novices. "Gentlemen, return to the pells. I'll be with you shortly . . ."

The new men saluted and parted to let him pass.

D'Urbot led the way to the far side of the yard. There he turned to face Isaac and Wallace. "So, what is this matter of grave urgency?"

Wallace bowed his head. "Sire, Isaac has this morning brought a most important matter to my attention."

Isaac stepped quickly forward. "I thought you should see this, sir." He handed the parchment to d'Urbot.

As the knight scanned it, his brow furrowed. "Is this what I think it is?" he murmured without looking up.

"It clearly treats on the strengths and weaknesses of the Acre garrison, sir." Isaac leaned closer and added in a whisper, "Moreover, I have learned that a copy has been delivered to the Mamluks!"

"What?" D'Urbot looked sharply at Isaac. "How came you by this knowledge?"

"I discovered this draft in the possession of my mentor, Rabbi Solomon Petit, and I know he has recently conveyed a finished copy of this to the Mamluks in Safed."

"Did the rabbi himself write this?" d'Urbot asked, staring at the parchment.

"No."

"Who did?"

"I have no idea, sir."

D'Urbot placed his hand on Isaac's shoulder. "You have done well in bringing this to me, Isaac." He folded the parchment, tucked it beneath his jerkin, and started across the yard. "I will bring this without delay to the Temple Master. *Adieu.*"

Watching d'Urbot go, Isaac sighed in relief. "That's done. Now let's away."

"First to the stable. I've had two old chargers brought from pasture. We'll load supplies and victuals in the cart." With long strides, Wallace moved down the lane.

"The disguises are at the yeshiva." Isaac panted as he ran to keep up. "We'll pass there on the way to the land gate. And that same crate the merchant brought from Safed will also serve us well."

The pungent smell of the stables grew stronger as they passed bales of hay and pools of standing water.

"There's one thing I don't understand . . ." Wallace said as he lifted the heavy bolt and pulled the stable doors open. "Who wrote that document you gave to Claude d'Urbot?"

"I did," Isaac replied.

Chapter Twenty-Six

כו

Acre
29 May, 1290
Midmorning

Wallace guided the wagon to the outer land gate just as the sun lifted its brow over the crenellated parapets of the city wall. Isaac didn't recognize the Knight Hospitallers who stopped them.

"Where do you think you two are going?"

"By your leave, Knight," Wallace said and inclined his head in a quick bow. "I'm a squire in Claude d'Urbot's service, sent by my master to keep an eye on this one." He tugged gently on one of Isaac's side locks.

"And you?" The knight squinted up at Isaac. "What's your business beyond the walls?"

Isaac pointed with his thumb at the crate in the wagon. "We carry the remains of a nameless Jewish pauper for burial, sir."

The knight peered over the side of the wagon at the coffin-like crate and the long-handled shovel next to it among burlap sacks. "Off with you, then! Can't have you clogging up the gate." He slapped the side of the wagon with a mail glove.

Wallace snapped the reins and drove the horses out the gate and onto the caravan road. Within minutes they were approaching the faded sign at the edge of the Latin frontier.

"Is this the border?" Wallace asked without slackening the pace.

"There's really no clear border between the Christian and Moslem lands. It's more a transition zone—a no-man's-land. The knights tell me they come out here when they get bored—to course hares and chase gazelles. And it's here Italian merchants like Buscarel pass freely to conduct their commerce."

"How far ahead is he?"

"Perhaps two hours. We'll need a brisk pace to have any chance of catching him." Isaac pointed forward to a point ahead where the road split. "Take the road to the left, William—that's the way to Safed. The southern fork runs along the shadow of Mount Carmel toward Jerusalem and Cairo."

Wallace kept the horses trotting swiftly forward, their hooves drumming, the wagon creaking, and the wooden wheels biting through the sand and stones.

Isaac began to relax. So far, all had gone well. They had managed to leave the city quickly and without incident. After readying the wagon with implements and supplies at the commandery, they had gone together to the yeshiva and loaded the crate into the wagon before Petit's return. Stopping briefly at his home, Isaac had told his parents of his desire to visit his grandfather's grave and to pray at the Cave of Elijah. Before they could object, he had kissed them goodbye and left.

And now, for the first time in his life, he felt free—free from Rabbi Petit's coercive expectations and free from his parents' surrounding love—the freedom of being no one's son.

After traversing a cultivated plain studded with rows of date palms, the road began to rise into the foothills. Isaac turned in his seat and looked back. Although they had traveled only a few leagues, Acre already seemed very far away, its bold western front seeming to rise up out of the sea, ringed by gray walls and studded by square towers. Beyond it, the bright Mediterranean stretched to the unbroken line of the horizon where the sea met the lighter blue of the sky.

He had never been so far outside the city, nor had he ever seen Acre at such a distance. Leaving aside his thoughts of Buscarel, he drew a deep breath. *What worlds lie beyond the far edge of that firmament?* He had heard of places with names that resonated in his imagination—Provençe, of the great Gershon ben Solomon; Spain, with scholars like Moses de Leon; and the island of Comino, where the brilliant apostate Abulafiya proclaimed himself messiah.

Acre looked small and gray against the sea, like a barnacle clinging to the shore between the blue Mediterranean and the onrushing tide of the Mamluks. He turned in the wagon and faced forward. In the distance, beyond hills covered with blue-green olive trees, he could see the stone walls of a village. He tapped Wallace on the arm and pointed. "Let's take that side road and change clothes."

Wallace guided the wagon between two stately cypress trees that stood like sentinels astride a rocky path that led through an olive grove and ended abruptly on a sheltered knoll by a ruined castle. After hours of noisy traveling, the sudden silence was profound, broken only by the breathing of the horses.

Isaac jumped down from his seat and surveyed the tumble-down castle wall, festooned with grasses and trailing vines. "I'll get the clothing," he announced. Opening a hempen sack, he pulled out a black velvet doublet lined with gold brocade. "This one's for me, and this one's for you." He handed Wallace a green velvet jerkin.

Wallace grimaced. "Why can't I have one like yours?"

"Because this was the largest I could find, and it goes with this." Isaac handed Wallace a green cotton velveteen hat.

Wallace winced as he took the hat and pulled it onto his

head, over his ears, almost down over his eyes. "You must be joking."

"It isn't worn like that." Isaac laughed. "Here, I'll show you." He took off his own black skullcap, reached up, pulled the hat off Wallace's head, and put it on his own. "You wear it like this, see?"

"Hanging off to the side like that?"

"Yes." Isaac handed the hat to Wallace. "Trust me. I've watched these merchants come and go for years. This is how they dress. I can't help it." He reached into the sack and brought out a scarlet sash. "And tie up the jerkin with this."

Rolling his eyes, Wallace took the sash.

Isaac took off his black frock coat, laid it to the side, and put the doublet on over his white shirt. He fastened the hooks closing the doublet and put on a black velvet cap. As he stuffed his own black frock coat into the sack, he found two leather arm cuffs. "Hold out your arms, William. These go with your outfit. They'll make your sleeves look puffier."

"I hardly think we need concern ourselves with puffy sleeves." Wallace fumed as Isaac tied the arm cuffs into place. "Besides, I still need to water the horses."

"Patience," Isaac replied as he cinched down a knot. "In these regions, it's imperative we look the part of Genoese merchants. There. Done."

"Wonderful," Wallace said as he grabbed a bucket from the wagon along with a water skin. Turning, he made his way toward the horses. "You're certain my sleeves are sufficiently puffy?" His voice dripped with sarcasm as he filled the bucket with water.

"Definitely." Isaac smiled. "Can I help with the horses?"

"No need. Just make sure everything in the cart is secure."

Isaac tucked his side locks beneath the velvet cap and peered into the wagon. The crate's cover was firmly in place, concealing its contents of old parchment and St. Clair's sword. The sacks with their supplies were still tightly closed and secured despite the bumpy ride.

Isaac noticed a feather in a corner of the wagon. Picking it up, he saw it was pure white, probably from a gull. He held it close, rotating it between his thumb and forefinger, studying it. Then he turned toward the sea and, straightening his arm high over his head, held it up against the blue sky, watching the wind ruffle its edges. He let it go, and the feather sprang free, soaring over the highest branches of the olive trees. He watched its flight until he could see it no more.

The long arc of the coastline was far away. Acre, on its lonely promontory, was barely visible against the wide blue water. For nineteen years his life had been bounded by the sea and the city walls, sealed off like the city itself, contracted like a clenched fist—closed, small, and hard. But now, like the feather, he was free.

The thought thrilled him. They could stay away for weeks, even months.

Feeling a little guilty, Isaac promised himself to get word to his parents—to reassure them. He was certain he'd be back by the coming winter—definitely before spring. Because in the spring the Mamluks would come.

For a siege needed fair weather. When the rains of winter ended, and the muddy water dried in the ditches and the ground became hard underfoot, they would come. When fresh winds cleared the sky, and the days grew long and warm, when wildflowers began to appear and all the earth rejoiced in new life, they would come.

Isaac saw that Wallace was still watering the horses. Leaning forward with his elbows on the wagon, he rubbed his eyes and yawned. The excitement of pursuing Buscarel had made him forget the night without sleep, spent preparing the report for

Petit. Now, fatigue hovered at the edge of every movement and every thought, beckoning him to rest. Pushing the feeling away, he opened his eyes wide. "All right, then," he announced, climbing back onto the wagon, "let's get going."

Wallace tossed the empty bucket and water skin into the wagon, reclaimed his seat, and guided the wagon back to the main road. "Do you think we have a real chance of catching him?"

"Most definitely. We might by this evening. Otherwise, we'll get him tomorrow."

"I'll be glad when this is over and we can get on to Jerusalem." Wallace glanced at Isaac and smiled. "Do I look as ridiculous as you in these clothes?"

"More so, I think."

Wallace flicked the whip lightly across the backs of the horses, spurring them forward. The wagon rattled and creaked, and the boys fell silent.

As the hours passed, the road rose, bending among terraced slopes with a dry streambed to their right and unbroken groves of olive trees on their left. Piles of rocks and standing stones marked the road's edge with a scattering of old pack frames, broken wheels, frayed harnesses, bones, and piles of dung. The time of the olive harvest was long past, and they met no one on the road.

In late afternoon, the sun stood a hand's breadth above the western horizon, a smudge of gold behind silver clouds. "Look there, Isaac," Wallace said, nodding forward.

In the distance, Isaac saw a flag of dust trailing away among the terraced hills. "Buscarel?" he asked.

"No. It's someone coming toward us." Wallace flicked the whip. "Now we'll see just how convincing these disguises are."

★ ★ ★ ★ ★

Galilee
29 May, 1290
Midday

The wind blew gloriously and the boat shot along the surface of the water with Shmuel's hand steady on the tiller. Zahirah, at the bow in her hooded robe, faced east, feeling the wind all about her. The eastern shore of the lake, though still far away, drew nearer.

"To what may the thing be likened?" the rabbi asked, raising his voice to make himself heard over the wind. "A man thinks he is at rest, as we are on this boat, yet day after day, he journeys forward—his life unfolds. If he acts or does not act, if he moves or remains still, if he speaks or is silent—life and destiny unfold. This is like to our condition. For here we lie without motion on a boat that flies on the wings of the wind."

Leaning forward on the bow, Zahirah drew a deep breath. She remembered a tapestry that hung in her home as a child in Safed—the likeness of a beautiful woman gracing the prow of a galleon. She closed her eyes and smiled. Her hood blew off, but she did not care if the fishermen saw her shaved head. Over the wind, she heard something else—shouting.

She opened her eyes.

Something was wrong.

"Make the sheet fast, Yosef!"

She saw fear darken the faces of the fishermen as the little boat was driven forward with great speed.

"Furl the sail!" Shmuel shouted over the roaring wind. "I'll jam the tiller . . ."

All about them, jagged waves rose up like mountains—canyon walls of water loomed below a darkening sky.

Yosef groped at the sail as water sheeted down, as in a drenching rain. Waves came upon the boat from all sides, striking with such blows that Yosef staggered and fell down.

Zahirah watched in mounting fear as the wind tore at the sail. Then part of the mast snapped off and flew into the water with a length of rope. Yosef lurched over the hull, reaching out to grab the rope. A huge wave crashed over the boat, and he was gone.

"Yosef!" Shmuel shouted as he searched the water.

Yosef surfaced just a boat-length away, flailing and gasping for air. The rabbi's disciple quickly grabbed an oar to reach him, but the waves lifted Yosef up and carried him away.

Horror filled Zahirah's heart as she saw him sink beneath the waves.

The disciple quickly cast off his boots and Mamluk robe. Huddled against the bow, Zahirah's breath caught as she saw his raiment—a shirt of mail and a splayed red cross on his white tunic. "Oh, my God," she whispered. "A Templar!"

The knight quickly stuffed his vestments beneath his robe next to the rabbi. Now wearing only drawers and leggings, he lifted a leather pouch from about his neck and gave it to the rabbi. Then he leapt headfirst into the flood.

For many minutes Zahirah searched with her eyes but saw neither the knight nor Yosef. She thought them both drowned and gave herself over to grief. The wind and waves buffeted the boat and water flooded the hull. Zahirah grabbed a wooden bucket and began to bail, but in her heart, she bade life farewell.

But as she bailed, Zahirah lifted up her eyes and saw the Templar holding Yosef in one arm, swimming toward the boat in a valley between mountains of water. The waves crashed over him but still he swam on, carrying Yosef. She bailed faster as the rabbi and Shmuel fought the oars. After many minutes, they rose up and dragged Yosef back into the boat.

The rabbi tended Yosef as the boat swung away from the knight. Shmuel jammed the oars, and Zahirah reached out to help the Templar from the water. A wave crashed upon him, driving him beneath the surface. Shmuel turned the boat about, again and again, searching the water.

Finally she saw him, about a furlong away, fighting the waves. "There he is!" Her hand shot out, pointing. "Over there!"

Shmuel managed to bring the boat near, and she reached out. To her amazement, the Templar ignored her hand and tried to catch hold of the gunwale. But he could not grasp it.

"Take my hand!" Zahirah shouted, but he would not. The Templar began to tire and sink down in the water.

She thrust her arm further toward him. "Take my hand!" she shouted. Instead, he again tried to catch the rail but could not. Then a huge wave washed over him, and he was gone.

"No!" she cried, weeping, her arm outstretched over the water. Tears and rain streaked her face. "No!"

Shmuel continued to turn the boat, searching the lake. Seconds crawled by as the waves rolled and tossed the boat.

Then the knight's head broke the surface once more. He was gasping for air.

"Take my hand!" she shouted, leaning far over the gunwale. "Now!"

He fixed her with his eyes, reached out, and grasped her outstretched arm.

Shmuel dropped the oars, took the knight's other arm, and together they brought him into the boat.

As soon as the Templar was aboard, he looked to Yosef, who was still blue and shaking from the cold. The woman stared at the knight's back, white and crossed with crimson scars. While his back was turned and without quite knowing why, she crouched and took his heavy mail shirt and his jerkin, stuffing them among her own robes.

Seeing that Yosef lived, the knight turned and lifted his cloak from where it lay to cover Yosef against the cold. Zahirah saw him looking for his vestments, and she saw he was vexed to find them gone.

The wind abated and the sea calmed. As the rabbi and the Templar worked the oars, she rose up and went to see how it was with Yosef. He lay in the boat, his head cradled by his brother, his body covered with the knight's robe. "How is it with your brother?" she asked Shmuel.

"Thanks be to God . . . and him." Shmuel nodded toward the knight. "Is he a Tem—"

"Shh!" Zahirah raised her hand and whispered, "You mustn't tell anyone or his life is forfeit." She held out her hand. "There's more silver for you—three dirhams for your silence, if you swear an oath."

Shmuel took the silver and nodded. "I swear."

Zahirah lifted up her eyes and beheld the shore, not more than a bow shot away. The rabbi had tired, and the Templar rowed alone. She looked at his muscular body, naked above his breeches, so very white and crossed by scars.

"There's the ruined tower of Ein Gofra!" Shmuel called.

She turned and looked. "Who lives there?"

"No one," Shmuel replied.

"Then why does a cooking fire burn on the shore?"

Shmuel looked up, squinting into the gathering dusk.

A clutch of Saracen fishermen stood upon the shore where several boats were moored, bobbing in the surf. Behind them, a haze of gray smoke hung above the orange flames of a cooking fire.

Shmuel called out to them. "Ahoy, there! I am Shmuel of Magdala."

"Ahoy, Shmuel!" A voice floated over the water. "I know you. I am Kasem of Kafr Harib. What brings you so far from Magdala?"

"We have given transit to three Mamluk scholars," called

Shmuel. "And what of you, *ya Kasem*? What seek you in this desolation?"

"Shelter from the storm."

Near shore, the boat moved forward with the breathing of the tide. The knight shipped the oars and quickly took up his cloak to cover his nakedness. Stepping into the shallows, he guided the boat to shore.

An Arab, with a short beard and robed in the manner of Saracen fishermen, stepped forward to help. "Come and warm yourselves by our fire, Shmuel—you and your company. We will give you warm broth and a hearty dinner. And tomorrow we'll help you repair your vessel. After the manner of our father, Abraham, we welcome you as brothers."

"We thank you, *ya Kasem*!" Shmuel called. Then, turning his head, he whispered to Zahirah, "Do not be troubled. As I swore to you, I will tell them nothing."

Chapter Twenty-Seven

כז

On the road to the khan of Er Rameh
29 May, 1290
Late afternoon

"Don't worry about the disguises," said Isaac as a Saracen merchant came into view, riding a donkey with loaded panniers. "Just let me do all the talking."

As they drew near, Isaac waved. *"As salamu 'alaykum!"* He greeted the man in Arabic with a Genoese inflection.

"Wa 'alaykum is salam!" came the reply with a broad smile. "You boys are new to this route, no?"

"We are, indeed, sir. My cousin, here, arrived with the west wind from Genoa, and I have, until now, tended my uncle's stalls in the great bazaar of Acre."

"Acre . . ." the merchant repeated as he adjusted his checkered turban. "May Allah restore it soon to the Moslems. How is it there?"

Isaac frowned. "The city is churlish, full of smells and filth. It teems with knights of the Crusade and frightened pilgrims. All will no doubt flee once the tide of Islam rises against the city walls."

"I know that you speak true." The merchant leaned forward and added in a conspiratorial whisper, "I have heard the sultan has left his royal court in Cairo, and even now leads his armies north." He raised his shoulders and sighed. "We can only hope it ends quickly so we can get back to business." He craned his head and tried to peer into the wagon. "You are bound for Damascus?"

"No, sir. We seek to join our uncle, Buscarel, upon this road."

"Buscarel of Genoa? I saw him just now!" He motioned backward with his stick. "But two leagues hence, and not far from the khan in Er Rameh. If you do not find him upon this road, seek him there."

"Then we'll bid you farewell, sir. May Allah in His beneficent offices grant you prosperity."

"*Alayk,* my young friend. There is no God but He." The merchant made a little bow, and with a few taps on his donkey's hindquarters, he moved down the road.

Wallace, who hadn't understood a word of the conversation, snapped the reins. "What was that about Buscarel?"

"He's just ahead, making for a caravansary. If we hurry, we might catch him before he gets there." As the wagon lurched forward, Isaac considered how they might get the scroll away from the merchant.

Wallace drove the horses at a near gallop. The shadows grew long and the air chilled as the sun dipped toward the horizon, setting the clouds afire. Rounding a curve in the road, they saw Buscarel with his little cart and donkey, plodding along, a furlong away.

"There he is!" Wallace called and snapped the reins, driving the horses forward.

"Wait!" Isaac shouted.

Wallace slackened the pace. "What's wrong?"

"That's what's wrong." Isaac pointed toward a sprawling stone building on the left side of the road. "That must be the caravansary."

Wallace cursed under his breath and pulled back on the reins. Together they watched Buscarel disappear through the gate, which closed behind him.

"Don't worry." Wallace patted Isaac on the knee. "We'll get the scroll from him tomorrow."

Isaac nodded as he stared at the closed gate. "We should find a place to watch for him." He raised his hand and pointed toward a stand of pine trees on a low bluff a bow shot from the caravansary gate. "Over there. We can hide the wagon among the trees."

Wallace guided the wagon forward and, well short of the caravansary, turned in among the trees. "I'm starved," he announced and hopped down from the wagon. He reached into a sack and handed Isaac some hard biscuit.

Staring out from behind the trees, Isaac murmured a blessing and took a bite. "We have to get that report . . ."

"You worry too much, Isaac." Wallace uncorked a skin and took a drink of water.

At that moment, the caravansary gate swung open and Buscarel burst out. He was on foot, turning as he ran, stumbling. He was followed by a dozen soldiers with yellow cloaks and yellow-plumed helmets.

"The emir's halka!" whispered Isaac.

"Stop or you're dead, Buscarel!" shouted a guard who held a drawn scimitar in his hand. The others carried long bows. "Give me the letter."

"I told you." Buscarel turned, pleading. "The emir instructed me to give it to his hand and his hand alone. How can I do otherwise?"

"And I told you the emir has instructed us to obtain the letter from you, and bring it swiftly to him."

"But what of my payment?"

"Once we have the letter, you shall receive your full reward.

You have the emir's word and my own."

"Please understand," Buscarel pleaded, backing away, edging closer to where Isaac and Wallace stood hiding among the trees, barely daring to breathe. "The emir instructed me in private counsel. I am to give the letter to no one but him. I am bound by my word, sir. I cannot do otherwise."

"Then you shall die." The captain of the guard raised his scimitar. "Archers!"

The soldiers drew back their bows.

"All right! All right!" Buscarel reached into his robe and walked back toward the guards. "Here! Take it."

"Thank you," the captain said and snatched the scroll from Buscarel's hand.

The merchant raised his shoulders. "So, worthy captain, you have the scroll. Now, what of my payment? The emir spoke of three hundred *dinars* for my service."

The captain tucked the scroll into his tunic and said nothing. The archers kept their aim, bowstrings taut.

"You have the scroll," Buscarel repeated.

The captain looked at the merchant, but made no reply.

"What of . . ." Buscarel took a hesitant step back, raising his arms and then letting them fall at his sides. "Let this service be my gift to his Excellency, the emir." His voice shook. Bowing at the waist, he took another step back. "Please convey the scroll to his eminence with my compliments and my blessings. Now, good captain, if I may take my leave . . ."

The captain shook his head wearily. "You cannot take what is not given to you." Looking past Buscarel, he seemed to be studying the trees. For a terrifying second, Isaac thought they were discovered.

The captain turned his gaze back to Buscarel and said, "Go."

"Go?" Buscarel raised his arms. "Go where?"

"That way." The captain pointed his scimitar toward the trees.

Tentatively, Buscarel shuffled backwards. Then, turning sideways, he took half steps as he watched the archers. He turned and began to run, weaving cleverly, dodging back and forth, ducking and zigzagging toward the trees. Isaac and Wallace watched, transfixed, as Buscarel drew closer to their hiding place, now but a few paces away.

He never reached them.

The archers loosed their arrows. Hissing through the gathering dusk, the bolts converged on Buscarel, thumping into his back.

The merchant stopped running. He stood very still.

Isaac could see his face through the tree branches. His eyes had the look of one who wrestles with a perplexing question. Then they emptied, he fell heavily forward, and lay very still. The arrows bristled along his back like the quills of a porcupine.

Isaac saw the halka returning to the caravansary. "The captain has the scroll!" he whispered and turned away. "Now all is lost!"

"Perhaps not," Wallace replied quietly. "Look again."

Isaac turned.

In the deepening twilight, he saw the captain drawing near, the scroll still stuck in his tunic. The rest of the guard had disappeared into the caravansary. "He comes alone," Isaac whispered, "no doubt to claim plunder from the dead merchant."

"And now's our chance," Wallace said and stepped back to the cart.

When he returned, Isaac saw that he had retrieved the shovel. Isaac leaned close and whispered, "Why didn't you take the sword?"

"Getting it out of the crate would make too much noise—this will do well enough."

The captain came briskly forward, quite close now as he approached Buscarel's body. Isaac's heart was pounding, while

Wallace, shovel in hand, waited in the shadow of the trees.

The captain knelt and began to rifle through the merchant's robes.

Isaac held his breath as Wallace lifted the shovel.

"Ahh! What have we here?" exclaimed the captain with a little laugh. He lifted a purse from the merchant's body and began to loosen the ties when one of the horses nickered.

The captain looked up sharply, his eyes searching the trees as he reached for his curved sword.

With a loud snapping of twigs, Wallace burst from the thicket and swung the shovel.

Chapter Twenty-Eight

כח

Khan of Er Rameh
29 May, 1290
Night

Buscarel, his back bristling with a dozen arrows, lay beside the captain of the halka, still clutching his curved sword. The captain's helmet lay on the ground a few feet away, dented by the blow from the shovel.

In the gathering dusk, Isaac stepped out from among the trees and knelt next to the captain's body. He put his hand to the man's neck, feeling for a pulse. There was none.

"Is he dead?" Wallace asked, his chest heaving, unable to catch his breath.

Isaac looked up at Wallace and nodded.

Wallace swallowed hard. "Turn him over and get the scroll."

Isaac gingerly pulled on the captain's shoulder. The body, heavy in death, barely moved. Shouts of raucous laughter rang out from the caravansary. Isaac looked up, his heart racing, afraid the halka might come looking for their captain. But the gates remained closed.

"Help me turn him, William."

Wallace tossed the shovel to the ground. Isaac saw that his large hands shook as he gripped the captain's shoulder and pulled. The head rolled over last, disjointed like a broken doll, the left side of the face slick with blood. “Oh, my God.” Isaac recoiled, staggering backwards.

Wallace pulled the scroll from the captain’s tunic and handed it to Isaac. “Is this it?”

Isaac saw in a glance that it was. He nodded and tucked the scroll beneath his doublet.

“Good.” Wallace exhaled. “Now let’s hide the body.” He pulled the scimitar from the dead man’s hand, picked up the plumed helmet, and tossed them into the darkness between the trees.

Isaac remained standing by the bodies, breathing heavily. Tattered crimson clouds faded to gray in the darkening sky.

Wallace bent and took hold of the captain’s flaccid arms. “Take the legs, Isaac.”

With his head turned away from the corpse, Isaac took hold of the ankles. Together, they lifted the body, which sagged heavily between them. Isaac staggered forward as fast as he could go, as they carried the captain’s body into the forest where the trees grew thick. The voices from the caravansary faded beneath the sharp snapping of branches underfoot. They covered the body with twigs and handfuls of pine needles. Then they made their way back to the clearing where the horses were still harnessed to the wagon.

“We must away with dispatch,” Wallace said as he slid the shovel back into the wagon next to the crate. He snapped the reins and the wagon creaked forward. The light was fading fast.

Isaac looked back at the caravansary, shrouded in darkness, with only the glow of cooking fires hovering above the walls. He could hear laughter and the occasional squeal of a woman’s voice. The guards wouldn’t come now. Indeed, they probably hadn’t even noticed the captain’s absence, occupied as they were with their own appetites and affections.

Once back on the main road, Wallace turned to Isaac. "Now that we have the scroll, we go to Jerusalem."

"Yes." Isaac looked down the road, a faint gray in the blackness. There was not yet any moon and only the stars for light. "I can barely see the way."

"We should walk," Wallace suggested. "I wouldn't want to stray into the rocks and break a wheel."

Climbing down from the cart and leading the horses, they traveled on foot, cautiously retracing their way down the mountain road.

Hours passed.

A thin crescent moon rose over the dark shoulder of the mountains and the road was illuminated by weak moonlight. They reclaimed their seats in the wagon, where Isaac promptly fell asleep, exhausted by the long march and lack of sleep.

He woke to Wallace's elbow in his side. "Isaac! Wake up."

"Where are we?" he asked, squinting into the half-light before dawn.

"Back among the olive trees."

Isaac could see the road dip at the edge of the foothills to the plain of Acre stretching to the sea. "Good. We should press on, William. I'll take the reins, if you like. You should sleep."

Wallace shook his head, "I can't sleep."

"Then let us make haste. If the emir's men find the captain's body, they will likely seek his murderers on this road."

"I'm not a murderer, Isaac," Wallace protested. "I didn't mean to kill him."

"I know that."

"I've had time to think about what I did while you slept." Wallace shook his head. "I never killed a man before."

"It was self-defense, William. You did nothing to feel guilty about. And besides, in reclaiming this scroll," Isaac tapped his doublet, "we have likely saved the lives of every man, woman, and child of Acre."

"But there's also this . . ." Wallace pulled a leather bag from within his jerkin and put it on Isaac's lap. "Buscarel's purse—I took it from the captain's body—like a common brigand."

"Nonsense, William. It was the captain who killed Buscarel, and it was he who robbed the body. Once Buscarel was dead, that purse became abandoned property—*hefker.* I'm glad you took it." Isaac untied the strap and poured the coins into his lap. His jaw dropped. "This is a king's ransom!" He had never seen such a treasure. Even in the poor light he recognized Venetian golden ducats among a hoard of silver French deniers and Moslem dirhams. Regaining his composure, he returned the coins to the purse. "If it will make you feel better, we can use this to give alms to the poor of Jerusalem."

"Like us." Wallace snapped the reins and shrugged. "We're poor."

Chapter Twenty-Nine

כט

The ruins of Ein Gofra
30 May, 1290
Well before dawn

As the whine of a mosquito sounded close to his ear, St. Clair covered his head with his robe. In the airless darkness, he closed his eyes and waited for sleep to come. His body felt heavy with fatigue, but alive with desire for the woman. The knowledge that she made her bed a few strides up the slope conspired with his blood and the warm night air to intensify his longing. The robe over his face grew intolerable. He pulled it off and sat up.

The rabbi lay nearby, snoring quietly. St. Clair looked up at the stars past the jagged blackness of a ruined tower. He began to recite the Vigils night office, *"Beatus vir qui non abiit in consilio impiorum . . ."* With a battle-tempered vigilance, he stopped. There was something moving in the darkness among the broken stones. He gripped his stave, but in the next moment, he saw it was merely feral cats, darting and playing among the ruins.

Zahirah was pleased to make her bed within the solitude of the ruins—on a little hill behind the broken wall of a tumbledown house. The rabbi had found the spot for her to make her pallet away from the men as modesty required. The Mamluk sailors had placed their beds by the cooking fire on the shore, claiming that the ruins of Ein Gofra were haunted by evil *jinns.*

In her heart, she scoffed at their fear. *I care not about unseen demons whose bodies are of smokeless fire. For I have known human demons to rival the jinn, and their bodies were of flesh.*

She had spread her robe upon soft grasses growing within the ruin, and sheltered by the remains of a wall. She lay on her back looking up at the sky. The storm and wind had passed, the air was cool, and the sky was crowded with stars.

She thought about the knight who made his bed with the rabbi next to a broken tower. Unable to sleep, she turned and peeked over the stones of the wall. She could just see him, faintly in the starlight, awake while the rabbi slept. She watched as he turned, sat up, lay back down, and turned again. *Perhaps the mosquitoes vex him,* she thought. *I shall tell him they do not trouble me since I have rubbed my skin with leaves of the lemon thyme.* She drew a deep breath as she watched him. *Perhaps I should tell him now.*

But, she did not move. *Not now, but soon I will tell him.* She felt her heart beating as the words of the poet rose in her mind: *I will be the night staying up till dawn, as the moon waits for the sun.*

She sighed and looked toward the lake—a blackness beneath the night sky. By the shore, the embers of the sailors' fire glowed soft orange. The knight moved again on his pallet. She wondered if he thought of her. She wondered if he pondered the fate of his mail shirt and tunic. These she had taken from the boat and dried over her little fire. Once dry, she had placed the tunic for a pillow beneath her head.

She lay down and closed her eyes, the fabric of the tunic soft upon her lips. *I will be the night staying up till dawn.*

★ ★ ★ ★ ★

St. Clair gave up trying to sleep and climbed to his feet. After donning his robe, he skirted the sailors' camp and picked his way among broken columns and boulders, heading toward the lake. Tall cedars loomed among the stars, spires of darkness against the sky.

He thought about the woman, glad she had followed them from Tel Hum. Though he had tried to feign outrage, she filled his heart with joy. He shook his head, pushing the thoughts away.

Sheltered by a stand of pine trees near the lake, he shed his robe, undershirt, and lambskin breeches. He remembered his lost tunic and mail hauberk with a frown. Through the years, the mail had saved him from many an arrow and scimitar stroke. *Ah well, it's gone and that's done. I'll get another when I return to Acre.*

Stepping carefully over the stones into the shallows, he lay forward, giving his body over to the caress of water, cooling the burning of his loins, cradling him in a smooth embrace. He swam for a dozen strokes and, a stone's throw from shore, he floated onto his back. The spring night was well on, and summer constellations had risen, wheeling above him like old friends.

Looking up at the sky Zahirah recognized the bright star, Vega, shining like a jewel in the constellation of the soaring eagle. A cool wind off the lake washed over her, yet she felt warm, unable to catch her breath. Sleep would not come. Turning over, she looked down to where the knight made his bed.

His pallet was empty.

Where has he gone?

She looked toward the lake, then threw off her blanket and stood up. Though covered only by the thin cotton of her nightshirt, she felt warm, as if the heat of a false summer rose from her own body. On the shore of the lake, the dying fire marked the sailors' camp. No one moved there. Indeed, all was silent except for the slow breathing of the tide upon the smooth stones of the shore.

She decided to cool her body in the waters of the lake, thinking the knight might be there. She descended the little hill and slipped among the trees. As she came near the shore her body shook and her heart pounded. Steadying herself against a tree, she tried to quiet her breathing. *It is with me as the poet has written—I was dead, now alive, weeping then laughing. The power of love came into me, and I became fierce like a lioness, then tender as the evening star.*

Standing by the quiet blackness of the lake, she listened for any sound before removing her nightshirt. All was silent, but suddenly, the sky lightened and shadows of the tall trees appeared upon the water. She looked past the trees and saw that it was not morning, but the dawning of the moon—a thin crescent risen like a chalice of bright silver over the eastern mountains.

She slipped off her nightshirt and entered the cool embrace of the lake.

St. Clair relaxed, his body undulating with the water, voluptuous and heavy, beneath a sky bannered with stars. Each bright star seemed a perfect silver bell of sound ringing out in the dark symphony of night. A sliver of moon appeared in the eastern sky and unbidden thoughts about the woman rose in his mind. He did not resist them. Closing his eyes, he drew measured breaths. But now, another current rippled along his flank. Turning, he saw a swimmer drawing near.

He straightened up, treading water. "Who comes?" he demanded, his voice a harsh whisper.

"I could not sleep, my lord."

It was the woman.

"You should not have come here." He edged away. "Return to your place."

"No one knows I am here, sir," she replied softly. "No one other than God makes a third with us." She turned in the water and pointed. "Look upon the rising moon, my lord. Is it not beautiful?"

"I am not permitted discourse with thee, maiden," he replied thickly and swallowed hard. "You must away."

"See how the ghost of the new moon rests upon the silver chalice of the dying crescent. It is as the poet has written, *the old moon with the new moon in her arms.*"

"Please. Away."

"I have always loved to look upon the moon—my mother was named for it—Badra."

St. Clair began swimming for shore, angling away from the woman and toward the stand of trees where he had left his clothing. He could hear her behind him, matching him, stroke for stroke. *Her mother's name—Badra—why is that familiar?* Then he remembered. *Je vais regarder al badra*—the nightly valediction of his dead master.

Thrashing to a stop, he turned and faced her. "Depart from me!"

"No, my lord," she whispered and lightly bit her lower lip as she treaded water. "I will not depart from thee."

For a moment, his eyes rested on her shorn head, the slope of her shoulders, her face shining in the silver light of the crescent moon. With a low cry, he turned violently away, his long hair spraying an arc of droplets over the smooth water of the lake. He gulped a lungful of air and dove down, beneath the surface.

The water, black and starless, held him. But now he felt her flesh, warm upon his arm. He turned and roughly took hold of her shoulders with his hands, feeling the smoothness of her skin, the smoothness of her body in the dark womb of the lake. He pulled her close and felt the fullness of her against his chest—a powerful warm current in the cool baptismal water of the Galilee. In the darkness, he sought her face and kissed her mouth.

They broke the surface together. And together they inhaled and kissed again, and again. Then, turning, they made for shore.

As he swam, the thick discipline of his abstinence fell away. He saw his chaste offering as a deformed sacrifice, a thing God had never requested.

Together, they stepped through the shallows. In the cool air among the trees, he took his robe from where it hung on a branch, and wrapped it about him and her, drawing their bodies together, feeling the warmth and smoothness of her.

She lifted her face and he brushed her mouth with his lips. Then, enfolding her in his arms, he kissed her ears and the hollows of her neck.

With a murmur of pleasure, she shivered.

"You are cold, dear maid?"

"I tremble with love for you, Knight."

"What?" He pulled away, his voice flat. With his hands on her shoulders, he looked into her eyes. "What did you call me?"

"I called you knight," she replied deliberately, her mouth smiling, challenging him, "for so you are—a Knight of the Temple."

"No." St. Clair shook his head. "You are mistaken . . ."

"Why do you deny it? It was I who took your shirt of mail and your tunic, and I have them still." She kissed his mouth. "Yet, even without these, I knew thee for a Templar."

"What do you know of Templars, dear one?" He sighed, holding her face softly in his hands, a sadness filling his heart. "What do you know of Templars, except that one such as I killed your father?"

"No." She shook her head, her eyes filling with tears.

He wiped droplets of water from her cheek and looked into her eyes. "It's true. I served at the Safed garrison during the battle when your father died—perhaps by my hand." He traced the curve of her cheek. "This hand." He felt a great tenderness for the woman. "Can you love me knowing this? Can you love me knowing that it was perhaps by my hand your father died?"

She took his hand and kissed it. "This cannot be."

"But you said he died at the citadel—"

"Shh." She placed her fingers against his lips. "My father, indeed, died there, sweet knight," she whispered, her cheeks wet with tears. "But he was not your enemy. He was your master."

Chapter Thirty

ל

Safed
30 May, 1290
Morning

My time is at hand, Viceroy Tewfiq Ayoub thought as he passed among the veined columns rising to the vaulted ceiling.

He tied a sash of yellow silk around his white cotton robe as he crossed the Hall of White Marble. *As it is written, one who digs an evil hole will fall into it.* He smiled at the image. *And I am delighted to assist the emir in digging a very deep hole in which to bury himself.*

For years, Ayoub had chafed beneath the arrogant whims of the emir. The years of flattery had gained him much, including the emir's confidence. And now, the time had come to bait the trap.

The bait was on its way—a thin strip of pigeon post placed on his prayer rug that morning in the palace mosque—the merchant Buscarel was returning to Safed. Within the space of a few days, the secrets of Acre's defenses would be in the emir's hand and the trap would be baited and set.

In truth, the emir was trapping himself. His lust for power would compel him to act—against Acre and against the sultan.

Ayoub felt no sense of disloyalty. Indeed, his ultimate loyalty was to the sultan, whom he was compelled to warn of the emir's machinations. It was the only honorable thing to do. It was not Ayoub who doomed the emir, but the emir's own perfidious designs. *As it is written—treachery will return to the betrayer.* Ayoub hurried down the long colonnade toward the throne room wondering how richly the sultan would reward him.

He could hear music as he neared the great beaten-copper doors of the throne room, and knew that the emir was enjoying his harem. It was for this reason he had not answered the muezzin's call to morning prayer. Clearly, his proclivity for debauchery knew no hour. Ayoub frowned. *How can one so faithless feign to be defender of the faith?*

Ayoub nodded to the guards, and they pushed the great doors open. As he stepped into the throne room, his senses were assaulted by a blaze of bright silk, throbbing music, and the combined aromas of perfume and tobacco. Pausing by the door, he watched a half-dozen girls dancing for the emir in front of the dais. Scantily clothed in colored silks, their bare arms encircled with gold bracelets, the dancers moved with the throbbing of the *bendair* and the *'ud,* as a eunuch with distended cheeks blew a lilting melody on the *zulami.*

The viceroy stepped forward. "Most resplendent emir," he proclaimed over the noise, "may Allah preserve you."

Lounging on the cushioned dais, the emir waved his hand to silence the musicians.

In a discordant cacophony, the music ceased, except for the eunuch who hadn't seen the emir's gesture and played a few lonely notes before he too fell silent.

"To disturb me thus, viceroy, you must have a very good reason or a wish to see your head severed from your body."

"My apologies, Great One, but I have this very hour received good tidings, and is it not written, that in delay there is only grief?"

"Even so, my most sapient advisor." The emir nodded and climbed to his feet. As was his custom when entertaining the harem, he wore a patch over his blind eye. Ayoub wished he always kept it covered. The bad eye was hard for one to look at, often red and weeping.

The emir stood up and clapped his hands twice. "Away with you all—except for . . . you." He lazily pointed at one of the dancers, then beckoned the girl forward as the other dancers, with the servants and musicians, filed out of the throne room.

Smiling shyly, she approached and bowed low.

"You dance well, my child." The emir reached out and hung a rope of black pearls around her neck. "My servants will see that you refresh yourself in a bath of asses' milk before I call upon you." When she was gone and the great doors closed, the emir took off the patch, rubbing his blind eye and turning to the viceroy. "Quickly now, what is the news?"

"Wonderful tidings, my lord." Ayoub stepped forward. "As we hoped, the good merchant, Buscarel, comes hither bearing the information you require from the Acre rabbi. He entered the western march this morning, and will call upon you before the sun sets twice."

"Excellent! With this device, the infidels will be crushed like garlic." The emir strode down the dais. "We will move before the winter rains abate, long before the engines of Ashraf Khalil are assembled in the spring."

"Begging your royal indulgence, Great One, there is one thing more. This same hour have I learned that the Sultan Qa'la'un left his palace in Cairo a fortnight ago. He has, even now, arrived in Ascalon, and will there encamp till spring."

"The hour has struck," the emir murmured. He drew himself up to his full height and beckoned the viceroy closer. "Fate has brought the dotard Qa'la'un within my reach, and I will soon strike him and his indolent son. Upon their deaths, the struggle for ascension will commence, and I will emerge alone among all claimants when Acre falls like a ripe plum into my hand."

"But, Sire, we have no engines for a siege."

"Ours is a siege of stealth, not of engines, and all Islam will rejoice upon our victory over the unbelievers. I will have succeeded where all before me have failed—even the great Saladin and the cunning Baybars. And Qa'la'un?" The emir spat his disgust through yellow teeth. "In such a sultan, the world makes a racehorse of an ass." The emir struck himself in the chest with a clenched fist. "It is I, Abdullah ibn Sayid ibn Elias—it is I, beloved of Allah, Master of Realms and Dominions," he pounded his chest again. "It is I who will be hailed as the instrument of fate and the ultimate victor over the Franks. When the Franks vanish from our shores like a storm chased by the wind, I will emerge as leader of the faithful!" The emir leaned closer. "So, listen well to me, my faithful viceroy. I will soon send forth our assassins to strike down Qa'la'un and his worthless son—hitting two birds with a single stone."

"But, Great One, the sultan is well-guarded."

"Bah! The slaves that surround him are like dogs that snarl at the approach of danger, then tuck their tails and flee. It is with them as it is written—when the wolf comes for the sheep, the dog goes to defecate."

"Indeed, Sire, but it is also said that one should stretch one's legs only as long as one's quilt can cover. Would it not insure our purpose, Great One, if I went first to the sultan and cleared a path for the assassins to follow?"

With a sly smile, the emir leaned back. "No, worthy viceroy. I have another job for you. Word has come to me that the Baghdad rabbi we have sought these many weeks has finally been discovered." He raised his shoulders and added with a chuckle, "Hiding among lepers in their colony by the great lake." He pointed a long finger at the viceroy. "You will direct our efforts to end his flight. I am resolved to finish what we set out to do."

"But Sire, we will soon have the report from Petit. What matters if the old man lives or dies?"

"Indulge me," the emir said dryly. "I'll take care of the sultan. You deal with the rabbi."

"Excellent well, Sire. I'll make preparations to depart forthwith." Ayoub bowed and left the throne room. *This faithless villain will answer for his treachery and betrayal! I will see to it that the sultan is warned and his life preserved.* Ayoub's heart pounded as he considered the dangers and rewards of the journey he was about to make. He could scarcely catch his breath.

Acre
30 May, 1290
Morning

The synagogue door shook with a knocking that did not brook delay.

The Jews at morning prayer fell silent and turned toward the door, not daring to speak.

Rabbi Solomon Petit broke the silence. "Menahem Mendel," he intoned quietly to his steward, "open the door."

Lurching from his stool at the back of the synagogue, Mendel shuffled quickly to the door. He opened it a crack, turned, and began to speak, "Knights of . . ."

The door flew open and four bearded Templars in full mail stepped into the synagogue, their boots thundering on the wooden floor.

"Is there among you a Rabbi Solomon Petit?" the sergeant asked pleasantly.

Someone coughed. Otherwise there was silence. After a few seconds, Menahem Mendel, who had the habit of nervous laughter, began to giggle.

"Silence, fool," barked the knight, his blue eyes flashing.

Mendel covered his large mouth with both hands. He returned to his stool and sat down, his shoulders shaking with barely contained laughter.

"We are constrained never to harm any Jew," the sergeant began smoothly. "So it was established by Saint Bernard of Clairveaux, and so it is today." He paused and paced down the aisle in his heavy boots. "However, I would not want to see some unfortunate accident occur—such as the reduction of this hovel of a synagogue to burnt cinder. So, I ask again, and for the final time. Is there among you a Rabbi Solomon Petit?"

Menahem Mendel jumped up from his stool, trying to catch his breath between small explosions of laughter, his eyes tearing. "My master is too modest." His hand shot out. "There he is! Rabbi Petit, the greatest scholar in all Acre."

At once trembling with rage and shaking in fear, the rabbi rose from his place on the front bench.

The knight stepped toward the door with an elegant bow. "Rabbi Petit, if you please, a word with you."

Perhaps my being old and frail will create compassion. Petit prayed as he slowly followed the knights out the synagogue door, blinking, into the bright morning sunlight.

The sergeant held out a scroll. "Would your holiness care to explain this?"

Petit took the scroll and opened it. *The draft by that bastard, Isaac, ee'mach sh'moe!* He shrugged, pretending to study it. "I have never seen this before."

"Really? Do you know what it is?"

"It appears to be an inventory of some sort."

"It is, indeed, an inventory, Rabbi—an inventory of every aspect of Acre's defenses. Your student, Isaac, informed us that a scroll such as this is now in the hands of the Mamluks."

"Isaac told you this?" the rabbi asked incredulously, then pretended to peer closer at the text. "This is definitely Isaac's hand. There is no question he wrote this, and I fear it is likely that Isaac himself has conveyed it to the Mamluks." Petit looked up at the sergeant. "Have you asked him about it?"

"It seems Isaac has gone missing."

Petit raised his shoulders. "He sometimes spends time at home with his family. Have you checked there?"

"We have, Rabbi. It appears he's left the city. But if you don't mind, I'll ask the questions." The sergeant snapped the scroll out of Petit's hand. "Why would Isaac tell one of our officers that it was you who conveyed this to the Mamluks?"

Petit sighed and stroked his beard. "I have my suspicions, though it pains my heart to speak of them."

"Pain or no, speak."

"Very well, Sir Knight. What you hold in your hand is manifestly the work of a traitor to his city and his people." Petit sighed deeply. "Isaac has joined with those who oppose me in an important controversy that pits Jew against Jew. In this dispute, Isaac and his ilk are on the side of the Levant—on the side of the Mamluks. I am on the side of Europe." Petit paused and added with special emphasis, "I'm on *your* side. This sedition against me also opposes your rule in Acre. If you want to find these traitors, seek them at Midrash Hagadol. For it is *they* who conspire to destroy your rule in Acre, just as they seek to destroy me."

Chapter Thirty-One

Along the Mediterranean Coastal Road
3 June, 1290
Midday

Viceroy Tewfiq Ayoub urged his little mare along the strand between the shoreline and the simmering desert, cursing himself for his lack of preparation. *Only four days out of Safed—no food and the water skins are empty!*

Above him, the sun made a glaring furnace of the sky, reflecting on the sand and touching the blue sea with fire. As far as his eye could see, no tree offered shade, and the dry thorn brush and brittle feather grass gave no moisture.

He looked down at his robes with disgust. The gold embroidery was almost hidden by layers of dust. After four days in the saddle and three nights on the ground, his fine silk *djellabah* was torn and dirty. For one accustomed to the well-favored comforts of palace life, such indignity was insufferable. He wondered if he would ever see the pavilions of the Sultan Qa'la'un. Indeed, only the lofty goal of saving the sultan's life sustained him. That, and the promise of a rich reward.

According to all accounts, the sultan and his host left Cairo early in the month of Jumada. By now, his court should be reestablished in

Ascalon. And what of the emir's assassins? Ayoub worried that he wouldn't be in time to save the sultan. Perhaps he was already too late. His hands tightened on the reins and he spurred the mare with his heels into a short lope across the shelving beach.

He had slipped away from Safed as quickly as he was able, knowing that the assassins were soon to be dispatched. Ignoring the emir's directive to descend east to the Galilee and chase after the old rabbi, he had taken some provisions and headed west, alone and under cover of darkness. He feared that, somehow, the emir knew of his plans. *Is he able with his one good eye to see into my heart? Or can he know my mind in the dark whiteness of his blind eye?*

Ordinarily, he would have stopped at the caravansary along the way, but, fearing for his life, he avoided the main roads. The emir's spies could be anywhere.

The mare's pace slowed.

With a curse, Ayoub slammed his heels into her flanks. Broken by thirst and heat, she sighed and stood still. He doubled up the reins and lashed the mare's neck until his arm grew weary, but she didn't move. Shading his eyes, Ayoub squinted into the distance. Along the silent coast nothing moved; no wind stirred the dust, and the brush and grass were gray with bitter salt. Listlessly, he sat on the horse and regarded an ancient pile of dung and a bleached camel skull, leering at him with broken teeth, half buried in the sand. His throat was raw and it was hard to swallow. He tried to spit but had none.

Ayoub would have preferred more commodious transportation—a litter born by slaves with cups of iced sherbet. Indeed, he had not endured such discomfort since he had briefly served as squire in the emir's guard. That unpleasantness ended when his father, a wealthy Bedouin sheik, purchased alternative service for him in the palace.

Again, Ayoub stuck his heels into the mare's flanks and,

thankfully, she began to move, but very slowly.

Having finished the last of his water and dates for breakfast, he began to worry about something other than warning the sultan. His throat burned with thirst. Shielding his eyes with his hand, he saw they were coming upon a hill. *Perhaps on the other side—a spring with sweet water . . .*

The hill was more a high sand dune studded with windblown scrub brush permanently bent away from the sea. The midday sun stared down from a cloudless sky, and the heat rose in waves from the sand. As Ayoub urged the mare forward, he felt a hitch in her stride. Midway to the top of the dune, she staggered and pulled up, refusing to move.

Cursing, he dug his heels into her flanks, but to no avail. He swung a leg across her withers, slid to the ground, and pulled on the bridle. The mare's mouth was flecked with foam, her eyes glassy. As he lifted his arm to flog her, she folded at the knees and collapsed. He stood, swaying on his feet, looking down at the horse. Her sides heaved, and her breath whistled on the dry sand. He dropped the reins. *She's finished and so am I.* Turning, he staggered up the hill, praying for a view of something other than empty wastes of sand along a maddening vastness of brackish water. He no longer cared about warning the sultan. All his grand designs had collapsed down to a single practicality. All his ambition was for something to drink.

As he reeled toward the summit, he saw the tops of date palms—fronds shining in the sunlight. He began to run, his feet churning ankle deep in the sand. He crested the hill.

A city spread out before him—between the desert and the sea. Beyond tilting remains of a tumbledown wall, tall date palms lined rows of stone houses, and broad lanes were crowded with people. Though he had never seen the city, he knew its name. "Ascalon," he whispered through parched lips. His spirits rose as he staggered forward.

Ascalon lay before him, clustered about its many wells. Here he would quench more than his thirst for water. For among the spires of tall cedars dotting a large central garden, he saw the pavilions of the sultan marked by royal banners hanging in the windless air. He was halfway down the hill when three riders emerged at a gallop from a grove of date palms.

"You!" shouted one of them. "Stand where you are."

Ayoub raised a hand in greeting as he pelted down the hill without slowing. He saw that one of the riders was of the wild clans of the northern hills, a Turkoman, his pointed helmet wrapped in black cloth. He held a javelin and a long curved sword hung at his side. The other two were dark Kurds of the east with lances and painted shields.

"I said stop, cur!" shouted the Turkoman, readying his javelin.

Ayoub staggered to a halt at the bottom of the hill, his chest heaving. He smiled and struck his chest. "I am Viceroy Tewfiq Ayoub, master of shields and cupbearer to the Emir of Safed."

The riders exploded with peals of laughter. Wiping his eyes, the Turkoman nudged his horse forward and made a flourished curtsy. "We bow before his eminence, the viceroy, master of scorpions and cupbearer to vultures."

Ayoub glanced at the tatters of his dirty robe, realizing how ridiculous he appeared. He jabbed his ring hand up for the Turkoman to see. "I speak the truth! Look at my seal. Brigands set about me. They killed my guard and took my slaves. Only I escaped."

Sobering slightly, the Turkoman asked, "What's your business here, sir?"

"I seek an audience with his eminence, the Sultan Qa'la'un, on a matter of the greatest urgency."

"Everyone has a matter of the greatest urgency," drawled one of the Kurds with a sly shrug.

Ayoub reached into his purse and produced shining coins,

glinting in the sunlight. "Perhaps a few silver dirhams will convince you of the urgency of my audience with the sultan. This is a matter that cannot wait." Stepping in among the riders, he handed each two coins. "My mount went down just beyond this hill. Which of you will tend to her?"

"I will, my lord," the Turkoman said.

"Good man, and more silver for you." Ayoub gave the man another coin.

One of the Kurds reached down to him. "Come, sir. Ride with me. I will take you to the sultan's pavilions."

Once mounted behind the Kurd, Ayoub began to relax. He was almost at his goal.

The beach stretched away toward the grove of palm trees. On his right, the waves, little more than ripples, paled from dark blue to a green as bright as Chinese stone along the shore. With the wind being light, several merchant dromonds stood at anchor within a stone's throw from the beach, rocking up and down in the surf. Ayoub could barely conceal his delight at how quickly his fortunes had changed.

As they approached a gap in the toppled wall, a few beggars staggered toward them, pleading for alms and scattering when the Kurd shook his lance. They rode past a man with a basket full of brown dates and a woman selling fish that shone like silver in her basket. A couple of boys ran alongside the horses, their hands uplifted, dangling strings of coral beads.

Once inside the city, the Kurd slowed his horse to a trot as they followed a cobbled street that ran along the broken wall and passed through another grove of palm trees where women were drawing water from a well. He resisted the urge to stop and slake his thirst, knowing he would soon refresh himself in the sultan's pavilion. Looking away from the well, he tapped the Kurd on the shoulder and pointed to a standing section of wall. "What happened to the fortifications?"

The Kurd scratched his chin, the dark stubble rasping beneath his fingers. "Ascalon was well-fortified by the accursed Franks, but it wasn't enough to stop Baybars. He took down their wall, just as Qa'la'un will bring down the walls of Acre, may Allah grant us a swift victory."

Ayoub pointed to a broken statue of weathered marble in an alcove of the wall. It was a human figure with no arms, its face obliterated and pockmarked by wind and sand. "Is that of the Franks?" he asked.

"More ancient than the Franks. It is said those are the pale ghosts of the Romans, frozen in marble."

They reached a terrace that bordered three sides of what appeared to be a ruined palace. Here the Kurd turned in his saddle and helped Ayoub slip to the ground before he himself dismounted. "The sultan's tents are pitched in the gardens of what was the Franks' palace."

"I thank you, sir," Ayoub said, offering the soldier two silver coins.

The Kurd held up a hand. "Does your lordship intend to seek audience with the sultan dressed as a beggar? For five dirhams I'll get you a bath and new clothes."

"Done," declared Ayoub. "But we must be quick about it."

Within half an hour, Ayoub, attired in splendid white robes, was seated with other supplicants about the carpet in a tent that stood beside the sultan's pavilion. Guards of the halka in yellow cloaks stood at the front of the tent where the flap was raised, allowing for a view of the pavilion festooned with banners sporting passages of the Koran in the ornate style. Around the tent emirs reclined in velvet kaftans and cloth-of-silk girdles. Bedouin in flowing robes conversed with Kadis wearing fur-trimmed *khalata.* Chieftains of Kurds and Turkomen chatted with Sayyids in green turbans who were said to have the blood of Mohammed in their veins.

Ayoub had nearly emptied his purse in bribing the sultan's secretary to secure an early audience. But still he waited. The minutes crawled by while slaves passed among the supplicants with beaked teapots and clinking cups of white porcelain. Ayoub took the cup offered him by a slave and drained it. He was anxious to stand before the sultan and reveal the emir's treachery. He had considered revealing all to the secretary, but had thought better of it. *I want the sultan to hear of this directly from my lips.*

He climbed to his feet and again approached the secretary. Taking the last of the coins from his purse, he pressed them into the secretary's hand, leaned down, and whispered, "In delay, there is only disaster. I *must* speak with his eminence *at once*!"

The secretary answered with a bow. "You will be the very next to enter, Viceroy."

Satisfied, Ayoub returned to his place on the carpet. He rehearsed his speech in his mind as slaves passed through the tent with trays of fruit and sweetmeats. When the tray was offered to him, he took some dates and considered how close he had come to death. *And now, praise Allah for His beneficent mercy, my goal is at hand.*

Around him, the other supplicants talked to pass the time. A Kurdish commander was showing off his sea eagle. The great bird gripped its wooden perch with sharp talons, its curved beak showing beneath a worn leather hood. The Kurd claimed to have taken the sea eagle young on the Red Sea coast, though on this he was challenged by a lean Turkoman who insisted that such birds were never found west of the Euphrates River. The men almost came to blows on the matter, and Ayoub helped calm the fray.

The Kurd thanked him and introduced himself. "I am Meshtub, chieftain of the Kurds. I was ransomed by the Crusaders for thirty thousand pieces of gold," he boasted. "Sit with me on the carpet."

Ayoub chose the side away from the eagle. "I am Viceroy Tewfiq Ayoub, master of shields and cupbearer to the Emir of Safed."

"The praise to God. Today we are an army of Islam able to defeat any adversary. Why do we wait here like women? We should take Acre now."

"By God, this is not possible," replied Ayoub. "The sultan's son, Prince Khalil, is even now building scores of siege engines. Only when these engines are ready and the spring rains pass, and the ground becomes firm—only then can the siege begin. And then great walls of Acre will crumble before us."

The Kurd thoughtfully chewed on a date, spitting the pit into his hand. "I saw such engines when I led my people with Qa'la'un against Tripoli. Most were burned with naphtha by the Franks. You say Khalil is building new ones?"

"Yes," Ayoub replied as he watched the secretary, praying to be summoned for his audience.

"Where is there wood enough to build them?"

"My master, Abdullah, the Emir of Safed, has given over two forests for this purpose."

"May Allah grant him long life and fine sons."

Lunch was announced and a huge brazier filled with rice and mutton was carried into the tent. The Kurd fell silent as honor prescribed. In the center of the brazier were the boiled, upturned heads of three sheep, propped up on severed stumps of neck, their jaws gaping open, their tongues still pink. Though Ayoub had no interest in food, he was obliged to join the others. Not to do so was unthinkable.

The men rose, came forward, and sank to one knee around the tray. Ayoub glanced at the sultan's secretary, who returned his gaze and smiled. He turned back his right sleeve to the elbow and, in unison with the other supplicants, murmured, "In the name of God the merciful, the compassionate." They dipped together, with the right hand, which alone was honorable.

As the meat pile wore down, a Bedouin, one of the chief Howeitat, drew his dagger, silver-hilted and set with turquoise. As he began cutting long diamonds of meat from a leg bone, there came the sound of shouting outside the tent.

Ayoub scrambled to his feet. Through the open flap, he saw guards running in and out of the great pavilion, their yellow cloaks spread out, their brass armor and drawn scimitars flashing in the sun. One of them darted into the tent, shouting and brandishing his weapon.

"The sultan has been killed! Assassins! Assassins!"

Ayoub's body sagged down to the rug next to the brazier. Blankly, he stared at the sheep's head facing him from the center of the plate.

Meshtub, Chieftain of the Kurds, caught hold of the guard. "Who has done this?"

"There were two of them. One we have killed. The other we will convince to tell us."

Ayoub saw Meshtub running across the lawn into the sultan's pavilion.

For a moment he considered trying to flee. But between the desert and the sea, there was nowhere to hide.

Meshtub emerged from the sultan's pavilion calling out the name Ayoub expected to hear. "Abdullah of Safed! The accursed dog who murdered our Sultan is none other than Abdullah, the Emir of Safed!" Meshtub drew his scimitar and pointed it at Ayoub. "And here sits his treacherous viceroy, the third assassin!"

Ayoub remained sitting by the brazier, staring at the sheep's head—the pink tongue, the half-closed eyes, the lips sneering away blackly from the white teeth.

From the corner of his vision, he saw Meshtub coming for him with his curved sword, and, beside him, the chief of the Howeitat raised his silver dagger set with turquoise.

Chapter Thirty-Two

לב

Ascalon
4 June, 1290
Dawn

The Sultan al-Mansur Qa'la'un was dead. His body lay in the funeral tent, ringed by candles and surrounded by imams who knelt on prayer rugs. With bowings and prostrations, they chanted from the pages of the Koran.

His eldest son, al-Ashraf Khalil, knelt within the ring of the candles beside the body. He wore a black camel-hair robe, and his head was crowned by a *kafiyah* of white silk with gold embroidery, itself crowned by a black *agal* of two woolen cords wrapped with silver and gold thread.

"My father, you are not yet avenged," he whispered, and raised his right hand. "But by this hand, my will, and my heart," he touched his head and placed his hand upon his chest, "I swear the traitorous dog, Abdullah of Safed, will be brought to me in chains. And on that glorious day, father, I will strike off his head and put it on a stake. Only then will the encumbrance of your murder be satisfied." He leaned forward and kissed his father's forehead. "And until then, my father, I will not rest." He rose to his feet, turned, and limped out of the tent.

Facing east, Khalil saw how the sky above the desert brightened before dawn. Great was his relief to see the morning after the long and terrible night. Beset by the two assassins after they had murdered his father, Khalil had been wounded in the arm and thigh before he managed to fend them off. But there was fear the blades were envenomed and the royal surgeon had ministered to Khalil through the night, drawing away pestilent blood with tourniquets and leeches. All the while, Khalil directed the interrogation and execution of conspirators. Before the surgeon departed in the late hours of the night, he declared that if the prince's wounds did not rankle by sunrise, he would live.

Khalil pushed aside his robes and checked the wounds in the morning light. The edges were clean, with no effluence and little pain. Surely, he would live. Closing his eyes, he whispered, "Praise Allah."

Though he had not slept, any notion of fatigue vanished with the exhilaration of seeing morning come. He felt the warmth of the rising sun on his face and the cool desert air tinged with the smell of the sea. From the west Khalil could hear the pounding surf along Ascalon's breakwater. His thoughts returned to the business of succession. It was no easy matter to lead men who hated to be led.

Having purged the camp of known accomplices, he resolved to assure his ascension and eliminate the traitorous emir of Safed. Then he would direct his efforts against the Franks in Acre. But first things first. He summoned the captain of the halka.

"I await your command, O Prince."

"I am no longer your prince, I am your sultan. Remember that, and so instruct the guard."

"To hear is to obey, O Sultan."

"Make haste and bring the halka to the great pavilion where

the leaders of the people are now gathered. I will go there and wait for you."

As the captain hurried off, Khalil strode toward the large tent of black goatskin, crossing a patch of dry grass dotted with worn flagging stones. From within, he could hear a chorus of excited voices. While he waited for the guards to assemble, he listened.

"By Allah, who has seen Abu Naila?"

"Is he here?"

"I do not see him, and neither do I see Ibn Hisham."

Khalil stepped away from the tent as the captain arrived with the guard. "Have your men compass the pavilion round," he whispered. "On my signal, raise the sides of the tent and the door flaps."

The halka was soon in place, the morning sun glinting off drawn scimitars and polished armor. The babble of voices within the tent continued.

"I contend this is all of the Franks."

"By God, you are a fool. This is manifestly the doing of Abdullah of Safed."

"How did he ever think to succeed?"

"You know Abdullah—tall as a palm tree, but his brain is as small as that of a sheep."

Standing by the entryway to the tent, Khalil silently raised his arm, then brought it down. The sides flew up, two guards parted the door flaps, and Khalil stepped into the pavilion.

"Greeting, my masters," he proclaimed, and flanked by guards, strode to the head of the carpet.

The emirs and generals fell silent. Some groped among their robes for dagger hilts as they turned, their eyes darting from Khalil to the guards surrounding them.

"In the name of God, the merciful, the compassionate," Khalil announced in a booming voice. "To the glory of Allah, and in trust of His mercy at the last, I call this council to order."

Whispering together, the men stood along the edge of the carpet.

Aboul Heidja the Fat stepped forward and bowed, his black robe the size of a small tent. "I am pleased to see you alive, O Prince! Yet, I have a grieving in my heart for your noble father, may Allah exalt him in paradise."

"The years of my father, the noble Qa'la'un, are ended. But in me," Khalil struck his chest, "his eldest son and rightful heir, the valorous struggle against the infidels will continue. The lives of some men are like a dream, vanishing in the light of day. But the memory of my father will live on as we banish the Franks from Acre and cleanse our Holy Land of traitors." Khalil spread his arms wide. "Content ye to sit in council, my masters."

Once all were seated, he continued, "As you know, the perfidious Emir Abdullah of Safed has drawn his dagger against us. While my father and I conducted matters of state, assassins stole into the royal pavilion. With long knives they murdered my father and assailed me. Praise to God, I prevailed against them! And now, with the guidance of Allah and with your good counsel, I take my father's place at the head of the carpet."

Khalil looked to a guard and said in a voice for all to hear, "Have slaves bring food and drink for these good men who are loyal to our person." He glanced around the carpet, confident that none would dare challenge his claim.

Slaves bearing trays piled high with sweetmeats and fruit swept into the tent, and the council members began to eat.

"Without doubt you have perceived that many faces are missing from our circle today. Look about you. Mark them by their absence. These same, my father trusted as friends, but they proved false. These same I have banished from this life. What say you?"

As the council roared its approval, Khalil took a scimitar

from one of the guards. Testing the blade, he made a few quick strokes in the air as he paced along the edge of the carpet. "My dear and faithful comrades, we will now settle things with the traitor Abdullah of Safed and with the Franks." As he spoke, he took an apple from a fruit platter. He tossed the apple high into the air and sliced it in half with a quick stroke of the scimitar. The two halves of the apple fell to the carpet at his feet.

"First, we strike Abdullah of Safed and his spawn." Khalil thrust the blade down, impaling half the apple. "Then, with siege engines on dry ground next spring, we move against the Franks in Acre." He raised the blade and brought it down again, impaling the second half. "Thus is my noble father avenged! And thus, we draw the poisoned barb of the infidels from the flesh of Islam!" He raised the sword with both halves of the apple on the point and shouted, "What say you?"

With salutes and shouts of acclamation, the men of the council rose to their feet.

Khalil brought the sword tip to his mouth and lustily took a bite of the apple.

Chapter Thirty-Three

לג

Al-'Ayzariyah (Bethany)
5 June, 1290
Before dawn

St. Clair awoke to the song of a thrush coming from within the apple orchard. He awoke as he had slept, beneath the shelter of a fig tree with Zahirah in his arms. Warm beneath woolen blankets, they lay cushioned by their robes upon a bed of fig leaves.

Almost a week had passed since they had left Ein Gofra on the eastern shore of the Galilee. Traveling through the Jordan Valley, they had been aided for most of the journey by gracious farmers and merchants. Rabbi Samuel's hip troubled him greatly, and he was regularly able to find a seat in a wagon or cart with Jonathan and Zahirah usually choosing to walk alongside. They had camped for the night outside Al-'Ayzariyah, which the Christians called Bethany. They were now within a league of Jerusalem.

The sky lightened toward dawn and other birds joined the song of the thrush, calling from within the apple orchard.

Wishing to give St. Clair and Zahirah a measure of privacy, the rabbi had made his bed on the far edge of the orchard. St.

Clair lifted his head and peered past the foliage of the fig tree, searching the orchard where a mist like milk softened the branches of the trees. He could not see the rabbi.

Turning from the cool air, St. Clair nestled close to Zahirah and looked at her face—her lips full and almost smiling in sleep. There was something of her father, his dead master, about her mouth.

Lightly, he kissed her lips.

She stirred but did not awaken.

He studied the light blush of her smooth cheeks and the soft shadow of eyebrows nearly grown back. These she had shaved with all her hair at Tel Hum. Her eyelashes lined the softness of her closed eyes like the filaments of a perfect flower.

"Henah yafa, ra'a'yatee," he whispered in Hebrew and kissed her closed eyes. " 'Behold, thou art beautiful, my love, your eyes like doves.' "

She smiled and stretched.

"Henah yafa," he repeated, savoring the words, the beauty and vibrancy of the Song of Songs, this vocabulary of love so long held hostage in the dark prison of his celibacy.

He leaned back, drawing his chest away from hers. The leather pouch with the scroll lay nestled between her breasts, the cord around his neck. Gazing down, he remembered his foolish argument with the rabbi. "Aaron and Moses, indeed!" he whispered with a soft laugh. Gently, he lifted the tether, rotated it about his neck, and let the pouch rest over his back.

Zahirah opened her eyes. "Good morning, my love," she murmured in Arabic and drew him close. "I also know passages from the Song of Songs." In Arabic-accented Hebrew, she whispered into his ear, "*Heen'ha ya'feh doe'dee, af na'eem.* 'You are beautiful, my love, and gentle . . .' "

"How do you know this?" he asked, touching the curve of her cheek.

"We had a book of Hebrew writings at my home in Safed. My father brought it there. He taught me to read Hebrew when I was small."

"I was thinking of him before you awoke. In some ways he was like my own father. I loved him as much."

She hugged him tighter. "Then you and I are like brother and sister."

"I think it is very fortunate we are not so related." He traced her body with his hand, smooth and warm beneath the blankets. He kissed her cheek, tasting the smoothness of her skin. Cradling her shorn head with his left hand, he felt the stubble of her hair, which was growing back.

He kissed her mouth very softly.

Her lips parted.

He gathered her in his arms and kissed her ravenously.

She made a little sound as she pulled away and drew a deep breath. Then, framing his face with her hands, she kissed him with an ardor that surprised and delighted him.

She leaned away and smiled up at him. "*Mee zote oleh min ha'midbar,*" she whispered and bit her lower lip. "Who is that coming up from the desert?"

Kuryat-el-Anab
5 June, 1290
Before dawn

It had been Isaac's turn to sleep in the wagon. He had made himself a comfortable bed, nestled among blankets against the wooden crate. He awoke to the sound of someone chopping wood. He opened his eyes and looked up. It was not quite dawn. Beyond the dark branches of pine trees overhead, stars were fading in a gray sky. He turned over and covered his head with the sack of clothing he used for a pillow. It didn't help. He could still hear the chopping. He pushed his hands against his ears and shut his eyes.

In the darkness, his mind brought forth images: the merchant Buscarel, his back bristling with arrows, his eyes as he stood dying. The captain of the guard—the supple heaviness of his dead body, his face slick with blood. Isaac began to pray, silently reciting the prescribed words for dreamless sleep. *"Vee'hee ratzon mil'fan'e'ha—God of my fathers, grant that I lie down in peace and that I rise up in peace. Let not my thoughts upset me, nor evil dreams . . ."* As the recitation poured from memory, other images arose in his mind.

Five days had passed since they left the plain of Acre and rounded the point of Carmel. Guiding the wagon over limestone ledges, through wastes of empty sand and dry thorn brush, they had stayed within sight of the coast for two days before turning inland. In the darkness of his closed eyes, he could see the sun as it had emerged each day from the ridge on the left-hand side, shining on the wet sand and touching the green-blue sea with fire. *"Blessed are You, God, whose majesty gives light to the world . . ."*

Turning inland, they had followed the wells, cultivated land, and watchtowers toward Er-Ramleh—passing orange groves heavy with fruit, and feather grass blowing brittle beneath clear skies. *"Low tee'ra mee'pa'had lie'lah . . . Fear not the terror of the night, nor the pestilence that stalks in darkness . . ."*

Outside the village of El Kubab, they had finally glimpsed the brown ramparts of Jerusalem's foothills, half-veiled through a haze of dust. *". . . spread over us the shelter of Your peace . . ."*

Traveling as they did in the guise of Genoese merchants, the farmers and peasants along the way had been either oblivious or friendly. When Isaac and Wallace waved their velvet caps toward soldiers manning the watchtowers, they were greeted in kind. But Isaac remained anxious and watchful, knowing their greatest peril lay with real merchants of Genoa who could easily expose their charade. Thankfully, they met none. *"Blessed be the Lord by day, blessed be the Lord by night . . ."*

Once past Latrun, they had advanced into the Mountains of Judah. Stopping for the night at Bab-el-Wad, the Gateway to the Valley, they had made camp by a highway shrine sheltered by ancient terebinths. *"Behold, the guardian of Israel neither slumbers nor sleeps . . ."*

Then, starting early in the morning, they began the ascent to Jerusalem.

The well-traveled pilgrim road twisted among barren gullies and around the shoulders of hills covered by tangled thickets of *alaka* with brown leaves and sticking thorns. Finally, as the sun set into a bank of purple clouds, the road gained the high ridges, crowned by the scattered remains of an old pine forest. As darkness fell, they had made camp on the outskirts of the small mountain village of Kuryat-el-Anab. *"Adonai lee, ve'low ee'rah . . . The Lord is with me and I am not afraid."*

Isaac gave up trying to sleep and sat up, rubbing his eyes. In the half-light, he saw that their wagon stood just off the rutted dirt road in a flat dell that sloped downward to the southwest. A bow shot in the opposite direction was the village, marked by a central house of two stories surrounded by little stone cabins with flat roofs. To the east, the silhouette of rolling hills edged the pink-blue sky. Dawn was approaching.

Recalling that Wallace had made his pallet next to the wagon, Isaac leaned over the side and saw that Wallace was gone. His blankets lay tangled on a bed of dry grass.

The chopping sound continued, irregular and unceasing.

That must be him, or someone from the village gathering firewood.

Isaac pulled on his boots, stuck the velveteen cap on his head, and climbed down from the wagon. After relieving himself in a clutch of pine trees, he donned the black doublet over his white shirt and started across the field. Looking at the sleeping village over the rocky table of land veined by streaks of red-brown earth, he whispered aloud, "If this is Kuryat-el-Anab, this field might be the site of Kiryat Ye'arim, where the Holy Ark rested on its way to Jerusalem."

The chopping sound was coming from somewhere beyond the rubble of a tumbledown wall at the far edge of the field. Threading a path through the dry bracken, Isaac thought about the armies and the generations of pilgrims who had passed this way to Jerusalem—walking where he now walked—Jews, Philistines, Babylonians, Assyrians, Greeks, Romans, and Christians. As Isaac passed through the field, a dry whisper rose from the thorn brush and barbed fingers caught and tugged at his black trousers. Words from a psalm rose in his mind: *a man's days are like grass, we flourish for a moment like a flower of the field, then a wind passes over and we are gone, and no one knows the place where we walked.*

As he neared the wall, the chopping grew louder, echoing among the hills. Beyond the wall, the high branches of an oak tree were hung with rags like the votive offerings he had sometimes seen on ancient trees around Acre. Traversing a gap in the wall, he emerged on the other side. At the base of the solitary tree, William Wallace, with his bright green jerkin and cap, wielded a stave, striking the thick trunk with heavy blows.

"What are you doing, William?"

"Practicing," Wallace replied and continued pummeling the tree.

"Where did you get the stave?"

"It was our shovel. I took off the blade."

"Why? It served you well enough at the caravansary."

"Too well, Isaac. I don't want to kill anyone." Wallace delivered a final series of blows, then turned, leaning against the oak. He took off his cap and wiped his forehead. "I need some water."

"We still have half a skin."

"Not anymore. The horses were thirsty this morning."

Isaac looked back in the direction of the village. "There must be a spring or well here. Let's fetch the water skins from the wagon and go into the village."

Wallace led the way back across the field to the wagon, carrying the stave over his shoulder. He began to whistle.

Isaac thought the melody beautiful—sad and full of yearning. "What tune is that?" he asked.

"An old song my father used to play on the pipes back in Scotland," Wallace replied as he slid the stave back into the wagon next to the crate. He knelt, picked his blanket off the ground, and shook it free of dry grass, whistling as he folded it.

"Could you teach me to do that?" Isaac asked.

"How to fold a blanket?"

"No, how to whistle," Isaac said, laughing. "Could you teach me?"

"You don't know how to whistle?"

"Whistling is considered bad form in these parts. Mamluks believe it an omen of evil—the manner by which jinn are called forth from the netherworld."

"Jinn?" Wallace frowned as he stuffed his blankets back into the wagon. "What's that?"

"*Ghuls, afrits,* demons—some Moslems believe the very air is peopled with spirits."

Wallace turned and looked back over the empty field. "Strange you should mention that. Out there, I felt I wasn't alone."

Isaac nodded. "I had the same feeling."

Wallace raised his eyebrows and smiled. "Then perhaps I shouldn't whistle."

"I think the dead don't wait upon a whistle, and we're far enough from the village that the living won't hear. Please, let me hear that melody again."

Wallace picked up the tune as he lifted the empty water skins from the wagon.

"Oos'kut!" came a voice from behind. "Silence, son of perdition!"

Wallace stopped whistling.

Behind a copse of tangled brushwood stood a woman covered in a black robe from head to foot. With one hand, she balanced an earthenware jug on her head, and with the other, she half-covered her face with a black headscarf. She was chanting in Arabic, ". . . I seek refuge in Allah, the King of men, the God of men, from the evil of the whisperer who whispers into the hearts of men . . ."

"Good morning, madam," Isaac said with a little bow. "My brother is newly come to the Holy Land. He did not realize that the practice of whistling might call forth evil. He will not do it again."

The old woman cautiously advanced along the path, balancing the jug on her head. The boys stepped aside to let her pass. Ramrod straight, she stared at them with amazingly blue eyes. "Are you Genoese or Venetian?"

"Genoese, madam," Isaac replied with a pleasant smile. The woman stopped walking and Isaac could hear the water lapping against the sides of the jug. "Please, lady," he asked, "could you tell us where we might water?"

She motioned with her hand, dropping the veil to reveal her brown face, covered by a maze of wrinkles. "There's a ruined Frankish church at the bottom of the *wadi.* Inside the church there are steps leading down to a spring."

"Thank you, *halati,*" Isaac said. "And one thing more. Is this, indeed, the village of Kuryat-el-Anab?"

"It is," she replied without moving her head. "And are you, indeed, Christians?"

"We are," Isaac replied quickly. "If we were not People of the Book, the Sultan Qa'la'un would not favor us."

"Qa'la'un favors whoever gives him money." Her blue eyes fixed on Isaac. "Where are you bound?"

"Jerusalem, *el Kuds.*"

"You behave as if this is your first trip."

"It is, *halati.*"

"Why weren't you with the caravan? They passed this way two days ago."

"We missed the departure from Acre," Isaac lied. "Tell me, *mid fadlick,* which way to Jerusalem is best? Through the wadi or along the ridge?"

"Keep to the ridge." She motioned with her hand as she walked away. "From the high ground, just past the village, you'll get your first view of El Kuds."

"Allah ma'ik, halati," called Isaac. "May God be with you."

"He is," she called back without turning.

"*Allons,* William," Isaac said, switching back to French. "There's a spring at the bottom of the ravine. The old woman said we reach it by going down some steps in a ruined church." He led the way along a well-worn footpath, past clumps of thorn brush and a tangled thicket of myrtle. The path dipped into the wadi, snaking downward between gaps in the ancient retaining walls that supported each successive terrace from the one below it. After descending a half-dozen levels, they reached a broad terrace, and followed the path around a huge hawthorn bush. Then they stopped short. Looming above them was an edifice of limestone blocks filling the width of the terrace. Fine grass sprouted from between dirt-lined stones with scattered sprigs of caper bush. A small cactus crowned a broken parapet.

"Would this be the ruined church?" Wallace asked.

"This must be the one," Isaac replied.

They stepped over shards of pottery and brittle weeds that

grew between the flagging stones. Cautiously, they entered the abandoned church.

The vestibule was dark, lit only with a gray light filtering through gaps in the high, wood-beamed ceiling. Looking up, Isaac could see small patches of sky. In the center of the vestibule was a stone font, green with moss and brimming with dirty water. Patches of muddy soil partially covered the stone floor, sprouting clumps of pale grass. Wallace stepped to the font, dipped his fingers, knelt, and crossed himself. To Isaac's sideways glance, he muttered, "God's house."

"Are you sure? I think He moved out."

"No. He's still here." Wallace straightened up and peered into the darkness. "Here and everywhere."

Together, they passed beneath an arched aperture into a large hall, their footsteps echoing in the brooding silence. "This was the main chapel," Wallace whispered and pointed at the wall above the dais. "Look. Shadows of frescoes." He crossed the room and traced his hand over the wall. "And these scratches here," he canted his head and looked closely. "Names of pilgrims who passed this way."

"How long has it been deserted?" Isaac asked quietly as he stepped to a west-facing window.

"About a hundred years. The last Crusader to be anywhere near here would have been Richard, Coeur-de-Lion. After he took Acre, he fought his way to within sight of Jerusalem, perhaps somewhere around here." Wallace fell silent as he walked the length of the chapel, his footsteps echoing in the empty darkness. "There's another room over here," he said and disappeared through a doorway.

Isaac remained at the window, resting his hand on a section of dressed stone along the sill. He looked out over an overgrown vineyard where a tall palm tree stood amid a tangle of vines.

"I think I found the stairs to the spring," Wallace called.

Isaac followed Wallace's voice into a dark cloister. In the silence, he could hear the sound of running water.

"Down here," Wallace said, disappearing into a stone stairwell.

Isaac followed, descending slowly because of the uneven steps and the darkness. The steps ended at the bottom of the ravine. Wallace was already kneeling by a stream of clear water that sparkled over the wadi's rocky bed.

"This one's full." Wallace lifted the dripping water skin that bulged against its patches, taking the shape of the goat that once occupied it. He handed the skin to Isaac.

After Wallace had filled the second skin, they both drank from the stream, scooping the cool water up with their hands. Then they made their way up the steps, through the church, and back to the wagon.

Rabbi Samuel had just finished morning prayer when St. Clair and Zahirah found him at the far edge of the apple orchard. "I'm ready to go," he announced as he stamped his fire to embers. He beamed at them. "Breakfast in Jerusalem, my children."

They left the orchard, wrapped in their cowled robes against the morning chill. St. Clair carried the rabbi's pack in addition to his own. The road wound through trailing mists among terraced hills and through the sleeping village of Al-'Ayzariyah. Well past the stone houses of the village, the road began to rise. The rabbi leaned heavily on his staff, limping painfully up the hill, struggling to keep up. Seeing this, St. Clair came to a stop. "Let's pause here awhile," he suggested.

"Is it much further?" Zahirah asked.

The rabbi leaned back on a smooth boulder by the side of the road and pointed with his stick. "If this is, indeed, the eastern face of the Mount of Olives, we'll see Jerusalem from the top of the ridge." The sun rose over the Jordan Valley, bathing the mountainside with light. The rabbi closed his eyes and drew a deep breath.

"How is it with you, Rabbi?" Zahirah asked, resting her hand on the old man's shoulder.

"The hip pains me, my child."

"I shall make for you another poultice of boiled nettles and cabbage leaf when we get to Jerusalem."

"Jerusalem . . ." St. Clair repeated, looking up the road. "We're so close. My order was born in Jerusalem with a calling to guard the Temple Mount, to guide and protect pilgrims to and from the city." He frowned and shook his head. "But we lost Jerusalem more than a hundred years ago. And now the order is more concerned with shipping invoices and banking loans. We lost our true calling when we lost Jerusalem."

"But many Mamluks believe the Templars will regain Jerusalem, Jonathan."

"No, Zahirah. The Wars of the Cross are finished. The Latin Kingdom of Jerusalem is like something we dreamed as children, a dream we can barely remember. Qa'la'un is poised to finish what Baybars began. Marghab and Tripoli have fallen—only Acre remains. Qa'la'un will fight the jihad to the end, and our banners will be swept from the Holy Land like dry leaves before a storm. It's finished."

"Peradventure, no." Rabbi Samuel had caught his breath after the climb. "In Baghdad it is said that the Mongol Il-khan Arghun calls for an alliance with Christendom against the Mamluks."

"Yes, Rabbi, but nothing comes of it. The letters of Il-khan are ignored, and the Mongol embassies to the papal court are given empty platitudes and dismissed as heathen barbarians. Meanwhile, the Holy Father and the princes of Christendom are absorbed with their petty intrigues and quarrels. They have no interest in the Crusades. Only the Templar fleet brings sustenance to our garrison. And the new recruits from Europe are naught but quarrelsome and ill-favored adventurers. Some of these have taken to killing Moslem merchants in Acre, and this, it is said, will serve as an excuse for Qa'la'un to break the truce. And when he attacks, no help will come. All Christians who do not leave Acre will die there. The only calling remaining to my order is to cover the retreat."

"I believe you are mistaken, Jonathan. Your calling will be renewed."

"Don't be ridiculous, Rabbi." St. Clair wearily shook his head. "I know of what I speak."

"The scroll you wear about your neck tells a different tale. That parchment holds the key to revive your mandate. Your banners may yet again fly over the battlements of Jerusalem."

"How can this scrap of parchment renew my calling?" St. Clair asked as he lifted the leather pouch from within his woolen robe.

"The scroll holds the key to unlocking the Jerusalem you came here to find. Not the Jerusalem of this world, Jonathan, but a city of pure light. It is for that reason I brought you here." He pushed himself away from the boulder and pointed with his stick. "Come. Let us see what lies beyond this ridge." With St. Clair's assistance, the rabbi resumed the climb. "It's always worse in the morning," he muttered, wincing with each step as he labored slowly up the hill.

They finally crested the summit and stood together, looking down. Beyond the Kidron Valley, filled with light mist, Jerusalem lay at their feet, ringed in part by a wall of pale stone, and crowded with domes, minarets, and towers shining like jewels in the light of the rising sun.

The rabbi fell to his knees. With trembling hands, he tore open his robe.

Zahirah laid a hand on his shoulder, "Rabbi," she said anxiously.

"Let him be," St. Clair whispered. "He does as tradition requires."

Kneeling in the dust, the rabbi smiled down at Jerusalem through his tears. *"Yerushalayim she'mama,"* he wept. "Jerusalem is a desolation. Our holy and our beautiful house where our fathers praised Thee is burned with fire; all our pleasant things are laid waste . . ."

By the time Isaac and Wallace reached the cart, the sun had risen and warm shafts of golden light lit the air. Birdsong rang from within a nearby mastic tree.

Facing into the sun, Isaac closed his eyes. *"Blessed are You, God, whose majesty gives light to the world."* He drew a deep breath and pointed. "The old woman said we might get our first glimpse of Jerusalem from that knoll."

Wallace snapped the reins and the wagon lurched forward.

Isaac sat in the cart without moving, squinting to the east. "I should warn you, William. Ancient custom prescribes that Jewish pilgrims weep when they behold Jerusalem for the first time."

"Thanks for warning me."

As they crested the hill, Wallace drew rein and the wagon rocked to a halt.

Isaac jumped down from the wagon. He could see domes and minarets shining beneath the morning sun on the edge of the horizon. Ripping open the fabric of his white shirt, he bared his heart. *"Arey kad'she'ha ha'yoo mid'bar,"* he wept, dropping to his knees. "Thy holy cities are become a wilderness, Zion is become a wasteland, Jerusalem a desolation . . ."

Chapter Thirty-Four

Safed
5 June, 1290
Morning

The master of the royal aviary pointed at the horizon. "She comes, my lord!"

Emir Abdullah of Safed shaded his good eye and squinted into the morning sun. Having moved his pavilion with a few courtiers to the roof of the citadel next to the aviary, he had anxiously waited to receive word of the success or failure of his bold move against the sultan, hardly sleeping for two days and two nights. With growing excitement, he spotted the pigeon, soaring over the rooftops of the city. His heart raced as he watched the bird flutter onto the outstretched hand of the keeper of the aviary. Now he would know.

"There's a good girl," cooed the keeper, gently stroking the bird's head, "You've had yourself quite a trip, my pretty. You—"

"Give me the bird," the emir snapped.

"Shall I detach the scroll, my lord?"

"I'll do it myself." The emir reached out, and the bird settled on his arm. Everything hung in the balance—unlimited wealth and power, or an ignominious death. Everything or nothing. He nodded at his courtiers. "Now leave me, all of you." He waited as they disappeared into the stairwell leading down from the roof.

Now he was alone.

The flags of the pavilion murmured in the wind, and the pigeons cooed softly in their cages. He drew his dagger and cut the thin cords binding the pouch to the bird's leg. Then, with the pigeon standing primly on his arm, he extracted the tiny scroll and spread it open.

The news was bad.

Though the Sultan Qa'la'un was indeed killed, his son and heir, al-Ashraf Khalil, lived.

In that moment, he knew all was lost; his role in the sultan's death would be known and the vengeance of the prince would be swift. His hand closed over the soft feathers of the pigeon's shoulders, and in a flash of anger, he sliced off its head.

But perhaps not all is lost, he thought. *Clearly, I must leave Safed with dispatch. But first . . .*

He went from cage to cage, calmly killing the rest of the pigeons. After wiping the blade clean on a tent flap, he returned the dagger to the jeweled scabbard that hung at his waist. Then he opened the hawks' cages, releasing the birds to guard the skies. There would be no more pigeon post in or out of Safed.

Within an hour, the emir rode out alone, unattended and unrecognized, bareheaded and attired in a simple gray robe, mounted on the Templar mare he had acquired from the academy. He headed east, his pace slowed by the heavy-laden donkey tethered to the pommel of his saddle. He had loaded the donkey with as much treasure as it could carry. After all, he would need something to start a new life.

In the early morning, the road was deserted, and the only sounds were the incessant creaking of leather and thudding of hooves into the soft earth. So Abdullah rode for hours, as the shadows grew short and the sun rose in a cloudless sky.

He drew rein and looked back at Safed for the last time, knowing he would never return. Then he jigged his mount about and dug in his heels. The mare lurched forward, but in the next moment slowed to a walk as it strained at the tether to the donkey, plodding unhurried behind. As he felt the tug of the lead rope, Abdullah wondered at the wisdom of bringing the donkey. To travel in this manner was agonizingly slow. But he did have a head start, and though he had gambled for the sultanate and lost, his winnings were still considerable.

Though he had long lived like a king, he had never truly succumbed to pampered luxury. He was, after all, a proud desert-bred fighter and a Tatar—kidnapped in childhood, sold as a slave in Damascus, instructed in the Faith, and groomed as a warrior of the Golden Horde. He had never forgotten the lean cunning of his youth, nor the fierce hunger honed on forced marches through empty desolation.

He had been the protégé of the Sultan Baybars, and, following the defeat of the Templars at the citadel, Baybars had given him control of Safed. That was more than twenty years ago. And now he was leaving, but with no regrets, and not as a broken king—though he fled alone and unattended—because Safed was not truly his home. It had never been his home. In the solitude of the open road, he was a wayward son finally returning to his true home—a land of the open steppe and the endless sky, far to the northeast of the Jordan.

Leather creaked, and the hooves of horse and donkey drummed steadily and softly on the dirt track. Thus he rode, as the sun climbed overhead and the day grew hot.

Finally, after passing the village of Khan Jubb Yusuf, he paused and looked out over the Galilee where a rippling path of gold shone upon the blue water. He was nearly there. It remained only to cross the Jordan to be beyond the reach of al-

Ashraf Khalil.

But when he looked back, he saw them coming—in the small cloud of dust hovering over the ridge road many leagues away. Within that dust, lights flashed, and he knew it was an armored column, bearing down upon him like a sword thrust out of the west.

They were yet at a good distance, and he did not doubt he could outrun them. But not with the donkey.

With a twinge of regret, he drew his scimitar and laid open each of the donkey's panniers. Coins and precious jewels spilled into the dust of the road, sparkling in the sun. Cutting the donkey free, he smacked its hindquarters with the flat of his sword, and the donkey skittered away, scattering a glittering path of treasure among the stones and thorn brush.

Satisfied that the riders would stop to fatten their purses, he spurred the mare and galloped down the road, standing forward in the stirrups, heading east, toward the Jordan River and freedom.

After riding for nearly an hour, the sun stood high over the lake and the horse was sweated. He drew rein, and looked back. The column was still far away, a soft blur against the dull brown slopes of the hills. He smiled as he turned and canted forward in the saddle, looking down at the verdant green lining the Jordan River, just north of the lake. He was close now, not an hour away. Once at the river, he would vanish into the tangle of rushes and marsh grasses, beyond the reach of Khalil's vengeance.

But now, he saw another cloud of dust between him and the lake. Within the cloud, sunlight flashed upon armor and scimitars. A second group of riders was coming from the east. There was no escape.

For a moment, fear gripped his heart—entrapped it in his chest like a hawk too long caged. But in leaving Safed, he had been released from the prison of his position and the burdens of office. He had already tasted a freedom he had not known since his youth, and he would not be caged again. Not by fear. Not by death.

He dug in his heels, and the horse bounded under him and shot forward. Standing in the stirrups, he brandished his scimitar and shouted with joyful terror, his soul lifting upon wings of a wild abandon beyond despair, flying forward, galloping toward the promise of pitched battle. He was, after all, a Tatar and a proud warrior of the Golden Horde.

Chapter Thirty-Five

Jerusalem
5 June, 1290
Morning

Approaching the walled city, St. Clair half slid down a tilting slab of weathered stone etched with a fading Hebrew epitaph—one of the thousands of gravestones scattered over the Mount of Olives' western slope. Then he turned to help the rabbi and Zahirah.

Breathing heavily, Rabbi Samuel sat on the flat surface of a broken gravestone. "I must rest for a moment." He pushed back the hood of his robe, wiping perspiration from his forehead.

Zahirah stood next to St. Clair, looking across the Kidron Valley. "I thought the city would be walled all about," she murmured.

"I expected as much myself," the rabbi agreed.

Turning, St. Clair saw that the city wall was intact to the south where it loomed high over the valley, but fragmented toward the north where tumbled-down stones lay scattered among ornate headstones. "More graves?" he asked.

The rabbi nodded. "That's the Moslem cemetery. In life as well as death, we reside in separate quarters. That's theirs, *this* is ours." He slapped the gravestone where he sat with the flat of his hand. "Yet we share a common expectation—the raising of the dead at the end of days—on Judgment Day. That's why this valley called Kidron, between Olivet and Jerusalem, is also called *Jehoshaphat,* meaning God will judge." He waved a hand toward the summit of the Mount of Olives. "Many Jews believe the Messiah will ascend this very mountain; Ezekiel will blow his trumpet and those buried here will be the very first to hear the call. They're like wedding guests who arrive early to the nuptial feast, hoping to be first at the banquet table." The rabbi smiled as he pushed himself up from the gravestone. "Such notions are idolatrous."

"You would not wish to be buried here?" Zahirah asked.

"Not just yet."

"I mean . . . someday."

The rabbi raised his shoulders. "One must be buried someplace, I suppose. And this certainly gives visitors a nice view . . ."

St. Clair offered the rabbi his arm and led the way down the slope into the Kidron Valley. He angled to the left, where the descent was more gradual and easier to negotiate. The sun shone through ribbons of clouds, casting a shifting pattern of light and shadow over the broken mosaic of gravestones.

Midway down, the rabbi paused to rest again, leaning against the trunk of an ancient olive tree. The morning wind keened through gnarled branches, so contorted they appeared to writhe. The rabbi pointed at a broken section of the city wall. "Jonathan, why isn't Jerusalem better fortified?"

"A number of reasons, Rabbi—Jerusalem is no longer a seat of power and there's little commerce here since it's no longer on any trade route. For a hundred years, Jerusalem has slumbered in the backwaters of the Mamluk Empire—just a city of mosques and *madrasas.* But the main reason they don't rebuild the wall is that they no longer have anything to fear from the armies of the Cross."

Finishing the descent of Olivet, they reached the valley road where clutches of peasants with donkeys and women balancing baskets on their heads converged from the south toward Jerusalem. "These crowds suit us well," said St. Clair. "Among them, we might enter the city without attracting attention."

The rabbi pulled his hood up to cover his head. "Listen well to me now, both of you. If we should become separated for any reason, we'll meet at the home of Abu Muhammad ibn Hasan, who is called al-Hasani. Commit that name to memory—al-Hasani. If you go there, tell him you are with me." He held out his hand. "I'll carry my pack now, Jonathan."

As he unshouldered the rabbi's pack, St. Clair asked, "But why would we go to the house of a Moslem, Rabbi? Isn't there a community of Jews here?"

"Yes, but there are none I know and trust as I do al-Hasani. We were close friends in Baghdad for many years. You may trust him as you trust me."

Reaching the trail along the valley floor, they moved along slowly with bowed heads, keeping close together among the other travelers. St. Clair peeked out from beneath his hood at the carved cliff face bordering the road on the right. "What are those?"

"Rock-cut tombs and funerary monuments—very ancient," the rabbi whispered.

Zahirah turned to look. "This one looks like an Egyptian temple with that pyramid on top."

"You are observant, my daughter. From pilgrims' drawings, I know this to be the Tomb of Zechariah. Let's stop here awhile and rest."

They stood together, just off the road, peering up at the solid stone monolith, graced with several columns in relief, each topped by a capital with an Ionic flourish beneath the capstone.

"Is the entrance on the other side?" Zahirah asked.

"Good question. Jonathan, go around and see."

St. Clair did as the rabbi asked and soon emerged from the shadow of the tomb shaking his head. "There's no entrance, Rabbi."

"Hmm. No entrance . . ." The rabbi's voice trailed off, distracted.

Staring up at the monument, St. Clair fingered the pouch that hung by the cord around his neck. "Do you see it, also, Rabbi?" he asked quietly.

"I do, Jonathan. The very form of that greater triangle inscribed upon your scroll."

"Is it a coincidence?"

"I don't think so."

"What does it mean?"

"I'm not certain. But al-Hasani might know."

"How so?"

"Among his other skills, he's a mathematician and a mapmaker. Al-Hasani might help us understand."

"What are you talking about?" Zahirah asked, looking from St. Clair to the rabbi.

"Perhaps the very reason we came here," the rabbi replied.

They resumed walking among the crowd, moving slowly up the road. St. Clair's heart pounded. He was certain the similarity of the triangles was no coincidence. His hand trembled as he tucked the pouch back beneath his robe.

The well-worn path led up the side of the valley to a broken section of the city wall where a high wooden gate was set among the rubble. The pace slowed as the crowd converged at the gate. St. Clair's breath caught as he saw the flashing armor of Mamluk guards. Lances at their sides, they eyed the crowd. Knowing he would stand out because of his height, St. Clair stooped and kept his head bowed beneath the hooded robe. As he neared the gate, he saw one of the guards snatch a carrot from a farmer's basket. He heard the guard snap off a loud bite.

"This is a sorry lot," the guard said with his mouth full. "How many more do we need for the work detail?"

"At least one, or we'll have to carry stones ourselves."

The guard snapped off another bite. "What about that one? He's big enough."

St. Clair was only a few paces from the gate.

"Hey, you! Come here," the guard called. "We've got work for you."

St. Clair kept moving, pretending not to hear.

"You with the hood," the guard shouted. "Come here at once!"

St. Clair didn't stop. He kept his head down, plodding slowly forward.

"I'm talking to you!"

He felt something hit him on the head, and saw the stump of carrot fall at his feet. He looked up, his jaw muscles working. He felt the rabbi's hand on his arm and heard him whisper: "Remember—al-Hasani."

St. Clair glanced back at Zahirah, then turned and pushed his way through the crowd. Approaching the guards, he bowed and smiled sheepishly, his head bobbing. "I apologize, O valiant soldier. I didn't think you meant me. How may I be of service?"

"There's a day's work for you at Birket Mamillah." The guard pointed with his thumb. "Get back there with the others."

"A thousand thanks, my master." St. Clair bowed his head up and down like a fool as he moved to join a group of men squatting in the rubble by the wooden gate.

"Wait a minute," a second guard said. "Push back your hood."

St. Clair complied, remaining stooped, a weak smile on his lips.

The guard's eyes narrowed as he studied St. Clair's face. "By God, this one has the look of a Templar . . ."

"Valiant soldier!" St. Clair knew the scar on his face and his gray eyes made him suspect. He smiled stupidly and raised his shoulders. "I know nothing of Templars—may Allah utterly reject them! I'm Circasian and a devout Moslem." He shuffled backwards to take his place among the other men."

"Really?" The guard stepped forward, challenging him. "Recite for me the first *kalima.*"

During his years in the Holy Land, St. Clair had studied the *kalimas*—declarations of faith, compiled for children to memorize. At one time he'd known all six of them. *"La ilaha ill Allah Muhammadur-Rasul Allah,"* he recited flawlessly.

"And the second?"

"The *Shahaadat*? Certainly. 'I bear witness that no-one is worthy of worship but Allah, the One alone, without partner, and I bear witness that Muhammad is His servant and Messenger.'." He hoped they wouldn't ask for any more. The first few were short, but the others were longer, and he wasn't sure he could remember them. Beneath his robe, his heart pounded. He continued to smile and bob his head.

"Let him be, Ahmed. He knows the Faith better than you. Besides, with this one, the work detail is complete. Let's go."

Two guards led the way away from the gate and into the darkness of a narrow lane filled with beggars, stray dogs, ragged children, donkeys, and women swathed to the eyes with bundles of laundry balanced on their heads.

Al-Hasani, St. Clair repeated, determined to remember the name.

Chapter Thirty-Six

לו

Birket Mamilla
Outside Jerusalem
5 June, 1290

With the sun warm on his back, St. Clair spent the day carrying heavy stones to skilled workmen who fitted them and repaired a long section of wall along the southern border of the Mamillah Pool. To the east, the walled city of Jerusalem was in constant view. As he worked, St. Clair wondered how the rabbi and Zahirah had fared. He wondered if they had made it to the home of al-Hasani. Throughout the day, the eyes of the guard who had questioned him at the gate seemed to challenge him, but St. Clair averted his gaze and kept to his work. Thus, the day passed.

Toward evening, the workers lined up and were given a few coins and a piece of flatbread. After receiving his wages, St. Clair hung back as the men of the work detail and the guards made their way down the dusty road to Jerusalem. Though he was anxious to rejoin Zahirah and the rabbi, he wanted to avoid any further challenges from the suspicious guard.

He sat on the pool wall as ribbons of clouds drifted into the western sky and reddened. Tearing off bits of flatbread, he ate and watched the men move toward Jerusalem, their voices fading in the distance. From an oak tree at the corner of the wall came the noisy chatter of jackdaws as evening approached. He tore off a final piece of bread, folded the rest, and put it into his pack. Leaning over the sun-warmed stones, he slaked his thirst with handfuls of cool water. Now that the others were gone, the pool was wondrously quiet. Except for the birds.

He shouldered his pack, and with his wooden staff in hand, made his way toward Jerusalem along the pool's southern wall. As he passed the oak tree, the birds startled and flapped noisily away, cackling and scattering into the air. The flock gathered and circled overhead, turning into the western sky streaked with purple clouds and then descending onto a barren hill north of the pool, where they began to forage. The birds suddenly rose into the air again as a horse-drawn wagon clattered over the road on the far side of the pool.

St. Clair saw two men in the wagon. By their clothing, he knew them to be Genoese merchants. One of them waved to him, and he waved back.

He pulled his hood up and watched the merchants climb down from their wagon. He was used to seeing Genoese merchants in Acre, walking about under parasols held by slaves, surrounded by men-at-arms, arrogant in their fancy clothes. These two were different—they were young and they were alone.

St. Clair paused at the corner of the pool and watched as the taller of the two loosened the harnesses of the horses and let them drink. He wore a bright green jerkin more suited for a ball than for commerce. The other, wearing black velvets, was busy filling a goatskin from the pool. Even from across the water, they looked like mere youths. He shook his head as he started down the road toward Jerusalem.

"*Ya sidi,*" came a voice in Italian-accented Arabic. "Is this the road to El Kuds?"

St. Clair's breath caught. *That voice—there's something familiar about it.* He stopped walking and turned around. Shielding his eyes from the late afternoon sun, he saw that the merchant in black velvet was waiting for a reply. He placed his hand by his ear, pretending he hadn't heard. *"Caman mara?"* he called back.

The young merchant repeated the question, and St. Clair answered by nodding and pointing toward Jerusalem.

As he turned down the road, he thought of all the merchants he had known in Acre, but none matched this voice. *And yet, so familiar to me.* Then, he froze. *Wait—I know that voice, and it doesn't belong to any merchant! But how can this be? I'll circle back and get a good look without the sun in my eyes.*

Leaving the road, he ducked behind a large domed tomb, then slipped behind scattered oak trees, moving back toward the pool.

"He's coming back this way," Wallace said in a low voice.

Isaac swiveled around. "Who?"

"That big fellow you spoke to." Wallace pretended to tighten a harness on one of the horses. "He's coming this way."

"Where? I don't see him."

Wallace glanced up. The stranger was no longer on the road. "I'll wager he's skulking about among the trees." He strolled to the back of the wagon and took the wooden stave from where it lay next to the crate. "You wait here. I'll go see."

"He's just a Mamluk holy man, William," Isaac reasoned.

"Don't you think he's . . . you know, a bit large for a Mamluk holy man?"

"And aren't you a bit large to be a Genoese merchant?"

"Exactly my point." Wallace, stave in hand, retreated toward a cluster of oak trees. "I'll look around. You wait here."

Well away from the pool, Wallace found a tree with a good view of Isaac and the wagon. He flattened himself against it, watched, and waited.

He didn't wait long.

The hooded Mamluk, himself carrying a stave, was moving quietly forward, intent on Isaac and the wagon.

Wallace didn't move. Hidden behind the tree, he gripped his stave tightly. *A good knock on the head will banish any notions he may have of robbing us.* He peeked out and saw the stranger pause, staring toward Isaac and the wagon. Then the big man lurched forward.

Wallace sprang from his hiding place and ran, quickly closing the distance between them. He drew back the stave and swung it with all his strength, hitting the Mamluk a glancing blow to the head.

The man sprawled on the ground and rolled over. He sprang to his feet, glaring at Wallace with feral eyes over his dark beard, a snarl on his lips. The hood of his robe was askew, the side of his head slick with red blood. His stave lay in the dirt at Wallace's feet, and the stranger lunged for it.

Wallace snapped his own stave upward, sending the brigand staggering back. But he didn't go down. Blood trickled down his face from a fresh cut over the eye. Like a wary animal, the Mamluk circled about, wiping his face with his sleeve. Suddenly, he sprang forward, spearing his head into Wallace's midsection and knocking him to the ground.

Wallace struggled to rise, but the man drew back his fist and struck him full in the face so hard he almost swooned. Then the man dashed back and retrieved his stave.

Wallace wiped his nose and saw his hand covered with blood. He climbed to his feet and brandished his stave in both hands, slantwise across his body, as he had practiced. Lunging forward, he flailed at the Mamluk, and the wooden staves clattered as they parried blows. Wallace missed a stroke and the stranger poked him in the stomach, then thrust the spar between his legs and tripped him, sending him down hard on his backside.

The stranger seemed to be toying with him. Furious, Wallace bounced up. Two-handed, he hacked a flurry of blows at the Mamluk's head, but the man easily turned the blows aside. Desperately, Wallace rushed at him and managed to strike a blow to the head.

This only seemed to raise the Mamluk's ire. Now he attacked Wallace in earnest, the stave whirling in his hands. Wallace's weapon flew from his grip as the Mamluk milled blows to his head and ribs. Under this drubbing, Wallace went down and covered his head.

Apparently satisfied, the Mamluk stepped back.

Wallace opened his eyes and saw the brigand roll the stave over his wrist, spin it in the air, and catch it with his other hand. He was clearly an expert with the thing.

It was no use.

Then the Mamluk spoke. *"Avete avuti abbastanza, ragazzo?"*

Wallace didn't understand what sounded like a question in an Italian dialect. He did understand the tone, though—threatening.

He staggered to his feet, steadying himself against a tree, breathing hard and wiping blood from his face. Then he turned and raced back to the wagon, pushed Isaac aside, and threw open the crate. He grabbed the hilt of the sword, pulled it from the scabbard, and turned to face his assailant, brandishing the heavy claymore in both hands over his head.

He expected the Mamluk to run away.

But the man didn't run. He came to a stop, a strange look on his bloodied face.

Wallace brandished the sword higher. He let out a wordless yell he hoped sounded frightening. But the stranger just stood there, looking at the claymore, more in amazement than fear.

With another blood-curdling yell, Wallace rushed forward,

swinging the blade.

The Mamluk stepped to the side. The sword sliced uselessly through the air and hit the dirt.

Wallace turned and lunged again, sword point first.

The Mamluk easily knocked the blade away with his stave, shouting, again in the Italian dialect, *"Come avete ricevuto questa spada?"*

Two-handed, Wallace hacked a flurry of blows at the man's head, but the Mamluk parried expertly, turning the blade aside so that the sword never bit and the stave never broke.

Wallace's strength ebbed and the heavy claymore looped through the air more and more slowly. His mouth was full of blood, his chest heaved, his arms ached, and he couldn't catch his breath. As he raised the sword for another futile stroke, the Mamluk caught his arm and wrenched the sword free. Then, with one blow of his fist, he knocked Wallace to the ground.

The Mamluk raised the sword to his eyes, turning the blade. Then he did the last thing Wallace expected. He smiled.

Wallace scurried backwards, crawling on his back, certain his end was at hand.

Casting the stave aside, the Mamluk advanced, almost casually.

Wallace saw Isaac creeping around behind the man, apparently trying to retrieve a stave. But it was no use. The Mamluk had the sword. In desperation, Wallace remembered what Isaac had told him about the Mamluks' fear of jinns and the manner in which they are summoned by whistling. He spit blood from his mouth and pursed his lips. He drew a deep breath and began to whistle, the same high lilting Scottish air that had so frightened the old woman.

The Mamluk froze in mid-stride, looking at Wallace, his eyes wide. "Sweet Jesus!" he exclaimed in perfect English edged with a Scottish brogue. "I know that tune—that's the Lament for

Brian Boru!" He thrust out his hand. "If ye be a Scot, lad, give me your hand!"

Wallace couldn't believe his ears. He reached up.

Just then, the Mamluk toppled forward.

Behind him stood Isaac, holding a wooden stave, smiling.

Chapter Thirty-Seven

Birket Mamilla
Outside Jerusalem
5 June, 1290
Evening

"What have you done?" Wallace shouted as he sat on the ground next to the unconscious stranger.

Isaac, still clutching the stave and barely able to catch his breath, looked down at the man. "Is he dead?"

"I hope not, Isaac. He spoke to me! I'll warrant this is a knight of Scotland, a knight of my own land. I'm sure of it!" Wallace got to his knees and turned the knight over. The man's face was covered with blood, his eyes closed. Wallace laid a hand on his chest. "Thanks be to God. He's still breathing."

"You can't blame me, William," Isaac said and threw down the stave. "I thought he was about to kill you."

"I know, I know." Wallace looked at the bloodied face. "We should try to revive him." He stood up, retrieved a goatskin full of water from the wagon, and handed it to Isaac. "Here, hold this." Then he knelt, lifted the man's shoulders, and slipped the sodden hood off his head. "Here, Isaac, splash some water on his face."

Isaac unstoppered the skin and sent a torrent of cool water over the man's face and head, washing away the blood. The man sputtered and his eyes fluttered open.

Isaac's jaw dropped. "Jonathan?"

"What? Who's Jonathan?" demanded Wallace.

The man sat up, wiping water from his eyes, blood still trickling down the side of his face.

Now Isaac was sure. "Jonathan!" he shouted.

St. Clair looked up and smiled. "So, it *is* you, Isaac. What are you doing here?"

"What am *I* doing here?" Isaac laughed and squatted down in front of St. Clair. "What are *you* doing here? And masquerading as a Mamluk holy man, no less!"

"At least I'm not the one dressed up like a Genoese courtesan," St. Clair said as he shook the water from his hair.

"You *know* each other?" Wallace cut in, looking back and forth between St. Clair and Isaac.

"Certainement!" Isaac exclaimed, clapping St. Clair on the shoulder. "This is my dear friend and my sometime student, Jonathan St. Clair!"

"Jonathan St. Clair?" Wallace straightened up, his eyes wide.

St. Clair nodded up at Wallace. "And you are . . . ?"

"William Wallace, sir. Newly come to the Holy Land, and honored to make your acquaintance."

"There, William," St. Clair extended his hand, "my hand in friendship. No hard feelings?"

"None, sir." Wallace grasped St. Clair's hand. "Let me help you up." As St. Clair got unsteadily to his feet, Wallace pointed to the side of St. Clair's head. "You're bleeding, sir."

"So are you." St. Clair smiled, pointing to Wallace's nose.

"You're both a sight!" Isaac muttered as he pulled a white muslin cloth from his trouser pocket. He tore it in two and handed half to each man.

Wallace held the cloth over his nose and said to St. Clair in English, "I struck you first, sir, and for that I'm sorry."

"Don't be. I'd have done the same." St. Clair pressed the bloodstained cloth against his temple. "You're a long way from home, lad. Did you come to fight in the Holy Crusade?"

"No, but now that I'm here, I might. When I left France, my only thought was to see Jerusalem."

"What was your business in France?"

"Sent there by my father, sir, to become a priest."

"Your father . . ." St. Clair fixed his eyes on Wallace. "Would he be called Malcolm Wallace of Ellerslie?"

"The same, sir. You know him?"

"Aye. I did once—long ago—as fine a man and patriot that ever broke bread. Is he well?"

"He is, sir."

"I would you remember me to him."

"I will, sir."

"Où avez-vous trouvé ceci?" St. Clair asked Isaac as he lifted his sword from the ground.

Isaac pointed to the crate in the wagon. "It arrived in that crate from Safed, Jonathan," he replied, "along with the bloodied vestments of Rabbi Samuel. Is he, indeed, dead?"

"Not when I left him this morning," St. Clair answered dryly. Fixing his eyes on Isaac, he added, "He's convinced it was Petit who bribed the emir to have him killed."

"In this he was correct," said Isaac.

St. Clair picked his claymore off the ground and slid it back into the scabbard. "But how did this crate come from Safed? Who brought it to Acre?"

"Do you remember the merchant, Buscarel?"

"Yes. Buscarel of Genoa—I know him well."

"It was Buscarel who went between Rabbi Petit and the Emir of Safed."

"And Petit bribed the emir?" St. Clair frowned. "I don't understand how he had the money for a bribe."

"It wasn't about money." Isaac shifted uncomfortably. "It was about information . . . information concerning Acre's defenses . . ."

"What would Petit know about that?"

"Someone gathered the information for him."

"Who?"

Isaac drew a deep breath. "I did."

"You? But why would you do such a thing?"

"Petit tricked me, Jonathan. I didn't realize what I was doing until it was too late."

"Oh, Isaac! How could you do this?" St. Clair slammed his fist against the wagon. Then, closing his eyes, he drew a deep breath. "So, Buscarel brought this supposed proof of our death to Petit, and returned to Safed with the information you provided—the secrets of Acre's defenses." He shook his head. "This is bad, Isaac. This is very, very bad."

"But Buscarel never got to Safed!" Wallace said. "He was killed on the way, and we retrieved the scroll! Show him, Isaac!"

Isaac reached beneath his doublet and drew out the scroll.

St. Clair spread the parchment open in his hands. *"Mon Dieu!"* he murmured and shook his head. "You even had maps and tables . . ."

"Rabbi Petit wanted everything in detail," Isaac answered weakly.

"Thank God this didn't reach Safed," St. Clair said as he rolled up the scroll and stuck it beneath his robe. "And how did Buscarel die?" He looked at Wallace. "Did you kill him?"

"No, no! We didn't kill him," Wallace protested.

"Buscarel was killed by the emir's halka," Isaac hastened to explain. "After the captain of the halka had taken the scroll from Buscarel, we took it from the captain."

"*Really?*" St. Clair laughed. "*You* took it from the captain of the halka?"

"He came alone to plunder Buscarel's body near where we were hidden," said Wallace. "I hit him with our shovel. I only meant to knock him out, but I hit him pretty hard—"

"You killed him?"

Wallace nodded.

"We had to retrieve the scroll!" Isaac said.

"When was this?" St. Clair asked.

"About a week ago."

"Did anyone see you kill him?"

"No."

"Were you followed?"

"No," Isaac replied. "It happened at dusk. After we hid the body, we left. By the time the sun rose, we were far away."

"You did well to reclaim the scroll." St. Clair lifted the cloth from his head. "Is it still bleeding?"

Wallace peered closely. "I don't think so, sir." He lowered the cloth from his own face. "What about my nose?"

St. Clair canted his head to the side. "It's a bit askew—broken, I think. Here, I'll straighten it out." He reached up, cupped Wallace's nose with his hands, and twisted.

"Ow!"

"There, good as new!" St. Clair smiled. "Press hard with the cloth till the bleeding stops." He patted Wallace on the shoulder. "So, Malcolm wanted to make a priest of you!"

Wallace nodded.

"I don't suppose you got much instruction with sword or stave at the scriptorium."

"No, sir." Wallace laughed and winced.

"Well, William, we shall have to remedy that, won't we?"

"I'd be honored, sir," Wallace said with a little bow.

Isaac spoke up. "It will be night soon. Shouldn't we go into

Jerusalem?"

"Not by my counsel," St. Clair replied, looking toward the wall's dull scarlet reflection in the gathering dusk. "The gates are guarded. We'll arouse less suspicion if we enter the city in the morning with the crowds." He placed his hand on the wagon. "And we can't enter Jerusalem with the horses and wagon—it's a city of narrow alleys and stairs." He leaned over the side of the wagon and ran his hand through the scraps of parchment in the crate. "We'll need to find a way to board the horses so that we'll have them for our return trip to Acre. And you two need some proper clothing. Was there anything of value in here that we might sell to secure what we need?"

"Nothing but old scrolls and worn-out religious articles," Isaac replied.

"But money isn't a problem," Wallace was quick to add.

"No, William." St. Clair smiled. "Not having money is the problem."

"But we have money," Wallace insisted. "Plenty of it."

"Really? *You* have plenty of money? I hardly think an aspiring priest and a yeshiva boy have anything but debt."

"William speaks true, Jonathan," Isaac said quietly. "We have a lot of money."

Bemused, St. Clair raised his shoulders. "All right, how much between the two of you?"

Wallace pulled Buscarel's purse from within his green tunic.

St. Clair's brow furrowed as he felt the weight of the sack. He loosened the straps and peered in. "*Mon Dieu!* How many years did you two save to gather such a hoard?"

"Actually," Isaac cleared his throat and the boys exchanged guilty glances, "we came upon it recently."

"Came upon it?"

Wallace nodded. "That money belonged to Buscarel."

St. Clair grimaced. "You took it off his body?"

"No, Jonathan, no," Isaac hastened to reply. "We told you—the captain of the halka pillaged Buscarel's body. *He* took the money."

A smile spread over St. Clair's face. "Ah! And when you recovered the scroll after the captain's *unintended* death, the money was just . . . there."

"Yes—*hefker,* abandoned. What should we have done?" Isaac asked. "Just left it there?"

"Certainly not. With this money we'll be able to get you out of those ridiculous clothes," St. Clair said as he stepped around the cart and patted the necks of the horses tethered by the pool. "And we'll be able to pay for the boarding and care of these old war horses in one of the villages near here. Come, William—let's hitch them to the wagon."

St. Clair lifted a bridle off the ground and began to place it on one of the horses. "There's just one thing I still don't understand. After you retrieved the scroll, why didn't you go back to Acre? You still haven't told me what you're doing here."

Wallace and Isaac exchanged glances.

"When Isaac and I met in Acre," Wallace said as he adjusted the horse's bit, "we discovered that we shared a common desire to see Jerusalem—"

"Indeed," said Isaac, "even before the business with Buscarel, we had already made all the arrangements to go."

"And once we reclaimed the scroll on the road to Safed," Wallace said as he picked up a breast collar from the ground, "and we were already away from Acre, we decided to continue our journey and fulfill our dream." He nodded toward Jerusalem.

"Om'dote hayu raglaynoo b'sha'ara'yih, Yerushalayim," Isaac added with a smile.

"That we will, boys—tomorrow morning we'll stand in the gates of Jerusalem," St. Clair said as he secured the reins to the bridle. "For tonight, though," he nodded toward the silhouetted hills against the scarlet sky, "we'll bivouac on yonder hill."

Chapter Thirty-Eight

Jerusalem
6 June, 1290
Morning

The brass bell at the apex of the arched doorway sprang to life with a sharp ring, dancing against the white plaster wall. Rabbi Samuel and the mapmaker, Abu Muhammad ibn Hasan, called al-Hasani, glanced up.

"Early customers?" the rabbi asked.

"Not this early." Al-Hasani shook his head, careful not to spill tea from the porcelain cup in his hand. A slight old man, he wore a white gown embroidered with silver thread around the hem and cuffs. His skin was deeply lined, like a map of heavily traveled trade routes in a brown desert. "My son will attend to it." He smiled over his cup.

The bell jangled again.

"That should be the knight I told you of, Jonathan St. Clair," said the rabbi.

"If so, I look forward to seeing that scroll of his . . ."

The two men sat together at morning tea on a low divan beneath a high-domed ceiling in the airy common room of al-Hasani's home within the walled city of Jerusalem. The ground level also housed the apothecary, library, and the map workshop.

"I recall you had five children, old friend." Rabbi Samuel made conversation as he waited to see if, indeed, it was St. Clair at the gate.

"Sad to say, Sha'ima and I lost two children to a catarrhal fever soon after we left Baghdad," al-Hasani said as he placed his cup on a hammered brass tray. "Our eldest son and daughter are gone to the great university in Salerno, and only our youngest son, Tarek, is with us." He leaned back, adjusting the silk *calotte* that crowned his unruly mane of gray hair. "I still can't comprehend why you closed your academy . . ."

"As you know from your own experience, old friend, it is precarious to live in the crevices between great empires—Mongol, Mamluk, and Christian. It is as the poet, Yehudah Halevi, has written: *Between the armies of Seir and Kedar, my army perishes and is lost . . .*"

Al-Hasani nodded. "The same was expressed by the great Thucydides in his histories: *The strong do as they wish, the weak suffer as they must.*"

"And now I travel with a Christian knight." Rabbi Samuel lifted his cup and smiled. "Ironic, no? After all these years, my only companion—a Knight of the Crusade."

"Not merely ironic, Samuel—unbelievable—" Al-Hasani stood up as a handsome young man with dark skin and sharp brown eyes strode into the room.

"My father, there are three strangers at the gate. They claim to be friends of Rabbi Samuel."

Rabbi Samuel got to his feet. "Are you certain there are *three*?"

"Yes, Rabbi, and all wear Mamluk robes."

"Are they armed?" al-Hasani asked.

"No, my father. Though two of them carry staves and have cuts and bruises upon their faces. What should I tell them?"

Rabbi Samuel touched al-Hasani's arm. "This troubles me

greatly. No one but Jonathan knows I am here."

"Perhaps he met some friends along the way?"

"He has no friends in these lands—only enemies."

Al-Hasani stepped toward the stairwell. "I will speak with them."

"Do you have any weapons here?" the rabbi asked.

"We do." Al-Hasani turned to his son. "Alert the apprentices, Tarek. Arm yourselves."

Isaac glanced furtively up and down the lane. "Are you sure this is the place?"

St. Clair pointed at the weathered sign hanging above them. "You worry too much."

"Why are they taking so long?" Isaac asked.

St. Clair raised his hand to give the bell chain another pull when the wooden door creaked open. The face of an old man appeared, with skin like wrinkled coffee-colored parchment, framed by white hair and a white beard.

"How may I help you?" came the reedy voice.

"We are friends of Rabbi Samuel, the Gaon of Baghdad," St. Clair said in Arabic. "We desire—"

The door flew open to reveal Rabbi Samuel standing next to the old Arab.

"Enter, Jonathan." The rabbi glanced past St. Clair at the two strangers. "You and your friends."

Once the three were through the door and standing in the inner courtyard, Rabbi Samuel clapped St. Clair on the shoulder. "Al-Hasani, this is the new disciple I told you of, Jonathan St. Clair."

"Ahlan wa'marhaban!" al-Hasani said with a bow of his head. "You are most welcome to my home, Jonathan. You and these gentlemen." His deep-set eyes fluttered over to Isaac and Wallace.

St. Clair rested his hand on Isaac's shoulder. "This is my young mentor, Isaac, from the yeshiva of Rabbi Solomon Petit of Acre."

Rabbi Samuel's smile faded at the mention of Petit's name. He eyed the young Jew warily.

Noticing the rabbi's reaction, Isaac bowed. "I assure you, Rabbi Samuel, you have nothing to fear from me. I am honored to meet the esteemed Gaon of Baghdad, whose reputation goes before him. I lately became aware of the machinations of my former mentor, Rabbi Petit, *ee'mach sh'moe,* and I offer my loyalty and my service to you. Indeed, before I left Acre a fortnight ago, I conveyed a working draft of your writ against Petit to Midrash Hagadol. It may be that Petit has, even now, been excommunicated and banished from the city."

This news seemed to reassure Rabbi Samuel, who took a step forward. "Isaac, is it? And from Petit's yeshiva? I have heard of a prodigy there known as Isaac of Acre." His eyes narrowed. "Might that be you?"

Isaac blushed. "I am he, though unworthy of any special distinction."

"Not according to the stories I have heard," Rabbi Samuel said. "But, tell me, Isaac, are you as well versed in gematria as you are in Talmud?"

"I am, indeed." Isaac smiled. "I'm adept at many permutations of gematria."

"That is well, Isaac. For I might soon require your assistance in this regard." Rabbi Samuel looked from Isaac up at Wallace. "And who is this young giant?"

"My friend and my protector," replied Isaac, reaching up to lay a hand on Wallace's shoulder. "A young Scot just arrived in the Holy Land, and though he is able to converse in many tongues, Arabic is not among them."

Wallace bowed. *"Je m'appelle William Wallace."*

"Vous êtes la soyez bienvenu ici, William," al-Hasani said, extending his hand. "Please join us for tea."

"Merci, monsieur," Wallace replied.

As the men crossed the courtyard, Rabbi Samuel asked St. Clair in Arabic, "What happened to your face?"

"The young Scot was protecting Isaac when I came upon them outside Jerusalem. We fought as enemies before we realized we were friends."

"Well, even with that face, Zahirah will be delighted to see you. She was very distraught when they led you away with the work detail."

"Where is she?"

The rabbi nodded toward a spiral staircase. "Her chamber is on the upper floor."

St. Clair paused, eyeing the staircase. "I should let her know I've come back."

"Very well, but be quick."

St. Clair heard a note of urgency in the rabbi's voice. "What is it?" he asked.

"The scroll. Al-Hasani and I wish to begin study of the inscription without delay."

St. Clair lifted the tethered pouch from about his neck and handed it to Rabbi Samuel.

CHAPTER THIRTY-NINE

לט

Acre
7 August, 1290
Evening

With quill in hand, Rabbi Solomon Petit bent over a *responsa* he was composing to Rabbi Simeon of Joinville. The question under review concerned whether one was permitted to carry a walking stick on the Sabbath when going from one town to another. Ever the rigid legalist, Petit was formulating a dissenting opinion. Light from a burning taper hovered over the parchment. He inked the quill and gathered his thoughts for a particularly compelling argument, when there came a heavy knock upon the study door.

"A man to see you, Rabbi," his steward Menahem called.

"A man, you clod of earth? What *manner* of man?"

"A Knight of the Cross, Rabbi."

"I'll be right out."

Petit wiped the nib clean with an ink-stained rag and pushed away from his desk. The responsa would have to wait. He took his striped robe from its hook by the door and went out into the hall, brushing past Mendel as he pulled on the robe. *One must never raise the ire of a Christian Knight by forcing him to wait . . .*

As he bustled out the door of the yeshiva, Petit saw that day had turned to evening, and the air had cooled. He tied his sash as he approached the gate.

"Chevalier, bonsoir!" he exclaimed, hoping the knight spoke good French. But at the gate was a common soldier who answered with a jabber of guttural Arabic mixed with Latin and stray bits of low French. From what Petit could gather, something about a goat at the city gate.

"Une chevre?" he asked. *"Je ne comprends pas . . ."*

The soldier patiently repeated his message, making no more sense—just plainsong and rasping—like one who clears the throat before expectorating. Nonetheless, if there was someone or something at the city gate, it was incumbent upon Petit to go.

He nodded, pulled a coin from his purse, and pressed it into the soldier's fleshy hand. *"Merci, de vos douleurs, monsieur."*

Hurrying along empty lanes of gray stone, he cursed Isaac. In the months since his former protégé had fled, it had fallen to Petit to examine all parcels addressed to Jews, and to meet all non-resident Jews coming to Acre through the land gate. So far, it had proved a complete waste of his time and energy.

An old man should not have to endure such hardship, he thought and cursed Isaac again. *Ee'mah sh'mo ve'zih'ro! Not only does he abandon me, but he tries to destroy me.* Petit knew it was Isaac who conveyed the excommunication decree to his enemies at Midrash Hagadol. And he had nearly succeeded. Only by marshaling his powers of persuasion and the support of a few allies had the council accepted Petit's contention; the document, full of corrections and erasures, was a crude forgery and could never have the force of law. Petit insisted he would be happy to answer all charges if and when Rabbi Samuel, himself, was present in the rabbinic court. For now, his enemies accepted his argument and were silent. But for how much longer?

I just have to hold them off for a few more months, he thought as he hurried toward the land gate in the gathering dusk. *By then the emir of Safed will have taken Acre and he will reward my service by granting me authority over the Jews of Acre, including the rabbinic court. Indeed, once the emir becomes sultan, I'll be the leader of all Jewish communities throughout the Holy Land! But until then, the threat of this decree hangs above my head like a sharp sword . . .*

At the land gate was a tall Jew in a skullcap and shapeless robe. He looked odd—his beard too short and his side locks barely of the prescribed length.

Two guards lounging in a wooden shack glanced up as the rabbi passed, then returned to their game of dice.

"Thank you for coming to my aid, Rabbi," the stranger called in Hebrew. "May I now enter the city?"

"Presently, my son," Petit said and took the opportunity to rest his weary back against the wall just outside the gate. "Have you traveled far?" he asked pleasantly.

"Yes, Rabbi. Two days have passed since I left the shores of the Galilee."

"And what is your purpose here?"

The man hesitated. "I . . . I have some documents I'm charged to deliver."

"Documents?" Petit held out his hand. "Let me see them."

"I'm sorry, Rabbi, but I have specific instructions as their delivery—"

"What instructions?"

The man hesitated, then replied, "One is to be given to the Master of the Templars, the other to the head of Midrash Hagadol."

Petit's breath caught. "For reasons of Acre's safety, I have been charged to speak with any Jew who wishes to enter the city. Believe me," Petit forced a smile, "it is not my wish to be in this position. They," he nodded in the direction of the guards, "have decreed that I must make a full inquiry before any Jew enters the city. I have no choice in the matter, my son. Neither do you."

The man stared at the ground "But my instructions—"

"I'm sorry, my son. But without the documents in my hand, you will not enter Acre. Shall I have the knights escort you back to the frontier?"

The Jew shook his head.

"What's your name, my son?" Petit asked kindly.

"Nehemiah, sir."

"Tell me, Nehemiah, you said you've come hither from the shores of the Galilee. Which village by that blessed lake do you call home?"

"Actually . . . ah," he stammered, "my . . . my home city was Jerusalem. I was living by the Galilee only for the past year, at . . . at a place called Tel Hum."

"That's a colony of the unclean!" Petit peered closely at Nehemiah's face. In the dusk, he could make out a scaling discoloration on the man's left cheek. He hadn't noticed it before. He took a step back. "On whose authority did you leave?" he asked.

"I assure you, Rabbi," Nehemiah said, pointing to his cheek, "This is not the affliction. Such was the attestation of a prominent scholar according to the laws of Israel. I do *not* have the leprosy. Here, I'll show you." Nehemiah bent, fumbled in a pack that lay at his feet, and held up a scroll. "This proves it."

Petit gingerly took the scroll and carefully unrolled it. In the waning light, he scanned down, his eyes settling on the signature at the bottom. There, in elegant Hebrew script, was the name of his tormentor, Rabbi Samuel ben Daniel Hakohen, the Gaon of Baghdad.

Petit's heart pounded. "You said there were two other documents. Give them to me." He stuck out his hand. "Now."

Nehemiah shifted his weight back and forth. "I was told—"

"I don't care what you were told!" Petit barked, then drew a deep breath and forced another smile. "Be assured, Nehemiah, once I have examined the documents, I will return them to you without delay."

Nehemiah cleared his throat and shook his head. "But I promised . . ." he said weakly.

"And I promise *you* that you will not enter Acre without giving me the scrolls!" Petit fixed his eyes on Nehemiah in the waning light. "And not only will you not enter Acre," Petit continued in a voice as dark as the sky, "but this document that supposedly declares you clean will vanish, and you will return to Tel Hum. You may not have leprosy now, Nehemiah, but after a few more years at Tel Hum, you will."

Nehemiah hesitated, then bent down, pulled two sealed scrolls from his pack, and handed them to Rabbi Petit.

Chapter Forty

מ

Acre
8 August, 1290
Morning

Rabbi Solomon Petit paced up and back the center aisle of the synagogue while he waited along with eight other congregants for a tenth man to form a *minyan* so they might begin morning prayer. He was preoccupied with two alarming bits of news. One had come yesterday with Nehemiah from Safed—*Rabbi Samuel still lives.* The other was whispered among the assembled men at synagogue—*the Emir of Safed is dead.*

The synagogue door creaked open and a clutch of men hurried in. The prayer service began.

Seeing they had more than enough for a *minyan,* Petit, feigning illness, left the synagogue. *I need time to consider my current situation,* he thought as he hurried back to his academy. *How might I repair my shattered fortunes?*

He moved as quickly as he could over the uneven paving stones, his mind racing. *The emir of Safed is dead. On one hand, that is well, because he lied to me about killing Samuel. On the other hand, I shall require a new patron if I am to become the leader of Acre's Jews. Where can I find a Mamluk prince who might be willing and able to strike a bargain with me?*

He opened the yeshiva gate and hurried through the front door.

And what other resources do I have? Petit asked himself as he entered his study, pushed the door closed, and stood, staring at the fire burning in the hearth. *I have Nehemiah! I'm sure he knows Samuel's whereabouts, and I'm sure he'll tell me.*

He had instructed his steward to lock Nehemiah in the cellar for the night and to tether him to a cot. Having no good rope, he had given Menahem Mendel an old set of phylacteries to use for its leather straps.

Kneeling by the hearth, Petit removed four of the bricks. He peered into the hidden compartment where he kept his wealth and important documents, removed the three scrolls he had taken from Nehemiah, and placed them on his desk.

Petit rubbed his eyes and settled into his chair. He had not slept well. Pulling his chair forward, he studied each scroll in turn.

First, he took the writ of excommunication. *Clearly, to have intercepted this is a divine attestation to the righteousness of my cause. Had this reached Midrash Hagadol, my excommunication would have been immediate and my exile permanent.* He examined the document's Hebrew date: 15 Sivan, 5050. *Well over two months ago.* He pushed back from the table and stepped to the hearth. *I should have destroyed the draft—I won't make the same mistake with this.* He tossed the parchment among the glowing coals and watched the flames spring up, licking the scroll with orange tongues, blackening and twisting the edges. After a minute, the flames guttered out, and the writ of excommunication was ashes.

Petit returned to his desk and looked at the second scroll. Like the first, it was a mixture of Hebrew and Aramaic—Samuel's attestation of Nehemiah's condition. Glancing through it, he found himself agreeing with the observations and conclusions; Nehemiah clearly had a non-leprous skin ailment. The document bore the same date as the first—15 Sivan, 5050.

He took the third scroll. It was written in an unusual blend of Provençal and proper northern French—clearly by the knight whose sword had been in the crate from Safed. Manifestly an intelligence report; the knight had traveled from Acre to Safed, and then to the northwest shore of the Galilee, though Tel Hum wasn't mentioned by name. The knight described Mamluk troop strength and fortifications in a number of towns of the northern Galilee, especially Safed. Petit pursed his lips and scanned the document. *It ends with an interesting clue—"I will travel south and try to report again in a fortnight." It's dated 5 May, 1290, which corresponds to 15 Sivan, 5050—the same date as Samuel's scrolls. And it's written on the same parchment Samuel used and delivered to Acre by the same courier. It is manifestly clear that this knight travels with Rabbi Samuel, though I can't imagine why . . .*

Petit leaned back in his chair, still studying the knight's scroll. *So, Samuel travels from Baghdad and composes the writ of excommunication against me. He stops in Safed about two months ago where he meets a Knight of the Crusades, and with the help of this knight he avoids the death I arranged for him at the hands of the emir.*

Petit placed the scroll on his desk and frowned. *That was no happy accident—the knight was hired by my enemies for that very purpose—to protect Samuel so that he might reach Acre alive and personally rebuke me.*

Petit pushed back his chair and stood up. He began to pace. *Samuel and the Templar leave Safed, but instead of making the journey to Acre, they travel in the opposite direction. Perhaps to hide from the emir, they stay for some weeks among the lepers of Tel Hum. But after leaving the scrolls for Nehemiah to deliver, why do they travel south? With the knight to protect him, why does Samuel not return here? And where are they going? Baghdad? Not likely. Tibe-*

rius? Jerusalem? Gaza?

He took the bell that stood on his desk and rang for his steward. *I'm certain Nehemiah knows. And I'm certain that he'll tell me.*

After a minute, the study door scraped open, filled by a hulking shadow. "Are you ready for your breakfast, Rabbi?" mumbled Menahem Mendel.

"Not now. Tell me, how fares our guest?"

"I did as you instructed, Rabbi," the steward said thickly.

"With the phylacteries?"

"Yes, Rabbi. I bound him, and I stood outside the door all night."

"And did he talk?"

"He never stopped talking, Rabbi." The steward's unshaven face creased into a smile. He motioned with his fingers and thumb. "All night—talk, talk, talk, talk, talk."

"Good. I would hear some of this talk. Bring me a candle."

Petit carefully led the way down the stone steps into the cellar, the light from the taper in his bony hand flickering over the rough-hewn walls. From within the cellar, he could hear Nehemiah's muffled voice, pleading. Petit raised the candle and the wavering light fell on the deeply grained wood of the cellar door. With a finger to his lips, he half-turned and motioned Mendel to remain silent. Then he leaned his head against the door and listened.

"Why do you shut me in a dark house?" Nehemiah wailed. "How can you treat me thus? I beg you, sir. Release me. Please. I cannot believe Rabbi Petit directed you to do this. The good rabbi would never leave a fellow Jew tethered like an animal. When he learns what you have done, you will be harshly punished. Release me now, and I'll say nothing. This is your last chance. Do you hear me?"

A short pause was followed by a howl of rage. "Why do you

not speak? Are you made of stone, or are you even there? Are you still there?"

Another pause. In the silence Petit could hear the soft hiss of his candle's flame.

"Are you there?" Nehemiah cried, his voice rising in pitch. "Is anyone there?" Shrieking dissolved into sobbing, and then silence.

After a few moments, Petit stepped back and began to motion for Mendel to lift the bolt, but stopped when Nehemiah spoke again, quite softly, seemingly to himself. Petit put his ear to the door, straining to hear.

"I only wished to return home. To return to Jerusalem and my bride—to go home after a year of a living death among the lepers—a year buried alive. I only wished to return to the life that was torn from me—to go home . . . to my wife . . ."

Petit smiled broadly. He stepped back and motioned to his steward.

Mendel lifted the bolt, opened the latch, and pushed on the door. Creaking on rusty hinges, the door opened.

"Please!" Nehemiah shrieked. "In the name of Abraham, Isaac, and Jacob, release me!"

Petit's candle guttered in the effluence of rank air from the cool darkness. In the flickering light, he saw Nehemiah sitting on the edge of the cot, bound hand and foot with the phylacteries' leather straps, his face haggard and wet with tears, blinking at the light.

"Menahem, what have you done?" Petit's voice rang with feigned anger. Turning he shouted at the steward whose huge body filled the doorway, and whose own candle illuminated his coarse visage, more monstrous in the half-light. "How could you do this to a brother Jew?"

"But . . . but, Rabbi . . ."

"Silence, fool," Petit thundered.

"It is even so, Rabbi," Nehemiah whined, squinting into the candlelight. "I am painfully bound here in darkness. I, who have already suffered so much—wrongfully cast into a leper colony. Should I now be tied like an animal in darkness with neither food nor drink?"

"Of course not, my son," Petit replied. The damp stench in the cramped cellar made him swoon. "Release this man immediately," he barked at Mendel. "Bring him a basin of fresh water, and when I ring, bring him to my study."

Petit toiled back up the steps to the main floor of the yeshiva. Once in his study he smirked. *At least I saw to it that Nehemiah fulfilled the mitzvah of binding with phylacteries.* He stepped to a basin set on a black cast-iron stand, washed his hands, and tapped some water on his face. After drying his hands, he rang for the steward.

After a minute, the study door shook beneath Mendel's fist.

"Come," Petit said as he sat behind his desk.

Nehemiah slumped in the doorway, the steward behind him.

"Bring our guest a chair."

"Your *guest*?" Nehemiah sputtered. "You have bound me in darkness—"

"That was *his* doing." Petit waved an arthritic finger at Mendel. "And for this, he will be severely punished." Petit gestured toward the chair. "Here, my son. Sit with me awhile." Petit glanced at Mendel. "Bring food and drink for this man who you have so grievously wronged."

"Yes, Rabbi," Mendel said and pulled the door closed.

"I know you have suffered, my son, and I wish to see you restored to your former state. But before I can help you, you must help me."

"What do you require of me?" Nehemiah asked, rubbing his wrists. "I'll do anything."

Petit smiled as he settled back in his chair.

"When we spoke last evening, you mentioned you had been with Rabbi Samuel at Tel Hum by the Galilee. You told me he left about two months before your departure. Unfortunately, you couldn't recall his destination. Perhaps now you can . . ."

Nehemiah drew a deep breath. "If I tell you this, will you release me?"

"Not only will I release you, Nehemiah, but I will fit you out for your journey home." Petit left off speaking and waited, scarcely daring to breathe, watching Nehemiah fidget, looking him in the eyes, then looking away. Finally Nehemiah spoke.

"Rabbi Samuel is bound for Jerusalem."

"Good." Petit nodded and exhaled. "Now tell me this; I know he travels in the company of a certain Christian knight. Who is this man?"

"A Christian knight? No. Rabbi Samuel travels with one of his pupils—a tall man called Yonatan. They left Tel Hum together."

"Yonatan," Petit repeated.

"Yes. By now they're probably in Jerusalem." He shifted in the wooden chair. "Rabbi Petit, I've told you what you wished to know. When may I leave?"

"Presently, my son, presently . . ." Petit leaned back in his chair as he turned the facts over in his mind. He recalled that one of the knights of the Acre garrison, a Jonathan St. Clair, had shown a bizarre interest in Jewish studies. Indeed, Isaac had tutored this same knight. *Could it be?* He fixed his eyes on Nehemiah. "This Yonatan—did he have a scar along the left side of his head—here?"

"He did. But how could—"

Nehemiah's question was cut short as the study door opened and Mendel appeared in the doorway. The rabbi waved him forward and the steward shambled into the room carrying a tray of salt fish, bread, and tea.

"Here you are, my son. We'll breakfast together." Petit stepped to the washbasin and poured water from a pitcher on one hand and then the other. After mumbling the requisite blessings, he pulled off a piece of bread, stuffed it into his mouth, and sat down at his desk. Leaving the salt fish for Nehemiah, he took only a crust of bread and a cup of tea.

Nehemiah quickly washed and then immediately fell to eating and drinking.

Petit sat back in his chair, sipping at his tea and watching Nehemiah. "There, my son, you must be so very hungry. Please—eat, drink," he murmured, his mind racing.

So, the Knight Templar, St. Clair, masquerading as a Jew, is with Samuel in Jerusalem. This same knight has had a long association with Isaac. This connects with Isaac's treachery and his sudden departure from Acre. The three of them might actually be together in Jerusalem, hatching their plans against me. Petit smiled into his beard. *Now is my chance. As I strike at Samuel, I can, perhaps, crush Isaac as well.*

Mendel was pulling the door closed when Petit called out, "Wait!"

"Yes, Rabbi?" Mendel's shaggy head poked back through the open door.

"Go to the caravansary of the Franks and fetch me that merchant . . ." Petit plumbed his memory for the name. "Buscarel. Tell him I have another very lucrative proposition for him. Have him come to me at once. Do you understand? At once!"

The elements of Petit's plan were now clear in his mind. He leaned forward and spoke to Nehemiah. "I'm sending my steward to bring a certain Genoese merchant who will lead you to Jerusalem in comfort. You see, Nehemiah? I keep my promises. You will be arrayed in fine clothing, and return to your bride as a splendid prince. However," Petit raised his index finger, "let me further enlighten you as to the condition of your restoration."

"Condition?" Nehemiah asked as he chewed on a piece of bread.

"A very simple condition. I will entrust to the merchant who accompanies you three letters. When you arrive in Jerusalem, you will simply point out Rabbi Samuel to the merchant and your work is done. The merchant will place in your hand this scroll, signed by Rabbi Samuel, that proves your health. You will then be free to return to your bride and to the holy community of our brethren in Jerusalem."

Nehemiah rubbed his chin. "You said the merchant would have two other letters."

"You listen well, my son." A greasy smile slid across Petit's mouth. "I will compose a second scroll to be employed if you fail to identify Rabbi Samuel."

Nehemiah's eyed narrowed. "What is the purpose of the second scroll?"

"Just this—if you fail to identify Rabbi Samuel, the second scroll sends you back to the leper colony. Forever."

Nehemiah opened his mouth to speak when there was a tapping at the door.

"Who is it?" Petit shouted.

"It's me, Rabbi," Mendel's dull voice sounded from the hall beyond the door.

"Did you fetch the merchant, Buscarel?"

"No, Rabbi. I met a man." The door creaked open and Mendel's head appeared.

"Why haven't you summoned Buscarel as I instructed?"

"I met another merchant. He told me Buscarel is gone."

"Where is this other merchant?"

"At the caravansary."

"Bring him to me at once."

"What if he won't come?"

"Tell him there will be gold for him. Now, go." Petit turned back to Nehemiah, "While I arrange for your escort to Jerusalem, take the tray and come with me. I will show you to a comfortable room where you may finish eating and refresh yourself." Petit stood up. "Come."

Holding the tray, Nehemiah asked, "And what of the third scroll?"

Petit smiled. "That scroll does not concern you. Now, come."

He led Nehemiah out of the study and down the hall. Stopping at the closed door of the room that had been Isaac's, Petit drew a heavy ring of keys from a pocket of his coat. He fitted a key to the lock. "Take as much time as you need." He motioned Nehemiah into the room, pulled the door closed, and locked it.

Back at his desk, Petit readied a quill and took a sheaf of parchment. *This missive will be quick work—just a brief note sending a leper back to Tel Hum.* Once done, he blotted the ink dry and set the parchment aside.

He sat back in his chair and closed his eyes. *This next letter will be a gesture of goodwill and a baited hook.* He took a fresh sheet of parchment and began to write. Ten minutes later he was finished and readying sealing wax when Mendel's knock sounded at the door.

"I've brought the merchant, Rabbi. He's at the gate."

"Bring him in here when I ring for you," Petit called out as he blotted the documents dry. "Tell him it will only be a minute."

"Yes, Rabbi."

Petit rolled up the scrolls, made a notation on each, and sealed them. Then he rang the bell and waited, sitting up straight in his chair, his hands folded before him on the desk.

The door soon opened and a man bustled into the study. Attired in a purple robe trimmed with gold brocade, he was squat and fat, yet had an air of elegance. Removing his velvet cap, he paused at the door and curtsied with a flourish. "*Cosimo de Pise à votre service,* your Holiness!" A bright smile flashed within his black beard.

"*Asseyez-vous si'l vous plait, monsieur.*" Petit gestured at the chair. "You have some news of Buscarel?"

"Actually, there's no news of Buscarel—which is equally troubling, your Holiness—"

"Please don't call me 'your holiness,' Monsieur Cosimo. 'Rabbi' will be sufficient. Tell me, good Cosimo, what do you know of Buscarel's whereabouts?"

"There's not much to tell, Rabbi. He was last seen on the road to Safed some months ago. Since then, no trace of him."

"Is that so strange? Perhaps he stays in Damascus or some other city."

"Without anyone knowing? Not a chance. There's a steady stream of merchants—Pisan, Genoese, Venetian, Saracen—flowing back and forth between Damascus and Acre. We all compete with each other, but we look out for one another." Cosimo leaned forward. "But Rabbi—until such time as Buscarel returns—perhaps I can be of some assistance to you."

"Perhaps you can." Petit reached out his hand and placed six golden dinars on the table, the coins clinking down heavily in a neat stack.

Cosimo quickly removed his velvet cap and covered the coins. He looked at Petit and smiled. "You have my attention, Rabbi."

"Merely that you escort a certain Jew, Nehemiah, to Jerusalem."

"That's all?" Cosimo lifted the cap and peeked at the coins. "For taking this man to Jerusalem, you give me six dinars of gold?"

"Yes, and that's just the beginning, good Cosimo. Nehemiah must perform a certain task for me in Jerusalem, and you are to stay with him until he has fulfilled his obligation."

The merchant's face darkened. "How long will it take?"

"A week, a month . . ."

Cosimo lifted his cap from the table and put it on his head. "Rabbi, my time is much too valuable to sit about waiting—"

"I'll pay you an additional gold dinar for every week you're in Jerusalem, and another six when you return with proof that you have successfully discharged your mission."

"This sounds too easy."

"It *is* easy, Monsieur Cosimo."

"In that case, Rabbi, I'd be a fool to question your generosity." He swept the coins off the table into his pudgy hand.

"Indeed, Monsieur, all I require of you is to take my friend, Nehemiah, to Jerusalem along with *these.*" Petit pushed three scrolls across the desk toward Cosimo.

The merchant frowned, suspicious. "What do I do with those?"

"Each has a purpose." Petit picked up one of the scrolls and leaned back in his chair. "This one, with the name 'Nehemiah' upon it, is to be given to him after he identifies a certain Jew, Rabbi Samuel of Baghdad, and only after the rabbi is arrested. Understand?"

"Yes, but what has this rabbi done?"

"That is not your concern, Monsieur. But I will tell you this much—this scroll certifies that Nehemiah is healthy and therefore able to rejoin the Jewish community in Jerusalem. Remember, he receives this only after the rabbi is arrested." Petit picked up a second scroll. "But for the rabbi to be arrested, you must first bring this scroll to the authorities in Jerusalem. You will tell them the indictment recorded herein against Samuel also applies to two men who may be found with him—a young Jew and a Christian knight who masquerades as a Jew. See?" Petit tapped the scroll. "I've inscribed their names here on the outside of the scroll next to the seal; Samuel, Isaac, and Jonathan."

"What are the charges against these men?" Cosimo asked.

Petit smiled and said nothing.

"That is not my concern?"

"Precisely, Monsieur. Just bring this to the Mamluk authorities once Nehemiah identifies the rabbi. Who knows? The Mamluks may pay you handsomely for delivering to them a Christian spy. And when you return here to me, I shall also fatten your purse accordingly."

"What of that one?" Cosimo nodded at the third scroll.

"This one you'll give to the authorities if Nehemiah fails to identify the rabbi. See here? I've marked it with the name of a leper colony, Tel Hum." Petit placed the scroll down with the others. "Now, good merchant, repeat what I've just told you of each scroll."

Petit nodded as Cosimo correctly recited the information. Then he stood and extended his hand. "So, *mon ami,* I wish you a pleasant and profitable journey."

Cosimo took the rabbi's hand. "When do we leave?"

"Immediately, Monsieur Cosimo."

"Impossible. I must return to the caravansary to make arrangements. The earliest I can leave is tomorrow."

"Very well. But I insist you lodge here at my academy tonight. Thus, you'll be able to leave with Nehemiah at first light tomorrow morning."

"Agreed, Rabbi. I'll return later this evening. Thank you."

Once Cosimo had left, Petit brought his steward into the study. "Menahem, you and I will leave Acre tomorrow at noon. Prepare your things."

"But Rabbi, what of your pupils? What of the instructors?"

"Don't trouble yourself with things that don't concern you. Tomorrow at noon."

As Mendel pulled the door closed, Petit sat at his desk and finished his tea. *Once I'm away from here, I'll contact the emir of Jerusalem regarding the secrets of Acre's defenses. Perhaps he'll be interested to bargain for what I have to offer . . .*

Chapter Forty-One

מא

Jerusalem
30 December, 1290
Evening

Rabbi Samuel studied the carved ivory chess pieces arrayed on the mother-of-pearl inlaid board, and stroked his beard. The chessboard rested on the edge of a broad table that was otherwise covered by a large map. While Samuel studied the chessboard, al-Hasani studied the map.

The two men had worked for the past five months, seeking to unlock a hidden portal into the Temple Mount. The rabbi had used every form of gematria to extract series of numbers from the inscription on St. Clair's scroll, and al-Hasani had applied different combinations of the numbers to link a map of Jerusalem with a variety of geometric patterns. For the past week they had remained sequestered in the map room night and day, sleeping little, buoyed by the emerging image of their goal and by strong tea delivered to the room by al-Hasani's wife.

Through a window lightly veiled by damask curtains, afternoon sunlight ignited the burnished brass of intricate astrolabes, and bright dust motes sifted lazily in columns of light that fell upon shelves crowded with worn leather-bound tomes and rolls of dusty maps.

Rabbi Samuel waited for al-Hasani to apply the last series of numbers to the pattern on the map. He reached out and moved a knight in the image of St. George slaying a dragon, taking al-Hasani's bishop in the form of a dour priest flanked by two boys. He looked across the table. "Your move."

Al-Hasani made no reply. With sleeves rolled up to the elbows, he rotated a cross-staff and traced a sliver of charcoal along its edge.

The rabbi stood up and stretched. "How are you coming with the map?" he asked.

"I'm not sure . . ." al-Hasani muttered.

The rabbi looked down at St. Clair's parchment that lay spread out next to the map. Yellowed with age, its frayed edges were secured by four smooth stones. The script they had deciphered was inscribed within the larger of two triangles. Written in the archaic Hebrew characters used during the restoration from Babylon, the text included passages from several sources. Lines from the prophet Zechariah: *For I am returned unto Zion and I will dwell in the midst of Jerusalem, the holy mountain.* A second passage read: *In that day there shall be a fountain opened to the house of David.* A third passage was from the Song of Songs: *A fountain in the garden, a well of living waters that flows from Lebanon.* Then followed two words from the psalms—*S'oo zim'rah—take up the song.*

The rabbi crossed his arms. "It's your move . . ."

Al-Hasani didn't look up. He etched a curved line with his compass and made a notation on the margin. "I don't think we'll finish this match today, my friend."

Samuel leaned forward. "You have something?"

"I think so."

"Finally!" Rabbi Samuel stepped behind him and looked over his shoulder. The map of Jerusalem was crisscrossed with lines and arcs. He thought he recognized the Dome of the Rock beneath the cluttered lines. "Is this . . ." No sooner had he begun to speak than a fit of coughing wracked his body. His turban fell to the floor.

Al-Hasani turned on his stool and looked up at him, while he did his best to stifle the paroxysm. "That cough, Samuel, it worries me."

"I'm fine . . . really."

"No, you're not. Your chest is full of cracklings and whistlings. And look," al-Hasani gently took one of the rabbi's hands, "the circles of your nails are blue. Will you please let me give you that nostrum I have in the apothecary?"

"Which one? You have so many."

"The embrocation of foxglove leaves and beet greens." Al-Hasani picked up the rabbi's turban from the floor and handed it to him. "I'm certain it will have a salutary effect."

"Not now. If we're close to finding the portal, I don't want to stop." Samuel pushed the turban down on his mane of white hair, cleared his throat, and pointed at the map, "Tell me—is this the Dome of the Rock?"

"No. That's over here."

"What scale is this?"

Al-Hasani waved his charcoal-blackened fingertips over the map. "Each of these markers is a hundred paces—one tenth part of a thousand Roman paces, a standard *mille passuum.*" He looked at the rabbi. "You promise to take all the medicines I give you?"

"Yes, I promise," the rabbi snapped. "Once we're done."

"Very well." Al-Hasani sighed and placed the cross-staff over the map. "I'm ready for those other numbers now."

"Ah, yes, the gematria I had Isaac do for us is right here . . ." Samuel said as he rummaged through the pockets of the slightly undersized striped robe al-Hasani had lent him.

"Have you told Isaac about the nature of our quest?"

"Not yet. When the time comes, we'll tell him everything," Samuel replied as he searched through his pockets. "It's odd, isn't it, old friend? The two of us and that bit of scroll." He nodded toward St. Clair's parchment. "Like a rare conjunction of planets."

"A rare conjunction, indeed," al-Hasani said as he sharpened the charcoal with a small blade and blew the shavings away. "You—steeped in Kabbalah, me—a mapmaker, and the knight's scroll. We endeavor to unlock the mystery of this parchment by combining the spirit of Pythagoras with the soul of Kabbalah."

"Are those worlds indeed separate?" Samuel asked as he continued to search through his pockets. "Before Moses led our people out of Egypt, he was an architect, full of the knowledge of ancient geometry. Many believe he encoded this knowledge into the Torah and particularly into the design of the Tabernacle and the Temple. In this manner, the secrets of sacred geometry were fused into the fabric of our lives, but so subtly that they're invisible. Through Kabbalah, we're able to glimpse them—but only vaguely. Perhaps the sacred geometry of Pythagoras will allow us to see clearly. Ah—here they are." He held up a piece of parchment. "Are you ready?"

Al-Hasani nodded and brushed a stray bit of paper off the map.

Samuel slowly dictated the series of numbers as the sunlight reddened with the approach of evening. With each number, al-Hasani wielded his cross-staff, rule and compass, making lines and arcs over the map.

"I think we're there!" al-Hasani exclaimed as he took the straight-edge and made a final line across the map. He straightened up and smiled as he looked down at it. "There it is! That's the gateway!"

Rabbi Samuel leaned forward. "Where?"

"You tell me." Al-Hasani placed his hand on the rabbi's

shoulder. “If you can find it, I’ll forfeit the chess game.”

“You’ll forfeit?” Samuel frowned as he studied the map. “You’ve already lost . . .”

“All right. If you can’t find it, you’ll forfeit to me.”

“Challenge accepted.” Samuel squinted at the lines and arcs forming patterns over the map of Jerusalem. “There’s something very familiar about this. It actually reminds me of a diagram from an ancient text of Kabbalah. But knowing you disdain mysticism, I imagine you came up with this on your own . . .”

“Quite so. I’m a mapmaker and a scientist, Samuel, not a mystic. What do you see?”

“This pattern represents the manner in which the forces of the divine settled on the tabernacle in the desert wilderness.”

“That’s an odd coincidence.”

“Hardly a coincidence, I think.” Samuel pointed. “Look at these arcs forming circles superimposed over the Temple Mount. In the traditions of Kabbalah, this larger central circle represents God, and this circle below it represents the power of divine judgment—the Angel Gabriel. And this one on the other side of God represents divine blessing—the Archangel Michael.” He looked up at al-Hasani. “You’ve never seen the diagram?”

“Samuel, my life is devoted to *rational* thought. What possible interest would I have in arcane notions of Jewish mysticism?”

“There may be more mystery in the world than is dreamt of in your rational thought, my friend.” The rabbi’s hand moved over the map as his excitement grew. “In the Kabbalistic diagram, these circles representing Gabriel and Michael are flanked by double rows of smaller spheres on both sides. They represent the agents of God’s presence in the world—intermediary powers between heaven and earth—angels, if you will. Each one brings a specific attribute into the world.”

“You’re telling me I’ve diagrammed a host of angels?”

“Some, indeed, call them angels. Each of their names signifies a divine attribute, and based on their nature, each attribute is paired with another. Here, for example, the angel who hears is paired with the angel of excitement, the angel of mercy with the angel of holiness, the angel of righteousness, *Tzadki'el,* with . . ." Samuel paused and tapped the map. "That's strange—*Tzadki'el* has no partner—or the partner is hidden. It should be right here." Samuel placed his finger on the spot and looked at al-Hasani from beneath his heavy eyebrows, "This is the place, isn't it?"

Al-Hasani nodded.

Rabbi Samuel looked down at the map. "The gateway to the house of God," he whispered, then frowned. "But wait—this isn't on the Temple Mount—it's in the Kidron Valley." He looked up at al-Hasani. "Are you sure there's no mistake?"

"There's no mistake, Samuel."

The rabbi looked back at the map, his finger resting on the spot. After a long silence, he said, "I think I know this place. This is Zechariah's Tomb."

"That's correct, Samuel."

"Interesting. We saw the tomb when we first entered Jerusalem—the capstone is in the shape of a pyramid, like the larger triangle on the scroll. And two of the inscriptions within the triangle are from the Prophet Zechariah . . ."

"Everything points to it," al-Hasani said. "This is the portal."

The rabbi frowned. "But the tomb is solid rock, al-Hasani. How can there be a gateway with no opening?"

As the men studied the map, a long high note, mournful and clear, sounded from the minaret of the Great Mosque. The voice of the muezzin formed words that tolled like somber bells above the huddled houses of Jerusalem. *Allahu akbar . . . Allahu akbar.* The words floated on the cool wind in the gathering dusk.

Chapter Forty-Two

מב

Jerusalem
31 December, 1290
Morning

Zahirah sat up in bed and adjusted a white cotton blanket across her shoulders. "What do you mean, they're gone?"

"Just that. They're gone." St. Clair crossed the small room in two paces and parted the goatskin curtains that covered the single window. "Tarek saw them leave before dawn." Resting his arms on the stone casement, he looked out over the domes and spires of Jerusalem. The sun felt warm on his face and a cool wind stirred the edges of his white linen robe. Overhead, heavy clouds lowered over the city, but to the east, the morning sky was a bright blue.

"Did they say where they were going?"

"Not a word." St. Clair turned from the window and sat on the edge of the bed.

She wrinkled her nose, frowning. "Do you think it has something to do with your scroll?"

"I think it has everything to do with the scroll." He leaned forward and kissed her on the nose. Her dark auburn hair had grown back, though it was still quite short. He gently passed his hand over her head and saw how her hair flattened and rose beneath his hand, like a wind moving through a field of wheat.

"I love the feeling of your hand upon me," she said, her eyes almost closed. She took his hand, brushed his fingertips with her lips, then placed his palm against her heart. "Jonathan," she whispered. "Make me your wife."

He kissed her forehead. "In God's eyes, you are already my wife."

"Then make me your wife in the eyes of men."

"That is not so easy. Men have religions—"

"How can religions separate us when we are one in God's eyes?" Her lips curved into a smile, teasing him.

"It's complicated." He shrugged. "My vow—"

"You have broken your vow."

He rested his chin on his hands and stared at the floor. "I know."

"Do Christians not have wives?"

"I'm not merely a Christian, my love. I'm a soldier of Christ."

"Soldiers have wives." She was relentless.

He thought of trying to explain the precepts of his order, canon law and church councils, the sacramental life and obedience. But the words that rose in his mind seemed empty of any real essence—like the dry husk of a pomegranate.

"Is it not true that many priests have wives?" she persisted.

"That's all past. It's now determined that priests and men of my order can never marry."

"Determined?" She reached out and stroked his back. "I have heard that the Holy Fathers kept concubines. Are these stories not true?"

Of course the stories were true. He drew a deep breath but said nothing. The hypocrisy was undeniable. Reformers, from the great Donatus to Peter Waldo, were branded as heretics for their efforts. *And for what?* The lavish extravagance of the papal court and the sham of clerical celibacy continued to infuriate the faithful. *The woman speaks words of truth. It is good that she challenges me.*

He stared at the floor and considered all the rules of his order. *We have replaced Grace with laws. We are become like the Pharisees—Pharisees with a new set of laws.* He thought about Templars he had known who had sworn their lives to the Sepulcher and to Christ, Templars who had kept women in secret. He remembered his dead master at the Safed garrison, living a double life—the order on one hand, a Saracen woman and child on the other. And that child was now the woman he loved. He felt her caress on his back and remembered what Rabbi Samuel had said about the beauty of the Sea of Galilee, about the sweet caress of the water. He drew a deep breath and exhaled slowly, enjoying her touch.

Zahirah broke the silence. "What say you, my love?"

He rested his hand on her knee. "Your tongue is as sharp as it is sweet, my darling." Taking her hand, he pressed his lips against the soft skin of her palm. "We will speak further of this."

"When?"

"Soon." He stood up, still holding her hand. "Will you come to breakfast?"

She bent forward, folding her arms around the blanket where it tented over her knees, "I think not, Jonathan. I feel sick again this morning. But perhaps, like yesterday, I shall feel well by midday. You go."

"No, I shall remain here with you and fast. And if I fast, I must sleep." Stepping to the door, he secured the latch, then sat on the edge of the bed, and pulled off his boots. "Did not Rumi write that there is hidden sweetness in the stomach's emptiness?"

She moved to make room for him in bed. "But did he not also write that the breeze at dawn has secrets to tell you, and therefore you mustn't go back to sleep?"

"Let us listen to those secrets together, my love." He removed his robe and slipped beneath the cotton blanket next to her. Closing his eyes, he folded his arms over his chest, feigning sleep.

He knew she was lying on her side, looking at him. He felt her hand tracing his beard, trimmed short, tracing the scars over his arms and chest. She had given up asking about campaigns and battles—he would never speak of them. He felt her lips brushing the jagged track of a scar that ran down the side of his arm, and he heard her whisper, "So much pain . . ."

He turned toward her, fixing her with his blue-gray eyes. "I account it all as a blessing." He reached out and touched the arc of her neck down to the shoulder, her skin smooth and the color of burnt gold.

"You account the pain as a blessing?" she asked.

"The blessing is to have gone through a life that has led me to you."

The blanket slid off her shoulders as she drew him close.

Rabbi Samuel and al-Hasani stood among patches of dry grass in the Valley of Kidron, looking up at the Tomb of Zechariah, carved out of the western escarpment of the Mount of Olives. A cold wind moved through the skeletal branches of ancient olive trees bordering the tomb, scratching the stone with a dry whisper. Above the tomb's pyramid-shaped capstone, heavy clouds crowded the evening sky and a light rain began to fall.

Al-Hasani cinched his robe closed and drew the cowled hood over his head. "It's solid rock all around."

"I told you as much before we came." Samuel squinted up at the tall gray monolith. "Are you certain of your calculations?"

"Yes. Are you certain of the gematria?"

"There's no question. This has to be the place."

"A gateway with no opening? How is one supposed to get in?"

"Perhaps we're overlooking something."

The sky opened and the rain came harder, heavy drops smacking against the tomb.

"Come, Samuel. If we stay here any longer, we'll only succeed in getting soaked."

A frigid north wind funneled down the valley, pulling at their robes as they trudged the rocky path toward the city.

Turning his face from the cold, Samuel looked at the sloping hillside below the city wall—crowded with gravestones and tombs. Above it towered an intact section of wall and the sealed Golden Gate, the old stones stacked like rows of sepulchers.

Clutching the sodden hood over his head, his fingers felt stiff and cold. His hip hurt and a heaviness held his chest in an iron grip. It was hard to catch his breath. He leaned into the wind as he limped painfully forward, yearning to stop and rest. But there could be no rest without shelter, and there would be no shelter until they entered Jerusalem.

Reaching the tumbledown remnants of the Sheep Gate, the rabbi saw the single guard dozing in the shelter of a black goatskin tent. The rain beat down in sheets, and the guard did not stir as they passed.

A few paces past the gate, al-Hasani turned into a sheltered alcove. Samuel followed with great effort, his heart beating out of his chest, the pain worse than he had ever known it. Once out of the rain, he leaned against the limestone wall, pressing his face against the stone's cool roughness, waiting for the pain to pass.

Al-Hasani was at his side, patting him gently on the back. "I want you to take this right now, old friend."

The rabbi took the glass vial al-Hasani placed in his hand and drained it. He turned and leaned his back against the wall.

As the pain ebbed away, he slowly exhaled a white plume of breath. He pushed back the hood of his robe and wiped the rain from his eyes. The alcove opened into a terraced alley, wet cobblestones shining in the wavering light of torches set at wide intervals. Through gaps in the vaulted archway over the alley, he could see patches of gray sky. A fine rain misted down, catching the torchlight in gleaming ribbons. He closed his eyes and sighed. The pain was gone.

"Feeling better?" al-Hasani asked gently.

"Yes. What was that you gave me?"

"Tincture of *khella* and hawthorn berry. When we get home, I'll give you another."

"I'd sooner have brandy," Samuel said with a weak smile.

Mounting the broad steps of the terraced alley, they came upon a lane lined on both sides by shuttered stalls. The sound of ringing hammers echoed among the walls. A stone's throw down the lane, a swath of light marked an open stall.

"I know that place," al-Hasani said. "That's the workshop of the silversmith, Abu Rahman. We'll be able to rest there."

As they drew nearer, the ringing of the hammers grew louder. Samuel felt there was something odd about the sound, though he did not know why. The narrow shop front was only five paces across and cluttered with shining silver platters, still on display from the day's commerce. Inside, showers of sparks cascaded from dark anvils where smiths, silhouetted against a bright forge, wielded iron hammers.

Al-Hasani leaned close and shouted, "These are the apprentices of the master smith, Abu Rahman. That's him working the bellows." He pointed to a giant of a man with a heavy black beard, his face shining in the light of the forge. "Like the patron god of smiths—the very image of Hephaestus, no?" Al-Hasani raised his hand and called in greeting, *"Mas il cher, ya Abu Rahman!"*

The silversmith peered out of the light, then raised a muscular arm. *"Ahlan ya Al-Hasani!"* Striding forward, he beckoned to them. "Come, my friends. Join me for tea. Come in."

The noise of the hammers echoed in the lane.

As they entered the workshop, Samuel realized what was odd about the sound.

It wasn't noise at all, but a tapestry of consummate harmony. It was flawless music. It was perfection.

Chapter Forty-Three

מג

Jerusalem
31 December, 1290
Late evening

Isaac and Wallace hurried across the broad precincts of the Temple enclosure in driving rain, making for the shelter of the Dome of the Rock. The paving stones were slick, wet with rain and scoured smooth by centuries of pilgrims' feet.

As Isaac threaded a path between the puddles in the shallow hollows of the smooth stones, he glanced up. Wallace was already in the shelter of the shrine, having covered the distance quickly with his long strides. The dome of the shrine was a dull gray beneath the darker gray of heavy clouds, and along the western horizon, there was a band of clear sky beneath the clouds where the setting sun stood like a scarlet sentinel over the hill country of Judea.

Isaac lowered his head and pelted forward. Reaching the shrine, he flattened himself against the wall of blue tiles, smooth and cool to his touch. Trying to catch his breath, he turned to Wallace. "I thought the dome was covered in gold leaf."

"Not for many years," Wallace replied. "The ravages of war and the greed of sultans stripped all the gold away."

Isaac looked out from beneath the dripping hood of his robe

at the rain falling on the city of crowded domes and minarets. "God certainly answers prayer—we've petitioned for wind and rain since autumn . . ."

Wallace smiled, flashing white teeth in the dusk. "In Scotland, we receive such blessings throughout the year." He paused, then said, "Tell me, Isaac, over the past months we've visited sites throughout Jerusalem—why was al-Hasani so surprised when he heard you were coming *here*?"

"Because he knows it is forbidden for Jews to venture upon the Temple Mount, lest they tread upon the place where the Ark of the Covenant stood in the Holy of Holies—the foundation stone in the sacred heart of the Temple."

"Doesn't that prohibition apply to you?"

"The prohibition was created because the exact spot of the foundation stone is unknown. The rabbis, therefore, prohibited Jews to go *anywhere* on the Temple Mount. They created restrictions to restrictions—we call this 'making fences around the Torah.' It's a way to make certain no one might transgress and desecrate the spot—*wherever* it actually is—"

"But aren't *you* worried about desecrating the spot?"

Isaac shrugged. "I may not know *exactly* where it is, but I know the only two possible sites. That's one over there." He raised his hand and pointed in the direction of a small cupola, a stone's throw away. "The Dome of the Tablets and Spirits."

"And the other?"

"Come. I'll show you."

Isaac led the way around the shrine to a high arched doorway bordered in flourishes of Arabic calligraphy. They stepped into a curved ambulatory, the air dark and close about them, smelling of old stone and mildew. Passing beneath a low archway, they entered a circular nave, lit by weak lamps. Thick carpets cushioned their steps. Beyond a decorative partition, they saw a rough expanse of stone in the lamplight, shining like a frozen sea.

"There it is," Isaac said in a barely audible whisper. "That's the other possible foundation stone . . ."

William's eyes were wide. "The center of the world—the omphalos connecting heaven and earth."

"Some hold to that belief. Either this rock or the one beneath the small dome."

"But you've never been here before, Isaac—how do you know these things?"

"Travelers' accounts and Talmud. Mostly Talmud. But the allusions are subtle."

Wallace stepped forward, then hesitated and turned back to Isaac. "You're not coming, are you?"

"Of course not. I'll wait here. You go."

Wallace turned and disappeared into the darkness.

Isaac squatted in the shadows, waiting.

"Welcome!" the silversmith exclaimed and led the way into the workshop.

"Thank you, esteemed Abu Rahman," al-Hasani said. "We were caught by the foul weather and wish to warm ourselves by your fire."

"You are most welcome, my friends! Let me help you out of those wet robes. They'll dry by the hearth in no time."

Al-Hasani handed his robe to the silversmith and gestured toward Rabbi Samuel. "Allow me to introduce my cousin, the worthy Saleh ibn Ali Bakr."

Samuel bowed his head and with his right hand touched his chest, lips, and forehead in the manner of the Moslems. "May Allah preserve the venerable Abu Rahman whose artistry is renowned even unto the eastern lands between the great rivers."

The silversmith returned the salute. "And may Allah smile

upon the esteemed and distinguished kinsman of my learned friend, who is thus my friend also. Warm yourselves by the forge, and allow me to offer you some refreshment."

The hammers of the apprentices rang out their harmony as the old men followed the silversmith toward the bright warmth of the forge in the back of the workshop.

Abu Rahman spoke to one of the apprentices. "Here you, mind the fire!"

The boy sprang to the task and the bellows breathed life into the forge, filling the shop with warmth and light. The silversmith drew chairs around a small table. "Sit here, noble sirs, and rest yourselves. Abdul!" he shouted to another apprentice. "Bring tea!"

Rabbi Samuel eased into one of the chairs, grateful for the opportunity to rest. The lighter striped cotton djellabah he wore beneath his woolen robe was fairly dry.

Taking the chair next to Samuel, al-Hasani held his hands out to the fire, rubbing them together. "This is better, no?" He nodded toward the apprentices. "Do you like the sound of their work?"

"I wanted to ask about that," said the rabbi. "It's not at all the noise of a workshop. It sounds more like music."

"That's your cousin's doing!" Abu Rahman patted al-Hasani on the shoulder, then pulled up a chair and sat down.

"How so, *cousin*?" The rabbi smiled. "I never knew you to be a musician."

"Musicians measure their craft in time, just as mapmakers measure space. So it was when I passed this shop a few years ago; I heard the noise of the smiths working, and I recalled a story told of the great Pythagoras. According to the tale, he once passed a smith's shop in Samos and heard the sound of hammering—the noise was dissonant and grating, just as it was here. It is said that Pythagoras entered the shop, gathered the smiths' hammers, and weighed them. He then had the smiths switch hammers and found that the tone of each hammer was determined by its weight, not by the strength of the smith. With this knowledge, he hung hammers of different weights upon strings of cat gut and found that different weights created different tones of the string when plucked—the greater the weight, the more taut the string. By making measured changes in weight, he found proportional changes in tone. He then determined which proportions were harmonious, and used these proportions to make hammers of specific weights which were in harmony."

"Thus did the venerable al-Hasani do with our shop," Abu Rahman cut in, gesturing with a blackened hand. "By adjusting the weights of my apprentices' hammers, he transformed noise into music. Amazing, no?"

The rabbi held his hands out to the fire. "I have heard of the wisdom of Pythagoras and his knowledge of sacred proportions. This knowledge spreads through the world like ripples through quiet water. The revered mathematician al-Kindi is said to have brought this wisdom to Baghdad and then, by the trade routes, it reached even to the furthest east where the Mongols have also become enlightened."

"I'm impressed, cousin," al-Hasani said, patting the rabbi's knee. "I did not know you had knowledge of such matters."

Samuel canted his head to the side and smiled. "I actually heard all this from you, years ago, during one of our long dinners at that teahouse by the Tigris."

Turning to the silversmith, al-Hasani explained. "When we lived in Baghdad, my cousin and I spent many a night till dawn in ecstatic conversation and eating . . ."

"Indeed," Samuel interjected. "You spoke endlessly—"

"And you ate endlessly," al-Hasani shot back.

Laughing, the rabbi stretched out his fingers, studying them against the light of the forge. "You told me how this harmony is embedded throughout the world, from the bones of our hands to the spiraling symmetry of a seashell—sacred proportions, you called them—the connection between sacred geometry and sacred music." The rabbi looked at al-Hasani, his eyes shining in the light. "I've never forgotten those nights. I've never forgotten those conversations."

"Nor have I," said al-Hasani.

The apprentice arrived with tea. "Here you are, my masters." Fragrant steam rose from three small cups.

"Well done, lad. Now, back to work." Lifting a cup, Abu Rahman declared, "To your health, noble guests!" He took a sip and placed his cup down. "So, the venerable al-Hasani gave my apprentices hammers of specific measure and created this music!"

"The thanks to you, Abu Rahman. You were enlightened enough to allow me to do this, though it interrupted the work of your shop for some days."

"You thank me? You took away noise and gave me music! For this I am forever in your debt."

"It is, indeed, pleasing to the ear," said the rabbi. "This resonance gives evidence of a sacred order that fills the universe—the perfect intention of the Mind of God."

"The architecture of many great mosques also reflects this perfect resonance," al-Hasani added. "The grand design of the Master Builder."

"So is it, also, even among the infidel Christians and Jews," said the rabbi as he lifted his cup. "In my travels I have witnessed this harmony in the churches and synagogues of many lands."

"Yes," Abu Rahman agreed. "These truths exist throughout the world. Indeed, the Temple of Solomon was crafted with these very principles, brought by Moses from Egypt."

"You are right, *ya* Abu Rahman," al-Hasani said. "The sacred geometry of Pythagoras is seen in all the world—from the pyramids in Egypt to the harmony of the hammers here in your shop." Al-Hasani finished his tea, and placing the cup down with a flourish, exclaimed, "*Daim'e!*—may our friendship always remain thus!"

"*Aa'mar!*" the rabbi added, setting down his cup. "But tell me, Abu Rahman, why do you work so late? All the other shops are shuttered and dark—"

"We strive to finish a large order for the emir of Jerusalem. He wishes to present rich gifts to al-Ashraf Khalil before he journeys north to lay siege to Acre."

"Why does his father, the Sultan Qa'la'un, not himself lead the final march upon the Franks?"

"You didn't know?" al-Hasani asked. "The Sultan Qa'la'un is dead—murdered months ago."

"Murdered?" Samuel asked, shocked he hadn't heard the news.

Abu Rahman leaned close. "It is widely known that Emir Abdullah of Safed did this wicked thing. But now, all praise to Allah, he is dead—killed in revenge by al-Ashraf Khalil."

"The Emir Abdullah of Safed is dead?" Samuel's heart was pounding in his chest.

"Yes—killed by al-Ashraf Khalil—months ago," Abu Rahman repeated, "along with other traitors and conspirators."

Samuel was overwhelmed. *The Emir of Safed dead! Jonathan and I are safe!* He heard Abu Rahman continuing to speak.

". . . to show his loyalty to the new sultan, my patron, the Emir of Jerusalem, has commissioned fine gifts. I've nearly finished the new sultan's sword and shield—a most exquisite marriage of silver and steel. Do you wish to see them?"

"Please," al-Hasani said. "Show us your artistry."

As Abu Rahman stepped away, Rabbi Samuel leaned back against the wall. Relieved to hear of Abdullah's death, he closed his eyes and listened to the music of the hammers, the perfect proportions of the hammers' song. Words from St. Clair's scroll rose in his mind: *S'oo zimrah, take up the song.*

Suddenly, the connection was clear. "I think I understand!" The rabbi sat forward and put his hand on al-Hasani's arm. "We must return to the map workshop at once."

"Certainly. In a few minutes . . ."

"No. We must go now!" The rabbi took their robes where they hung drying by the hearth. "Let us bid our host goodbye and away with all haste. We have work to do."

Abu Rahman was just returning to the table with the sword and shield in burlap sacks. "What is this, my masters? You're leaving?"

"An urgent matter has just come to our attention," al-Hasani said as he helped Samuel with his robe. "We thank you for your hospitality, and we'll soon return to view your handiwork."

"The music of your workshop has been an inspiration," the rabbi added.

Chapter Forty-Four

מד

Jerusalem
31 December, 1290
Late evening

When Wallace emerged from the nave, he saw Isaac still crouched in the shadows of the ambulatory. He sat on the rug next to Isaac. "I wish you could have been there with me!"

"What was it like?"

"Wondrous! After a few paces, I came to a balustrade with a wrought-iron screen, put there to keep pilgrims from chipping away pieces of the rock to take home. I circled around and came to a gateway, which was open. Once inside, the rock was right there. I just reached out and touched it."

"How did it feel?"

"Like a rock—rough, cool to the touch—but just knowing that *this* was Mount Moriah—where Abraham offered Isaac for sacrifice, perhaps the very spot where the Ark of the Covenant once rested . . ." He leaned back. "I walked all about it and came to some stone steps that led down into a little cave." Wallace turned to Isaac, his eyes shining. "A cave beneath the rock!"

"What did you see there?"

"Nothing at first. It was murky and smelled of old wax and

incense. But once my eyes grew accustomed to the darkness, I found a round stone set in the floor. I was able to move it away, though it was quite heavy. Beneath it, there was another chamber! I went down into it but there was no light and I had no torch." He shook his head as he stood up. "Next time, I'll bring one. Who knows? Perhaps I'll find a passage to the very chamber where King Hezekiah hid the Ark before the Temple was plundered by the Babylonians."

Isaac sighed as he got to his feet. "How I wish I could have been with you! I've heard of that cave and the passage. Some believe it leads to a treasure chamber. Others contend it's nothing more than a system of aquifers carved in the rock to drain away the blood from Temple sacrifices . . ."

Wallace and Isaac stepped from the Dome of the Rock to find the Temple courtyard bright with torchlight and filled with worshippers streaming out of al-Aqsa Mosque. The rain had stopped and the crowd was in high spirits, joining responsively in a boisterous chant as they moved toward the northern edge of the sacred precincts beneath the dripping branches of spreading pine trees.

In their gray Mamluk robes, the boys blended into the throng, descending into the lower city through well-lit alleys washed clean by the rain. They ducked into a teahouse hung with bright lanterns. The air was filled with laughter, shouted salutations, and the rattle of dice.

Isaac led the way among the crowded tables, searching for an empty one through the fragrant haze of tobacco smoke. Seeing none, he led them to a side door and stepped out to a patio where a few tables were set in the open air along the side of the shop beneath a striped canopy.

"I'd rather be away from all that noise and smoke anyway," Wallace said and settled into a chair.

"It will go on like this 'til the third watch of the night."

After a minute a thin boy not older than ten appeared at the table clutching a large round tray in his hands. He wore a fancy embroidered vest over a tattered robe. He was barefoot and sported an oversized tasseled cap.

"Masa'a al khir, ya sa'da," he said solemnly.

Isaac ordered tea and two slices of honey cake. Once the boy was gone he noticed two men sitting at a nearby table.

How odd, those two—they sit together and yet seem so different from each other. One was squat and fat, a bright smile flashing within his heavy black beard. In his attire—a broad purple cap and matching robe trimmed with gold brocade—Isaac recognized the gaudy clothing of an Italian merchant. His tall companion, half-hidden within a hooded robe, seemed watchful and furtive, scanning the crowd as if looking for someone, but not wanting to be seen. The two whispered together with thinly veiled intensity.

Wallace also noticed the pair. "What's with those two?" he asked in a low voice.

Isaac strained to overhear their animated conversation. As he watched out of the corner of his eye, the fat one slipped a flask from his robes and discreetly tilted it to his lips.

Then the conversation apparently flared as the tall one raised his voice. "Stop asking me, already! I'll tell you when I see him—"

"Don't you use that tone with me, my friend!" the merchant shot back. "Don't forget, I hold your fate in my hands."

Isaac noticed the merchant's Arabic was accented with the inflection of one of the Italian states, probably Pisa. He saw the Pisan sneak another sip from his flask.

"What are they saying?" whispered Wallace.

Isaac raised his hand, straining to hear.

"You need to look about, that's what you need to do," the

Pisan declared as he stuck the flask back inside his robes.

"You know I'm trying," the tall one replied. "I'll tell you straightaway when I see the rabbi."

The rabbi? Isaac's blood froze in his veins.

"Well," the fat one said, laughing without mirth, "you better hope you see him soon, or you'll never see that bride of yours again."

"You don't need to remind me of that—"

"I suppose I also don't need to remind you that we've been in Jerusalem over *four months*!"

"What do you care? You're being paid well enough—"

"I have a business to attend to in Acre! I'll give you one more week." He raised a sausage-like finger. "One week and then I leave you to your fate. It's no matter to me, my friend. I'll be back in Acre collecting my gold. That's where I'll be. Where will *you* be? In the arms of your bride? Or rotting away in a leper colony? It's your choice."

"My choice? What more do you want me to do? I've asked every shopkeeper in the city a dozen times."

"You haven't asked among the Jews."

"You know I can't! How many times do I need to tell you? They still regard me as unclean. Give me the scroll that clears me, and I'll be able to search among the Jews."

"Oh, you'd like that, wouldn't you? I give you the scroll, and you disappear. I don't think so. But if *you* can't ask among the Jews, then *I* will. You leave that to me." The merchant took another sip from his flask, then wiped his mouth with the back of a pudgy hand. "You see? I'm not such a bad person. During this final week in Jerusalem, I'll help you out."

The merchant left off speaking as the serving boy emerged from the shop, balancing a tray loaded with cups and plates. He approached the table of the two strangers and set down two cups and a double piece of *baklava* for the fat Pisan. Then the boy stepped to the table where Isaac and Wallace sat. Extending a thin arm, he set out a teapot, two porcelain cups, and a small plate with two thick slices of honey cake. Isaac tossed a few copper coins on the tray.

At the other table, the tall man had pushed back the hood of his robe to reveal a short red beard and a scarlet discoloration on his cheek. As the man glanced his way, Isaac leaned forward and took a bite of his cake. From the corner of his eye he watched the merchant finish his tea, then refill the cup from his flask.

The merchant reached across the table and gave the tall man a gentle slap on the shoulder. "Cheer up! We'll find him!" Then he attacked the *baklava* with both hands, quickly finishing the sweet pastry. Licking honey from his fingers, he added, "Like I told you, the old man keeps company with a renegade knight. That should make them easy to find—a pair like that. Relax!" He winked. "You'll soon be back with that little wife of yours."

Chapter Forty-Five

מה

Jerusalem
31 December, 1290
Night

Rabbi Samuel stood in the map room, leaning on the table, staring at St. Clair's scroll. The candles wavered as al-Hasani entered and pulled the door closed.

"Any ideas?" he asked hopefully.

The rabbi made no reply.

"At the shop of the silversmith, you seemed so certain—"

"I was. Isaac and I have done every type of gematria that exists. I don't know what other numbers I can come up with."

"What are you looking for?"

"I'm not sure, but I'll know when I see it."

One of the candles guttered and went out, leaving a trail of black smoke twisting in the air above the table. Al-Hasani relit the candle and peered over the rabbi's shoulder. "Why are those letters larger than the others?"

"Which letters?"

Al-Hasani pointed. "These three. They're slightly larger than the rest."

The rabbi squinted at the scroll. "I do believe you're right. That's odd."

"Is it significant?"

"Everything is . . ." Succumbing to a fit of coughing, the rabbi tried to stifle the paroxysm and managed to blurt out, "Everything . . . is significant."

"That's it! No more excuses!" al-Hasani exclaimed as he opened the door and stepped out of the study. "I'm going to fetch those nostrums for you right now."

Once his coughing subsided, the rabbi leaned over the table, staring at the scroll. He looked up when al-Hasani returned to the map room. "You're right about these three letters—they're clearly larger. I can't believe I missed that."

"Do you know what it might mean?"

"I think I do. Here, I'll show you—"

"First, some refreshments." Al-Hasani raised three shiny glass vials and handed one to Samuel.

Rotating the vial in his hand, the rabbi saw it held a green liquid. "What's this?"

"Essence of foxglove leaf. I'm going to prepare doses for you to take each morning and evening. And you'll take them, just as you promised. Go ahead, drink."

Samuel threw his head back and drained the vial. He grimaced and handed it back empty.

The mapmaker held out a second vial. "Now some khella and hawthorn berry—to avoid any more discomfort of the chest."

The rabbi, muttering under his breath, took the vial and drank.

Al-Hasani held out the last vial.

"Is this really necessary?" the rabbi snapped. "I'm breathing easily now."

"It's not your breathing that worries me, Samuel, it's your heart."

"What's my heart got to do with it?"

"I believe dropsy is primarily a question of the heart. This will help—a tincture of parsley root and dandelion leaf."

"I've had that before," the rabbi said, taking the vial in his hand.

"I want you to take it four times a day."

"I can't do that." Samuel frowned. "I'll be up all night making water."

"All right, three times a day. But tonight we'll be up anyhow, so drink." His eyes narrowed as Samuel hesitated. "Now."

Samuel downed the vial. "Can we please get back to work?" He pointed at the scroll. "The three letters you noticed form a triangle. At its apex is a *kav.* This one down here is a *het* and over here at the other corner of the triangle is a *bet.*"

"What does it mean?"

Samuel waved his hand over the scroll. "The arrangement resembles another Kabbalistic diagram—the manner in which God descends and dwells among us. Based on their arrangement, these three letters seem to be the initials of three divine attributes. The *kav* stands for *keter*—crown, the *het* for *hohma*—wisdom, and the *bet* for *beenah*—understanding. Please, old friend, take ink and inscribe the numbers I will tell you." Calculating quickly, he rattled off a few sets of numbers based on several different systems of gematria.

"Do you believe this will change the location of the portal?"

"No. I believe this will unlock the portal."

"What?" Al-Hasani frowned. "How?"

"I think it has something to do with the last two words on the scroll—*take up the song.*"

"The key involves music?"

"Possibly. As I listened to the harmony of the hammers at the silverworks of Abu Rahman, I was struck with the idea that there may be a connection between that music, this scroll, and the sacred geometry of Pythagoras. These three letters might be that connection. They might provide the key. And by using this key, perhaps we'll open a portal into the tomb—"

"What are you saying? It's solid rock! You said so yourself. There's no portal there."

"So it is—solid rock." Samuel clasped his hands behind his back and stepped to the window. Through the open casements, he could see a few bright stars shining through gaps in the canopy of clouds. He inhaled deeply, tasting the cool night air—like clear wine and pine-scented. "During one of our long dinners at that café by the Tigris, you told me another story about Pythagoras—about how he demonstrated the nature of matter to his disciples. He lifted a stone from the ground and said, *this is frozen music.*" Samuel turned from the window. "An interesting notion—the stone is frozen music. Do you remember?"

"Of course I remember, but what's the relevance?"

"I want you to take these numbers and do with them as you did with Abu Rahman's hammers." Rabbi Samuel stepped to the table and pointed. "These can be looked upon as proportions, correct? I want you to find sets of three notes using these proportions that we might use to open the gateway."

"Have you gone mad?" al-Hasani snapped. "Are you insinuating that the solid stone of the tomb can somehow melt away and present a doorway? Besides," he jabbed a finger at the scroll, "this diagram is nothing more than allegory—"

"This is no allegory!" the rabbi shot back. "Those of us who study Kabbalah don't look upon this *as if.* We believe God was actually present within the desert tabernacle, and later, within the Temple, and right now, here with us."

Al-Hasani rolled his eyes. "Samuel, you know I love and respect you. But what you *believe* is of no consequence. When Pythagoras uttered those words—*that stone is frozen music*—he wasn't speaking literally. He was merely pointing out that rock is, in essence, a perfect geometric arrangement of crystals."

"Are you so certain he was speaking metaphorically?"

"Samuel, I'm a practical man, and I don't believe the earth melted away beneath Korah any more than I believe Mohammed ascended to heaven by jumping off the foundation stone."

"Wasn't he on a horse?"

"With or without the horse—stories that defy natural law lie beyond the realm of science. Such notions may be interesting metaphors, but they're of no consequence to a man of science!"

"Then of what consequence is sacred geometry?"

"Sacred geometry is a language of shapes, numbers, and angles—relationships based on the qualities of the circle and the triangle, the sphere and the pyramid—the inner workings of nature. Sacred geometry *orders* the natural world. It does not operate outside of nature. Sacred geometry obeys natural law—"

"And who interprets natural law? You?"

"Why not me? I am a man of science. I don't claim to understand the totality of creation, Samuel, but I know the difference between fact and fantasy."

"Do you? On one hand, you state that you are a master of sacred geometry, and this is a blueprint of creation—the inherent order that pervades the known universe."

"Yes . . ." al-Hasani replied carefully.

"And does this order not extend to the boundaries of your knowledge?"

"Yes, but where are you going with this?"

"Why do you stop looking at that point?"

"At which point?"

"At the point where you are forced to turn your face from what you know, to what you do not know—at the furthest edge of your knowledge—when you stand on the threshold of that darkness, why do you look away?"

"Because that is a realm of idle speculation! I pursue knowledge based on fact, Samuel, not a hunch. The tree of knowledge must be bathed in light lest it wither. That dark land of which you speak is barren."

"Barren? In the dark gestation of the womb there is no light, yet a world of promise. *That* is the fertile darkness of which I speak."

"Bah! The Greek mystery school strayed into that darkness and never emerged."

"I cannot speak for them, al-Hasani, but *this* I can tell you. In the half-light of Kabbalah, we bring together the physical creation with the spiritual essence behind it. We seek the meeting place between the seen and the unseen, the manifest and the unmanifest, the finite and the infinite—the point where one kind of knowledge ends and another kind of knowledge begins. How else can we move from what we are to what we are not? How else can one be born into a new knowledge, if not as a fetus that moves in the darkness toward the light? And in this quickening, we experience the divine in every aspect of creation. As it's written in the psalm, *Ve'laila ke'yom ya'ear*—for night shines as the day, and darkness is as light."

"That's an abstraction—mere words!" al-Hasani lashed back.

"For me it's *not* an abstraction! I believe creation extends beyond the limits of our senses, and beyond the limits of your knowledge. Why is that dark realm any less real simply because of our own limitations?"

"Because that's all I have!" al-Hasani shouted. "I cannot hope to comprehend that which is beyond comprehension."

"Yet we must *try*. For us there is only the trying." The rabbi gestured toward the table where the scrolls and maps were spread. "Come, my friend, let us venture into that darkness."

"No, Samuel. I cannot go there . . ."

"But I can," the rabbi whispered and laid his hand on al-Hasani's shoulder. "You leave that part to me, old friend. Just help me unlock the door."

Chapter Forty-Six

מו

Jerusalem
1 January, 1291
Before dawn

Zahirah awoke in the cold darkness with a wonderful and terrible knowledge. She reached out to St. Clair with a pounding heart, but the pillow where his head had rested was cold. She sat up, clutching the blanket around her shoulders with one hand, searching the bed blindly with the other.

"Jonathan?" she whispered, suddenly afraid.

"What is it, my love?" St. Clair asked, his voice a beacon of comfort.

She had forgotten that he sometimes left her bed and slept on the floor. He claimed it was a habit, after years of campaigning in the field. She suspected it was something else—perhaps guilt over being too comfortable and too close to her. But she wanted him close to her now.

"Come back to bed, Jonathan. I would speak with you."

"How can I refuse such an invitation?"

She heard him stirring, and now she felt him, warm and strong, next to her beneath the cotton blanket. She put her arms around him. "I am so filled with love for you!" she whispered.

"And I for you." He encircled her body with his arms.

She thrilled at his gentle power, drawing her close, the roughness of his hands on her skin. "When I say I am filled with love for you, I speak of more than the feeling of love."

"Is love not sufficient?"

"Aye, it is sufficient. But it is more than a feeling that fills me." She took his hand and placed it against her belly.

"Do I understand you aright, my lady?" He bent his head down, searching the darkness for her face, kissing her forehead, then her nose. "Is this some glad news?"

"Yes, my love." Lifting her face to his, her breath caught as she felt his mouth on her lips. "Yes, yes."

Al-Hasani opened his workshop door to find Isaac and Wallace sleeping on the floor in the hallway. "What's this?" he asked as he lifted his lamp.

Rabbi Samuel looked over al-Hasani's shoulder. "I thought you made them a pallet by the fire."

"I did." The mapmaker bent down and gently shook Isaac's shoulder. "Wake up, lad. Wake up!"

Isaac stirred and sat up. "Is it morning?" Next to him, Wallace, wrapped in his robe, snored quietly.

"No. It's but the third watch of the night. You and your friend shouldn't lie in this freezing corridor. Come by the fire in the main hall."

"I'm sorry, sir. But Tarek told us you weren't to be disturbed."

"Thank you for not disturbing us, but why are you sleeping on the floor?"

Isaac rubbed his face with his hands and forced his eyes open. "I must speak with Rabbi Samuel—"

"I'm right here. What is it?" Samuel crouched down next to Isaac. "Do you have more gematria for me?"

"No, Rabbi. I finished all the text you gave me yesterday. Did I do well?"

"Yes, Isaac, very well."

"I must speak with you now on a matter of great urgency." Isaac paused, glancing from Samuel to al-Hasani. *"De'vareem rak le'oz'necha rabee,"* he whispered, switching from Arabic to Hebrew. "Words only for your ears."

"Nah'noo ih'wa." Samuel straightened up and rested his hand on the mapmaker's shoulder, turning the conversation back to Arabic. "Al-Hasani and I are as brothers. Whatever you have to say to me, may be spoken in his hearing."

Al-Hasani raised his lantern. "But must we remain here shivering in the cold? Wake up William and let's to the hearth where there is warmth and light." He led the way down the corridor into the main hall. "Come. I made a pallet for you by the fire."

In the main hall, the men settled on cushions, their faces illuminated by the red glow of the hearth. Wallace, barely awake, went back to sleep by the fire. Al-Hasani hung a copper pot of water to boil.

The rabbi looked at Isaac, "What is it, my son?"

"William and I went to a teahouse last night—we heard two men talking together—a Pisan merchant and a Jew. They spoke of seeking after a rabbi. I'm certain they spoke of you. And they also mentioned a knight who travels with you—"

"What's this about?" al-Hasani asked as he sat on a cushion by the hearth.

"A certain rabbi in Acre—" Samuel began.

"What are you all doing up so early?" St. Clair's voice cut in, calling down from the darkness of a second-floor balcony.

"Ta'al huna!" Samuel called back. "This concerns you, Jonathan." He looked back at al-Hasani. "There's a certain rabbi in Acre with whom we've had a bitter dispute over the great Mai-

monides, he who you call Abu Amran. Along with most other rabbis of the Levant, I am on the side of Maimonides. Solomon Petit of Acre is on the other side. But he so vehemently opposes the teachings of Maimonides that he burns his manuscripts and sends his proxies to vandalize Maimonides' tomb. Because of this, it fell to me, as Baghdad Gaon, to discipline the man. Since he has refused to desist from his attacks, I had no choice but to issue a writ of excommunication."

"Which is why he sent these men to Jerusalem," al-Hasani said as he checked the water in the pot. "To stop you."

"No, to kill me—"

"They said nothing of killing, Rabbi," Isaac cut in. "They only spoke of finding you."

"Trust me." Samuel glanced at Isaac. "It is even so. To this end, Petit made an unholy alliance with the Emir of Safed—to have me killed."

"But the silversmith told us the Emir of Safed is dead," al-Hasani said as he spooned black tea leaves from a clay jar into the boiling water. "Doesn't that change anything?"

"Apparently not. Petit has evidently enlisted others for the same purpose—"

"What's this about, then?" St. Clair asked as he descended the staircase, his face illuminated by the stub of a lighted candle in his hand.

Rabbi Samuel raised his eyes. "Petit has sent men to find me, Jonathan."

St. Clair crouched in his long nightshirt by the fire. "I was afraid of this. How many?"

"I saw two," Isaac answered. "A Pisan merchant and a Jew."

"How do you know he's a Jew?"

"From parts of the conversation I overheard."

"What manner of man was he?"

Isaac raised his shoulders. "Of early middle age, tall."

"Anything else?" St. Clair prodded.

Isaac thought for a moment, then waved his hand over the side of his face. "He had a reddish mark here, on the left half of his face—"

"Nehemiah," St. Clair whispered through clenched teeth.

Samuel drew a deep breath. "Petit must have stopped him before he had the chance to deliver my writ to Midrash Hagadol."

"And before he conveyed my report to the commandery." St. Clair's mouth twisted into a snarl as he paced. "And with Nehemiah hanging about in Jerusalem, it's only a matter of time before he sees us." He stopped and shot a look at Isaac. "He hasn't seen us yet, has he?"

"No, sir," Isaac replied quickly. "And there's this—the merchant said something about Nehemiah only having one more week to find you. After that, the merchant leaves for Acre."

"Excellent!" al-Hasani said brightly as he stirred the tea. "You only have to lay low for a week, then the merchant's gone."

"The merchant is of little consequence," St. Clair said. "Nehemiah is the problem. The churl knows us, and he'll likely remain in Jerusalem—this is his home. As long as he's about, the danger to the rabbi abides."

"Neither Nehemiah nor the merchant will dictate what I do," Rabbi Samuel snapped. "I can't stay cooped up even *one* day in hiding. We must go back to the tomb before sunrise *today.*"

"The tomb?" St. Clair asked. "What tomb?"

"The Tomb of Zechariah in the Kidron Valley," the rabbi explained. "It's the one with the pyramid-shaped capstone. Do you recall it?"

"Yes. But why expose yourself to Petit's villainy just to make a pilgrimage to some tomb?"

"This is not a pilgrimage to *some tomb,* Jonathan."

St. Clair fixed his eyes on the rabbi. "Does this have

something to do with my scroll?"

"Yes, but the full significance is not yet clear. Which is why we must go there at sunrise. We must know for certain." He took a breath and added, "You're a part of this, Jonathan. Your scroll guided our every step."

St. Clair nodded, feeling the full weight of the rabbi's words. "Granted," he said, looking down at the rabbi. "But why not wait a week, until the danger is less?"

"Two reasons, Jonathan. The first is that my health fails. Despite the able ministrations of my friend and physician, al-Hasani, I don't know how much more time I have left . . ."

The color left St. Clair's face. He stepped to the mapmaker who stood by the glowing hearth, tending the tea. "Is this so?" he asked.

Al-Hasani sighed. "If my hopes and my nostrums were all that mattered, Samuel would live to one hundred and twenty. But . . ." he raised his shoulders and left off speaking.

"I can't afford to waste a single day or even a single hour," the rabbi said. "But there's another reason, Jonathan. We must finish our business in Jerusalem because of you."

"Because of me?"

"You're the reason we came here."

"Me?" St. Clair stuck his face forward, striking his fist against his chest as one doing penance. "No, Rabbi. It's the scroll. You said so yourself. I just happened to possess it."

"Do you really believe you just *happened* to possess the scroll, Jonathan? Do you believe your having the scroll is mere coincidence?" The rabbi's face was suffused with color as he jabbed a finger at St. Clair, his voice rising. "It was no *coincidence* that the scroll came to your forebears in Petra of the Nabateans. It was no *coincidence* that it found its way to you through seven generations. It was no *coincidence* that you were drawn to the academy of Rabbi Joseph in Safed, and it was no *coincidence* that you were the only Templar to survive the slaughter of your garrison." The rabbi planted himself in front of St. Clair and put his hands on the knight's shoulders. "Jonathan, it's no coincidence that you and I are here—now and in Jerusalem. I tell you that at the root of all coincidence is the hand of God. *You* are the steward of the scroll, Jonathan, and you *must* share in its secrets. You *must* be part of this."

"Then *make* me a part of this!" St. Clair shouted, grasping the rabbi's shoulders. "Reveal to me what you know!"

"You're right. Come with me."

"Come with you? Where?"

"For the present, what I have to say is for your ears only." The rabbi lifted a lighted lamp from the floor and turned toward the stairs leading to the upper floors. "Bring blankets."

Chapter Forty-Seven

מז

Jerusalem
1 January, 1291
Before dawn

The rabbi paused on the second-floor landing to catch his breath.

"Why the blankets?" St. Clair asked.

"We're going up to the roof to talk." The rabbi raised his lantern and disappeared into the dark maw of a hooded alcove.

St. Clair followed, gray blankets draped over his arm. Lamplight flickered on walls of flaking white chalk and rough-hewn steps that ended at a closed door of weathered wood.

Rabbi Samuel grasped the latch and pushed. "It's stuck," he said, and stepped aside. "You try."

St. Clair put his shoulder against the door and it creaked open, scraping upon the jamb. Through his nightshirt, he felt the rush of chill night air on his skin. He stepped out upon a flat stone roof. There was no moon and the open sky was crowded with stars.

The rabbi walked forward, the lamplight illuminating crenellated battlements of the city wall bordering the roof on one side. St. Clair could see regularly spaced embrasures that narrowed into arrow slits. On the other side, toward the city, the roof sloped away into darkness.

The rabbi placed the lantern at his feet and settled into one of the embrasures. "Come and sit with me, Jonathan."

St. Clair unfurled a blanket and draped it around the rabbi's shoulders. "I didn't realize al-Hasani's home was flush with the wall. It feels like being on the leads of a high castle." Wrapping himself in another blanket, he sat cross-legged at the rabbi's feet, anxious to hear what he had to say.

The rabbi cinched the blanket about his shoulders and looked down at St. Clair. "It is said," he whispered, "that the Templars held Jerusalem for a hundred years. And in that time, they explored—digging down into the holy mountain—from above and from the sides. Is this not so?"

"It is even so."

"Do you know what they sought, Jonathan?"

"We are sworn to silence on these matters, Rabbi."

"Another of your vows?"

St. Clair looked away and said nothing.

"Hear me, Jonathan. We have only a little time together. You must be round with me if we are to accomplish the task that flows from your scroll. Tell me, my son—what did the knights seek?"

St. Clair stood up and walked a few paces away, down the sloping roof. He drew a deep breath, tasting the crisp night air, and looked up. The sickle of the great lion stood high in the western sky—its body, a bright triangle of stars, almost directly overhead.

"It's wondrous, isn't it?" the rabbi murmured. "How the sky before dawn in winter shows us the stars of spring. I didn't think I'd see them again . . ."

The rabbi's words pierced the armor of his silence like an arrow from a longbow. In the months since they had first met in Safed, St. Clair had watched the old man grow steadily weaker.

Turning, he stepped back to where the rabbi sat in the embrasure of the battlements. He crouched down and whispered, "They sought artifacts of the Temple, Rabbi. They sought the Ark of the Covenant—"

"Indeed, they did. And what did they find?"

"They found nothing—empty passages leading nowhere, leading to aquifers, to cisterns, to other aquifers, leading to nothing. No Temple. No Ark. Only darkness."

The rabbi's eyes shone in the lamplight beneath his heavy brows. "Are you quite certain, Jonathan? Didn't they find anything at all?"

St. Clair stood up. He raised his shoulders. "Some told of a cavern . . ."

"Ah!" A smile spread across the rabbi's face. "I knew it!"

"But there was nothing there, Rabbi. It was dark, empty—"

"But it was vast, wasn't it, Jonathan?"

"How could *you* possibly know this? Is it mentioned in the Talmud?"

"No. The Talmud hints of the Ark, but there's no mention of this cavern—"

"Then how could you know? You couldn't have been there. No one can. A channel leading to the cavern from the Pool of Bethesda was sealed before Jerusalem fell to the Saracens a hundred years ago—"

"But with the help of your scroll, Jonathan, we may find another way."

"Is that why you're going back to the Tomb of Zechariah? Is that the other way?"

"I believe it is, and at dawn I hope to unlock the portal."

"I should go with you."

"Impossible."

"Why not?"

"Because once we go through, I'm not certain we'll be able to return."

"Then I *must* be with you," St. Clair said, his voice rising. "You just said I should be a part of this—"

"But you are." The rabbi rested his hand on St. Clair's shoulder. "Are you no longer a Knight of the Temple?"

"Of course. Which is another reason you must let me come. This concerns me."

"Jonathan, I learned something yesterday from a silversmith in Jerusalem that *also* concerns you. This spring the sultan will march on Acre with siege engines and a vast army. You must warn the garrison. You must—"

"What? Why didn't you tell me?" St. Clair jerked out from under the rabbi's hand, stood up, and lurched away "I must leave at once!"

"Soon, Jonathan, but not yet. We're almost finished here, and you'll have a few months' time to warn them—"

"You vex me, Rabbi! You learned that the siege is imminent and told me *nothing*?"

"I've told you now—"

"Enough of your talk, old man. I'm through!" St. Clair turned to leave.

"I charge you, stay! Did you not swear to serve me?"

"I serve the Temple!"

"Do you not first serve God?"

St. Clair hesitated, the blanket billowing around his shoulders in a sudden gust of wind. He turned back to the rabbi and drew a deep breath. "How can I not warn the Temple in Acre?"

"Because you must first deal with the Temple in *Jerusalem.*"

"*What* temple in Jerusalem? Do you speak of the *Order* of the Temple?"

"No. I speak of the Temple itself—the Temple of Solomon."

"What are you *talking* about? That Temple has been gone for a thousand years!"

"I speak of a Temple not made with hands, Jonathan, and a Jerusalem not of stone. I speak of *Yerushalayim shel ma'la*—an Upper Jerusalem, a gateway between this world and the next. Just as I told you when you first came to me in Safed asking to unlock the secrets of your scroll. The inscription led us to Jerusalem to find a gateway. This we have done. The inscription has also given us a key to unlock the gateway. This remains to be done."

"Then I *must* be with you," said St. Clair almost wearily as he sat back down at the rabbi's feet. "When my order was first established upon that very mountain, this was our original calling—to guide and to protect pilgrims seeking that connection."

"Which is *precisely* the high purpose you are to assume."

"And I tell you that I must assume it *now*!" Even as St. Clair shouted the words, he knew the rabbi was right. He knew he could not go. It was not only the matter of warning the Acre garrison. It was also the matter of the woman. He shut his eyes against a torrent of thoughts and the shards of his broken vows, his anger ebbing away. "How can I not be among you?" he asked, almost sadly.

"Because we must insure that you survive to answer your calling. Jonathan. You understand, don't you? I'm certain we'll be able to enter the chamber, but I'm not certain we'll be able to leave—"

"Then what good is all your work? If you don't come back, the secrets of the Temple Mount will disappear with you."

"Not so. Al-Hasani and I have labored through the night to make ready—to make sure you will have all the knowledge we possess. This knowledge will pass to you, whether we return or not."

"But—" St. Clair began.

"No." The rabbi cut him off and placed his hands on St.

Clair's shoulders. "No. You shall not please yourself with adventures as if you were a private person. You said it yourself. You are a Knight of the Temple, and you must live to warn the garrison and to fulfill your destiny." Samuel rested a hand on St. Clair's head, as if in benediction. "We once spoke of death, Jonathan—you said you wished to die with a sword in your fist, do you remember?"

St. Clair nodded.

"You will go on from here, Jonathan. When the time comes, you will do your part." Samuel drew him close.

St. Clair held the rabbi in a fierce embrace, his shoulders shaking.

The rabbi stood up and pointed at the sky. "Look, Jonathan. See how the stars begin to fade? Come with me now. Al-Hasani and I must leave well before sunrise."

St. Clair looked to the east where the sky grayed almost imperceptibly over the shadows of the city, slumbering in darkness.

"Before we leave," the rabbi continued, "you must see something of what we have found."

"There's time for that?"

"Yes. We'll explain other matters after we return this evening or tomorrow at dawn—"

"*If* you return . . ."

"If we don't, you'll have this knowledge, and you'll carry it with you to Acre. And there you'll do what is necessary to preserve and to transmit what we've found. All of you will do what's necessary—"

"All of us? What do you mean—all of us?"

"You and Zahirah, Isaac and Wallace—when the time comes, each of you will do your part."

Chapter Forty-Eight

מח

Jerusalem
1 January, 1291
Before dawn

St. Clair followed al-Hasani out of the study and down the darkened hallway carrying four burlap sacks. The lantern lighted the way to the main hall where the hearth glowed. On the divan sat the rabbi, his face shining in the ruddy light.

"Put the sacks here, Jonathan." He pointed to a spot on the carpet near where Isaac and Wallace lay huddled on cushions by the hearth, sleeping. "We must show you something of what we've found, and time is short."

Al-Hasani sat on the other end of the divan. "When should we leave, Samuel?" he asked.

"Within the hour. We should be there before dawn."

"Why is that important?" asked St. Clair as he sat on the divan between them.

"The portal can only be opened at the rising and the going down of the sun."

"Why is that so?"

"It flows from gematria applied to your scroll's inscription and from sacred geometry. We'll explain more of the details when we come back."

If you come back, St. Clair thought as he turned his eyes away from the rabbi.

"*If* we come back," al-Hasani said and rested his hand on St. Clair's shoulder. "I know that's what you're thinking, Jonathan. It's only natural to consider that possibility. We certainly have. Which is why we've done all this." He gestured toward the sacks. "We've duplicated all the scrolls and instruments."

"Instruments?" St. Clair asked.

"Yes," replied the rabbi. "And it is the use of the instruments that we must show you before we leave." He bent to pick up a sack, but was seized with a fit of coughing.

"This will never do, Samuel." Al-Hasani stood up, stepped over to the rabbi, and patted him on the back. "You're in no condition to go like this. I'll be back with your nostrums in a few minutes." He lifted the lamp and disappeared down the hall.

The rabbi's coughing subsided. He leaned forward, took hold of one of the sacks, and lifted out a box-like stringed instrument of dark wood with a slender neck. "This is a monochord. See? It has but a single string."

"What kind of music can be made with one string?"

"Peradventure, the music of the spheres." The rabbi smiled and placed the monochord across his knees. "Watch carefully. I'll demonstrate the stops you must use to create the particular tones we have derived. See here? We've marked each of the three stops with a letter. First, you press here." The rabbi plucked the string, emitting a clear note. "Then here." He plucked the string again. "Then here." As the rabbi sounded the third note, the three tones seemed to meld together and resonate. "Now you try." He passed the monochord to St. Clair.

When St. Clair mastered the sequence, he looked up at the rabbi and smiled. "The tones are pleasing to the ear, but what's their purpose?"

"To open the portal."

"And these exact notes are required?"

"Yes."

"But if the string of the monochord is loosened, what then?"

"It will need to be made taut to the proper degree. For that, we have panpipes—"

"The panpipes must wait," announced al-Hasani as he returned to the main hall, glass vials in each hand. Handing one to the rabbi, he said, "Here, drink to your health."

The rabbi downed the potion, grimacing. "Must it be so bitter?"

The wrinkles at the corners of al-Hasani's eyes deepened with amusement. "Perhaps you'd prefer a concoction from the hags who dwell in the caves by the Dead Sea. They make their draughts with the vital parts of snakes and bats. I assure you, Samuel, mine are much pleasanter drinking." He smiled broadly and handed the second vial to the rabbi. "And they're kosher . . ."

The rabbi drank, wiped his mouth, and handed the empty vials back to al-Hasani. "I was just about to show Jonathan the panpipes. Will you demonstrate? I haven't the breath."

"Certainly." Al-Hasani held the pipes for St. Clair to see. "I fashioned the reeds according to the same proportions of sound we used for the monochord. Hold the pipes thus, with your finger and thumb. Give each of the three reeds breath with your mouth." Blowing evenly, al-Hasani sounded the three notes; a low note followed by a high note, and then one between.

"Might the human voice create the same notes?" St. Clair asked.

"As long as they're the exact resonance," replied the rabbi. "It doesn't matter how the tones are created."

Al-Hasani handed the pipes to St. Clair. "Now you try."

After reproducing the tones, St. Clair asked, "If these give the same notes, why bother with the monochord?"

"I fashioned the monochord first," al-Hasani replied, "from the proportions of weights. The pipes came later."

"And all for greater confidence, Jonathan," the rabbi added. "These instruments are fashioned of wood. They can be broken, warped by water, or burned with fire. We want to have more than one key to open the portal."

"And look here." Al-Hasani unfurled a parchment. "I've rendered the tones into musical notation. This will also be in the sack."

St. Clair raised his shoulders. "But I cannot read the music."

"If necessary, you will find someone who can. For now you have the pipes and the monochord." The rabbi pointed at the sacks on the carpet. "These two sacks we take with us, the other two stay with you." He looked at al-Hasani. "Have we remembered everything?"

"Have you remembered to eat?" Al-Hasani's wife, Sha'ima, bustled into the main hall carrying a tray. "Please, gentlemen, I have brought tea and refreshments."

"Thank you, my dear wife."

Above her white linen robe adorned with a breastplate of blue, violet, and black embroidery, her bright eyes shone from a face furrowed with lines and folds. She placed the tray by the divan and looked at al-Hasani. "I've also prepared a lunch for you and the venerable rabbi." She clasped her work-worn hands together. "When will you depart, my husband?"

"Very soon." Al-Hasani handed a cup to St. Clair and one to Rabbi Samuel.

The rabbi made a little bow. "We thank you, Lady Sha'ima, for your hospitality, your graciousness, and," he raised his cup, "for the tea."

"You are more than welcome, honored guests," she murmured and bowed in response, then looked back to al-Hasani. "When will you return?"

"I don't know," he replied and walked over to where she stood. "Perhaps tonight, perhaps tomorrow morning, perhaps . . ." He left off speaking and drew her close.

As they embraced, St. Clair looked away and finished his tea.

After Sha'ima left, the rabbi turned to St. Clair. "Go back to bed, Jonathan. We have said all that is necessary for now. We will speak more when we see you this evening, or tomorrow morning, at the latest."

"And if not then?"

"Then we have said all that needs be said."

Chapter Forty-Nine

מט

Jerusalem
1 January, 1291
Before dawn

The stars were fading in the sky overhead as al-Hasani pulled the gate closed. "This way," he whispered.

"Where?" asked the rabbi, squinting into the uncertain half-light. "I can barely see the lane."

"I'll walk with you."

The rabbi limped along next to the mapmaker. Though he carried two burlap sacks over his shoulder, his load was light; one sack containing only scrolls, the other a spare repast. "Do you have the sack with the flints and candles?" he asked.

"Yes, but we don't need them now. I'll go slowly and guide you."

They left off speaking and moved through the uncertain darkness, cloaked with hooded robes against the wind and the eyes of any who might be watching. Al-Hasani paused frequently to help the rabbi along the uneven lane that was more a stairway than a street. Passing the shuttered stalls of the sleeping cotton market, they trod the pavement in a silent patrol.

"*Ya* al-Hasani," the rabbi whispered. "Let us speak together while we walk. Conversation will draw my attention away from the hip, which pains me. Tell me your thoughts."

"My thoughts are already at the tomb, Samuel. Within the hour we will sound the notes, and something will happen or nothing will happen. In either case, I shall be vexed. If nothing happens, I'll be disappointed that we labored in vain. On the other hand, if a portal opens, I'll be vexed because the whole fabric of my logical world will crumble. I don't know which will vex me more—"

"I don't believe you for a moment," the rabbi said with a little laugh. "You want to see the portal open as much as I do. And when it opens, I'm sure you'll enter with me."

"You know me too well, Samuel. Of course I will, even though it will challenge every scientific notion I have." Al-Hasani paused, his face shrouded by his hooded robe. "What will it mean for you, old friend?"

"Apart from the culmination of a lifetime of study, it will be the chance to draw healing and light out of the brokenness of Jerusalem—"

"The brokenness of Jerusalem? All ancient cities are broken, Samuel—fallen towers, tumbledown walls, shards of pottery—Jerusalem is no more broken than Baghdad or Alexandria—"

"Not so, my friend. I contend that Jerusalem has a brokenness beyond other cities—layers upon layers—houses built and rebuilt upon the brokenness of old houses, layer upon layer. More than other cities, Jerusalem is a city broken by the currents of time, and rebuilt again and again. And beneath the layers of broken houses, the deep rock of Mount Moriah itself is cleft by chasms and riven with hidden channels, caves, and springs. Thus, at its very core, Jerusalem is a place rich in brokenness—one of the most wounded places of this earth. It is because of *this* that Jerusalem is a city of light—"

"A city of light?" al-Hasani cut in. "How can you say that? You speak of a city built upon layers of broken houses, a city of underground channels and hidden caves. You describe a city of darkness, not light."

"Jerusalem is a city of light *precisely* because of its brokenness—that's how the light gets in." Rabbi Samuel paused and looked up at the graying sky past the shadows of cactus and caper bush that grew from crevices in the looming walls above them. "Is it not written in the psalms that *the night shines as the day, and darkness is as light?* Thus in the midst of darkness I believe we will find wellsprings of light. In this manner, Jerusalem is a place rich in healing and wholeness."

"I don't grasp this notion of healing and wholeness, Samuel, but I agree that Jerusalem has been broken and rebuilt again and again—the tragedy of a city at the crossroads of trade and empire. So many have claimed her—Canaanites, Philistines, Hebrews, Assyrians, Greeks, Romans, Christians, Mamluks—all have claimed her as their own . . ."

"And most of these claimants of Jerusalem are moved not by love for her, but by greed."

"Is greed not part of our nature?" al-Hasani asked as he helped the rabbi up a step.

"As in the story told of King Solomon," said the rabbi. "The child claimed by two mothers."

"And should Jerusalem be divided among all who claim her?"

"Not all who claim Jerusalem are her true children, al-Hasani. Only Jerusalem's *true* children love her enough to share her. And the very attributes of the Divine we will use to unlock the portal—wisdom and understanding—are reflected in men and women of *all* nations. It gives one hope for something better—people willing to live peacefully together as with an open vineyard with grapes for all to share."

"A noble thought, Samuel, but *this* world is ruled by those who desire the whole vineyard for themselves."

"Yes," said the rabbi. "And by their hunger, they destroy

what they would claim. As it is written in the Song of Songs, these are the foxes that spoil the vineyard. Sadly, they ruin things for all of us, devouring the good fruit, turning men and women against each other, sowing discord . . ." The rabbi left off speaking as his breathing became labored. He leaned back against a wall and looked up. He saw that al-Hasani had led them to one of the wider alleys, open to the sky, away from the midnight darkness of narrow lanes with vaulted ceilings.

Al-Hasani handed him a vial. Without objecting, he drank the liquid. Pocketing the empty vial, al-Hasani leaned against the wall next to the rabbi. "So much for this world."

"So much for *this* Jerusalem," the rabbi said. "We're about the business of the *other* Jerusalem. And in seeking *that* Jerusalem, we join those who seek the healing of the world."

"You believe there are others about this business?"

"Without a doubt. While Abram's family was worshiping idols in Ur, a wise Melchizedek ruled over a shining city on this very mountain. It is whispered that the children of Melchizedek are with us even today, these firstborn of Jerusalem—a hidden fellowship stretching back for a hundred generations. The knowledge we have struggled to decipher lives in their bloodline, and though they are unknown to us, we are bound to them in mind and heart."

Al-Hasani stepped away from the wall and looked up at the sky. "Come, Samuel. Dawn is but an hour away. We should go."

As they walked together, the rabbi saw that the sky had indeed lightened and details of the cobblestone pavement and limestone walls emerged from the darkness in sharp relief. "You are bound to the children of Melchizedek by way of Pythagoras, through your knowledge of the heavens and mapping of the earth. And I am bound to them through the study of Torah and Kabbalah. In this manner our dedication to a lifetime of study is folded together in a common purpose. Our learning flows together like tributaries of a mighty river."

"But what of other rivers, Samuel? What of distant tributaries? Do you believe Jerusalem is the only city? The Tomb of Zechariah, the only portal?"

"I'm under no such illusion, my friend." The rabbi pushed back the hood of his robe and wiped perspiration from his forehead as he walked. The air was cool on his face and he left the hood down. "I've seen enough of the world to know there are diverse people in distant lands who have their own paths and their own portals. I've glimpsed the wisdom of Confucius, Buddha, and Zarathustra from scholars in Baghdad. But we are bound by birth and circumstance to follow our own path." The rabbi pointed toward a swath of orange light filling the lane a stone's throw away. "What light burns there?"

Al-Hasani glanced up. "A teahouse for laborers; those who finish working through the night, and those who begin early. It's quite close to the Sheep Gate."

"Should we avoid the place?"

"Most decidedly. I know a way around it."

As they approached the teahouse, Samuel felt the wind increase as dead leaves rattled toward them. Passing a wooden door recessed between two columns of a façade, they came to a narrow alley.

"This way," al-Hasani said and led them into the deeper shadow of a sheltered lane bordered by tall buildings with latticework boxes over upper windows almost meeting above them. The cool air was quiet with no wind. From around a corner twenty paces down the lane, two men appeared, moving toward them.

The rabbi, his hood still down about his shoulders, quickly lowered his head. Out of the corner of his eye, he saw al-Hasani fix the men with pointed scrutiny as they moved to the side and the two men passed by.

After a few paces, the rabbi stopped and turned. The lane was empty. "Did you recognize those two?" he asked in a low voice.

"No. Probably just a couple of porters going for tea," al-Hasani replied as he reached out and pulled the rabbi's hood up to cover his head. "Let's stand here awhile and see if they follow."

Looking up at the sky, the rabbi shook his head. "Dawn approaches. We must go."

Emerging from the alley, they left the walled city through the Sheep Gate. The red-brown earth of the road, studded with pebbles, wound into the Kidron Valley among scattered tombstones, olive trees, and the dry grasses of winter. The air was filled with birdsong and the music of crickets. Moving down the road, they paused frequently for the rabbi to catch his breath and to cast a watchful eye on the path behind them. Eventually they left the main road and approached the looming stone tomb, a dark silhouette against the russet sky. The grasses and trees rang with birdsong, swelling toward morning.

Al-Hasani readied the panpipes.

From the minaret of al-Aqsa, the muezzin's call to prayer floated over the walled city like a mist, drifting down into the valley.

Day was breaking.

Al-Hasani sounded the three notes.

Chapter Fifty

נ

Jerusalem
1 January, 1291
Dawn

"I'm sure it was him!" Nehemiah said in a tense whisper. "We must follow them—now!"

Cosimo hesitated. "Rabbi Petit said nothing about Rabbi Samuel in the company of another old man—he spoke of a young Jew or a Templar—"

"What matters is Rabbi Samuel, Cosimo, and I'm sure it was him. For God's sake, man, I spent two weeks with him at Tel Hum. I tell you it's him!" Nehemiah turned and began walking back in the direction the two old men had taken.

"All right—but slow down and let me walk with you apace. We must decide how to inform the Emir of Jerusalem—for it is he who must apprehend the rabbi." Struggling to keep up with Nehemiah, Cosimo continued speaking. "If you're sure it's Samuel you saw, I'll go to the emir and so inform him according to the instructions I received from Rabbi Petit, but be warned, if you're wrong, I will not face the emir's wrath alone. I will make sure you pay—"

"Cosimo, there is no question in my mind. Be assured—that was the rabbi."

The men reached the Sheep Gate, and Nehemiah signaled Cosimo to stop. He carefully peeked out the gate. "Good. They travel slowly and are heading into the Kidron Valley. We'll easily be able to follow them—"

"No," Cosimo cut in. "*You* follow, keeping the old men in your sight. I will straightway to the palace and inform the emir. Once the emir understands the importance of apprehending this rabbi, I'm certain he will immediately dispatch the palace guard. I will then bring them into the valley. Just make sure you keep them in your sight."

As Cosimo turned to go, Nehemiah took his arm. "Wait! What of the scroll you are to give me?"

Cosimo smiled. "It seems you'll be receiving it soon—once Rabbi Samuel is apprehended, not before."

The Emir of Jerusalem, Karim Abu-het, was preparing to join the Sultan al-Ashraf Khalil in Ascalon—well before the siege of Acre, which would take place late in the spring. In addition to a company of the palace guard, he was also hoping to bring a large contingent of volunteers as well as a personal gift for the new sultan. He had yet to see either.

From his bedchamber in the palace, the emir looked out through loops of ornamental stonework at the mountains of Moab, veiled in a blue mist. "Scribe, were copies of our letter requesting volunteers distributed throughout the provinces?"

"They were, Sire," replied the scribe. "Soon after cock's-crow, riders left to deliver the dispatch. Surely, many volunteers will emerge from the provinces to swell our ranks."

"With or without them, we shall make a great showing of devotion to the new sultan with a large company of the palace guard and our gifts." The emir turned to the scribe. "Indeed, what of the sword and shield we commissioned from the silversmith? I have yet to see a single piece. Why does Abu Rahman not apprise me of his progress?"

"Great One, the venerable silversmith works day and night to fulfill your commission. He swears an oath that he will soon complete the handiwork and present it to your lordship."

"Very well." The emir rose to his feet. "Have my meal made ready now, good scribe, for I perceive the onset of hunger."

"Certainly, Sire . . ." The scribe hesitated and cleared his throat. "There is a final matter of great urgency, if it please your lordship."

"It would please his lordship to eat," the emir said dryly.

"Of course, Sire. Of course," the scribe murmured and turned to leave.

The emir drew a deep breath, a pained expression flitting across his face. "Great urgency, you say? What is it?"

The scribe raised his shoulders. "At the door since rooster crow stands a Pisan merchant—Cosimo by name." The scribe pulled a scroll from within his white robe. "He wishes you to have this missive, Sire, sealed by a rabbi in Acre."

Karim stared at the scroll in the scribe's hand. "From Acre, you say?"

"Yes, Great One."

"Give it me." Karim put out his hand. "And while I peruse, fetch the man, that I may know his purpose." Breaking the red wax seal, the emir found there were actually two scrolls. They were both written in the language of the Franks, and he could not read them. "Wait!" he called before the scribe left the bedchamber. "You know how to read the language of the accursed Franks. Come and tell me the contents of these missives."

The scribe studied both parchments for several minutes before speaking. "This first letter is from a rabbi in Acre named Petit. He offers your lordship three spies who are even now in Jerusalem; one is a Knight Templar by the name of Jonathan St.

Clair, the second is a young Jew named Isaac, and the third, the worst of the lot, is a rabbi from Baghdad named Samuel.

"Rabbi Petit offers you these three enemies and spies, and in return for their arrest and execution, he offers to give you secrets pertaining to the defenses of Acre." The scribe held up the second parchment. "Petit treats on these secrets in this report, which includes various details—the number of knights, the number and nature of their weapons and engines, the height and thickness of Acre's walls, the times and positions of patrols, along with other details. And finally, Rabbi Petit promises to provide your lordship with further details of Acre's defenses if Rabbi Samuel's head is delivered to Petit's steward, who will daily wait at midday by the signpost marking the border between the Mamluk and Christian lands . . ."

The emir's dark eyes grew large, and a smile spread across his thin face. *This is yet the most precious gift I can offer the sultan.* "I will speak with this man, scribe. Bring him in."

The scribe left and quickly returned, proclaiming at the door, "I present the honorable Cosimo of Pisa to the Great Emir, Karim Abu-het, protector of Jerusalem and its sacred precincts, may his beneficent rule endure forever."

The portly merchant curtsied on his pudgy legs, sweeping the floor with his large velvet hat. "I bow before the glorious Emir of Jerusalem, may Allah grant thee long life," he said in flawless, though Italian-accented, Arabic.

"And long life to you also, good Cosimo." The emir raised the scrolls in his hand. "Do you know the substance of this matter?"

"I am but a poor messenger, Sire, who humbly delivers the scroll to your lordship on behalf of my patron, Rabbi Petit of Acre. I beg your royal pardon if the matter displeases your lordship."

"Actually," the emir said smoothly, "the missive much pleases me, but also puzzles me. For, like a bird of ill omen, it brings words of treachery. It treats on a rabbi by the name of Samuel, who travels as a perfidious agent of the Mongols from Baghdad to our dominions. What know you of this?"

"Only this, Great One. I was charged by Rabbi Petit of Acre to conduct a certain Jew, Nehemiah, to Jerusalem, since he knows Rabbi Samuel to identify him. This, Nehemiah has done this very morning upon the fourth watch. My task was then to convey the scroll hither."

"The missive states that the rabbi may be in the company of a young Jewish spy called Isaac and a Templar spy. What know you of these two?"

"Nothing, Sire. We observed the rabbi in the company of an old Arab, neither Jew nor knight. They left the city by the Sheep Gate before dawn and descended into the Valley of Kidron. There I left Nehemiah to keep them in his sight, and came I straightway hither."

"You have done well, merchant. For this and future service to our person you will be richly rewarded." The emir looked past Cosimo at the scribe.

"This good merchant is our friend, scribe. Take him with you at once to the barracks and there instruct the captain of the guard to lead a patrol, with the help of good Cosimo, to the place he will show them. Once they apprehend this rabbi, have them bring him to me in chains, or failing that, they are to bring me his head—whatsoever is the more expedient." The emir turned back to Cosimo and waved him away. "Go now, merchant, and await my scribe without."

"Certainly, Sire," Cosimo replied with a sweeping bow. Scuttling backwards, he continued to curtsy, stumbling and bumping into a wall before groping along a tapestry and finding the door. He pushed it open, bowed again, and left the bedchamber.

The emir turned to the scribe, his eyes feral with excitement.

"While the guard fetches Rabbi Samuel, I will make ready to depart for Ascalon in the space of two days." Seeing a look of confusion cross the scribe's face, the emir smiled beneath his beard and he raised the scrolls in his fist. "Do you know what rare gift the merchant has given us?" He leaned forward and whispered, "The keys to Acre!"

"I see your meaning, Sire."

"Once you have conveyed my instructions and the merchant to the captain of the guard, good scribe, return to me with dispatch. I would you render an Arabic translation of this document, detailing Acre's defenses. I cannot wait to see the sultan's face when I present this to him in Ascalon!"

"But Sire, what of your appeal to the provinces? What will the volunteers do when they answer your call and come to Jerusalem?"

"When they come—*if* they come—have them dispatched to join us in Ascalon." The emir spoke rapidly as he stepped behind a decorative screen by his wardrobe. Draping his robe over the screen's curved wooden border, he fixed his eyes on the scribe. "Once we have secured the head of the rabbi, I will straightway provide a detachment of the guard to give the merchant, Cosimo, safe conduct to the Acre frontier—the border is well known to us." The emir disappeared behind the screen as he dressed. "The captain of the guard will give Samuel's head to Petit's steward and will receive the further details Rabbi Petit has promised us. The guard will then make their way to Ascalon without delay."

"Very well, Sire, but, what of the work you have commissioned of the silversmith?"

"Cancel the commission. What need we of silver trinkets when we have gold?" The emir's head appeared above the screen, his face wearing a broad smile. "But now, good scribe, away! Have the guard fetch us the rabbi's head, which sits like a flower of rare beauty in the Valley of Kidron, ready to be plucked. Away! For the eye can see, but the hand cannot yet reach."

Once the captain of the guard had received the emir's instructions from the scribe, he turned his attention to Cosimo. "Come, merchant. Lead us to our quarry."

"Aye, sir. I am at your disposal." The merchant's rich clothes rustled as he bowed.

A contingent of guards was soon gathered in the yard, their armor shining in the bright winter sunlight, their yellow robes snapping in the morning wind. The captain stood before them.

"Follow me, faithful servants of the emir, on a mission of great moment. This good merchant will reveal to us the Jewish spy who is the object of our quest. Let us make haste."

The entourage set out with Cosimo struggling to stay in front as they traversed vaulted alleys and flights of cobbled steps to the Sheep Gate.

Cosimo came to a stop at the gate and pointed. "The two old men went that way." He took off his fine cap and mopped his forehead with the sleeve of his velveteen doublet.

The captain shaded his eyes against the morning sunlight. Amid the scattered boulders, olive trees, and scrub brush, the road wound in languid curves down the valley between the Temple Mount and Olivet. Apart from a woman with a basket on her head, the road was deserted.

The captain frowned. "I see them not."

"How far can two old men get?" Cosimo adjusted his cap and started down the hill.

"Very well. Let us proceed."

After several minutes, Cosimo rounded a bend in the road and saw Nehemiah in the distance, standing on a rock, waving his arms over his head. Behind him loomed a tall monument capped by a stone like one of the pyramids the merchant had once seen by the Nile at Ghiza. "There he is—just as I told you. The two old men must be close at hand!" Cosimo took off his cap and waved it.

The captain turned to the guard. "Let's get this rabbi, gentlemen."

As they started forward, Cosimo saw Nehemiah coming forward at a dead run, his gray robe spreading out behind him. From the branches of an olive tree, a flock of black birds startled into noisy flight at his approach.

"A man's job," Cosimo called out. "Now our work is done."

"No, I am undone!" Nehemiah shouted and jabbed his arm in the direction of the monument. "They were right there. I tell you, right there. I saw them clearly, and then they were gone!"

"What do you mean, gone?" asked the merchant. "Gone where?"

"Gone nowhere!" Nehemiah shrieked. "Gone—as if the earth swallowed them."

"What are you babbling about?" the captain snapped.

"Calm yourself, Nehemiah," Cosimo cautioned. "You are in the presence of the captain of the emir's guard."

"Pardon me, Sire." Nehemiah bowed. "I followed Rabbi Samuel and the other old man to yonder monument. But now, I see them not. I'm certain they must still be about." He looked back at the tomb and shrugged. "I just don't know where."

"Leave that to us." The captain turned and motioned to the guards. "Spread out and sweep the valley. We want the old rabbi alive, but dead will do just as well."

Chapter Fifty-One

Jerusalem
1 January, 1291
Midday

"Hold the stave like a weapon, not a broom," St. Clair said as he adjusted Isaac's hands. "See how William holds it?"

The three wore white burnooses borrowed from al-Hasani's son, Tarek, as they stood in a patch of sunlight warming the courtyard. High above them rose sunlit walls of rough-cut limestone, the color of cream—one wall covered by the dark green leaves and bright scarlet flowers of a climbing vine. Just past midday, sunshine filled half the courtyard, leaving the other half in cool shadow.

Isaac looked at St. Clair over the wooden stave. "It's hard for me to concentrate, Jonathan, not knowing what's happening with the rabbi and al-Hasani—"

"The waiting is difficult for all of us. But you must concentrate. The time may come when you'll need to fight."

"Do you think they'll come back tonight?" Isaac persisted.

"I told you—tonight or dawn tomorrow. Now concentrate! Hold it at this height, and prepare to defend yourself." Stepping back, he waved Wallace forward.

As the boys practiced, the courtyard echoed with the clatter of the staves. The burnoose St. Clair wore fit him well enough, though Isaac's was ill-fitting, brushing the smooth paving stones, and Wallace's was too short, barely reaching his knees.

"Better, but not quite right. Here, I'll show you." St. Clair took the stick from Isaac, rolled it over his wrist, caught it with the other hand, spun it back again, and gripped it, holding it away from his body. "Hold the stave like this."

"Why can't you teach us to fight with real weapons?" Isaac pouted. "Why must we play with sticks?"

"How many times do I have to tell you? If you know what you're doing, a solid piece of wood can parry any blade. Let me show you again." He turned to Wallace. "William, use your stave like a sword and have at me."

Wallace readily flailed away, St. Clair easily parrying the blows. "Like this. Like this. See? Now you try it."

"Only this time, Isaac," Wallace warned, "don't actually hit me or I shall strike you where it hurts."

Isaac glared back. "That was an accident. I would never strike a lady."

Wallace snorted. "*You're* the one dressed like an old woman."

"At least I have some modesty," countered Isaac.

"Gentlemen!" St. Clair barked. "Stop jousting with your tongues and begin!"

St. Clair watched as Wallace made a few thrusts at Isaac. "First from your right and then your left. Good! Parry the blows with a glancing stroke, and then show me your counter. Good!"

The brass bell jangled, and St. Clair crossed the yard and lifted the latch.

Draped with a dark shawl that covered her head but for her gray eyes, Zahirah pushed through the tall wooden gate. The shawl, like her richly embroidered black dress, was borrowed from Al-Hasani's wife, Sha'ima. In each hand, she carried a bulging sack of hemp netting.

"I was beginning to worry about you," St. Clair said, taking the sacks from her and glancing toward the gate. "But where are the Lady Sha'ima and Tarek?"

"They went to the Kidron Valley," Zahirah replied and pushed the gate closed. "It's whispered in the marketplace that the emir himself has joined the search."

"Which can only mean they haven't been found."

"Not a trace. They've searched the whole valley." She pulled the shawl off her head and fixed her eyes on St. Clair. "Where could they have gone?"

For a moment, he considered telling her. Instead, he turned and led the way across the courtyard, a sack in each hand. As he passed Isaac and Wallace, who stood leaning on their staves, St. Clair said, "We'll be eating soon. Go wash up."

"Won't Lady Sha'ima and Tarek be joining us?" Wallace asked.

"No," Zahirah replied. "They plan to keep a vigil through the night. I'll go out later and bring them food—"

"No, Zahirah," St. Clair cut in. "Neither you nor the Lady Sha'ima should be out in such weather. The boys and I will join them toward sunset, and if the rabbi and al-Hasani haven't come by then, Sha'ima and Tarek will return here and we will keep watch in their stead through the night." He shot a glance at Isaac and Wallace. "We'll bring blankets, and we'll bring staves . . ."

"I used to be quite good with those," Zahirah said.

"Really?" St. Clair smiled down at her. "When did you learn?"

"When I was a girl." She smiled at Wallace and held out her hand. "May I try?"

St. Clair put the bags down and took up his own stave, as Wallace handed his to Zahirah.

She gripped the stave lightly in one hand, seeming to test its weight and balance as she paced across the courtyard, her pregnant belly barely showing beneath her long dress.

St. Clair followed her out of the shadows, watching as she rolled the stave over her wrist and spun it in her hands, as he himself was wont to do. Noticing this, he laughed. "I see we had the same teacher."

"Defend yourself, my lord." She sprang at him, the stave whirling in her hands.

Surprised, he parried the blows and retreated, a broad smile on his face.

She swept a blow upward, knocking his stave away. Rotating the other end, she struck him softly on the buttocks.

"I am undone!" He raised his arms. "Grant me quarter, my lady!"

"Granted, my lord." She threw back her head and laughed.

St. Clair drew her close and whispered, "I saw my old master in you just now."

"As I see him every day in you, my love." She touched his face with her hand, her eyes shining.

Suddenly aware of the boys, they stepped apart.

St. Clair tossed the staves to the boys. "We'll call you when lunch is ready." He lifted the bags and led the way into the house.

"Please let me come with you tonight," Zahirah said as she closed the door.

"No, my darling. The weather may turn foul and you with child." He set the sacks down on the long wooden table that ran the length of the pantry.

"I wonder where they could be . . ." she mused as she hung a black iron pot to boil.

St. Clair knew the pot was heavy and he marveled at the strength and beauty of her hands. He leaned against the counter, feeling a great tenderness toward her, watching as she added kindling to the cooking fire and fanned the embers with a dry palm frond. There was a puff and a flare as the wood began to burn, drawing brightly at the draft from the hole in the wall behind the hearth. He felt a warmth filling his own heart as he reached out and drew her to him, kissing her mouth. Then, holding her, he felt her body against him, the pregnant belly against his loins.

"After lunch, I should rest," she whispered. "Will you rest with me, my lord?"

"Most decidedly, my darling. I will rest with you before I go to see Rabbi Samuel—"

"He couldn't have gone far, not with his bad hip," she said as she stepped back to the kitchen counter. "He can barely walk up a flight of stairs."

"They didn't have far to go," St. Clair said as he hung a large cheese covered in a cloth net from a hook over the counter.

"What do you mean by that?" Zahirah asked as she placed green cucumbers and red tomatoes on the counter. "What do you mean—they didn't have far to go?"

"I meant nothing."

"Jonathan," she said and pushed herself between the counter and his body, her hands around his waist, her face upturned. "What aren't you telling me?"

He bent down and kissed her mouth.

She pouted. "Tell me."

He fixed her with his eyes, a smile playing on his lips. "They did it," he whispered. "I didn't think it possible, but they did it!"

"Did what? What are you talking about?"

"The rabbi and al-Hasani—I believe they're inside the tomb!"

"What are you saying, Jonathan?" Her eyes quickly brimmed with tears. "Inside the tomb? Oh, God, they're dead?"

"No, no, no—it's not like that. Not dead." He cradled her face in his hands. "The rabbi is certain the tomb is a portal—"

"A portal?" Zahirah wiped her eyes with the palm of her

hand. "A portal to where? What are you talking about?"

"I'm not entirely sure. We'll find out when they come out." *If they come out,* he thought.

"When will that be?"

"This evening or tomorrow at daybreak, according to Rabbi Samuel." He bent and kissed her forehead.

She turned back to the counter and took leaf-wrapped parcels out of the sack. "But where are they?"

"The rabbi spoke of an Upper Jerusalem."

"The upper city? But you just said they entered the tomb in the Kidron Valley. That is far from the upper city—"

"He didn't mean the upper city of *this* Jerusalem," St. Clair said as he drew a deep breath. "He was referring to a Jerusalem not of this world." St. Clair raised his shoulders. "I know it sounds crazy."

Zahirah dried her eyes. "No more so than legends about Jerusalem in Islam. My favorite is about a great tree that blooms in heaven with its roots descending down into Jerusalem. The tree has three roots, each nourished by a river—one river is Judaism, one Christianity, and one Islam."

"Rabbi Samuel has spoken to me of such a river, but he spoke of only one river."

"Perhaps the three rivers are joined into one," Zahirah said as she lifted the lid on a wooden box filled with soft-colored hen's eggs nestled in straw. Carefully, she placed each egg in the water she had set to boil.

The kitchen door creaked open and Isaac's head appeared, wet hair plastered on his forehead. "When can we eat?" he asked.

"A few minutes," St. Clair replied. "Go prepare your blankets."

"Why?"

"We leave before the sun sets, and we'll likely spend the night in the valley."

Zahirah turned to St. Clair, watching as he drew a knife across the open end of the white cheese, cutting off thick slices. "Jonathan, we were speaking now of legends; a heavenly Jerusalem, a tree in the sky, all beautiful images, but you still haven't told me where the rabbi and al-Hasani actually are."

He turned and looked at her. "Haven't I?"

"Here you are, good Cosimo, tea chilled with ice from the snows of Hermon." Nehemiah held out a goatskin bag and smiled.

"Why, thank you, Nehemiah." The merchant seemed surprised. He unstoppered the cork, raised the skin, and with the spigot a hand's breadth away, he propelled an amber stream of tea perfectly into his mouth for an impossibly long minute. His thirst finally slaked, the stream stopped, and the merchant closed his mouth in a smile. "That," he sighed, "was heavenly."

Nehemiah sat down on a gravestone next to Cosimo, watching the guards search the valley. He was surprised they hadn't yet found the rabbi, but he knew they would, and his mind was greatly troubled. *This is how I repay the man who freed me from Tel Hum—who brought me back from the dead, and gave me back my life—with treachery and betrayal.* He dreaded the moment when the guards would lead the rabbi out, no doubt shackled and beaten. *But what choice did I have?* He shook the thoughts away as he reached into his purse and carefully took out a parcel wrapped in a large fig leaf. "I also brought you this—warm baklava."

"You're full of surprises today." Cosimo unfolded the leaf and gazed at the sweet confection packed with pistachio nuts and dripping with honey. He took a bite. "Mmm!" He closed his eyes, then looked at Nehemiah and smiled. "I do believe you're trying to bribe me."

"No . . ." Nehemiah wagged his head, "I merely . . ."

"Yes, you are." Cosimo chuckled and took another bite. "And it's working. So, tell me, how can I possibly repay you for such kindness?"

"You know how you can repay me . . ."

"We're not going to have that conversation again, are we?" the merchant said as he brushed flakes of crust off his beard and licked honey off his fingers.

"I've done my part, Cosimo. I pointed out the old man."

"That you did."

"So give me the scroll and let me return home."

"Well," Cosimo replied, still chewing, "they haven't yet apprehended him . . ."

"My charge was to point him out, and this have I faithfully done. Why must I sit here and wait? I haven't seen my wife in more than a year. It's not like I'm leaving Jerusalem. You'll know where to find me."

Cosimo took another drink of the cold, sweet tea. Then he turned to Nehemiah. "You'll be in the Jews' Quarter?"

"Of course! Where else would I go?"

"And if I should call upon you?"

"I'll come. You have my word." Nehemiah frowned. "You also have that other scroll . . ."

Cosimo seemed to mull the idea over in his mind as he finished the baklava and licked the honey and crumbs off the fig leaf. "This is, without doubt, the best baklava I've ever tasted." After another draught of tea, he reached into the purse that hung at his side. He pulled out a scroll and handed it to Nehemiah. "I believe this is yours."

With trembling hands, Nehemiah broke the seal and unrolled the parchment. He scanned it in a glance. "Thank you, good Cosimo! Finally, to return to my bride! Thank you!" Rolling up the scroll, he climbed to his feet. "A thousand times, thank you."

The merchant waved him away. “Go to that little wife of yours. Off with you, now!”

Nehemiah sprinted up the valley and soon disappeared around a bend in the road.

Cosimo took another long drink of sweet tea.

CHAPTER FIFTY-TWO

נב

Jerusalem
2 January, 1291
Long after midnight

Nehemiah ben Azariah staggered to a stop in a pale patch of torchlight along a deserted lane that ran beside the city wall. He leaned against the wall, feeling the cold roughness of stone beneath his cheek. *What am I to do?* His mind repeated the question. Numb with fatigue and despair, he stared blankly down the length of the wall. Torches marked the lane with islands of light as far as he could see. *What am I to do?*

He lurched forward, watching his shadow stumbling darkly before him, growing long and faint as he moved on, until it disappeared into the darkness between the torches.

He remembered a Mamluk guard calling the third watch, but he wasn't sure how long it had been—*a few minutes or a few hours?* He came to another circle of torchlight and saw stone steps mounting the wall. He pulled the torch from its bracket and climbed the mural steps to the top of the wall. A brisk wind whistled along the battlements, and the torch's blue flame flickered but did not go out.

The sky was clear now, moonless and crowded with stars. Facing Jerusalem, he raised his arms, giving himself over to the full force of the wind. His robe spread out, billowing and snapping behind him. The torch in his hand licked the night with a flickering blue tongue. Then he turned his back to Jerusalem and, reeling slightly, he stood, staring down into the darkness, where the valleys of Kidron and Hinon met far below, a blackness beneath the frozen stars.

Now is my hour—the dead of night in the dead time of the year. How fitting for a dead man . . .

The memory swept over him again, chilling him beyond the cold wind that swept around and through him. Again, the questions rose in his mind as tears coursed down his face. *How could she have known that I would ever return? Who ever returns from that place? And she, so beautiful, and the child at her breast . . . not my child, not my child. Yet I tried to reason with her. I showed her the scroll. I know she saw the scroll . . .*

He began to scream, screaming into the wind, without words, screaming over her voice that spoke in his brain. Then the voice left him and he stopped screaming.

He pulled the scroll from his belt—the scroll that was to have changed everything. He held it up to his eyes, turning it this way and that. How it mocked him. He drew back his arm and cast it into the darkness, imagining the scroll not falling but rising, rising in the wind, floating high in the air, high over the city, like a feather on the breath of God.

A feather on the breath of God—where did I hear that?

He couldn't remember. Closing his eyes, a memory flickered—at Tel Hum, an old Christian priest, disfigured by disease, reading poems and stories in a hoarse voice. That was it—words written long ago by a nun from some north country—*a feather on the breath of God.* He smiled and imagined himself rising, light as a feather, sailing high over the sleeping houses, flying on the wings of night. He began to feel a little better.

He lifted his eyes to the indifferent sky burning with stars, and a fierce joy filled his heart. Things were becoming clearer—his life was a weight grappling him to a world of pain. But now he was on the verge of a transformation—growing lighter, slipping out from beneath the weight of the night and the stars—the burden of his life, a huge stone, slipping away.

He breathed in, tasting the cold air. He felt as light and as cold as the air, already rising. The wind was all around him, in his ears, but not only in his ears. Like a harp of dry grass, the husk of his body sang beneath the fingers of the wind. The sound became a voice, and the voice rose, louder and louder, a great voice rising, really many voices.

With a fearful exaltation swelling in him, he lifted off the wall and plunged down—the night flowing over and around him in waves of dark air, the song of dry grass flowing through him, the voices vast and perfect.

The blue flame plunged down with him, fluttered, and went out.

And all the voices stopped.

It must be well into the third watch of the night, St. Clair thought as he sat cross-legged on a broken gravestone and looked up at the sky. "Orion has already set," he whispered, his breath marked by white mist in the cold air. He cinched the blanket about his shoulders and looked toward the place where Isaac and Wallace slept. He couldn't see them in the darkness, but he could hear them breathing as they slept in the shelter of the tomb.

St. Clair's thoughts turned to the rabbi, and his heart clenched. Samuel had assured him that he and al-Hasani would yet emerge from the tomb, either by sunset or by dawn. Sunset had passed and with dawn a few hours away, doubts stabbed through his mind. He feared he would never see the rabbi again, and the legacy of the scroll would remain sealed, like the Tomb of Zechariah. Yawning, he looked up at the sharp outline of the tomb against the stars. He yearned to sleep. *I'll just rest my eyes for a short time . . .*

He awoke to the noisy chattering of birds in the thorn brush. Light filled the valley. Morning was breaking, and there was no sign of the rabbi or al-Hasani. He stared at the stone face of the tomb. A great sadness filled his heart.

Climbing to his feet, he winced at the dull pain low in his back, the ache and stiffness of his knees. He rubbed the sleep from his eyes and saw that Isaac and Wallace still lay at the base of the tomb, wrapped in their robes and blankets. St. Clair knelt and, in lieu of Matins, muttered a *Pater Noster,* not taking his eyes off the tomb.

He thought he heard someone speak, but it was only the whisper of dry thorn brush blowing against the tomb in the morning wind. A sudden movement on the hill caught his attention. Shading his eyes, he saw it was only the branch of an olive tree nodding in the breeze. He lifted the blanket from his shoulders and shook it out. "Wake up, boys. Time to go."

Isaac stirred and propped himself up on one elbow. "Is the rabbi here?"

"I'm afraid not," St. Clair said as he folded the blanket.

Isaac sat up. "So, now what?"

"Now we do as we promised Rabbi Samuel. We return to the workshop of al-Hasani and take up the song—"

"It's only first light," Isaac protested as he climbed stiffly to his feet. "Shouldn't we wait a bit longer?"

"Not by my counsel." St. Clair stuffed the blanket into his pack. "The halka will soon return. They must not find us here."

He reached down and patted Wallace on the shoulder. "Wake up, William," he said in English. "It's time we were off, lad. Come now, or ye'll sleep yer brains inta muckle watter," he added, lapsing into Scottish vernacular.

"Must I, sir?" Wallace mumbled as he rolled onto his back, covering his face with an arm. "I hardly slept."

"Up with you, lad. We must be off."

"We could hide among the rocks," Isaac argued.

"Rabbi Samuel gave us a job to do and we must do it." St. Clair turned and nudged Wallace with his foot. "Come, William, up with you."

Wallace sat up. "It seems a shame not to give them more time."

"I also leave with a heavy heart," St. Clair said as he shouldered his pack. "But Rabbi Samuel knew that once he and al-Hasani entered the tomb, they might not be able . . . to leave. . . ." His voice trailed off. Squinting into the distance, he saw a group of men moving out of the mist that still shrouded the northern reaches of the valley. "What's this, then?"

Isaac stood next to St. Clair. "Why does light flash from them?"

"They bear weapons," St. Clair whispered through clenched teeth.

"Is it the emir's guard?"

"No."

"Brigands?"

"We're about to find out."

"Shouldn't we run?"

"If they mean us ill, running will only enrage them. So, listen well. Isaac—go fetch our staves from where they rest by the tomb. Then stand by me and say nothing." He stepped forward and raised an arm. "Good morning, gentlemen!" he called out in a cheerful voice.

The men either didn't hear or ignored his greeting. They were now near enough so St. Clair could see their shabby clothing streaked with grime. Several carried swords and shields.

"Here, sir," Wallace whispered and passed a stave to St. Clair.

"We may need to put these to use, boys. Follow my lead." Planting the stave like a staff, St. Clair waved again.

Several paces away, a huge Arab, apparently their leader, came to a stop, and the others drew up short behind him. A giant of a man with a full black beard and heavy-muscled arms, his leather vest, face, and arms were smeared with black grease. A silver sword hung at his belt and on his left arm he carried a round shield.

The morning sun reflected brightly off the shield and St. Clair shielded his eyes with his hand. "Good morning!" he called again.

The Arab nodded toward the Tomb of Zechariah. "Why are you here?" The question sounded like a challenge.

St. Clair raised his shoulders and smiled. "We are but wandering mendicants, good sir. We possess nothing you would have other than our blessings."

"I would have an answer. What do you seek here?"

"Nothing more than we have found, sir—shelter for the night—nothing more."

The Arab nodded toward Jerusalem. "Then, go."

"Certainly, good sir."

But even as St. Clair took a few steps up the valley, motioning Isaac and Wallace to follow, he was troubled by the presence of these men at the tomb. *What are they after?* He paused and turned. "Are you gentlemen come this fine morning to honor a revered ancestor or master?" he asked casually and pointed. "Is this the tomb?"

"Leave." The Arab took a step forward, his hand on the hilt of his sword.

St. Clair didn't move. He was keenly interested to know their purpose. He smiled amiably and shrugged. "I merely suggest that . . ."

"I have not drawn against you, sir, but if you do not leave at once, I will."

"We will leave, sir. Of that you may be certain." St. Clair bobbed his head submissively. "We mean no disrespect, but merely beg to offer you our prayers. Please accept them in the humble spirit in which they are offered. Does the prophet not exhort us to honor the memory of the righteous, and to give solace to the wayfarer—"

"I'm warning you . . ." the Arab said menacingly as he drew his sword.

St. Clair rotated the stave, gripping it with both hands, as he backed away. "No need for that, sir. If it pleases you, we—"

"Jonathan!" cried a familiar voice. "Abu Rahman! What foolishness is this?"

St. Clair spun around to see the rabbi and al-Hasani coming from the direction of the tomb. Without thinking, he stepped forward and shouted, "Rabbi!"

"Rabbi?" the Arab repeated, pointing his sword at Samuel. "Rabbi?"

St. Clair readied the stave to knock the sword away, but saw in a glance that the Arab's threatening countenance had given way to a look of bemused confusion.

"*Ya al-Hasani!*" the Arab exclaimed. "You told me this man was your cousin!"

In confusion, St. Clair's eyes darted between the Arab, the rabbi, and al-Hasani. Then, as with a chorus, St. Clair and Abu Rahman pointed at each other and asked in unison, "You know this man?"

Laughing, the rabbi opened his arms and embraced St. Clair in a fatherly hug. Then he turned to Abu Rahman. "Silversmith! How good to see you, and with your apprentices! But, how is it you came here this morning?" He canted his head and smiled. "How did you know?"

Abu Rahman folded his arms across his chest. "I'm not sure

what to tell you."

"I think I know." Al-Hasani rested his hand on the rabbi's shoulder. "Do you remember how we spoke of the hidden guardians of the holy mountain—the children of Melchizadek?" He fixed his eyes on the silversmith. "What say you, *ya* Abu Rahman?"

The silversmith smiled. "This is neither the time nor the place for us to speak of these matters. It is certain that the emir will search here today. We must away with all haste." He started up the valley road and hadn't gone ten paces, when he stopped. "Too late."

St. Clair could see the yellow robes of the emir's guard filling the Sheep Gate. "Should we do battle?" he asked.

Abu Rahman shook his head. "Only if we wish to die. I suggest we hide."

"In there?" St. Clair nodded back toward the tomb.

"That's not possible now," the rabbi said. "It is only given to us to enter or leave at set times, and the hour has passed."

"Then, where?"

"This way." Abu Rahman retreated behind the tomb and the others followed. "We'll hide in the garden of the oil press, that some call Gethsemane."

They followed a sheltered path between olive trees and gravestones up the Mount of Olives. As was his habit, St. Clair stayed close to the rabbi to assist the old man over rocks and steep terrain. But the rabbi seemed to require no assistance. To St. Clair's amazement, the rabbi's limp was gone and he stepped as lightly as a young man.

Chapter Fifty-Three

נג

Jerusalem
2 January, 1291
Midmorning

The guards lounged in the sun outside the Sheep Gate. Arrayed in shining armor and yellow robes, they waited upon the emir's arrival before setting out to renew the hunt for the rabbi. Many of them secretly questioned the wisdom of another day's search, having spent the preceding day scouring the valley and finding nothing. Word of their fruitless search had spread throughout the city, and a boisterous crowd gathered near the gate, making sport of them. Women veiled to the eyes along with farmers, merchants, and porters traded barbs with the soldiers.

The merchant Cosimo stood apart from the crowd, looking over the valley. The morning wind tugged at his white silk parasol, nearly pulling it from his grasp. He folded the parasol and stuck it under his arm. He was anxious to get started, anxious to see the day end and to collect his reward from the emir. He straightened his velvet cap and frowned. Petit had also promised to pay him well, but not so well that he could afford to waste any more time away from his trade.

With a flourish, the emir's litter arrived at the gate, and a smattering of cheers rose from the crowd. Bearers lowered the litter to the ground and the emir emerged, robed in white silk, scarlet slippers on his feet. He tossed coins into the crowd, and the cheering grew louder.

A guard stepped forward and shouted, "His eminence will address you."

When the crowd quieted, the emir began to speak. "Good people of Jerusalem, tomorrow I depart to join the sultan in Ascalon as we prepare for the final battle with the Franks. There is yet time for all able-bodied men to join our person. Know that Allah will richly favor all who join us, and will bless all who fall in battle with a place of prominence in the world to come."

Cheering and shouts of "God is great" filled the air. When the noise subsided, someone called out, "O Emir, what of the old men you seek?"

"We will find the Mongol spies today. But enough talking! Has not the poet said that loquacity is the pale stepchild of action? So, to the hunt! May Allah bless you and grant you peace, morning and night." He waved to the crowd and tossed another handful of coins.

Turning from the crowd, the emir approached Cosimo with an admiring glance at the merchant's silk parasol. "Good Cosimo, tomorrow we part ways; I for Ascalon and you for Acre. So listen well to me now." He drew close and fixed the merchant with his gaze. "I do not believe we will find the old rabbi, but it is of no matter. We will provide a head for you to bring to Acre—be it the head of Rabbi Samuel or that of some other old Jew.

"You will journey to Acre with a few guards, and when you reach the Western March near Acre, you will find Petit's steward waiting at the border marker at midday. You will present him with the head and demand that his master, Rabbi Petit, provide you with the information he promised. Be certain to inform Petit that I expect him to honor his word in full. Tell him I will remember him for good or ill when I lead the sultan's legions into Acre. He will either share in the spoils as the head of the community of Jews, or his flesh will be torn from his bones by the birds of the sky. The choice is his. Tell him this." The emir patted Cosimo on the back.

"Once my guards receive the information from Petit, your reward will be great." The emir smiled. "If you do this, Cosimo, you are my friend." The smile faded. "I'm your sworn enemy else. Do you understand?"

"I am most unreservedly in your service, Great One," the merchant declared as he dropped heavily to his knees. "My loyalty is yours."

"As is that delightful parasol?"

"Yes, Sire. It is yours!" Cosimo held it up.

The emir took the parasol and stepped back. "Thank you, good merchant. Now rise."

"I can't, Sire." Cosimo extended a pudgy hand. "Could you give me some assistance?"

The emir rolled his eyes and barked to an attendant as he stepped back to his litter, "See to the merchant." He drew the curtain, then removed his slippers and pulled on leather boots. He emerged with a crossbow in hand and took his place at the head of the halka. "Follow me!" he called and led the way into the valley.

St. Clair peered out from among the pine trees bordering the Garden of Gethsemane. He saw the column moving in their direction. "This doesn't look good."

"Do you think they saw us?" Rabbi Samuel asked.

"We'll know soon enough," al-Hasani whispered.

St. Clair's jaw muscles bunched as he saw them draw nearer, their armor shining in the sunlight. "How many swords do you have?" he asked Abu Rahman.

"Six, and you?"

"Three . . ." St. Clair paused and added, "Staves."

"We'll have the advantage of surprise."

St. Clair drew a deep breath as the halka reached the valley road. He exhaled in relief when the column turned sharply to the right.

"See?" Abu Rahman clapped him on the shoulder. "All that worry for nothing."

St. Clair watched the column descend into the valley. "They may yet search here later in the day—"

"Which is why," Rabbi Samuel said, "we must use the time we have to continue showing you what we have learned."

Relieved of the fear of discovery, St. Clair turned to look at the rabbi and al-Hasani. The old men were transfigured—their skin glowed and their eyes shone with youthful vigor. "You were both inside the tomb, and you came out!" he said breathlessly "You both look rejuvenated! What did you find there? Have you partaken of some new potion?"

The rabbi smiled at the mapmaker. "There is a balm in Gilead—not only in the apothecary of al-Hasani!"

The mapmaker nodded. "It is well known that warmth and light have power to heal—but I think it was more than that—"

"There is no time to explain," the rabbi cut in. "We must instruct you. Come, al-Hasani, we'll need a few minutes to arrange the scrolls and charts." The rabbi leaned down and easily picked up a heavy sack.

"My men will watch the valley," Abu Rahman offered. "If the guards begin to move in this direction, we'll give you ample warning."

"That is well, Abu Rahman."

The two walked briskly away, the rabbi showing no trace of his limp. They quickly crossed the clearing and settled at the base of an ancient olive tree.

Watching the old men, St. Clair shook his head. The change in Rabbi Samuel was beyond belief. Not only had he emerged from the tomb, but he had changed—his old body infused with life. *Something happened in there.* He started at the sound of Abu Rahman's voice.

"You will have ample time here, I think. This is the last day the emir will search for the rabbi. Tomorrow he leaves for Ascalon."

"Is the emir in need of a holiday by the sea, that he hastens to Ascalon?" St. Clair asked dryly.

"No." Abu Rahman laughed. "He goes to bring a rare gift to the sultan—a scroll containing the secrets of Acre's defenses—like so many keys . . ."

"That's impossible," Isaac cut in. "Wallace and I intercepted that scroll!"

"What could you know of such matters?" asked Abu Rahman.

St. Clair hastened to explain. "Isaac was duped into compiling a chronicle of Acre's defenses. This is, perhaps, contained in the scroll of which you speak."

"But Wallace and I got it back. I swear it! We retrieved the scroll, and at the first opportunity, we burned it!"

Abu Rahman shrugged. "My spies in the palace tell me that a scroll from Acre with this very information has arrived in Jerusalem."

"But that's not possible!" Isaac insisted.

St. Clair frowned. "Perhaps Petit reconstructed it from memory."

"No. He never read the final draft."

"*Final* draft?" St. Clair fixed his eyes on Isaac. "So there was an earlier draft?"

"Yes, that's the one I found in Petit's study—the one I brought to the Templars in Acre so they would know what the

Mamluks might learn."

"But Petit read that earlier draft," St. Clair prodded.

Isaac's jaw dropped. Realizing the truth, he buried his face in his hands. "I thought I had repaired the damage. Now I see that I failed."

"Not at all, Isaac." St. Clair rested his hand on the boy's shoulder. "You did well in carrying the draft to the Temple. They will, without doubt, make necessary adjustments in Acre's defense to confound the enemy." St. Clair glanced at Abu Rahman. "No disrespect intended, sir."

"None taken." Abu Rahman smiled. "Our only allegiance is to God and to the eternal Jerusalem, as is yours, being a true and original Templar."

"An *original* Templar? What's your meaning?"

"Such were the knights who founded your order. We remember them to this day—good stewards of the Temple. They learned much from us, but when they lost Jerusalem, they lost this knowledge. Templars became enamored with vows, uniforms, war, and gold. Nowadays, it seems knights of your order have little connection with this original and true calling." Abu Rahman put his arm around St. Clair's shoulders. "It is good to see one of you return."

"How have you maintained the calling?" St. Clair asked.

"Our stewardship of the eternal Jerusalem was enhanced by our appearing completely unremarkable. Thus, we lead our lives in this world as artisans, householders—"

"Jonathan! Bring Isaac and Wallace." Rabbi Samuel gesticulated from across the green. "We're ready to begin."

"What of breakfast, Rabbi?" Abu Rahman asked. "You've had nothing to eat."

"We have no time for that." Rabbi Samuel brushed the notion aside.

"Nonsense! I'll have one of my men go into the city and

fetch food and drink."

"Thank you, good Abu Rahman," said al-Hasani. "And if you might, please inform my wife that I am well, and make certain to tell her that she and my son should remain at home until I return."

"And also," St. Clair added, "please convey to the woman, Zahirah, that I shall see her soon."

"Wait, Abu Rahman," the rabbi said suddenly. He stood up and approached the silversmith. "Do not give this message to the woman."

"Why not?" asked St. Clair.

Ignoring the knight's question, the rabbi stood on his toes and whispered something in Abu Rahman's ear.

Chapter Fifty-Four

נד

Jerusalem
2 January, 1291
Midday

While Zahirah assisted al-Hasani's wife with the usual household chores—washing linens, preparing the pallets, pressing oil for the lamps, and pounding spices—she saw the fear rising in Sha'ima's eyes. She felt it herself—a growing fear gripping her heart. Jonathan and the boys had left yesterday—the rabbi and al-Hasani, the day before. Sha'ima's son, Tarek, was also gone, having left before sunrise to gather brushwood. With all the men gone, the house was empty and quiet. As the hours passed, they listened for the bell to sound.

The afternoon found them in the wind-swept courtyard where Zahirah pushed dead leaves with a broom toward Sha'ima, who gathered them into a sack for kindling. Zahirah wore only a cotton shirt beneath her tunic, and she could feel the cold fingers of the wind touching her body. Within her belly, she felt the baby sleeping warm and quiet. From time to time, the wind shook the bell that hung by the gate—a false messenger. She prayed for the bell to sound in earnest, for Jonathan to return.

Sha'ima turned back to the house, dragging the bag of leaves.

"Please, Lady Sha'ima, allow me to assist you."

"Thank you, child." Pausing at the door, the old woman raised her eyes to the sky. "They shouldn't be out in such weather."

Zahirah took the bag and followed Sha'ima into the house. Kneeling at the hearth, she took a stick and stirred the ashes but found no glowing embers. With leaves for kindling and a few sticks of brushwood, she struck a flint and coaxed a fire. She sat at the wheel and began combing yarn for the spindle. She looked at Sha'ima and saw that her hands shook as she tried to string the loom with flaxen threads.

"How can I sit here when my husband is being hunted?" Sha'ima said suddenly and stood up. "I must go to the valley and see what transpires there!" She took a woolen shawl from a hook by the hearth and pulled it about her shoulders.

"Please, my lady, don't go," Zahirah said as she followed her to the door. "It is dangerous for you to go there."

"Why? The emir seeks the rabbi from Baghdad, not my husband."

"But your husband and the rabbi travel together."

"They speak only of an old man who accompanies the rabbi. Trust me, if the emir knew it was al-Hasani, his guard would even now be at our gate." She lifted the latch.

"I beseech you, allow *me* to go in your stead. I will soon return and bring you word."

"I will happily allow you to go, my dear, but *with* me, not in my stead."

"Very well. I will go with you."

"But not like that." Sha'ima frowned. "Your robe is too thin, and you with child. I'll fetch you something that will keep away the chill." She led the way to the parlor. From a wardrobe she took a robe of black wool.

Zahirah lifted her arms to put on the robe and her belly rose beneath her smock.

"I have some knowledge of midwifery, my girl, and from your mounting belly I think that you have but three months to your time of confinement. Is this not so?"

"You are correct, my lady." Zahirah blushed and pulled the robe over her head. With her hand, she freed her hair, now grown long, from beneath the robe.

"You must not leave the house with your hair loosed in this fashion. I will braid it."

As she took a brush from the wardrobe, the bell sounded, and the two women rushed into the courtyard.

Sha'ima gripped the hairbrush like a weapon. "Who might it be?" she whispered.

Zahirah held her breath as she raised the latch, exhaling with relief when she saw Tarek, bent beneath a bundle of brushwood, peeking out from beneath the edge of his hood.

"Have they returned?" he asked.

"No, my son, and our hearts are greatly troubled."

Zahirah stepped forward. "Is there any word of Jonathan and the boys?"

"No. I heard nothing of them."

Tarek placed the wood on the floor by the hearth. Straightening up, he pushed back his hood. His hair, black as pitch, hung in ringlets beside his dark eyes.

"Warm yourself by the fire, my son, and tell us the news."

"There is much talk of the search for father and the rabbi in the Valley of Kidron. But they have found nothing. It is said this is the last day of the search since the emir leaves tomorrow to join the sultan's army in Ascalon."

"That is well," Sha'ima said as she ladled out a cup of hot tea and handed it to Tarek. "You rest here and mind the house, my son. Zahirah and I will go to the valley to watch for them."

"You must not go there, mother. People will become suspicious—"

"Suspicious of what?"

Tarek lowered the cup from his lips. "They say Rabbi Samuel is a spy sent from Baghdad by the Mongols, and it is well known that we are from Baghdad. Thus, your presence in the valley might raise questions. Besides, mother, it is bitter cold. I wish you would stay here."

"And I tell you I must go."

Tarek rose to his feet with a sigh. "Then I shall go with you,"

"Good. Bring blankets from the guest room." Sha'ima turned to Zahirah. "Come, my child. Let us prepare food and drink. And I shall braid your hair before we leave."

Just as the women entered the kitchen, the bell sounded again. As they crossed the courtyard, Tarek was already at the gate. He lifted the latch.

Zahirah stepped around Tarek and saw a stranger, clad in a dirty shirt, his face and arms smudged with grease. She thought him a beggar.

"Your business, sir?" Tarek asked warily.

The stranger leaned forward. "I am sent by my master the silversmith, Abu Rahman, to bring word to the wife of al-Hasani—"

"Enter, and quickly. I am the wife of al-Hasani."

"Thank you, lady." Bowing, the man removed his leather cap and stepped through the gate into the courtyard.

Tarek pushed the gate closed and secured the latch.

"Your husband wishes you to know that he is well and will soon come home."

"Does he even so?" Her eyes sparkled above the scarf. "And where is my master?"

"In that place known as the Garden of Gethsemane. I am to

return there after I go to market, where I am to acquire food and drink."

"Do not trouble yourself, sir. My larder is full. I will provide all they might require. Furthermore, we will come with you."

"I'm sorry, my lady. The master al-Hasani says you and your son must remain here and await his return."

"Very well." Sha'ima sighed and raised her shoulders. "I shall prepare victuals and drink that you might bring to them. How many are there?"

"Between your husband, the rabbi, and their company, they number five."

Zahirah's heart beat fast, sure that Jonathan was among them. She stepped forward. "In their company, is there a tall man, who has a scar here?" She traced a line along the side of her face.

"Yes. I know the man. That same gentleman requested to give a message to his woman, but the rabbi denied him."

"Denied him, you say? I am that man's woman, sir, and I charge you to tell me. What was the message?"

"I am sorry, lady, but I am constrained by Rabbi Samuel not to tell you."

"What foolishness is this? Why would the rabbi keep this from me?"

"Because instead of carrying a message, the rabbi bid me bring *you* to the garden."

"All of us?" asked Sha'ima hopefully.

"No—only her." He nodded at Zahirah.

"Very well." Sha'ima sighed and turned to Tarek. "Show this man to the hearth where he may warm himself while we prepare food and drink." She turned and stepped toward the kitchen. "Come, my daughter."

In the kitchen they emptied the larder of bread, honey wafers, fig cake, dried fruit, nuts, olives, dried cheeses, and curds.

Zahirah was certain she would soon see Jonathan, and her heart was glad. Within her womb she felt the baby leap.

Once all was ready, she turned to Sha'ima. "My lady, might you now braid my hair?"

"Certainly, dear."

Zahirah sat in a high-backed chair and Sha'ima brushed her hair, but suddenly stopped. "I hope I did not hurt you."

"Not at all."

"That's strange. There's a sore here at the nape of your neck. Doesn't it pain you?"

"No, mother," she replied as a cold dread began to enfold her.

"You don't feel this?"

"I feel nothing there." The fear rose in her heart, pounding in her chest. "I think I should go now."

"But I have not yet braided your hair."

"Do not bother with it, my lady. I shall keep myself covered with the hood. It is not necessary to braid the hair." She pulled the cowled hood over her head and took hold of two sacks of food. Her hands shook and it was hard for her to catch her breath.

From her time at the leper colony, she knew the meaning of painless sores.

The rabbi will know at a glance. I must ask him. I must know for certain.

Oh, Jonathan, my love. I am so afraid.

Chapter Fifty-Five

נה

The Garden of Gethsemane
2 January, 1291
Afternoon

Huddled in woolen robes by an ancient olive tree, the rabbi and the mapmaker instructed St. Clair, Isaac, and Wallace. Oblivious to the cold wind, they perused a dozen scrolls and reviewed the use of the panpipes and the monochord. Past midday, the high clouds thinned, and bright patches of sunlight drifted through the garden.

St. Clair glanced up from a scroll and saw the silversmith approaching. "What news, Abu Rahman? Does the halka come this way?"

"No, my masters. For now, they search along the southern march, perhaps a two-hour's journey. But the danger remains great." His face darkened. "The emir has decreed death to any who venture into the valley, and he has set a watch. Because of this, my men and I cannot move freely. We have therefore devised signals with flags; a white flag means they are moving up the valley toward Jerusalem and a black flag means they are coming to the garden."

"Master Abu-Rahman . . ." Isaac asked tentatively. "What of the food you spoke of?"

"My apprentice will no doubt skirt the valley to the north and will soon bring all you require. Be patient and farewell." He turned away, crossed the garden, and vanished into the thicket at the garden's edge.

Al-Hasani raised the panpipes toward Wallace. "Does your friend wish to try this again?" He directed the question in Arabic to Isaac who was translating everything into French for Wallace.

"Oui," Wallace replied. He took the pipes and carefully sounded the notes. Then he asked, "*Je ne comprends pas*—do these three notes summon someone to raise a portcullis and open a gate?"

"No, my dear boy." Al-Hasani laughed and shook his head. "The notes work through sacred geometry."

Wallace's eyes narrowed. "Is this some form of magic?"

"Yes, but only if you believe there is magic in the natural laws of the universe." Al-Hasani smiled and raised his heavy eyebrows. "Sacred geometry describes the manner in which nature orders itself. It gives evidence to the symmetric patterns we see around us—in a crystal or a flower or a seashell—the order that fills the universe."

"In certain respects," Rabbi Samuel added, "this order reflects the Mind of God."

"The Mind of the God of Israel?" asked Isaac.

"Is the God of Israel not the God of all nations and all worlds?" the rabbi asked as he smoothed his beard. "We speak of Divine principles beyond those of any one religion, Isaac. Indeed, in every land there are those who perceive the fabric of harmonious patterns embedded in the created world. The examples are all about us—in the wings of a butterfly, these pipes, or a great cathedral. The principles are the same."

St. Clair nodded his assent. "I have myself witnessed such things—the giant ring of stones on the island of Britannia, cathedrals in France, the Great Pyramid at Ghiza, the Dome of the Rock—"

"Precisely, Jonathan," al-Hasani cut in. "And just as these are the expressions of sacred geometry we can *see,* music is the expression we can *hear.* This knowledge flows freely between all peoples—from Pythagoras of Samos, to al-Kindi of Kufah, to Sa'adiah Gaon of Sura, to Lao Tzu of the eastern lands. All these, and men and women like them, in diverse times and places, have explored the fabric of this knowledge."

"Listen to me, Isaac," Rabbi Samuel said, leaning forward. "As Jews, we must recognize that our own story as a people is just that—*our* story. People of different faiths have *their* stories. Is it not written that the beauty of Japheth might dwell in the tents of Shem? Thus, all the stories—theirs and ours—inform and nourish each other. For us as Jews, the mystery is here in Jerusalem. But for others, it may reside upon some other mountain or in some other city—"

"But special blessing often brings a special curse," al-Hasani said with a frown. "Just look at what Jerusalem's election has brought." He turned his eyes to St. Clair. "The yearning that drew knights of the Crusade here plunged the Holy Land into centuries of bloodshed."

"And why, Jonathan?" the rabbi asked. "Because you saw a shining city on a hill, and confused the symbol with the actual place."

"I'm not sure I understand . . ."

"We speak of the *real* Jerusalem, Jonathan, not that city." He pointed. "Not that city of stone and dirt and bad smells and noise. We speak of a place of the heart, where people meet their better selves, where heaven and earth connect. But this great truth is hidden within myth."

St. Clair frowned. "Is the position of Jerusalem among the nations just a myth?"

"What is myth, Jonathan, but an artful lie that draws one to the truth? Most Jews, Christians, and Moslems have received this myth on its face value—that the Jerusalem of *this* world is the *actual* place. But we mustn't embrace the myth too fervently, lest we lose sight of the truth behind the myth—"

"But, Rabbi," Isaac cut in, "what you call myth is central to Judaism. Without Jerusalem we have no center."

"True, Isaac, but the key is the murmur of the city we hold in our hearts. To hear *that* Jerusalem, we must become still, and in that silence she will whisper her song to us. And wherever we are in the world, we will have the song of that quiet city." The rabbi pointed across the Kidron Valley. "*That* Jerusalem is a part of the song—but only a part. If we affix our hearts solely upon this particular place as the true and only shining city on a hill, we only succeed in creating a bone of contention that people will fight over, that people will kill for." He shook his head sadly. "That's our nature, isn't it? Whether the goal is power or gold or Jerusalem, people will fight and die for it."

"Surely, Rabbi," Isaac protested, "the Jerusalem of *this* world is more than an object of contention. Jerusalem holds a special place in the heart of every Jew."

"And also in the heart of every Moslem and every Christian, Isaac. It is as in the story told of King Solomon—and the child claimed by two mothers—a city claimed by many nations."

"And if I may invert the allegory," said al-Hasani, "the *true* children of Jerusalem are those who love her enough to share her. And it is our purpose to make that possible. This is the burden of our stewardship in this world—to guard the gateway—to protect pilgrims. This was the original calling of your order, Jonathan, and this is the calling we all now claim."

St. Clair picked a scroll off the grass and spread it out on his knee. He passed his hand over the pattern of circles and connecting lines inscribed on the parchment. "And you determined the location of the gateway from *this*?"

"Yes." The rabbi nodded. "For months we delved into the secrets of your scroll. By combining my knowledge of Kabbalah with al-Hasani's knowledge of sacred geometry and cartography, we found the point of entry."

St. Clair's heart pounded as he looked over the diagram with a dawning understanding and joy—almost a sense of homecoming.

"These names in the circles," he pointed, "crown, glory, and the others—you called these emanations of the Divine. What is your meaning? Are these entities, like angels?"

"No. The emanations are not intermediaries. They're identical to God's essence. Each of the ten is drawn from the Divine source just as water is drawn from a well, or light from the sun."

"Or, perhaps," St. Clair said with a smile, "as a candle is lit from another candle without being diminished. I remember you spoke to me thus at Tel Hum."

"Yes, Jonathan. As the radiant essence of the Divine, the emanations are the substance between the one and the many, between the hidden and the revealed. They emerge from within God—the *ayn sof*—and yet they are all equally close to the source."

"Then why do you arrange them in this manner?"

"Because the created world is not accidental. It's a structured intention of the Divine. There is a specific order to these attributes. In this manner the emanations are joined within the hidden life of God. Indeed, the inner foundation of every created being reflects this intention. In this manner God moves from concealment to revelation, from silence to speech."

The rabbi leaned toward St. Clair and placed his hand on his shoulder. "And silence is the key, Jonathan, because revelation is subtle, and Divine speech can be heard only when one knows how to listen. Thus, the heart of Kabbalah is becoming quiet and learning to listen, learning to hear that small voice—"

"My masters! My masters!" An apprentice of Abu Rahman burst from the thicket at the edge of the garden, shouting, "Someone comes!"

St. Clair stood up, his stave in his fist. "What flags?"

"There are no flags."

"Who comes?"

"Two people—not guards—approach from the north! They carry sacks and will soon be here."

"Be not troubled, Jonathan," said al-Hasani. "It's only Abu Rahman's apprentice and someone who helps him bring food and drink from market. Let's continue. We should speak to you of the portal—"

"Indeed," said St. Clair. "You've told us how you located the portal, but how were you able to unlock it?"

"The key was your scroll, Jonathan, and something I learned from you in Safed."

"Something you learned from *me*?"

The rabbi nodded. "You told me of your meeting Abraham Abulafiya long ago in Acre. That guided me in the right direction. I had always thought he came to Palestine to learn the wisdom of the Sufis, but you told me the reason he came was to find the River Sambatyon." The rabbi turned to Isaac. "What do you know of this river, Isaac?"

"I know of legends." Isaac raised his shoulders. "They tell of a torrent of rushing water and boulders among the mountains of darkness in Lebanon, a river that separates the ten lost tribes from Judah, a river that is said to behave like a living thing—even to keeping the commandment of Sabbath rest. But many have searched for it and found nothing. Most believe there is no such river."

"Ah, but there is," the rabbi whispered. "But it's not in Lebanon."

"Not in Lebanon?" Isaac asked and pointed at St. Clair's scroll. "But in this passage it's clearly stated—*a fountain in the garden, a well of living waters that flows from Lebanon.*"

"That's only the surface meaning, and that was Abulafiya's mistake. He had not yet perfected his abilities to derive layers of meaning from gematria. Otherwise, he would have understood that this river of living water wasn't in Lebanon at all. This was clear to me the first time I saw the scroll in Safed. It was then I knew we had to seek the sacred river here, in Jerusalem."

"But how?" Isaac asked.

"I'll show you." The rabbi pointed at the inscription. "Using gematria, this passage equals the number one thousand and five, which is exactly the number that derives from *y'rushalayim ha'kdosha*— sacred Jerusalem."

"But there's no river here—"

"Isn't there?" The rabbi smiled. "Listen to the text! The river we seek is not one of *water,* but *living waters,* a river of sacred light. And it is not hidden in Lebanon among mountains of darkness, but within a mountain of light." He raised his hand, pointing toward the Temple Mount. "*That* mountain—"

"My masters!" Abu-Rahman's apprentice shouted and pointed as he ran toward them. "The apprentice is almost here along with a stranger—"

"Who could this be?" asked Isaac.

"Someone who requires our assistance," the rabbi said and patted Isaac on the shoulder. "Go help them with the sacks."

"I'll also go—" St. Clair turned.

"No, Jonathan," the rabbi said. "Come and walk with me."

Rabbi Samuel led St. Clair into the garden. Stopping by an olive tree, he looked up at St. Clair and smiled. "I've watched you and Zahirah since Tel Hum, Jonathan. I've seen how the love grows between you."

Taken aback, St. Clair raised his shoulders. "Why are we

speaking of this now?"

"Have you asked her?"

"What?"

"To betroth—"

"Is this really the time to speak of such matters?"

"It is—we may not have another opportunity. Have you asked her?"

"We have spoken of the matter, and of my vow . . ."

"Ah, yes—your vow. So, what is your intention—to remain with the order and keep the marriage hidden?"

"No. I'll never conceal her. When we return to Acre, I shall lay the matter at the feet of the Templar masters, and I'll wait upon their word."

"Wait for what? You know they'll deny you an open marriage. You'll have to choose, Jonathan—the order or the woman."

"If it comes to a choice, Rabbi, I've already made it. I cannot live without Zahirah."

"Are you so resolved?"

"I am."

"Good. Then go to your bride, my son. It is she who comes hither."

Chapter Fifty-Six

נו

The Garden of Gethsemane
2 January, 1291
Late afternoon

"Rabbi Samuel! Jonathan! We have food and drink! Come and partake!"

St. Clair saw Isaac emerge from the thicket at the garden's edge holding up a burlap sack. He was followed by Wallace and Abu Rahman's apprentice. Then St. Clair's breath caught. Trailing behind, her face framed by the hooded robe, was Zahirah, her eyes downcast.

St. Clair crossed the clearing in long strides. Approaching Zahirah, he resisted the desire to catch her up in his arms. "My lady," he said softly.

"Darling," she said without looking up, "I must speak with the rabbi." As she moved past him, she raised her arms to push back the hood of her robe, her rich auburn hair falling to her shoulders.

Puzzled, he followed her with his eyes. *Perhaps she conspires to speak with him about our marriage. That is well.* But as he watched them speak, he saw the rabbi's countenance change, like a cloud blotting out the sun.

Something was wrong.

He watched as they turned and walked quickly away—to the further reaches of the garden where he could not see them. A terrible thought rose in his mind. *Oh, Lord, I pray that the baby is well.*

"Jonathan!" Isaac called from behind. "Come join us. Look, there are even honey cakes!"

He half-turned and saw Isaac, Wallace, and al-Hasani sitting among tufts of brown grass with parcels of food, clay jugs, and water skins around them.

"At least taste the fig cake before we finish it," called al-Hasani. He drew back his arm and tossed a parcel in a high arc through the air.

St. Clair caught the fig cake in his hand. Absently, he took a bite as he turned and searched for Zahirah and the rabbi with his eyes, pacing back and forth.

What are they talking about, and why so long?

He finished the fig cake and ambled over to where the men were eating. Realizing how hungry he was, he tore off a piece of flatbread and wrapped it around a square of yellow cheese. The sun felt good on his back, but his heart was filled with dread. After a long drink of water from a skin, he took a few olives. He ate, sitting on his heels, looking across the garden.

"What troubles you, Jonathan?" Wallace asked.

"I am worried how it is with Zahirah," he replied and spit an olive pit into his hand. "I don't understand why—"

He saw the rabbi come into view, followed by Zahirah, her head down, covered by the hooded robe. He started forward, then broke into a run across the clearing. As he approached, he saw Zahirah's cheeks were wet with tears. "Is it the baby?" he whispered.

The rabbi put his hands on St. Clair's shoulders. "No, Jonathan, the baby is fine. It's Zahirah, my son. It's Zahirah. The leprosy—"

"No!" St. Clair cried and fell to his knees at Zahirah's feet. He held her about the waist, feeling the fullness of her belly beneath the robe, pressing his face against her body. "No!" he cried again. Jerking his head to the side, he shot a look at the rabbi. "But you were *certain*—"

"There was no blemish before, Jonathan. None." The rabbi raised his shoulders. "Sometimes it takes months . . ."

"I must see for myself." St. Clair jumped to his feet. "Where is it?"

"Here." The rabbi pointed. "On the neck. I'm sorry, Jonathan. There is no doubt."

St. Clair gently pulled down the hood, and pushed aside Zahirah's rich dark hair. He stared at the spot—round and faint as the midday moon, a whitish plaque with slightly raised edges. He'd seen such lesions before.

She stood facing away from him, sobbing quietly.

He wrapped her in his arms and held her close, weeping, his tears wetting her hair.

"Jonathan." He felt the rabbi's hand on his shoulder. "You must be careful—"

"Careful?" He spit the word out, his eyes feral and filled with tears. "For what? I want also to have the leprosy!"

"No, my love," Zahirah protested and pulled away. "You must be healthy to care for our baby."

What of the baby? The question seared his mind. He drew back, his gaze darting to the rabbi. "What . . . what of the baby?" he stammered.

"The disease does not pass from mother to child in pregnancy. But after the birth, Zahirah will give the infant to a wet nurse and have no contact. Only thus will the child be spared."

Zahirah's shoulders shook as she wept.

Again, St. Clair wrapped her in his arms, and again, she pulled away.

"You mustn't touch me," she whispered.

St. Clair pressed his hands over his eyes. He wanted to scream. Instead, he came near her and spoke softly. "I will not touch you, but I will not leave your side—ever."

"When the time comes, you will leave."

"No." He watched how the sunlight shone on her hair. "I am also you now. We are one flesh. Your fate is my fate. I will never leave you."

"What foolish talk is this, Jonathan? Who will care for our child?"

"I will. And I will keep the baby always within your sight." He stepped around and fixed her with his eyes. "It is my desire that the rabbi will marry us now."

"Now?" Wiping tears from her cheeks, she gave a bitter laugh. "Do not vex me with such talk, Jonathan. My heart is torn and flayed."

"Yet I will marry you—"

"No, Jonathan. There can be nothing other than your choice from day to day. But let me depart now. I must keep my own counsel for a little time." She turned away and crossed the clearing toward the eastern edge of the garden.

St. Clair stood next to Rabbi Samuel, watching her until she disappeared among the olive trees, his head crowned with pain—like thorns piercing the bone case of his skull. His throat was parched and it hurt to breathe. Within the furnace of his chest, his heart burned. Stifling a scream, he tore his robe open and looked down at his chest—the battle scars crimson against his skin. "No hurt in battle felt worse than this," he whispered through clenched teeth and crushed his fists against his heart. "What am I to do?" He shut his eyes and gulped a lungful of air. "What am I to do?"

"You know exactly what you will do," the rabbi replied evenly.

St. Clair nodded. "I will see to it our child is born safely in

Acre. I will protect and care for Zahirah and the child."

"Yes. And you will be a good steward of the secrets of the pure Upper Jerusalem."

"The pure Upper Jerusalem," St. Clair said bitterly. "What good is that now?"

"What good, Jonathan? What good are the uses of this world *without* that connection? You have regained the knowledge, which the original Templars held in trust and lost. You must do your part to insure it is not lost again. This is your calling as a Knight Templar, and this is your calling as *my* knight." The rabbi rested a hand on his shoulder. "Zahirah is ill, Jonathan. This is a terrible, terrible blow. But I know you. And I know you will be with her in this sickness—"

"As I watch her die, bit by bit?"

"Jonathan, you know it may be many years—"

"Until she finally dies?"

"We all die—one way or another. You know this better than most. If the emir has his way, we'll all die today. But we decide how we *live*. What springs will you discover in this valley of weeping, Jonathan? I know you will love and care for Zahirah, and now without touching. You will practice the celibacy you practiced before."

St. Clair's jaw muscles bunched beneath his beard. He nodded but said nothing, glancing over to where Isaac and al-Hasani sat on the lawn. They had stopped eating, and sat without moving.

"Jonathan, since the first day I met you in Safed, I saw the struggle within you, between the man and the Templar. And the Templar always had his vows . . ."

"But I have renounced my vows, Rabbi." St. Clair rubbed a hand over his face. "Now I am only a man."

"*Only* a man, Jonathan? With or without your vows, you are God's man! You are a true Templar!"

"A Templar strives to be more than mere man," St. Clair said weakly.

"You strive to be like Christ?"

"Of course not. That would be blasphemy."

"But in your heart, you reach further. You have told me as much. In your chastity, your poverty, your sacrifice—you strive to be like Christ."

St. Clair stared past the olive trees and said nothing.

"It's ironic, no? He, as you, suffered here, agonized here—*in this very garden*—"

"This is blasphemy, Rabbi. You must not speak thus—"

"Leave off, Jonathan. In being the man that God ordained in the clutch of circumstance, you are God's man, not a man *presuming* to be God. You are uniting all aspects of your life—your heart and your mind, your insight and intention into a vehicle of wholeness—a chariot of God. This is the real journey we've made together, not merely a journey to Jerusalem, Jonathan, but a journey of rectification—of *tikun.*

"Long ago you committed your life to guide and to protect those who search for holiness. This you have done. You have stood in the breach, willing to sacrifice unto death. This also you have done. This is the calling of your order. But your order is larger than you know, Jonathan." The rabbi tapped his chest, his voice rising. "*I* am of your order." He raised his arm and pointed. "The mapmaker and Isaac and Wallace are of your order. So too Zahirah, Abu Rahman, and his apprentices. Ours is a fellowship of diverse people throughout time and throughout the world, bound together in a silent devotion to that calling—"

"White flags!" An apprentice of the silversmith called Khaled burst from the thicket, pointing. "The halka moves up the Valley of Kidron!"

St. Clair lurched forward. "Can you see them?"

"No, only the flags."

Isaac was at his side. “Shall we arm ourselves? What should we do?”

“Calm yourself,” St. Clair replied. “They may merely be returning to their barracks in Jerusalem.” He bent down and lifted his stave off the ground. “However, it would be prudent to move toward the eastern edge of the garden. It will be dark soon, and if they come to the garden, we’ll hide in the forest.”

“Come, boys,” al-Hasani said as he headed back to where the parcels were spread on the ground. “Let’s gather up the food and away.”

“I’ll see to the scrolls,” said the rabbi.

As St. Clair knelt to help the rabbi, he called to the silversmith’s apprentice, “Khaled, watch for the black flags. Tell us the moment you see them.”

“I will, sir.” The apprentice bowed and disappeared into the thicket.

“Do you have the panpipes in that sack?” the rabbi asked.

St. Clair nodded. “Both of them.”

“Give me one.” The rabbi tucked the panpipes among his robes and stood up.

“Why do you—?” St. Clair began.

“Let’s away!” The rabbi slung a sack over his shoulder.

As they crossed the garden, St. Clair anxiously watched for Zahirah, and was greatly relieved when she joined them, walking a few paces behind. Along with sadness and despair, there was a hope now rising in his chest—a hope that she might be healed. *After all, the rabbi was restored within the Holy Mountain! I’ll ask him at the very next opportunity. Might not Zahirah be restored there as well? Is it possible . . . ?* The hope made his heart beat faster.

The ground sloped upward. Olive trees gave way to cedar and pine with a low cover of thorn brush. They were now well concealed among the trees. Zahirah remained apart, her gaze downcast.

St. Clair came to a stop. "Let's remain within sight of the garden and see what further news the apprentice brings."

The rabbi put down the sack he carried. "We must speak further now, and we have little time, so listen well! We told you of a small pyramid that must be built on the coast of Provençe after taking ship from Acre. The dimensions of the pyramid are here—also the map showing the spot. Study these. The captain of the ship must put to shore at the port of Nice. From there it is but a short distance to the place."

Al-Hasani nodded. "One need only follow the map. The name of the place is Falicon—a small village in the mountains not far from the sea."

"The exact site and the details of the structure are of the utmost importance," admonished Rabbi Samuel.

"But why must we do this? What's the purpose?" Isaac asked.

"It's a beacon," al-Hasani replied, "a guide for others to follow—like the capstone of Zechariah's tomb, like the Pyramid at Ghiza. It falls to us to show others the way."

"But how—?"

"It's all in the scrolls," the rabbi cut in. "We've given you all you require to fulfill your part of the story. And, as I told you, Isaac, your part also includes separating from the others after the work of the pyramid. You're for the island of Comino—there you'll find Abulafiya. You must learn from him, Isaac."

"But there are fine teachers of Kabbalah in Provençe, Rabbi. And everyone knows Abulafiya is mad—"

"His is a holy madness, Isaac. Learn from him."

"Look!" al-Hasani pointed past the trees. "Isn't that the apprentice?"

St. Clair turned and saw Khaled walking slowly toward them. Much too slowly.

"What news, Khaled?" St. Clair called out from their hiding place among the trees.

The apprentice stopped walking. He looked up, swaying slightly. "The emir . . . the emir comes," Khaled breathed out, then pitched forward, a half-dozen arrows in his back.

"This way, now!" St. Clair pointed deeper into the forest.

Rabbi Samuel grabbed Isaac's arm. "Give me your stave."

Isaac held out his stave, panic and confusion etched on his face.

St. Clair turned to see the rabbi take the stave from Isaac. "What need you of *that,* Rabbi? We must away!"

"No—"

"What do mean, no? If we stand and fight, we die, and the knowledge will die with us."

"*You* have the knowledge now." The rabbi put his hand to his chest. "It's *me* the emir wants, and I will lead him away from you—"

"You must not do this!" St. Clair whispered through clenched teeth, scanning the garden through the trees. "I will not allow it!"

"You presume too much on your long service, my son. I tell you I must, and I will! And what I do, I must do alone. And I must do it *now.* There's no time to argue." Fixing St. Clair with his gaze, the rabbi smiled. "You will go on from here, Jonathan—for Zahirah and the baby." He glanced at Isaac, speaking quickly. "You will all go on. All of you." Quickly grasping al-Hasani's hand, the rabbi whispered, "Goodbye, brother!"

St. Clair stood, his face streaked with tears.

The rabbi backed away and raised the stave in a kind of valediction. "Go now!"

Chapter Fifty-Seven

נז

The Garden of Gethsemane
2 January, 1291
Evening

Once in the garden, the rabbi wasted no time. He bent over Khaled's body and unhitched the shield, belt, and sword. He noticed the device on the sword and the shield—the two interlocking triangles, glowing in the russet evening light—the same as on the scroll. He fastened the belt about his waist and sheathed the sword.

Evening sunlight poured across the rim of the sky. Squinting past silhouetted olive trees, he saw them, their yellow robes billowing in the wind.

"Here I am, O Emir!" he called out. "Your search is over, but your fight has just begun. I challenge you to single combat!"

The rabbi continued forward, passing the dark shapes of olive trees and the moving shadows of the emir's guard, like wraiths converging about him.

"Stand where you are, or you're a dead man!"

"We are all dead men, O Emir," the rabbi said and slowed his pace. Holding his stave with one hand, he shielded his eyes with the other. "Do you accept my challenge?"

"What idle boast is this, old man? Single combat? With you?"

He could see the emir now, a bolt set in his crossbow. "Ancient dotard—have the years left you witless that you dare make such a brazen and empty challenge?"

The sun had not yet set, and he still hoped to bring them to the tomb. There, he might sound the panpipes and lead them into the chasm of the mountain—that place of light for those of kindred spirit, a living Temple. But not for the emir—for those of dissonant nature, the chasm was a grave. He might yet lead them there, though the tomb was half a league away, and the sun was but a finger's breadth from the horizon.

He stopped walking and raised the stave. "Though I am old, I have some skill—my stick against your scimitar."

The guards roared with laughter.

The emir raised his crossbow. "Old fool, I have no time for your ravings. I profit only by your death."

"Ah, but by my death, you shall lose more profit than you think to gain."

"Of what profit do you speak?"

"Merely the greatest of treasures," Rabbi Samuel said. "Follow me, and I'll show you."

"No," the emir said quietly, almost wearily. "We will not follow you, and you will not show us. Stand and speak."

"There is no time for talk. The light fails and the night is soon upon us. Come." Rabbi Samuel edged away. If they came quickly, he might yet lure them to the tomb. "Follow me quickly, and you shall see."

The emir's voice rose. "I charge you to stand and explain yourself!"

"Shall I drop him, Sire?" a guard asked.

"No. The old man is my sport."

Rabbi Samuel reached the wooded edge of the garden and slipped among the trees.

"Stand where you are! Stop!"

But he did not stop. He angled away from the emir's voice, away from the heavy footfalls of the guards. He moved as swiftly as he could, out from among the trees, and down the slope of Olivet. The fiery disk of the sun, framed by crimson clouds, touched the line of the firmament. He wiped sweat from his forehead and felt the evening air, cool upon his face.

Now he was among the gravestones, crouching and weaving.

"Very well." The emir's voice floated down the hill from above. "I will wound you till you speak more."

A bolt grazed a headstone and sang off into the dirt.

"The next one will taste your flesh, old man. I order you to halt!"

But he kept moving, dodging between the stones, knowing he had the emir's complete attention, leading him away from the others.

"Halt, I say!"

He reached the valley road. Now he was in the open. He began to run.

The evening grew suddenly dark as a cloud moved in front of the setting sun.

How strange and fortunate is this darkness, though it is not yet night. Words of the Prophet Zechariah rose in his mind: . . . *and there shall come a day . . . lo yom ve'lo layla . . . not day, and not night.* He saw the words in his mind, the letters moving between their meaning and their gematria, numbers connected in shifting combinations, from one significance to another.

With a sudden thump and searing pain, a bolt struck his back.

He stumbled, staggering forward, his chest on fire. But he did not stop.

With a sudden blaze of light, the sun broke through the clouds—a sheet of gold shining over Jerusalem, the air rising in waves of light, shining on the headstones of Olivet, no longer day but not yet night.

A fierce joy filled his heart as the prophet's words streamed before his eyes, the letters cascading—*Ve'haya le'ate erev yi'hyeh or . . . in the evening there will be light. And living waters shall go forth from Jerusalem . . .*

A second bolt plunged into his back. No pain now—only the clarity of the gravestones, glowing in the evening, and the birds calling, and the wind in the thorn brush, and his own breathing. His mouth felt wet. He wiped with his hand and saw the redness of his blood. And now there was no blood and no hand, but only the letters streaming, only the letters shifting in a tapestry of blazing colors, or perhaps the last rays of the sun painting the sky, and the path of red earth winding down Kidron like a river of perfect fire. Caught in the blast of light, his soul leapt as another bolt struck.

In the silence between heartbeats he remembered the last words of Rabbi Hanina ben Tradyon, who perished at the hands of the Romans, wrapped in a burning Torah scroll. *The parchment is burning, but the letters are flying free.* Falling to his knees, he lifted his face to the burning sky, his eyes filled with tears.

Drawn into the circle of a living God, he understood that perfect travail, the quickening before birth. There was no beginning as there was no end—only an endless unknowable alphabet, stretching before and after, forming the world—a world alive with God—in the ground beneath him, in the wild skirling of the air, in the blaze of the setting sun; God piercing him through and through.

Drawn into the measureless power of that love, the letters flying free and love flowing through him in a tide of light.

Chapter Fifty-Eight

נח

The Garden of Gethsemane
3 January, 1291
Before dawn

"*Ya* al-Hasani! Where are you?" In the gray darkness, someone was calling from the garden.

St. Clair awoke as he had slept, wrapped in a blanket on a litter of pine needles within the forest bordering the garden. Instantly on his feet, he stared into the shadows past the trees.

The voice came again. "*Ya* al-Hasani!"

The mapmaker sat up.

Isaac was at St. Clair's elbow. "Is it the rabbi?" he asked hopefully.

St. Clair knew it wasn't and shook his head.

"It's Abu-Rahman," al-Hasani said, climbing to his feet.

"Are you certain?" Isaac asked.

"Yes. Let's hear what news he brings."

St. Clair turned to Isaac. "I'll go with al-Hasani. If it's safe, I'll call to you. If you hear nothing, remain hidden." He saw Zahirah was already up, standing apart in the bleak shadows, her cowled robe covering her head. He was filled with the hope that she might be healed of the leprosy within the mountain. But he didn't want to mention this to her without first speaking with the rabbi, if he still lived.

St. Clair and the mapmaker groped among the dark trees. Moving as silently as they could, they came into the garden.

The silversmith stood by his slain apprentice, a gray blanket covering the body, tented over the arrows in his back.

"Is it safe for us now?" St. Clair asked.

"Here in the garden it's safe, but not in the valley. In a few hours the emir will leave for Ascalon. Where are the others?"

"In the forest." St. Clair motioned with his head, then cupped his hand around his mouth and called softly, "Isaac! It's the silversmith, Abu-Rahman."

"How is it with Rabbi Samuel?" al-Hasani asked anxiously.

Abu Rahman shook his head. "I'm sorry, my friends. The rabbi is dead—killed by the emir, like my poor apprentice here."

The words staggered St. Clair like a sword stroke. He lowered his eyes. "Where's the rabbi's body?"

"On the valley road, halfway to the Tomb of Zechariah. He was leading them away from you."

St. Clair cleared his throat. "Please take us to him."

"No, my friend. It's too dangerous. When it is light, and we're certain the emir has left the city, then we may go . . ." Abu Rahman hesitated. "But I . . . I should tell you—"

With the sound of snapping twigs, Isaac, Wallace, and Zahirah emerged from among the trees.

Isaac anxiously looked from Abu Rahman to St. Clair. "What news?" he asked.

"Rabbi Samuel is dead," St. Clair replied quietly.

Zahirah began to sob. He looked at her, apart and alone by the trees, her face buried in her hands. He yearned to hold her, to comfort her, and to tell her of his hope for her. But he couldn't. Not yet.

Abu-Rahman stepped forward and put his hand on St. Clair's shoulder. "When you see the body . . ." He shook his head and turned away. "I should tell you." He sighed and gathered himself. "They struck off his head, and we can't find it. We searched for hours—all over the hillside." He raised his shoulders. "The head is gone."

"I know why," Isaac said as he dried his eyes with his sleeve. "The emir has sent the rabbi's head to Acre as proof of his death."

St. Clair shut his eyes against the tears. "When it is light, we shall take up his body and bury him on the Temple Mount, as befits a warrior of God."

"No," Isaac said gently but emphatically. "Rabbi Samuel would never approve of a Jew's burial within the Temple precincts. He would not walk there in life, and he would not wish to be buried there in death."

"Very well. If not on the Temple Mount, then next to it, along the wall known as the Wailing Place of the Jews." He looked at Isaac. "Is that permitted?"

"Yes."

St. Clair sighed and looked down at Khaled's body. "Now, let us honor and bury this noble apprentice."

When the sun stood over the Mountains of Moab, word came that the emir had left the city. Abu Rahman led the way down the slope of Olivet and into the gray haze that lay like a shroud over the Valley of Kidron.

At Isaac's suggestion, they wrapped the rabbi's body with a prayer shawl, and upon the body they placed sword and shield as St. Clair thought fitting, and covered all with a gray robe.

St. Clair pointed. "Let us proceed down this road, passing the Tomb of Zechariah—"

"That's impossible," Abu Rahman cut in.

"Why? The emir is gone from the city."

"Yes. But something the rabbi said about the tomb caught

the emir's ear, and before he left for Ascalon, he posted an entire division of the guard to watch the place both day and night. They have orders to kill any who approach. We cannot go near there—impossible."

"How long will the guard remain in place?"

"I don't know—at least until the emir returns—"

"From Ascalon?"

"No. After Ascalon, he'll join forces with the sultan at Acre. He'll be gone for months, perhaps years . . ."

"And the guard will remain in place all the while?"

"Yes. The emir was adamant about the need to guard the spot. Why do you ask?"

"I was hoping to go to the tomb later today, at sunset—"

"And I tell you this cannot be done. The guards have orders to kill anyone who even comes near . . ."

Standing by the rabbi's body, St. Clair shut his eyes as his hopes for Zahirah departed, leaving him empty.

They carried the rabbi's body into the walled city, to the wailing place of the Jews. At the southern end of the ancient wall, they found a spot beneath a stone arch, and there they buried Rabbi Samuel, in the shadow of the Temple Mount.

This done, they bade farewell to Abu Rahman and his apprentices, to al-Hasani and to his wife and son, and they slipped out of the city.

A few leagues west of Jerusalem, they stopped at the cottage of a farmer in the village of Ayn Karem. There they reclaimed the horse and wagon used by Isaac and Wallace months before to reach Jerusalem. After compensating the farmer for his pains in tending the horse, they left the village. St. Clair and Wallace went on foot with Isaac guiding the wagon, Zahirah sitting comfortably behind. Thus they traversed the Mountains of Judah and descended toward the coastal plain.

Chapter Fifty-Nine

נט

Jerusalem to Acre
January, 1291

It was the season of the latter rains when the earth began to shake off winter and transfigure into spring. Fine grass covered the wet slopes of the hills and muddy channels rutted the roads.

The journey was slow but uneventful, and after seven days, they entered Acre through the tall gates.

Isaac's family had given him up for dead, and great was their rejoicing when he returned home. They were, however, puzzled by his new friends—a Knight of the Crusade, a pregnant Mamluk woman, and a young giant from an island nation on the western edge of the world. Nonetheless, all were made welcome. Zahirah's affliction was not yet known to them.

Accommodations were plentiful since many of Acre's residents had left the city. Zahirah requested and received quarters separate from the others, which was thought fitting since she was with child.

Isaac learned that Rabbi Petit had disappeared many months before. Some thought him dead. Others were sure he had returned to France. No one knew for certain. Rabbi David Maimuni had also left the city, returning to his community in Egypt. The controversy over Maimonides was all but forgotten.

On the day after they arrived, St. Clair donned his white jerkin, mail shirt, and black cape. He looked, once again, very much the Knight Templar despite his short beard and shoulder-length hair. As he traversed the well-remembered stone lanes of Acre to the commandery, he spoke to Rabbi Samuel within his mind.

"Do you know where I'm going?" he asked.

"Dressed as you are? To meet with your brother Templars."

"Do you know what I'll do there?"

"You're going to tell them of the Mamluks that will soon lay siege to Acre."

"There is something else, Rabbi. I'm going to do as you suggested."

"Which suggestion? I made so many . . ."

"After I give my report, I'll seek an audience with the Master of the Temple."

"Oh, yes, I remember. You'll beg his sanction to live openly with Zahirah."

"No, Rabbi. I will inform him that I'm leaving the order."

After a brief pause, the rabbi's voice asked, *"Are you certain of this—"*

The voice was interrupted by the rattling of a wagon loaded high with the members of a large family and their household items, heading toward the harbor. St. Clair flattened himself against the stone wall as the wagon passed, and the lane grew quiet. He remained standing, his back against the wall, his eyes closed. "It's at such times I miss you, Rabbi."

"How can you miss me? I'm with you even now! You'll never be rid of me."

"Is it wrong, then, that I mourn for you?"

"Would you mourn the broken shell when the baby bird emerges? Would you mourn the dry chrysalis when the butterfly dries its wings in the sun and lifts into the air?"

★ ★ ★ ★ ★

In the long refectory, draped with the black and white banners of *Beause'ant,* the Master of the Temple, William de Beaujeu, met with St. Clair in open session with the high council. St. Clair presented the certainty of the coming siege, along with other matters, such as the absence of Mongol troops along the eastern march, the gathering of every emir from Damascus to Cairo for the campaign, and the harvesting of scores of trees for the construction of siege engines. This done, he requested and was granted a private audience with de Beaujeu.

St. Clair followed the Templar Master from the refectory through narrow passages of the keep. With his flawless vestments and trimmed beard, the Master had the look of a wellborn man. Climbing a spiral stair, they came to a cramped room in a high turret, weakly lit by sunlight through narrow embrasures. Looking out, St. Clair could see part of the inner ward where knights were working the pells. He took comfort in the familiar pounding of sword on wood.

"You didn't come up here for the view, St. Clair." De Beaujeu's voice echoed in the cramped chamber.

"No, sir. I wished to speak with you in private."

"There is no more private place in all the compound. Speak your mind."

St. Clair drew a deep breath, gathering himself. "My lord, I must request separation from the order."

For a moment de Beaujeu said nothing. He stood, looking out at the inner ward. Then he turned to St. Clair. "Jonathan, you are one of the most dedicated knights to ever wear the cross. How have you come to this?"

"There's a woman, sir. A Moslem woman, and she is with child."

De Beaujeu raised his eyebrows. "Do you wish to confess and repent?"

"I only confess, my lord. I do not repent."

The Master nodded. "You are no novice, St. Clair. You've been in the Holy Land longer than I have. You know others before you have been, how shall I say it? . . . discreet . . ."

"I will not be discreet, sir. I have renounced my vows, and I am resolved to separate from the order."

"I see you are so resolved," the Master said as he stood facing St. Clair, hands clasped behind his back, the red cross upon his surcoat, the somber mantle upon his shoulders. "But Jonathan, consider that we find ourselves at the hour of our greatest peril, at the threshold of destruction. Therefore, I would ask you this—if you will not pray with us, stand with us."

"My lord, in leaving the order, I will also leave the Holy Land. And I will do this *before* the hour of Acre's destruction. I am bound to be with my wife and child—"

"I understand. But for the present you are here, and the siege, as you have told us, is perhaps three months away." De Beaujeu stepped forward. "Your experience with the younger knights and the novices is invaluable. So, while you are yet here, I ask that you contribute to the defense of Acre."

St. Clair held the Master's gaze. "It is yet a few months until my wife's date of confinement, and she wishes for our baby to be born here. So do I. Therefore, so long as I am here, I will contribute to the defense of Acre. But I will leave upon the hour of my own choosing."

Chapter Sixty

ס

Acre

February to April, 1291

Within days of returning to Acre, Isaac obtained an audience with the rabbinic court. There he bore witness to the intention of Rabbi Samuel to excommunicate Solomon Petit. In this manner, the draft of the writ they held gained credence, and Petit was summoned to appear before the court. But he did not come. He had disappeared without a trace.

As St. Clair had promised, and notwithstanding his separation from the order, he became a regular visitor at the Templar commandery, instructing novices and helping to plan for the defense of the city. Wallace accompanied him, joining in training exercises and quickly proving himself a natural warrior. With his height and strength, he was issued a larger and heavier sword, a claymore, which he soon mastered.

By mid-March, the long shadow of the Sultan al-Ashraf Khalil began to form on the broad plain within view of Acre—a sprawling tent city. Siege engines of every size and shape began to rise, growing in number and size by the day. Two engines towered above the rest—trebuchets the Mamluks called *Victorious* and *Furious.* These were designed to hurl giant boulders and cart-sized orbs of burning naphtha. A host of smaller mangonels for hurling rocks and bolts, known as Black Oxen, also appeared. Facing the wall at regular intervals, wooden skeletons of siege towers took shape, their jagged scaffolding clawing at the sky as they rose in height.

The spring rains diminished, the water dried in the ditches, and wildflowers covered the plain of Acre. Some of the smaller catapults were moved forward, and, to test them or merely out of boredom, carcasses of diseased cattle and bodies of captured prisoners were occasionally launched into the city. The people of Acre began to watch the sky.

Zahirah's melancholy seemed to lift as soon as she entered Acre, living as the city did on the edge of a death more imminent than her own. At the threshold of her eighth month of pregnancy, the true reason for her separate living quarters was revealed to Isaac's family. At first they panicked, gripped by the dread of leprosy's contagion. But Isaac explained the rational precautions as taught to him by Rabbi Samuel, and their fears were largely assuaged. It was agreed that she might stay, remaining apart but not in isolation. Her secret affliction would remain within the circle of the family's trust, so long as there were no outward signs of the disease.

The baby came early—a tiny boy, a month before the expected time. The birth was an easy one, and, despite his size, the child had a lusty cry. Isaac's older sister, Hannah, who was weaning her own child of eighteen months, readily agreed to suckle the infant, small as he was. Zahirah's sadness yielded to resignation as, unable to hold or nurse her son, she watched him grow plump with Hannah's milk. William, they called him—after her father, St. Clair's beloved master and mentor.

As the host of Islam gathered beyond the city walls, March gave way to April, and the days grew long and warm. Zahirah thrilled in taking young William for strolls in a carriage St. Clair fashioned with small wooden wheels. To reduce the risk of contagion, she took to wearing gloves of white cloth, and, lest there arise any need to tend to the baby, she never went out alone—St. Clair usually in her company. They walked side by side, delighting to appear like any other proud couple with their baby. Embracing this joyful illusion and lost in a happy oblivion, they came close to touching, but never did. And all the while the siege engines and towers of al-Ashraf Khalil kept rising beyond the city walls.

In the face of the mounting threat, many of Acre's residents secured passage for Cyprus and Europe, and the port teemed with galleons. Yet Acre remained crowded. For just as a rainstorm washes dead leaves and dry branches down from the hills, so the storm of Islam swept pilgrims, priests, and crusaders to the shores of the great sea, and such as these gathered within the walls of Acre.

Every new arrival brought hopeful rumors; an impending attack against the Mamluks by the Mongols, an armada led by King Henry of Cyprus, another Crusade raised from Europe. Such tales encouraged a belief the city might be spared. Clinging to this hope, many elected to stay, and Acre was gripped with a feverish gaiety. Lords and knights with their wives and courtesans caroused in careless indolence, and the taverns thronged with revelers—gambling, feasting, and drinking far into the night.

But St. Clair knew no help would come. He contracted with Templar mariners for sure passage on a galley for Zahirah and the baby, for Wallace, and for Isaac and all of his family. To seal the pact, he paid in advance, and he paid well. But the siege engines were not yet finished, and it was not yet time to leave.

On the third day of April the weather was fair. Zahirah took young William out for a stroll, and as always, she wore white gloves. Since St. Clair was occupied at the commandery, it fell to Isaac, who looked like Zahirah's younger brother, to accompany her in the knight's stead. Through the crowded lanes of Acre, they passed the palaces belonging to the great families of Outremer, with fountains and lush gardens behind ornamented iron grille gates. They passed stalls of merchants beneath fluttering silk awnings, where trade remained brisk in fine carpets, embroidered dresses, silk, spices, and precious stones. Everywhere, Genoese and Pisan merchants could be seen in their fine clothes, guarded by men-at-arms, haggling over bargains. They hurried past the stalls of the meat sellers, festooned with the pungent carcasses of skinned sheep and goats.

Rounding a corner, Zahirah and Isaac came upon a crowd filling a narrow lane. It was not uncommon for a merchant to draw such a crowd with some curious object from a faraway land, or for a sleight-of-hand game to draw a throng of raucous bettors. But as they moved forward, snatches of the conversation told a different tale. One of the Black Oxen had launched another body into Acre.

"Who is it?" someone asked.

"I've seen that one before, I think."

"How can you be sure? There's not much to judge by."

"It's an old rabbi, I'll warrant. Look at that beard and striped robe."

Isaac pressed through the crowd and looked down at the twisted lump of flesh and bone—all that remained of his old master and teacher. Removing his dark frock coat, he placed it gently over the battered body.

Rabbi Solomon Petit had returned to Acre.

Chapter Sixty-One

סא

On the seventeenth day of May, St. Clair was atop Acre's inner wall, waiting for Wallace to finish climbing the steep mural stairs to the battlements. It had become St. Clair's daily habit to view the Saracen siege preparations, and today was no exception. However, this was the first day Wallace had come along. St. Clair looked over the domes and towers of Acre as he waited for Wallace to join him. The city on its promontory was shaped like a triangle, with two sides open to the sea, and the sea-lanes unchallenged, ruled by the Templar fleet. The third side, facing landward, was well fortified, guarded by the tall double wall.

Wallace reached the top, stepped onto the wall walk, and let out a low whistle as he looked down the length of the lane, wide as two wagons, running along the top of the wall in both directions. "How long is it?" he asked.

"Just short of a league," St. Clair replied as he crossed the lane toward the crenellated battlements of the parapet.

Leaning against the warm stone, he looked over the gap between the inner and outer wall; a stone's-throw distance, filled by trebuchets, catapults, and ballistas—armed and ready for the defense of Acre. The outer wall mirrored the inner wall in length and height and was additionally reinforced by nineteen towers. Beyond the outer wall, the plain of Acre was covered by the tents of the sultan's legions—with cavalry, siege engines, towers, and fluttering banners of every color as far as the eye could see.

Wallace stared, his mouth agape. When he spoke, his voice was a tense whisper. "What are they waiting for?"

"The ground is not quite hard enough, and it seems they have more work to do, such as covering that tower with copper plates." St. Clair pointed at a huge wooden skeleton well beyond the outer wall. "If left exposed, the scaffolding will burn like a torch." He scanned the plain and frowned. The Saracens stretched in unbroken ranks from the northern to the southern shore of the sea and back as far as the foothills. "They seem to have their divisions in place, though. Do you see that section there?" He pointed. "Kurdish lancers. And those there, between the two black banners? That's the sultan's personal guard. Each of the camps over there are troops of lesser emirs. In front of them are the Sufis. They'll serve mainly to make noise when the siege begins—with drums, trumpets, and the like. Next to them in the white robes near the black tents are Bedouin—" St. Clair suddenly jerked Wallace down. "Take cover!"

A black cloud of arrows arced across the sky.

The siege had begun.

After salvos of arrows and a dozen large stones cracked against the city walls, there came a lull. St. Clair and Wallace broke from the shelter of the parapet and raced down the mural steps. They sprinted along stone lanes toward the Jewish Quarter as another wave of arrows clattered about them and the air was filled with the cries of the wounded. The roar and crack of huge stones echoed against the walls and red-orange balls of blazing naphtha exploded in showers of flame. And there was another sound, faint and far away—the ululations of the Sultan's host, with a chorus of trumpets, drums, and cymbals.

Darting between doorways and alcoves, St. Clair led the way through the cobbled lanes of Acre, empty but for the dead and dying, filled with acrid smoke. Within his heart another battle raged; for the husband and father the time had come to leave, for the Templar the time had come to fight. And yet a third voice spoke.

"Stop entertaining the foolish notion of fighting for this doomed city."

"But my calling—"

"Your calling is to your wife, your child, and to the Heavenly Jerusalem. Remember that, Jonathan."

"So I am sworn and promised, and I will keep these promises, Rabbi."

"Good. Now away with you. And no more confusion!"

St. Clair dashed forward, followed hard upon by Wallace. They slipped beneath an arched doorway as a ball of flame scorched the sky above them, smashing into a palm tree, which ignited like the wick of a gigantic candle. Black smoke twisted into the sky, a shower of fire cascading onto the houses below.

"Where are we going?" Wallace asked.

"To Isaac's house and then to the quay. We'll gather the others. I've arranged with Templar sailors for a longboat and oarsman. There will be room for all."

"What? We will not stay and fight?"

St. Clair gripped Wallace's shoulder. "This is no longer our war, William. We have a calling beyond these shores. Come. We must gather the others."

The lanes by the harbor were beyond artillery range and choked with crowds of clawing fugitives. Mad with fear, they poured onto the quay.

St. Clair, with baby William bundled in his arms and Zahirah by his side, led the way along the edge of the mob, keeping the others in his sight. They paused in a sheltered street above the harbor and looked down.

Like an onrushing tide of roiling water, the mob flooded the harbor lanes, voices rising in desperation, washing over the quay in waves of panic, scattering a flotsam of household items and thrashing fugitives into the water. Out in the harbor, placid galleys waited under sail beyond the breakwater.

In a boat well away from the quay and approaching the outer harbor, St. Clair saw men and women he recognized from their dress as Jews. Isaac pointed to the boat and shouted, "Look, William! The Jews of York with Reb Yosef."

In another boat just launched from the quay, St. Clair spotted the patriarch in his rich robes with his entourage. Dozens of frantic people were trying to get aboard, and the sailors were beating them away with the oars. The boat moved into the harbor with a dozen fugitives clinging to its sides and a few managing to clamber aboard. Others flailed away in the water and, one by one, went under. The boat was soon in the outer harbor, moving slowly toward the galleys, but over-weighted and sitting low in the water. Then, as St. Clair watched in horror, the boat was swamped by heavy swells and quickly sank.

"Follow me. Now!" he shouted.

Leaving the noisy despair of the harbor, they were soon at a small jetty where St. Clair had arranged to meet the Templar mariners. But there was no boat—just one old sailor, pacing on the dock, a faded cap upon his head.

"Are you St. Clair?" he asked.

"Yes, but where's the boat I arranged for with your fellows?"

"With this madness about?" The old man shook his head and his rheumy eyes looked past St. Clair at Zahirah and the others resting in the shade by the jetty. "We'll launch in a week. Go back home for now."

"Are you insane?" St. Clair asked with mounting rage. "The siege . . ."

"Yes, I know," the sailor cut in. "The siege will go on for a *month*! I've seen this before—in Jaffa and Tripoli—everyone thinking they have to leave on the first day. We have *plenty* of time—"

St. Clair wheeled to face the old man, his voice raw with anger. "We had an arrangement—"

"And we'll honor that arrangement, sir, but not today. Have you seen what's going on over there?"

St. Clair's heart clenched like a fist. "We'll not wait a week. Do you understand me?" He planted his index finger in the middle of the old man's chest. "We'll leave today."

"Impossible! We need time to prepare." The old man paled and backed away. "Give us a few days . . ."

"One," St. Clair countered. "We leave tomorrow!"

The old sailor drew a deep breath and gathered himself. "All right. Tomorrow at sunset. But for now, you have more to fear from that mob than from any Mamluk." The old man turned and tipped his weathered cap. "Tomorrow," he repeated and left the jetty.

Chapter Sixty-Two

סב

Acre
18 May, 1291

The old sailor was wrong. The end came quickly.

Teams of Mamluk diggers had been working secretly for weeks, tunneling under the outer wall, and two towers collapsed in a day. The outer wall was breached, and with the ceaseless summons of the drums and blare of trumpets, the host of Islam surged forward.

Scaling ladders were set against the inner wall but the sultan's legions were driven back again and again with arrows, Greek fire, and hot oil from the parapets. The moat between the walls filled with the dead. But some slipped through. Like tendrils of a malevolent vine, they probed and advanced, slowed by pitched resistance and their own looting; yet they moved slowly forward, toward the harbor.

St. Clair, Wallace, and two Knights Hospitallers had fought since morning. Theirs was one of many patchwork bands of knights charged with stopping the advance. Knights Templar, Knights of the Hospital, and Teutonic Knights joined forces as old rivalries fell away.

St. Clair's band had routed a raiding party, and with evening approaching, the appointed hour of their departure was at hand.

With a rattle of chain mail and rasping of heavy boots on paving stones, they moved through smoke-filled lanes toward the jetty where Zahirah, baby William, Isaac, and his family waited.

Reaching a gap in the sea wall, St. Clair stepped aside and waited for Wallace and the two knights to pass before following them onto the quay. Removing his coif of shining mail, he shook his hair free and wiped sweat from his eyes. The flames above Acre reddened the sky and sparkled on the waves where the boat pitched on the breaking swells. He saw in a glance that Zahirah and the others were ready—huddled on benches with the sailors in a four-oared skiff that would carry them to the safety of the galley. The Knights Hospitallers planned to disembark at their stronghold in Malta, while the others would go on to the south of France.

One of the sailors beckoned. "Hurry, my masters," he shouted. "Hurry! Let's away!"

"Do not be troubled, friend," Wallace replied calmly as he stepped into the boat. "We have beaten the Mamluks back. They dare not raise their heads again this night."

"Not so, my young friend. Do you not see yonder light?"

All eyes turned toward a faint orange glow against the high walls bordering a lane. The light was moving in their direction.

"That's naught but a cooking fire," Wallace said without conviction.

"No, sir. I know that light—Mamluk torches—made of rushes soaked in pitch. And see how it moves! We must quickly away! For if we are not well into the harbor and out of their range, they will burn our boat and kill us all! Hurry, I say!"

"How far can they throw those torches?" Wallace said dismissively as he took his seat on the bench.

"The torches don't concern me, young sir. But there are naphtha throwers with clay jars of quicklime that burns upon the water—flames that cannot be quelled. Therefore, hurry, I say!" He waved to the last of the Knights Hospitallers to enter the boat, his voice rising. "Hurry, lest our lives be forfeit!"

St. Clair readied his hands on the prow, waiting for the last knight to enter the boat. He acknowledged Zahirah with a nod, and saw that Isaac was holding little William in his arms. He smiled as he saw how his son would not be still, kicking his small legs free from the blanket, the perfect little toes, the membrane delicacy of his skin, his bright astonished eyes.

The Knights Hospitallers took their place in the boat. Now all was ready.

He leaned down to push on the prow when a sailor leaped from the bench, his eyes filled with terror, "Wait, knight! Look!"

"What is it?" St. Clair shot back.

"The torches move quickly hither! We're doomed! They'll soon be at the sea wall, and we'll be in range of their naphtha. There's no way we can escape!"

"No, friend. There *is* a way." St. Clair beckoned to the knights. "Quickly, *mes frères*! Once more into the breach."

In a heartbeat, the two knights were out of the boat and on the quay.

"Here, take these!" the sailor shouted and heaved extra swords, bows, and quivers of arrows onto the landing. "Just hold them off so that we might reach the middle of the harbor."

Wallace stood up and moved to join the knights.

"Sit ye down, William!" St. Clair shouted as the knights climbed out of the boat.

Brandishing the claymore above his head, Wallace shouted in reply, "Nae, I will fight by your side!"

"No, William!" St. Clair pushed him back into the boat. "You must abide to bring my wife and son to Roslin in Midlothian! You swore as much! You must abide to build the pyramid. You know Isaac cannot do it alone!"

"But how can I leave you?" Wallace asked, his eyes brimming with tears.

St. Clair placed his hand over his heart as he moved toward the prow. "I'm proud of you by my side, William, but this is not your war, and now is not your hour. Draw your sword for Scotland, William. *Alba gu bràth!*"

St. Clair turned his eyes to look upon Zahirah one last time.

But she wasn't in the boat.

He straightened up, searching for her.

In disbelief, he saw the boat was already moving, water lapping the bow. And now he saw her—pushing on the prow, pushing the boat away from the landing.

"Pull!" she shouted to the sailors. "Pull for your lives!"

"Zahirah!" he cried.

"No! No!" Isaac and Wallace stood, shouting from the boat.

But the mariners rowed and the boat was away from the landing, moving and rocking on the swells.

Those on the jetty and those on the boat fell silent, looking at each other through a pale mist that lay upon the water, listening to the dip and splash of the oars.

"Goodbye, William," Zahirah called out. "Goodbye, my darling son!"

And now St. Clair was beside her.

The boat, wreathed in mist, moved slowly away.

Zahirah looked up at St. Clair, smiling through her tears. "I have no place in this world but at your side, my husband." Turning, she lifted a sword from the landing and stuck it point first into the wooden planks. Then she quickly slung a quiver of arrows over her shoulder.

St. Clair saw that the Mamluks were drawing near. Reaching over his shoulder, he unsheathed his broadsword. He looked down at Zahirah as she tested the bow. "Do you know how to use that?"

"My father taught me well enough! And when the arrows are gone, you shall see how well I use the sword."

Now St. Clair heard the drums, the trumpets, and the ululations. They would very soon be at the sea wall. The two knights stood ready at each side of the breach.

"Deus lo volt!" he called to them, and turned to Zahirah. With his free hand, he pushed back her hood. Her dark hair, loosed, fell about her shoulders—her face in the light of the burning sky, the tears on her cheeks, mirroring his own.

He touched her face and she drew back.

But then she took his hand and pressed it hard against her cheek. "I have waited so long to feel your touch . . ."

Drawing her close, he looked into her eyes. There was only this love and only this death. He bent down and kissed her mouth.

And now she returned his kiss, holding him with all her despair and all her longing.

And now the Mamluks drew near the breach.

St. Clair raised his sword.

Zahirah set an arrow and drew back her bow.

Together they turned.

ABOUT THE AUTHOR

Michael Cooper emigrated to Israel after graduating from high school in 1966. He lived in Jerusalem during the last year the city was divided between Israel and Jordan, and remained in Israel for the next decade. He studied at Hebrew University in Jerusalem and graduated from Tel Aviv University Medical School.

Now a pediatric cardiologist on the faculty at University of California San Francisco Medical Center, he returns to Israel/Palestine Authority frequently to volunteer his services to children who lack adequate access to care. His first novel, set in 1948 Jerusalem, *Foxes in the Vineyard,* was grand prize winner of the 2011 Indie Publishing Contest. *The Rabbi's Knight* is his second novel. He lives in Northern California with his wife and two cats. Three adult children occasionally drop by.